FLOWING GOLD

Rex Beach

1st WORLD
LIBRARY
Literary Society

Flowing Gold

Rex Beach

© 1st World Library, 2006
PO Box 2211
Fairfield, IA 52556
www.1stworldlibrary.com
First Edition

LCCN: 2006938099

Softcover ISBN: 978-1-4218-3402-3
Hardcover ISBN: 978-1-4218-3302-6
eBook ISBN: 978-1-4218-3502-0

Purchase *"Flowing Gold"*
as a traditional bound book at:
www.1stWorldLibrary.com/purchase.asp?ISBN=978-1-4218-3402-3

1st World Library is a literary, educational organization
dedicated to:

- Creating a free internet library of downloadable ebooks

- Hosting writing competitions and offering book
  publishing scholarships.

1st World Library Literary Society

Giving Back to the World

"If you want to work on the core problem, it's early school literacy."

- James Barksdale, former CEO of Netscape

"No skill is more crucial to the future of a child, or to a democratic and prosperous society, than literacy."

- Los Angeles Times

Literacy... means far more than learning how to read and write... The aim is to transmit... knowledge and promote social participation."

- UNESCO

"Literacy is not a luxury, it is a right and a responsibility. If our world is to meet the challenges of the twenty-first century we must harness the energy and creativity of all our citizens."

- President Bill Clinton

"Parents should be encouraged to read to their children, and teachers should be equipped with all available techniques for teaching literacy, so the varying needs and capacities of individual kids can be taken into account."

- Hugh Mackay

TO THE ONE WHOSE FAITH, ENTHUSIASM, AND DEVOTION CONSTITUTE A NEVER-FAILING SOURCE OF INSPIRATION, MY WIFE, SWEETHEART, AND PARTNER.

CHAPTER I

Room service at the Ajax is of a quality befitting the newest, the largest, and the most expensive hotel in Dallas. While the standard of excellence is uniformly high, nevertheless some extra care usually attaches to a breakfast ordered from the Governor's suite—most elegant and most expensive of all the suites—hence the waiter checked over his card and made a final, fluttering examination to be sure that the chilled fruit was chilled and that the hot plates were hot before he rapped on the door. A voice, loud and cheery, bade him enter.

Would the gentleman wish his breakfast served in the parlor or —No, the gentleman would have it right in his bedroom; but first, where were his cigarettes? He hoped above all things that the waiter had not forgotten his cigarettes. Some people began their days with cold showers—nothing less than a cruel shock to a languid nervous system. An atrocious practice, the speaker called it—a relic of barbarism—a fetish of ignorance. Much preferable was a hygienic, stimulating cigarette which served the same purpose and left no deleterious aftereffects.

The pajama-clad guest struck a light, inhaled with abundant satisfaction, and then cast a hungry eye over the contents of the rubber-tired breakfast table. He, too, tested the temperature of the melon and felt the cover of the toast plate.

"Splendid!" he cried. "Nice rooms, prompt service, a pleasant-faced waiter. Why, I couldn't fare better in my best club. Thanks to you, my first impression of Dallas is wholly delightful." He seated himself in a padded boudoir chair, unfolded a snowy serviette and attacked his breakfast with the enthusiasm of a perfectly healthy animal.

"Is this your first visit here, sir?"

"Absolutely. Dallas is as foreign to me as Lhasa. It is the Baghdad of my dreams and its streets are strange. Perhaps they are full of adventure for me. I hope so. Anything exciting can happen in a town where one has neither friends nor acquaintances, eh? You are a well-read man, I take it."

"I? Why—"

"At any rate, you have heard it said that this is a small world."

"Yes, sir."

"Good! I merely wish to deny authorship of the saying, for it is false. This is a large world. What is more, it is a world full of cities like Dallas where men like you and me, Heaven be praised, have neither friends, acquaintances, nor relatives. In that respect, it is a fine world and we should devoutly give thanks for its Dallases and its—Dalsatians. Jove! This ham is delicious!"

The waiter was accustomed to "morning talkers," but this gentleman was different. He had an air of consequence, and his voice, so deep, so well modulated, so pleasant, invested him with unusual distinction. Probably he was an actor! But no! Not in the Governor's suite. More likely he was one of the big men of the Standard, or the Gulf, or the Texas. To make sure, the waiter inquired:

"May I ask if you are in oil, sir?"

"In oil? Bless me, what a nauseating question—at this hour of the day!"

"'Most everybody here is in oil. We turn dozens away every day, we're that full. It's the boom. I'm in oil myself—in a small way, of course. It's like this: sometimes gentlemen like— well, like you, sir—give me tips. They drop a hint, like, about their stocks, and I've done well—in a small way, of course. It doesn't cost them anything and—some of them are very kind. You'd really be surprised."

"Oh, not at all." The occupant of the Governor's suite leaned back in his chair and smiled widely. "As a matter of fact, I am flattered, for it is evident that you are endowed with the money-making instinct and that you unerringly recognize it in others. Very well, I shall see what I can do for you. But while we are on the subject of tips, would you mind helping yourself to a dollar out of my trousers pocket?"

The waiter proceeded to do as directed, but a moment later announced, apologetically: "Here's all I find, sir. It's mostly pennies." He exposed a handful of small coins.

"Look in my coat, if you will."

But the second search resulted as had the first. "Strange!" murmured the guest, without rising. "I must have been robbed. I remember now, a fellow crowded me as I left my train. Um—m! Robbed—at the very gates of Baghdad! Dallas *is* a City of Adventure. Please add your tip to the check, and— make it two dollars. I'd like to have you serve me every morning, for I cannot abide an acid face at breakfast. It sours my whole day."

Calvin Gray finished his breakfast, smoked a second cigarette as he scanned the morning paper, then he dressed himself with meticulous care. He possessed a tall, erect, athletic form, his perfectly fitting clothes had that touch of individuality affected by a certain few of New York's exclusive tailors, and when he finally surveyed himself in the glass, there was no denying the fact that he presented an appearance of unusual distinction. As he turned away, his eyes fell upon the scanty handful of small coins which the waiter had removed from his pocket and for a moment he stared at them reflectively, then he scooped them into his palm and, with a smile, announced to his image:

"It would seem that it is time for us to introduce ourselves to the management."

He was humming a tune as he strode out of his richly furnished quarters.

The Governor's suite at the Ajax is on the mezzanine floor, at the head of the grand staircase. As Gray descended the spacious marble steps, he saw that the hotel was indeed doing a big business, for already the lobby was thickly peopled and at the desk a group of new arrivals were plaintively arguing with a bored and supercilious room clerk.

Some men possess an effortless knack of commanding attention and inspiring courtesy. Calvin Gray was one of these. Before many moments, he was in the manager's office, explaining, suavely, "Now that I have introduced myself, I wish to thank you for taking care of me upon such short notice."

"It was the only space we had. If you wish, I'll have your rooms changed as soon as—"

"Have you something better?"

Haviland, the manager, laughed and shook his head. "Scarcely! That suite is our pet and our pride. There's nothing to beat it in the whole Southwest."

"It is very nice. May I inquire the rate?"

"Twenty-five dollars a day."

"Quite reasonable." Mr. Gray beamed his satisfaction.

"It is the only suite we have left. We've put beds in the parlors of the others, and frequently we have to double up our guests. This oil excitement is a blessing to us poor innkeepers. I presume it's oil that brings you here?"

Gray met the speaker's interrogatory gaze with a negative shake of the head and a smile peculiarly noncommittal. "No," he declared. "I'm not in the oil business and I have no money to invest in it. I don't even represent a syndicate of Eastern capitalists. On the contrary, I am a penniless adventurer whom chance alone has cast upon your hospitable grand staircase." These words were spoken with a suggestion of mock modesty that had precisely the effect of a deliberate wink, and Mr. Haviland smiled and nodded his complete comprehension.

"I get you," said he. "And you're right. The lease hounds would devil you to death if you gave them a chance. Now then, if there's any way in which I can be of service—"

"There is." Gray's tone was at once businesslike. "Please give me the names of your leading bankers. I mean the strongest and the most—well, discreet."

During the next few minutes Gray received and swiftly tabulated in his mind a deal of inside information usually denied to the average stranger; the impression his swift, searching questions made upon the hotel manager was evident when the latter told him as he rose to go:

"Don't feel that you have to identify yourself at the banks to-day. If we can accommodate you—cash a check or the like—"

"Thank you." The caller shook his head and smiled his appreciation of the offer. "Your manner of conducting a hotel impresses me deeply, and I shall speak of it to some of my Eastern friends. Live executives are hard to find."

It is impossible to analyze or to describe that quality of magnetic charm which we commonly term personality, nevertheless it is the most potent influence in our social and our business lives. It is a gift of the gods, and most conspicuous successes, in whatever line, are due to it. Now and then comes an individual who is cold, even repellent, and yet who rises to full accomplishment by reason of pure intellectual force or strength of character; but nine times out of ten the man who gets ahead, be he merchant, banker, promoter, or crook, does so by reason of this abstract asset, this intangible birthright.

Gray possessed that happy quality. It had made itself felt by the waiter who brought his breakfast and by the manager of the hotel; its effect was equally noticeable upon the girl behind the cigar counter, where he next went. An intimate word or two and she was in a flutter. She sidetracked her chewing gum, completely ignored her other customers, and helped him select a handful of her choicest sixty-cent Havanas. When he finally decided to have her send the rest of the box of fifty up to his room and signed for them, she considered the transaction a tribute to her beauty rather than to her ability as a saleswoman. Her admiring eyes followed him clear across the lobby.

Even the blase bell-captain, by virtue of his calling a person of few enthusiasms and no illusions, edged up to the desk and inquired the name of the distinguished stranger "from the No'th."

Gray appeared to know exactly what he wanted to do, for he stopped at the telephone booths, inquired the number of the leading afternoon newspaper, and put in a call for it. When it came through he asked for the city editor. He closed the sound-proof door before voicing his message, then he began, rapidly:

"City editor? Well, I'm from the Ajax Hotel, and I have a tip for you. I'm one of the room clerks. Listen! Calvin Gray is registered here—got in last night, on gum shoes.... Gray! *Calvin Gray*! Better shoot a reporter around and get a story.... You *don't*? Well, other people know him. He's a character— globe trotter, soldier of fortune, financier. He's been everywhere and done everything, and you can get a great story if you've got a man clever enough to make him talk. But he won't loosen easily.... Oil, I suppose, but—... Sure! Under cover. Mystery stuff! Another big syndicate probably.... Oh, that's all right. I'm an old newspaper man myself. Don't mention it."

All American cities, these days, are much the same. Character, atmosphere, distinctiveness, have been squeezed out in the general mold. For all Calvin Gray could see, as he made his first acquaintance with Dallas, he might have been treading the streets of Los Angeles, of Indianapolis, of Portland, Maine, or of Portland, Oregon. A California brightness and a Florida warmth to the air, a New England alertness to the pedestrians, a Manhattan majesty to some of the newer office buildings, these were the most outstanding of his first impressions.

Into the largest and the newest of these buildings Gray went, a white tile and stone skyscraper, the entire lower floor of which was devoted to an impressive banking room. He sent his card in to the president, and spent perhaps ten minutes with that gentleman. He had called merely to get acquainted, so he explained; he wished to meet only the heads of the strongest financial institutions; he had no favors to ask—as yet, and he might have no business whatever with them. On the other hand—well, he was a slow and careful investigator, but when he moved, it was with promptitude and vigor, and in such an event he wished them to know who he was. Meanwhile, he desired no publicity, and he hoped his presence in Dallas would not become generally known—it might seriously interfere with his plans.

Before he left the bank Gray had met the other officers, and from their manner he saw that he had created a decided impression upon them. The bank president himself walked with him to the marble railing, then said:

"I'd like to have you wait and meet my son, Lieutenant Roswell. He's just back from overseas, and—the boy served with some distinction. A father's pride, you understand?"

"Was Lieutenant Roswell in France?" Gray inquired, quickly.

"Oh yes. He'll be in at any minute."

A shadow of regret crossed the caller's face. "I'm sorry, but I've arranged to call on the mayor, and I've no time to lose. What unit was your son with?"

"The Ninety-eighth Field Artillery."

The shadow fled. Mr. Gray was vexed at the necessity for haste, but he would look forward to meeting the young hero later.

"And meanwhile," Roswell, senior, said, warmly, "if we can be of service to you, please feel free to call upon us. I dare say we'd be safe in honoring a small check." He laughed pleasantly and clapped his caller on the back.

A fine man, Gray decided as he paused outside the bank. And here was another offer to cash a check—the second this morning. Good address and an expensive tailor certainly did count: with them as capital, a man could take a profit at any time. Gray's fingers strayed to the small change in his trousers pocket and he turned longing eyes back toward the bank interior. Without doubt it was a temptation, especially inasmuch as at that moment his well-manicured right hand held in its grasp every cent that he possessed.

This was not the first time he had been broke. On the contrary, during his younger days he had more than once found himself in that condition and had looked upon it as an exciting experience, as a not unpleasant form of adventure. To be strapped in a mining camp, for instance, was no more than a mild embarrassment. But to find oneself thirty-eight years old, friendless and without funds in a city the size of Dallas— well, that was more than an adventure, and it afforded a sort of excitement that he believed he could very well do without. Dallas was no open-handed frontier town; it was a small New York, where life is settled, where men are suspicious, and where fortunes are slow in the making. He wondered now if hard, fast living had robbed him of the punch to make a new beginning; he wondered, too, if the vague plans at the back of his mind had anything to them or if they were entirely impracticable. Here was opportunity, definite, concrete, and spelled with a capital O, here was a deliberate invitation to avail himself of a short cut out of his embarrassment. A mere scratch of a pen and he would have money enough to move on to some other Dallas, and there gain the start he needed— enough, at least, so that he could tip his waiter and pay cash for his Coronas. Business men are too gullible, any how; it would be a good lesson to Roswell and Haviland. Why not—?

Calvin Gray started, he recoiled slightly, the abstracted stare was wiped from his face, for an officer in uniform had brushed past him and entered the bank. That damned khaki again! Those service stripes! They were forever obtruding themselves, it seemed. Was there no place where one could escape the hateful sight of them? His chain of thought had been snapped, and he realized that there could be no short cut for him. He had climbed through the ropes, taken his corner, and the gong had rung; it was now a fight to a finish, with no quarter given. He squared his shoulders and set out for the hotel, where he felt sure he would find a reporter awaiting him.

CHAPTER II

The representative of the Dallas *Post* had anticipated some difficulty in interviewing the elusive Calvin Gray—whoever he might be—but luck appeared to be with him, for shortly after his arrival at the hotel the object of his quest appeared. Mr. Gray was annoyed at being discovered; he was, in fact, loath to acknowledge his identity. Having just returned from an important conference with some of the leading financiers of the city, his mind was burdened with affairs of weight, and then, too, the mayor was expecting him—luncheon probably —hence he was in no mood to be interviewed. Usually Mr. Gray's secretary saw interviewers. However, now that his identity was known, he had not the heart to be discourteous to a fellow journalist. Yes! He had once owned a newspaper—in Alaska. Incidentally, it was the farthest-north publication in the world.

Alaska! The reporter pricked up his ears. He managed to elicit the fact that Mr. Gray had operated mines and built railroads there; that he had been forced into the newspaper game merely to protect his interests from the depredations of a gang of political grafters, and that it had been a sensational fight while it lasted. This item was duly jotted down in the reportorial memory.

Alaska was a hard country, quite so, but nothing like Mexico during the revolution. Mexican sugar and mahogany, it transpired, had occupied Mr. Gray's attention for a time, as had Argentine cattle, Yucatan hennequin, and an engineering enterprise in Bolivia, not to mention other investments closer to home.

Once the speaker had become reconciled to the distasteful necessity of talking about himself, he suggested an adjournment to his rooms, where he would perhaps suffer less embarrassment by reason of his unavoidable use of the personal pronoun.

Gray noted the effect upon his visitor of the Governor's suite and soon had the young man at ease, with a Corona between his teeth. Then followed a full three-quarters of an hour, during which the visitor discoursed in his very best style and his caller sat spellbound, making occasional hieroglyphic hen tracks upon his note paper and congratulating himself upon his good luck in striking a man like this in one of his rare, talkative moods. Gray had set himself deliberately to the task of selling himself to this gentleman of the press, and, having succeeded, he was enough of a salesman to avoid the fatal error of overselling.

Alone at last, a sardonic grin crept over his features. So far, so good. Now for the rest of those bankers and the mayor. Gray was working rapidly, but he knew no other way of working, and speed was essential. It seemed to him not unlikely that delay of the slightest might force him to turn in desperation to a length of lead pipe and a mask, for—a man must live. As yet he had no very definite plans, he had merely undertaken to establish himself in a position to profit by the first opportunity, whatever it might be. And opportunity of some sort would surely come. It always did. What is more, it had an agreeable way of turning up just when he was most in need of it.

Gray called at several other banks that morning. He strode in swiftly, introduced himself with quick incisiveness, and tarried only long enough to fix himself indelibly in the minds of those he had come to see, then he left. There are right and wrong ways of closing a deal or of ending an interview, and Gray flattered himself that he possessed "terminal facilities." He was very busy, always a bit pressed for time, always a moment late; his theory of constant forward motion never permitted an awkward pause in conversation. On the street, his long legs covered the ground at something less than a run, his eyes were keenly alert, his face set in purposeful lines. Pedestrians turned to look after him.

At the mayor's office he was denied admission to the chief executive, but insisted so peremptorily as to gain his end. Once inside, he conveyed his compliments with such a graceful flourish that his intrusion assumed the importance of a ceremony and the People's Choice was flattered. He inferred that this Calvin Gray made a practice of presenting his formal respects to the dignitaries of all the large cities he visited and deemed it a favor to them. No doubt it was, if he so considered it, for he appeared to be fully aware of his own importance. After all, it was an agreeable practice. Since no man in public life can risk offending people of importance, His Honor unbent. Gray turned a current jest upon Texas politics into a neat compliment to the city's executive; they laughed; formality vanished; personal magnetism made itself felt. The call ended by the two men lunching together at the City Club, as Gray had assumed it would, and he took pains that the bankers upon whom he had called earlier in the morning should see him in company with the mayor.

He returned to his hotel that afternoon pretty well satisfied with his efforts and hopeful that some of the seed he had sown broadcast would be ripe for the reaping ere-long. But he received an electric shock as he approached the desk, for the bell captain addressed him, saying:

"Mr. Haviland wishes to see you at once, in his office."

"Indeed? Anything important?"

"Very important, sir. I've been waiting for you to come in." There was something ominous about this unexpected summons, or perhaps about the manner of its delivery. At any rate, suspicion leaped into Gray's mind.

So! Haviland was wise! Quick work that. Evidently he had investigated, through those mysterious sources of information available to great hotels. Or perhaps some one had seen and recognized him. Well, that was the way his luck had run, lately —every break against him.

Now—Gray's shoulders lifted in a shrug of resignation—there was nothing to do except wave aside the blindfold and face the firing squad like an officer and a gentleman. But it was a pity that the crash had come so soon; fortune might have given him at least a short interval of grace. Haviland was probably in a cold rage at the discovery of the fraud, and Gray could only hope that he wouldn't get noisy over it, for scenes were always annoying and sometimes they ran to unfortunate lengths.

There was a curious brightness to the imposter's eyes, a reckless, mocking smile upon his lips, when he stepped into the manager's office and stood beside the desk. He declined Haviland's invitation to be seated—it seemed more fitting that a man should take sentence on his feet.

"Have you seen the Post?" the manager inquired.

"No."

Haviland handed him a copy of the leading afternoon paper, and Gray's eyes flashed to the headline of an article reading:

CALVIN GRAY, HERO OF SENSATIONAL EXPLOITS, IN DALLAS ADVENTURES READ LIKE PAGE OF ROMANCE FAMOUS FINANCIER ADMITS LARGE OIL INTERESTS BEHIND HIM

From the opening paragraph Gray judged that he had impressed the reporter even more deeply than he had supposed, but he took no satisfaction there from, for Haviland was saying:

"I've read the whole story, but I want you to tell me something more about yourself."

"What do you wish to know?"

"Were you in France?"

Over the visitor's face there came a subtle change. Whereas, upon entering, he had worn an expression of careless defiance, now he appeared to harden in every fiber and to go on guard.

"I have been many times in France."

"I mean during the war. Did you serve?"

There was a pause. "I did." Gray's eyes remained fixed upon his interrogator, but they had begun to smolder.

"Then you're Colonel Gray. Colonel Calvin Gray."

"Quite so." The speaker's voice was harsh, and it came with an effort. "But you didn't read *that* in the *Post*. Come! What's the idea? Out with it."

The interview had taken an unexpectedly disagreeable turn. Gray had anticipated an unpleasant moment or two, but this—well, it was indeed the crash. Calamity had overtaken him from the very quarter he had least expected and most dreaded, and his mind raced off at a tangent; a dozen unwelcome queries presented themselves.

"Strange what circles we move in," Haviland was saying. "Do you know who owns the controlling interest in this hotel? Surely you must know or can guess. Think a moment. It's somebody you met over there and have reason to remember."

A sound escaped, from the throat of Colonel Gray—not a cry,

but rather a gasp of amazement, or of rage.

"Aha!" Haviland grinned in triumph. "I thought—"

His guest leaned forward over the desk, with face twitching. Passion had driven the blood from it, and his whole expression was one of such hatred, such fury, the metamorphosis was so startling, that the hotel man stiffened in his chair and stared upward in sudden amazement.

"*Nelson!*" Gray ejaculated. "Nelson! By God! So! He's *here!*"

During the moment that Haviland sat petrified, Gray turned his head slowly, his blazing eyes searched the office as if expecting to discover a presence concealed somewhere; they returned to the hotel man's face, and he inquired:

"Well, where is he?"

Haviland stirred. "I don't know what you're talking about. Who's Nelson?" After a second he exclaimed: "Good Lord! I thought I had a pleasant surprise for you, and I was gracefully leading up to it, but—I must have jazzed it all up. I was going to tell you that the hotel and everything in it is yours."

"Eh?"

"Why, the Ajax is one of the Dietz chain! Herman Dietz of Cincinnati owns it. He left for the North not an hour ago. At the last minute he heard you were here—read this story in the paper—and had bellboys scouring the place for you. You must know why he wanted to see you, and what he said when he found that he'd have to leave before you came in."

Colonel Gray uttered another exclamation, this time an expletive of deep relief. He fought with himself a moment, then murmured an apology. "Sorry. You gave me a start-decidedly. Herman Dietz, eh? Well, well! You made me think for a moment that I was a guest in the house of some other—friend."

"*Friend?*"

"Exactly!" Gray was himself again now. He ran a loosening finger between his collar and throat. "Quite a start, I'll admit, but—some of my friends are great practical jokers. They have a way of jumping out at me and crying 'Boo!' when I least expect it."

"Um-m! I see. Mr. Dietz told me that he was under lifelong obligation to a certain Colonel Calvin Gray. Something to do with passports—"

"I once rendered him a slight favor."

"He doesn't regard the favor as 'slight.' He was about to be imprisoned for the duration of the war and you managed to get him back home."

"Merely a matter of official routine. I felt sure he was a loyal American citizen."

"Exactly. But he makes more of the incident than you do, and he gave me my instructions. So—what can I do for you on his behalf? You have only to ask."

Gray pondered the unexpected offer. He was still a bit shaken, for a moment ago he had been more deeply stirred even than Haviland suspected, and the emotional reaction had left him weak. After all the hollow pretense of this day a genuine proffer of aid was welcome, and the temptation to accept was strong. Herman Dietz was indeed indebted to him, and he believed the old German-American would do anything, lend him any amount of money, for instance, that he might ask for. Gray wondered why he had not thought of Dietz before he came to Texas; it would have made things much easier. But the offer had come too late, it seemed to him; at this moment he could see no means of profiting by it without wrecking the flimsy house of cards he had that very day erected and exposing himself to ridicule, to obloquy as a rank four-flusher.

The scarcely dry headlines of that afternoon paper ran before his eyes—"*Famous Financier Admits Large Oil Interests Behind Him.*" Probably there were other things in the body of the article that would not harmonize with an appeal to Haviland for funds, nor sound well to Mr. Dietz, once he learned the truth. The more Gray pondered the matter, the more regretfully he realized that he had overplayed his hand, as it were.

Here was a situation indeed! To be occupying the most expensive suite in the hotel of a man who wished to lend him money, to be unable to pay one day's rent therefore, and yet to be stopped from accepting aid. There was a grim irony about it, for a fact. Then, too, the seed he had sown in banking circles, and his luncheon with the mayor! Haviland had a sense of humor; it would make a story too good to keep—the new oil operator, the magnificent and mysterious New York financier, a "deadhead" at the Ajax. Oh, murder!

"Well, name your poison! Isn't there something, anything we can do for you?" Haviland repeated.

"There is, decidedly." Gray smiled his warm appreciation of the tender. "If it is not too great a drain upon the Dietz millions, you may keep a supply of cut flowers in my room. I'm passionately fond of roses, and I should like to have my vases filled every morning."

"You shall dwell in a perfumed bridal bower."

Gray paused at the door to light one of those sixty-cent cigars and between puffs observed: "Please assure Mr. Dietz that—his obligation is squared and that I am—deeply touched. I shall revel in the scent of those flowers."

That evening, when Calvin Gray, formally and faultlessly attired, strolled into the Ajax dining room he was conscious of attracting no little attention. For one thing, few of the other guests were in evening dress, and also that article in the *Post*, which he had read with a curiously detached amusement, had been of a nature to excite general notice. The interview had jarred upon him in only one respect—*viz.*, in describing him as a "typical soldier of fortune." No doubt the reporter had intended that phrase in the kindest spirit; nevertheless, it implied a certain recklessness and instability of character that did not completely harmonize with Gray's inchoate, undeveloped banking projects. Bankers are wary of anything that sounds adventurous—or they pretend to be. As a matter of fact, Gray had learned enough that very day about Texas bankers to convince him that most of them were good, game gamblers, and that a large part of the dividends paid by most of the local institutions of finance were derived from oil profits. However, the newspaper story, as a whole, was such as to give him the publicity he desired, and he was well content with it.

Its first results were prompt in coming. Even while the head waiter was seating him, another diner arose and approached him with a smile. Gray recognized the fellow instantly—one of that vast army of casuals that march through every active man's life and disappear down the avenues of forgetfulness.

After customary greetings had been exchanged, the newcomer, Coverly by name, explained that he had read the *Post* article not five minutes before, and was delighted to learn how well the world had used Gray. He was dining alone; with alacrity he accepted an invitation to join his old friend, and straightway he launched himself upon the current of reminiscence. In answer to Gray's inquiry, he confessed modestly enough:

"Oh, I'm not in your class, old man. I'm no 'modern Gil Blas,' as the paper calls you. No Wall Street money barons are eating out of my hand, and I have no international interests 'reaching from the Yukon to the Plate,' but—I stand all right in little old Dallas. I'm the V. P. of our biggest jewelry house, and business is great." After their order had been given, he recited in greater detail the nature of his success.

Gray was interested. "Texas is booming," he said, at the conclusion of the story. "I'm told the new oil towns are something like our old mining camps."

"Except that they are more so. The same excitement, the same quick fortunes, only quicker and larger. Believe me, it's fine for the jewelry business. Look here." Coverly drew from his pocket a letter written in a painfully cramped hand upon cheap note paper, and this he spread out for his companion to read. "There's an example in point."

The letter, which bore the Ranger postmark, ran as follows:

DERE SIR—Your store has bin rekomend to me for dimons and I want some for my wife and dauter. Send me prises on rings of large sises.

Yours truley GUS BRISKOW.

"Um-m! Who is Mr. Briskow?"

Coverly shrugged. "Probably some nester who never saw a hundred dollars all in one place until recently. When they strike oil, they buy diamonds, nice large yellow ones, as a rule; then as the money continues to flow in, they pay off the mortgage and buy a bank—or an interest in one."

"In Heaven's name, introduce me to the opulent Gus Briskow."

"I wish I might. But I don't expect to make his acquaintance. The head of our firm is away and I haven't a man I'd dare trust to send out into the field. Usually I handle these inquiries myself when the victim can't tear himself away from contemplating the miraculous flow of liquid gold long enough to come here. I take an assortment of gems with me and beard the *nouveau riche* right on his derrick floor. Why, I've carried as much as a hundred thousand dollars' worth of merchandise on some of my trips." Coverly sighed regretfully. "Tough luck!

Too bad you're not a good jewelry salesman?"

"I am," Gray declared. "I can sell anything. As for diamonds—
I've bought enough in my time to know their value."

Coverly laughed in ready agreement with this statement. "Gad!
I'm sore at missing this sale."

"You needn't miss it. I'll go."

"Don't kid an unfortunate—"

"I'm not joking. If it's worth while, pack up your saffron
solitaires—all that you dare trust me with—and I'll be your
gentlemanly representative."

"Worth while? Good Lord! I'd probably get a ten-thousand-
dollar order!"

"Very well. It's settled." Gray's decision had been quickly
made. Opportunity had knocked—he was not one to deny her
admission, no matter how queer her garb. A hundred thousand
dollars' worth of gems! The very figures intrigued him and—
diamonds are readily negotiable. There would be a natural risk
attached to the handling of so large an amount. A thousand
things might happen to a treasure chest of that size. Gray
began to believe that his luck had changed.

"Where does Mr. Briskow live?" he inquired.

"Out beyond Ranger, somewhere. But—"

"I'm going to visit that field, anyhow. This will give me an
excuse."

"Nonsense!" The jeweler did not like to have fun poked at
him. For some time he refused to take the offer seriously, and
even when his host insisted that he would enjoy the lark, he
expostulated: "Why, the idea is ridiculous! You—Calvin Gray,

the financier, peddling jewelry? Ha! Outside of the fact that you wouldn't, couldn't do it, it's not the safest thing in the world to carry a small fortune in stones through the oil fields."

"Of course you insure it against theft?"

"That's the point. We can't. Have you ever heard of 'high-jackers'? That's the Texas term for hold-up men, robbers. Well, the country is full of them."

"Excellent! There no longer is any question about my going," Gray announced, firmly. "I am bored; I am stale; a thrill, of whatever sort, would stir my blood. Animated by purely selfish motives, I now insist upon a serious consideration of my offer. First, you say I 'wouldn't, couldn't'; I assure you that I would, could—and *shall*, provided I can qualify as a salesman."

Coverly admitted without much argument that anybody could probably effect a sale in this instance, if the diamonds were plainly marked with their prices; it would be a mere question of displaying the goods. That was not the point. Gray was a rich, a busy man—the idea was fantastic.

"Why, you're offering to do this as an accommodation to an old friend, and your time is probably worth more than our whole profit on the sale would amount to."

"My time is worth nothing. If you hesitate to intrust this king's ransom to me, I'll go personally responsible for its value. That's fair, isn't it?"

"Don't be silly. How could I pay you if you did go?"

"Um-m!" This idea, it seemed, had not occurred to Mr. Gray. It was plain that money meant nothing to him.

"You see? We couldn't permit—"

"I have it. We'll divorce friendship and sentiment entirely from the discussion and reduce it to a strictly business basis. You shall ease your conscience by paying my traveling expenses. The emotional suspense that I undergo shall be my reward. I'll take my commission in thrills."

This offer evoked a light laugh from Gray's guest. "You'd get enough of 'em," he asserted. "I'll advance a mild one, on account, at this moment. Notice the couple dining at the third table to your left. "Gray lifted his eyes. "What do you see?"

"A rather well-dressed, hard-faced man and a decidedly attractive woman—brunette. There's a suggestion of repressed widowhood about her. It's the gown, probably. I am not yet in my dotage, and I had seen her before I saw you."

"She's living here. I don't know much about her, but the man goes by the name of Mallow."

"No thrill yet."

"He's been hanging about our store for the past month, making a few purchases and getting acquainted with some of the clerks. Wherever I go, lately, there he is. I'll wager if I took to-night's train for Ranger, he'd be on it."

"And still my pulses do not leap."

"Wait! I got a sort of report on him and it's bad. I believe, and so does the chief of police, that Mr. Mallow has something to do with the gang of crooks that infests this country. One thing is certain, they're not the native product, and our hold-ups aren't staged by rope-chokers out of work."

Calvin Gray turned now and openly stared at the object of Coverly's suspicions. There was an alert interest in his eyes. "You've cinched the matter with me," he declared, after a moment. "Get out your diamonds to-morrow; I'm going to take the night train to Ranger."

Later that evening, after his guest had gone, Gray took occasion deliberately to put himself in Mallow's way and to get into conversation with him. This was not a difficult maneuver, for it was nearly midnight and the lobby was well-nigh deserted; moreover, it almost appeared as if the restless Mr. Mallow was seeking an acquaintance.

For the better part of an hour the two men smoked and talked, and had Coverly overheard their conversation his blood would have chilled and he would have prematurely aged, for his distinguished host, Calvin Gray, the worldly-wise, suave man of affairs, actually permitted himself to be pumped like a farmer's son. It would have been a ghastly surprise to the jeweler to learn how careless and how confiding his friend could be in an off moment; he would have swooned when Gray told about his coming trip to Ranger and actually produced the misspelled Briskow letter for the edification of his chance acquaintance. Any lingering doubt as to his friend's honesty of purpose would have vanished utterly had he heard Mallow announce that he, too, was going to Ranger, the very next night—a curious coincidence, truly—and Gray's expression of pleasure at the prospect of such a congenial traveling companion. The agitated Coverly no doubt would have phoned a frantic call for the police, then and there.

Once Gray was in his rooms, however, his manner changed, and into his eyes there came a triumphant glitter. Hastily he rummaged through one of his bags, and from a collection of trinkets, souvenirs, and the like he selected an object which he examined carefully, then took into the bathroom for further experiment. His step was springy, his lips were puckered, he was whistling blithely when he emerged, for at last those vaguely outlined plans that had been at the back of his mind had assumed form and pattern. His luck had turned, he had made a new start. Mallow was indeed a crook, and Gray blessed the prompt good fortune that had thrown both him and Coverly in his way.

It had been a busy day; he was well content with its fruitage.

CHAPTER III

Old Tom Parker was a "type." He was one of a small class of men at one time common to the West, but now rapidly disappearing. A turbulent lifetime spent in administering the law in a lawless region had stamped him with the characteristics of a frontier officer—*viz.*, vigilance, caution, self-restraint, sang-froid. For more than thirty years he had worn a badge of some sort and, in the serving of warrants and other processes of law, he had covered, first in the saddle or on buckboard, later in Pullman car or automobile, most of that vast region lying between the Arkansas and the Pecos, the Cimarron, and the Sabine—virtually all of what is now Texas and Oklahoma. He still spoke of the latter state, by the way, as "the Territory," and there were few corners of it that he had not explored long before it ceased to be a haven of hunted men.

That is what Tom Parker had been—a hunter of men—and time was when his name had been famous. But he had played his part. The times had caught up with and passed him, and no longer in the administration of justice was there need of abilities like his, hence the shield of his calling had been taken away.

Now Tom did not reckon himself obsolete. He was badger-gray, to be sure, and stiff in one knee—a rheumatic legacy of office inherited by reason of wet nights in the open and a too-diligent devotion to duty—but in no other respect did he believe his age to be apparent. His smoke-blue eyes were as bright as ever, his hand was quick; realization that he had been shunted upon a side track filled him with surprise and bewilderment. It was characteristic of the man that he still considered himself a bulwark of law and order, a *de facto* guardian of the peace, and that from force of habit he still sat facing the door and never passed between a lighted lamp and a window.

Among the late comers to Wichita Falls, where he lived, Tom was known as a quiet-spoken, emotionless old fellow with an honorable past, but with a gift for tiresome reminiscence quite out of place in the new and impatient order of things, and none but old-timers and his particular cronies were aware of the fact that he had another side to his character. It was not generally known, for instance, that he was a kind and indulgent father and had a daughter whom he worshiped with blind adulation. This ignorance was not strange, for Miss Barbara Parker had been away at college for four years now, and during that time she had not once returned home.

There was a perfectly good reason for this protracted separation of father and daughter; since Old Tom was no longer on pay, it took all he could rake and scrape to meet her bills, and railroad fares are high. That Hudson River institution was indeed a finishing school; not only had it polished off Barbara, but also it had about administered the *coup de grace* to her father. There had been a ranch over near Electra with some "shallow production," from which Tom had derived a small royalty—this was when Barbara Parker went East and before the Burk-burnett wells hit deep sand—but income from that source had been used up faster than it had come in, and "Bob," as Tom insisted upon calling her, would have had to come home had it not been for an interesting discovery on her father's part—*viz.*, the discovery of a quaint device of the law entitled a "mortgage." Mortgages had to do with a department of the law unfamiliar to Tom, his wit, his intelligence, and his dexterity of hand having been exercised solely in upholding the dignity of the criminal branch, but once he had realized that a mortgage, so called, was no more than a meaningless banking term used to cloak the impulsive generosity of moneyed men, he availed himself of this discovery and was duly grateful.

Tom carried on a nominal fire-insurance business, but as a matter of fact the tiny two-roomed frame structure that bore his painted sign was nothing more or less than a loafing place for him and his rheumatic friends, and a place in which the owner could spend the heat of the day in a position of comfort to his stiff leg—that is to say, asleep in a high-backed office chair, his feet propped upon his desk. It was here that Tom could usually be found, and when one of those hateful statements arrived from the East he merely roused himself, put on his wide gray hat, limped around to the bank, and pledged more of his oil royalties or signed another mortgage. What insurance policies he wrote were brought to him by his old pals; the money derived there from he sent on to "Bob" with love and an admonition to be a good girl and study hard and hurry home, because he was dying to see her. This office, by the way, no longer suited Tom; it was becoming too noisy and he would have sold it and sought another farther out had it not been mortgaged for more than it was worth. So, too, was the house where he lived amid the dirt and disorder of all bachelor establishments.

Now Old Tom would have resented an accusation of indolence; the bare implication of such a charge would have aroused his instant indignation, and Tom Parker indignant was a man to shun. As a matter of fact, he believed himself sadly overworked, and was forever complaining about it.

The time came, however, when he was forced to shed his habit of slothfulness as completely as a snake sheds its skin, and that was during the week before "Bob's" arrival. Then, indeed, he swept and he dusted, he mopped and he polished, he rubbed and he scrubbed, trying his best to put the house in order. Never in all his life had he labored as he did then, for four years of "batching" will make a bear's nest out of the most orderly house, but he was jealous of his task and he refused to share it with other hands. Pots and pans, rusty from disuse or bearing the accumulated evidence of many hastily prepared meals, he took out in the back yard and scrubbed with sand, leaving his bony knuckles skinned and bleeding from the process; he put down a new carpet in "Bob's" room, no easy task for a man with an ossified knee joint—incidentally, the "damn thing" kept him awake for two nights thereafter; he nailed up fresh curtains, or they looked fresh to him, at her windows, and smashed a perfectly good thumb-nail in doing so. This and many other abominable duties he performed. But love means suffering, and every pang gave Old Tom a thrill of fierce delight for—"Bob" was coming. The lonely, hungry, aching wait was over.

Constant familiarity with the house had mercifully dulled the occupant's appreciation of its natural deterioration and the effects of his neglect, so when he finally straightened his aching back and regarded the results of his heroic efforts, it seemed to him that everything shone like new and that the place was as neat and as clean as on the day "Bob" went away. Probably Hercules thought the Augean stables were spotless and fragrant when he had finished with them. And perhaps they were, but Tom Parker was no demigod. He was just a clumsy old man, unaccustomed to indoor "doings," and his eyes at times during the last few days had been unaccountably dim—as, for instance, while he was at work in Barbara's chamber.

He did not sleep much on the night before the girl's arrival. He sat until late with the framed photograph of Barbara's mother on his knee, and tried to tell the dead and gone original that he had done his best for the girl so far, and if he had failed, it was because he knew nothing about raising girls and—nature hadn't cut him out to be a father, anyhow. He had been considerably older than Barbara's mother when he married her, and he had never ceased to wonder what there had been in him to win the love of a woman like her, or to regret that fate had not taken him instead of her. Heaven knows his calling had been risky enough. But—that was how things went sometimes—the wheat was taken and the chaff remained.

And in the morning! Tom was up before daylight and had his dishes washed and his things in order long ere the town was awake. Then he went down to the office and waited—with the jumps. Repeatedly he consulted his heavy gold watch, engraved: "With the admiration and gratitude of the citizens of Burlingame. November fifth, 1892." It was still two hours of train time when he locked up and limped off toward the station, but—it was well to be there early.

Of course he met Judge Halloran on the street—he always did—and of course the judge asked when "Bob" was coming home. The judge always did that, too. Old Tom had lied diligently to the judge every day for a month now, for he had no intention of sharing this day of days with a tiresome old pest, and now he again made an evasive answer.

"Mendacity is at once the lowest and the commonest form of deceit," the judge indignantly announced. "You know perfectly well when she's coming, damn you!"

"Honest, I don't—not exactly."

But the judge was unconvinced. "You've been as mysterious as a bootlegger for the last week, but I could always read you like a book, Tom Parker. You know, all right. Mrs. Halloran wants to come over and fix things up for her. She said so this—"

"Oh, I got everything fixed," Tom hastily declared. "Ha! What did I tell you?" The judge glared; Tom could have bitten his tongue for that slip. "Your pitiful attempts to mislead Barbara's admirers expose you to ridicule, and offend those of us who tolerate you out of regard for her." (The judge had a nice Texas drawl, and he pronounced it "reegy'ad.") "You're on your way to the train at this moment and—I propose to accompany you."

"What would I be going to the train for, now?" Tom inquired, in a deceitfully mild tone. Inwardly he was raging, and he cursed the judge for a meddlesome old fool.

"Hm-m! Thought you'd sneak down there, unobserved, probably." There was a pause; then the speaker went on in an altered tone: "D'you suppose she has forgotten all her native accomplishments, Tom? I wonder if she can still ride and rope and shoot, or if those thin-blooded Eastern schoolma'ams have taught her that such things are unladylike and coarse."

"Pshaw! You never forget how to do those things."

"She could handle a horse or a rope or a gun as well as you at your best."

"*Better!*" Tom declared, with swelling pride.

Halloran wagged his white head in agreement, an unusual procedure, inasmuch as he never agreed with Tom on any subject which offered possible ground for disagreement. "A wonderful girl! And I'll wager they haven't spoiled her. Even *you* couldn't spoil 'Bob.'" He raised his red, belligerent eyes and fixed them upon his old friend, but there was now a kindly light in them. "You made a real son of her, didn't you, Tom?"

"Almost. I was mighty disappointed because she was a girl, but—I don't know as a boy could of turned out much better. Well, Judge, I got to be moving."

"You are neither grammatical nor precise," snapped Judge Halloran. "You mean *we* must be moving." He linked arms with Tom and fell into step with him; he clung to that rigid arm, moreover, despite Tom's surly displeasure. Not until a friend stopped them for a word or two was the distracted parent enabled to escape from that spidery embrace; then, indeed, he slipped it as a filibustering schooner slips its moorings, and made off as rapidly and as unobtrusively as possible.

Judge Halloran stared after the retreating figure, then he showed his decayed teeth in a smile. "'Bob' is coming home to-day and the old Mountain Lion is on edge," he explained. "I must warn the boys to stay away from the station and give him his hour. Poor Tom! He has held his breath for four years."

Tom Parker had heard of children spoiled by schooling, of daughters educated away from their commonplace parents and rendered disdainful of them, but never for one instant did he fear that his girl was that sort. He just knew better. He could no more have doubted "Bob's" love for him than his for her, or-God's love for both of them. Such love is perfect, absolute. He took no thought, therefore, of the changes time and poverty had wrought in his appearance: "Bob" wouldn't notice. He bet she wouldn't care if he was plumb ragged. They were one and indivisible; she was *his*, just like his right arm; she was his boy and his girl; his son-daughter. The old gunman choked and his tonsils ached abominably. He hoped he wasn't in for another attack of quinsy sore throat. But—why lie to himself? The truth was, he wanted to cry and he wanted to laugh at the same time, and the impulses were crossed in his windpipe. He shook his watch like a child's rattle, to be sure it was still running.

Barbara did not disappoint her father. On the contrary, she was perhaps more deeply moved than he at their meeting. At sight of him she uttered a strangled little cry, then she ran into his arms and clung there, tightly, her cheek pressed against his breast. It was only upon occasions like this that "Bob" kissed her father, for she had been reared as a boy and taught to shun emotional display. Boys kiss their mothers. She snuggled close, and Tom could feel her whole body shaking; but she kept her head averted to conceal a distressingly unmasculine weakness. It was a useless precaution, however, for Tom was blind, his eyes were as wet as hers, and tears were trickling down the seams in his wrinkled face.

"Oh, daddy, it has been a long time!" Those were the first words either of them had spoken.

Tom opened his lips, then he closed them. He patted Barbara clumsily, and finally cleared his aching throat with a loud "*Harrumph!*" He dashed the tears from his eyes with the heel of one harsh palm, then leveled a defiant glare over her head, directed at anyone who might be looking on at his weakness. It was a blurry glare, however, andnot nearly so ferocious as he intended it to be. After several efforts he managed to regain control of his vocal powers.

"Well, son!" he cried, huskily; then, "*Harrumph!*"

Barbara's clutch tightened appreciatively. "Such a long, long time!" Still with her cheek pressed close against him, she ran a small gloved hand into the pocket of his coat and brought forth a bandana handkerchief which she thrust into his palm, saying: "It's a good thing I'm home, for you've caught another cold, haven't you? Now blow your nose."

Barbara was anything but boyish to look at; quite the opposite, in fact. She was delightfully feminine from the crown of her smart little traveling hat to her dainty French heels, and although her suit was not expensive, it was worn with an air and was perhaps as fetching as any that had ever come to Wichita Falls. It gave the impression of perfectly setting off a figure and a personality that required no setting off. She had the Parker eyes of quenchless blue.

"Well, son, there's a boom on and the town has grown some; but I guess things here are about the same as when you left 'em." Tom spoke with pride and satisfaction as he paid the driver, took Barbara's suitcase, and opened the gate for her.

The girl turned from her first long, appraising gaze at the modest home. No change, indeed! The paint on the house was peeling, gutters had rusted out, some of the porch flooring had rotted through, the yard was an unkempt tangle of matted grass and weeds and neglected shrubbery. The sight of it was like a stab to her, for she remembered the place as it had been, and the shock was akin to that of seeing a loved one in the garb of a tramp. But she smiled up at the gray face above her—Tom, too, was as seedy as the premises—and she nodded.

"It hasn't changed a mite," she said, bravely.

A moment later she paused upon the threshold, tense, thrilled, apparently speechless. Tom was reminded of a trim little wren poised upon the edge of its nest. This time it was more difficult to counterfeit an exclamation of joy, but the catch in "Bob's" voice, the moisture in her eyes, was attributed by her father to gladness at the sight of old familiar things. This was pay for the thought and the love and the labor expended, truly.

"Why, everything is right where it belongs! How *wonderfully* you've kept house! You must have a perfect jewel of a girl, dad!"

"I let Aunt Lizzie go 'bout three years back," Tom explained. "She got—shiftless and I been sort of batching it since. Clean, though, ain't it?"

Barbara turned; blindly she walked to the center table and buried her face in a bouquet of wild flowers garnered from the yard. She held it there for a moment before she spoke. "You—didn't even forget that I love bluebonnets, did you, dad?"

"Pshaw! I 'ain't had much to do but remember what you like, son."

"What's the matter? Business bad?" "Bob's" face was still hidden.

"Oh no! I'm busy as usual. But, now you're home, I'll probably feel like doing more. I got a lot of work left in me yet, now I got somebody to work for."

"So you fixed everything with your own hands."

"Sure! I knew how you like the place to look, and—well, a

man gets used to doing without help. The kitchen's clean, too."

Side by side the two moved from room to room, and, once the girl had regained control of herself, she maintained an admirable self-restraint. She petted and she cooed over objects dear to her; she loved every inch of everything; she laughed and she exclaimed, and with her laughter sunshine suddenly broke into the musty, threadbare interior for the first time in four years.

"Bob's" room was saved for the last, and Old Tom stood back, glowing at her delight. He could not refrain from showing her his blackened thumb-nail—the price of his carpentry—for he hoped she'd kiss it. And she did. Not until she had "shooed" him out and sent him downstairs, smiling and chuckling at her radiant happiness, did she give way to those emotions she had been fighting this long time; then her face grew white and tragic. "Oh, daddy, daddy!" she whispered. "What *have* I done to you?"

Tom Parker had raised his girl like a son, and like a son she took hold of things, but with a daughter's tact. Her intuition told her much, but she did not arrive at a full appreciation of the family affairs until she had the house running and went down to put his office in order. Then, indeed, she learned at what cost had come those four expensive years in the East, and the truth left her limp. She went through Tom's dusty, disordered papers, ostensibly rearranging and filing them, and they told her much; what they did not tell her she learned from Judge Halloran and other old cronies who came in to pay their garrulous compliments.

Tom was mortgaged to the hilt, his royalties were pledged; a crow could not pick a living out of his insurance business.

Such a condition was enough to dismay any girl who had never seriously considered money matters and who had returned home to take up a life of comparative ease and superlative enjoyment where she had left it off, but "Bob" said nothing to her father. She knew every one of his shortcomings, and they endeared him to her, quite as a son's faults and failures deepen a mother's love, but she knew, too, that he was cantankerous and required careful handling. Tom's toes were tender, and he forever exposed them where they were easily trodden upon, therefore the girl stepped cautiously and never even referred to his sacrifices, which would have cruelly embarrassed both of them.

But something had to be done, and quickly; a new hand needed to mend the family fortunes. Barbara determined to lend that hand.

A great change had come over the town and the whole country round about, a change which the girl believed afforded her an opportunity to prove that she was not a mere daughter, not an ornament and a drag, but a real son-daughter such as Tom considered her. Wichita Falls was overcrowded with oil man, drawn thither by the town-site strike at Burkburnett, a few miles northwest, and excitement was mounting as new wells continued to come in. Central north Texas was nearing an epoch-making petroleum boom, for Ranger, away to the south, had set the oil world by the ears, and now this new sand at "Burk" lent color to the wild assertion that these north counties were completely underlaid with the precious fluid. At any rate, the price of thirsty ranch lands was somersaulting and prosperity was apparent in the homes of all Barbara's girl friends. Her admirers of the opposite sex could talk of little except leases and bonuses and "production"; they were almost too busy making money to call upon her.

Barbara knew something about oil, for she had watched the drilling of every one of those shallow wells that had kept her in college, and what is more, she knew most of the property owners in this part of the state. In that advantage she believed lay her chance of accomplishment.

After a fortnight of careful consideration she decided to enter the oil business and deal in leases.

"Good idea," Tom declared, when she had made known her plan. "The town's so full of scamps it looks like Rodeo Day, and most of 'em are doing well. If they can make good, it seems like an honest firm could do better."

"We'll be partners, dad. You run the insurance and I'll be the lease hound."

"Say—" Tom's eyes brightened. "I'll put a desk right alongside of mine—a little feller, just your size—and a nice lounge in the back room, where you can lay down when you're tired. You been away so long it seems like I can't have you close enough." Another thought presented itself, and he manifested sudden excitement. "I tell you! I'll get a new sign painted, too! 'Tom and Bob Parker. Real Estate and Insurance. Oil Prop'ties and Leases.' *Gosh!* It's a *great* idea, son!" His smile lingered, but a moment later there came into his eyes a half-regretful light.

Barbara read his thought almost before he was aware of it, and, rising, she laid her hand upon his shoulder. Wistfully she said, "I'm awfully sorry, too, dad—"

"Eh?"

"—that I disappointed you so by not being a boy. But—it wasn't my fault, and maybe I'll show you that a daughter can help as much as a son."

CHAPTER IV

A year before this story opens the town of Ranger, Texas, consisted of a weatherbeaten, run-down railroad station, a blacksmith shop, and a hitching rail, town enough, incidentally, for the limited number of people and the scanty amount of merchandise that passed through it. Ranger lay in the dry belt—considered an almost entirely useless part of the state—where killing droughts were not uncommon, and where for months on end the low, flinty hills radiate heat like the rolls of a steel mill. In such times even the steep, tortuous canyons dried out and there was neither shade nor moisture in them. The few farms and ranches round about were scattered widely, and life thereon was a grim struggle against heartbreak, by reason of the gaunt, gray, ever-present specter of the drought. Of late this particular region had proven itself to be one of violent extremes, of extreme dryness during which flowers failed to bloom, the grass shriveled and died, and even the trees refused to put forth leaves; or, more rarely, of extreme wetness, when the country was drowned beneath torrential rains. Sometimes, during unusual winters, the heavens opened and spilled themselves, choking the narrow watercourses, washing out roads and destroying fields, changing the arid arroyos into raging river beds. At such times life for the country people was scarcely less burdensome than during the droughts, for the heavy bottom lands became quagmires, and the clay of the higher levels turned into putty or a devilish agglutinous substance that rendered travel for man or beast or vehicle almost impossible.

Rex Beach

There appeared to be no law of average here. In dry times it was a desert, lacking wholly, however, in the beauty, the mystery, and the spell of a desert; in wet times it was a gehenna of mud and slush and stickiness, and entirely minus that beauty and freshness that attends the rainy seasons in a tropic clime. It was a land peopled by a hard-bitten race of nesters—come from God knows where and for God knows why—starved in mind and body, slaves of a hideous environment from which they lacked means of escape.

Geologists had claimed for some time that there must be coal in these north Texas counties, a contention perhaps based upon a comfortable belief in the law of compensation, upon a theory that a region so poor aboveground must of necessity contain values of some sort beneath the surface. But as for other natural resources, they scouted the belief in such. Other parts of the state yielded oil, for instance, but here the formation was all wrong. Who ever heard of oil in hard lime?

Nevertheless, petroleum was discovered, and among the fraternity that dealt in it Ranger became a word of contradiction and of deep meaning. Aladdin rubbed his lamp, and, lo! a magic transformation occurred; one of those thrilling dramas of a dramatic industry was played. A gypsy camp sprang up beside the blacksmith shop, and as the weeks fled by it changed into a village of wooden houses, then into a town, and soon into a city of brick and iron and concrete. The railroad became clogged with freight, a tidal wave of men broke over the town. Wagons, giant motor trucks, caterpillar tractors towing long strings of trailers, lurched and groaned and creaked over the hills, following roads unfit for a horse and buggy. Straddling derricks reared themselves everywhere; their feet were set in garden patches, in plowed fields, in lonely mesquite pastures, and even high up on the crests of stony ridges. One day their timbers were raw and clean, the next day they were black and greasy, advertising the fact that once again the heavy rock pressure far below had sent another fountain of fortune spraying over the top. Then pipe lines were laid and unsightly tank farms were built.

Ranger became a mobilization point, a vast concentration camp for supplies, and amid its feverish activity there was no rest, no Sundays or holidays; the work went on at top tension night and day amid a clangor of metal, a ceaseless roar of motors, a bedlam of hammers and saws and riveters. Men lived in greasy clothes, breathing dust and the odors of burnt gas mainly, eating poor food and drinking warm, fetid water when they were lucky enough to get any at all.

This was about the state of affairs that Calvin Gray found on the morning of his arrival. He and Mallow had managed to secure a Pullman section on the night train from Dallas; the fact that they were forced to carry their own luggage from the station uptown to the restaurant where they hoped to get breakfast was characteristic of the place. En route thither they had to elbow their way through a crowd that filled the sidewalks as if on a fair day.

Mallow was well acquainted with the town, it appeared, and during breakfast he maintained a running fire of comment, some of which was worth listening to.

"Ever hear how the first discovery was made? Well, the T. P. Company had the whole country plastered with coal leases and finally decided to put down a fifteen-hundred-foot wildcat. The guy that ran the rig had a hunch there was oil here if he went deep enough, but he knew the company wouldn't stick, so he faked the log of the well as long as he could, then he kept on drilling, against orders—refused to open his mail, for fear he'd find he was fired and the job called off. He was a thousand feet deeper than he'd been ordered to go when— blooie! Over the top she went with fourteen hundred barrels.... Desdemona's the name of a camp below here, but they call it Hog Town. More elegant! Down there the derricks actually straddle one another, and they have to board them over to keep from drowning one another out when they blow in. Fellow in Dallas brought in the first well, and it was so big that his stock went from a hundred dollars a share to twelve thousand. All in a few weeks. Of course, he started a bank.

Funniest people I ever saw, that way. Usually when a rube makes a winning he gambles or gets him a woman, but these hicks take their coin and buy banks.... Ranger's a real town; everything wide open and the law in on the play. That makes good times. Show me a camp where the gamblers play solitaire and the women take in washing and I'll show you a dead village. The joints here have big signs on the wall, '*Gambling Positively Prohibited*,' and underneath the games are running high, wide, and fancy. Refined humor, I call it.... There were nine killings one day, but that's above the average. The last time I was in town a couple of tool dressers got into a row with a laundryman—claimed they'd been overcharged six cents. It came to a shooting, and we buried all three of them. Two cents apiece! That was their closing price. The cost of living is high enough, but it isn't expensive to die here."

In this vein ran Mallow's talk. From the first he had laid himself out to be entertaining and helpful, and Gray obligingly permitted him to have his way. When they had finished breakfast, he even allowed his companion to hire an automobile and driver for him. They shook hands finally, the best of friends. Mallow wished him good luck and gravely voiced the hope that he would have fewer diamonds when he returned. Gray warmly thanked his companion for his many courtesies and declared they would soon meet again.

Thus far the trip had worked out much as Gray had expected. Now, as his service car left the town and joined the dusty procession of vehicles moving country-ward, he covertly studied its driver and was gratified to note that the fellow bore all the ear-marks of a thorough scoundrel. What conversation the man indulged in strengthened that impression.

The Briskow farm, it appeared, lay about twenty miles out, but twenty miles over oil-field roads proved to be quite a journey. During the muddy season the driver declared, it might well take a whole day to make that distance; now that the roads were dry, they could probably cover it in two or three hours, if the car held together. Traffic near Ranger was terrific, and how it managed to move, even at a snail's pace, was a mystery, for to sit a car was like riding a bucking horse. If there had been the slightest attempts at road building they were now invisible, and the vehicular streams followed meandering wagon trails laid down by the original inhabitants of pre-petroleum days, which had not been bettered by the ceaseless pounding of the past twelve months. Up and down, over armored ridges and into sandy arroyos, along leaning hillsides and across 'dobe flats, baked brick hard by the sun, the current of travel roared and pounded with reckless disregard of tire and bolt and axle. In the main, it was a motor-driven procession. There were, to be sure, occasional teams of fine imported draft horses, but for every head of live stock there were a dozen huge trucks, and for every truck a score of passenger cars. These last were battered and gray with mud, and their dusty occupants were of a color to match, for they drove blindly through an asphyxiating cloud. Even the thirsty vegetation beside the roads was coated gray, and was so tinder dry that it seemed as if a lighted match would explode it.

The sun glared cruelly, and the pyramidal piles of iron pipe chained to the groaning trucks and plunging trailers were hot enough to fry eggs upon, but neither they nor the steaming radiators gave off more heat than the soil and the rocks.

Detours were common—testimony to man's inherent optimism—but each was worse than the other, the roadbeds everywhere were rutted, torn, broken up as if from long-continued heavy shell fire.

From every ridge skeleton derricks were in sight as far as the eye could reach, the scattered ones, whose clean timbers gleamed in the sunlight, testifying to dry holes; the blackened ones, usually in clumps, indicating "production"—magic word.

There were a few crossroads settlements—"hitch-rail towns" —unpainted and ramshackle, but nowhere was there an attempt at farming, for this part of Texas had gone hog wild over oil. Abandoned straw stacks had settled and molded, cornfields had grown up to weeds, what few head of cattle still remained lolled near the artificial surface tanks, all but dried into mud holes.

It was a farm of this character that Gray's driver finally pointed out as the Briskow ranch. The house, an unsightly story-and-a-half affair, stood at the back of what had once been a cultivated field, and the place was distinctive only in the fact that it gave evidence of a good water well, or a capacious reservoir, in the form of a vivid green garden patch and a few flourishing peach trees immediately behind the residence—welcome relief to the eye.

Nobody answered Gray's knock at the front door, so he walked around the house. Over the garden fence, grown thick with brambles, he beheld two feminine figures, or rather two faded sunbonnets topping two pairs of shoulders, and as he drew nearer he saw that one woman was bent and slow moving, while the other was a huge creature, wide of hip and deep of bosom, whose bare arms, burnt to a rich golden brown, were like those of a blacksmith, and who wielded her heavy hoe as if it were a toy. She was singing in a thin, nasal, uncultivated voice.

Evidently they were the Briskow "help," therefore Gray made his presence known and inquired for the master or mistress of the place.

The elder woman turned, exposing a shrewd, benevolent face, and after a moment of appraisal said, "I'm Miz' Briskow."

"Indeed!" The visitor smiled his best and announced the nature of his errand.

"Lawsy me!" Mrs. Briskow planted her hoe in the soil and turned her back upon Gray. "Allie! Yore pa has gone an' done it again. Here's another of his fool notions."

The women regarded each other silently, their facial expressions hidden beneath their bonnets; then the mother exposed her countenance a second time, and said, "Mister, this is Allegheny, our girl."

Miss Allegheny Briskow lifted her head, nodded shortly, and stared over the hoe handle at Gray. Her gaze was one of frank curiosity, and he returned it in kind, for he had never beheld a creature like her. Gray was a tall man, but this girl's eyes met his on a level, and her figure, if anything, was heavier than his. Nor was its appearance improved by her shapeless garment of faded wash material. Her feet were incased in a pair of men's cheap "brogans" that Gray could have worn; drops of perspiration gleamed upon her face, and her hair, what little was visible beneath the sunbonnet, was wet and untidy. Altogether she presented a picture such as some painter of peasant types might have sketched. Garbed appropriately, in shawl and sabots, she would have passed for some European plowwoman of Amazonian proportions. Allegheny! It was a suitable name, indeed, for such a mountainous person. Her size was truly heroic; she would have been grotesque, ridiculous, except for a certain youthful plasticity and a suggestion of tremendous vigor and strength that gave her dignity. Her ample, ill-fitting dress failed to hide the fact that her robust body was well, even splendidly molded.

Gray's attention, however, was particularly challenged by the girl's face and eyes. It was a handsome countenance, cut in large, bold features, but of a stony immobility; the eyes were watchful, brooding, sullen. They regarded him with mingled defiance and shyness for an instant, then they avoided his; she averted her gaze; she appeared to be meditating ignominious flight.

The mother abandoned her labor, wiped her hands upon her skirt, and said, with genuine hospitality: "Come right into the house and rest yourself. Pa and Buddy'll be home at dinner time." By now a fuller significance of this stranger's presence had struck home and she laughed softly as she led the way toward the dwelling. "Di'mon's for Allie and me, eh? Land sakes! Pa's up to something new every day, lately. I wonder what next."

As Gray stepped aside for the younger woman to precede him, his curiosity must have been patent, for Allegheny became even more self-conscious than before, and her face flamed a fiery red. As yet she had not spoken.

There were three rooms to the Briskow residence, bedrooms all, with a semi-detached, ramshackle, whitewashed kitchen at the rear and separated from the main house by a narrow "gallery." Into the front chamber, which evidently did service also as a parlor, Mrs. Briskow led the way. By now she was in quite a flutter of excitement. For the guest she drew forth the one rocking chair, a patent contraption, the rockers of which were held upon a sort of track by stout spiral springs. Its seat and back were of cheap carpet material stretched over a lacquered frame, and these she hastily dusted with her apron; then she seated herself upon the edge of the bed and beamed expectantly.

Allegheny had carelessly brushed back her sunbonnet, exposing a mane of damp, straight, brown hair of a quantity and length to match her tremendous vigor of limb; but she remained standing at the foot of the bed, too ill at ease to take a chair or perhaps too agitated to see one. She was staring straight ahead, her eyes fixed a foot or two over the caller's head.

Gray ignored her manifest embarrassment, made a gingerly acquaintance with the chair of honor, and then devoted his attention to the elder woman. At every move the coiled springs under him strained and snapped alarmingly.

"We don't often see jewelry peddlers," the mother announced; "but, sakes alive! things is changin' so fast we get a new surprise most every day. I s'pose you got those rings in that valise?" She indicated Gray's stout leather sample case.

"Precisely," said he. "If you have time I'd like to show them to you."

Mrs. Briskow's bent figure stirred, she uttered a throaty chuckle, and her weary face, lined with the marks of toil and hardship, flushed faintly. Her misshapen hands tightly clasped themselves and her faded eyes began to sparkle. Gray felt a warm thrill of compassion at the agitation of this kindly, worn old soul, and he rose quickly. As he gained his feet that amazing chair behaved in a manner wholly unusual and startling; relieved of strain, the springs snapped and whined, there was a violent oscillation of the back, a shudder convulsed the thing, and it sprang after him, much as a tame rabbit thumps its feet upon the ground in an effort to bluff a kitten.

The volunteer salesman spread out his dazzling wares upon the patchwork counterpane, then stepped back to observe the effect. Ma Briskow's hands fluttered toward the gems, then reclasped themselves in her lap; she bent closer and regarded them fixedly. The Juno-like daughter also stared down at the display with fascination.

After a moment Allegheny spoke, and her speaking voice was in pleasing contrast to the nasal notes of that interrupted song. "Are them *real* di'mon's?" she queried, darkly.

"Oh yes! And most of them are of very fine quality."

"Pa never told us a word," breathed the mother. "He's *allus* up to some trick."

"Please examine them. I want you to look them all over," Gray urged.

Mrs. Briskow acted upon this invitation only after she had dried her hands, and then with trepidation. Gingerly, reverently she removed a ring from its resting place and held it up to the light. "My! Ain't it sparkly?" she gasped, after an ecstatic pause.

Again the girl spoke, her eyes fixed defiantly upon Gray. "You could fool us easy, 'cause we never saw *real* di'mon's. We've allus been too pore."

The man nodded. "I hope you're not disappointed in them and I hope you are going to see and to own a great many finer ones.

"We've never seen noth—anything, nor been anywhere, yet." It was Mrs. Briskow speaking. "But we're goin'. We're goin' lots of places and we're goin' to see everything wuth seein', so Pa says. Anyhow, the children is. First off, Pa's goin' to take us to the mountains." The mother faced the visitor at this announcement and for a moment she appeared to be gazing at a vision, for her wrinkled countenance was glorified. "You've seen 'em, haven't you, mister?"

"Mountains? A great many."

Allegheny broke in: "I dunno's these di'mon's is just what *I* expected 'em to be. They are and—they ain't. I'm kind of disapp'inted."

Gray smiled. "That is true of most things that we anticipate or aspire to. It's the tragedy of accomplishment—to find that our rewards are never quite up to our expectations."

"Do they cost much?"

"Oh, decidedly! The prices are all plainly marked. Please look them over."

Ma Briskow did as urged, but the shock was paralyzing; delight, admiration, expectancy, gave place to horrified amazement at the figures upon the tags. She shook her head slowly and made repeated sounds of disapproval.

"Tse! Tse! Tse! Why, your pa's crazy! Plumb crazy!"

Although the mother's principal emotion for the moment was aroused by the price marks on the price tags, Allegheny paid little attention to them and began vainly fitting ring after ring to her fingers. All were too small, however; most of them refused to pass even the first joint, and Gray realized now what Gus Briskow had meant when he wrote for rings "of large sises." Eventually the girl found one that slipped into place, and this she regarded with complacent admiration.

"This one'll do for me," she declared. "And it's a whopper!"

Gray took her hand in his; as yet it had not been greatly distorted by manual labor, but the nails were dull and cracked and ragged and they were inlaid in deep mourning. "I don't believe you'll like that mounting," he said, gently. "It's what we call a man's ring. This is the kind women usually wear." He held up a thin platinum band of delicate workmanship which Allegheny examined with frank disdain.

"Pshaw! I'd bust that the first time I hoed a row of 'taters," she declared. "I got to have things stout, for me."

"But," Gray protested, in even a milder voice, "you probably wouldn't want to wear expensive jewelry in the garden."

Miss Briskow held her hand high, admiring the play of light upon the facets of the splendid jewel, then she voiced a complacent thought that has been variously expressed by other women better circumstanced than she—"If we can afford to buy 'em, I reckon we can afford to wear 'em."

Not until Gray had suggested that her days of work in the fields were probably about ended did the girl's expression change. Then indeed her interest was arrested. She regarded him with a sudden quickening of imagination; she revolved the novel idea in her mind.

"From what my driver has told me about the Briskow farm," he ran on, "you won't have to work at anything, unless you care to."

Allie continued to weigh this new thought in her mind; that it intrigued her was plain, but she made no audible comment.

CHAPTER V

For perhaps half an hour the women tried on one piece of jewelry after another, exclaiming, admiring, arguing, then the mother realized with a start that meal time was near and that the menfolks would soon be home. Leaving Allie to entertain their guest, she hurried out, and the sound of splitting kindling, the clatter of stove lids, the rattle of utensils came from the kitchen.

Gray retired to the patent rocker, Miss Briskow settled herself upon a straight-backed chair and folded her capable hands in her lap; an oppressive silence fell upon the room. Evidently the duties of hostess lay with crushing weight upon the girl, for her face became stony, her cheeks paled, her eyes glazed; the power of speech completely failed her and she answered Gray with nods or shakes of her head. The most that he could elicit from her were brief "yeps" and "nopes." It was not unlike a "spirit reading," or a ouija-board seance. He told himself, in terms of the oil fields, that here was a dry well—that the girl was a "duster." Having exhausted the usual commonplace topics in the course of a monologue that induced no reaction whatever, he voiced a perfectly natural remark about the wonder of sudden riches. He was, in a way, thinking aloud of the changes wrought in drab lives like the Briskows' by the discovery of oil. He was surprised when Allegheny responded:

"Ma and me stand it all right, but it's an awful strain on Pa," said she.

"Indeed?"

The girl nodded. "He's got *more*

 nutty notions."

Gray endeavored to learn the nature of Pa's recently acquired eccentricities, but Allie was flushing and paling as a result of her sudden excursion into the audible. Eventually she trembled upon the verge of speech once more, then she took another desperate plunge.

"He says folks are going to laugh *at* us or *with* us, and—and rich people have got to *act rich*. They got to be elegant." She laughed loudly, abruptly, and the explosive nature of the sound startled her as greatly as it did her hearer. "He's going to get somebody to teach Buddy and me how to behave."

"I think he's right," Gray said, quietly.

"Why, he's sent to Fort Worth for a piano, already, and for a lady to come out for a coupla days and show me how to play it!" There was another black hiatus in the conversation. "We haven't got a spare room, but—I'm quick at learnin' tunes. She could bunk in with me for a night or two."

Gray eyed the speaker suspiciously, but it was evident that she was in sober earnest, and the tragedy of such profound ignorance smote the man sharply. Here was a girl of at least average intelligence and of sensitive makeup; a girl with looks, too, in spite of her size, and no doubt a full share of common sense—perhaps even talents of some sort—yet with the knowledge of a child. For the first time he realized what playthings of Fate are men and women, how completely circumstance can make or mar them, and what utter paralysis results from the strangling grip of poverty.

History hints that during the Middle Ages there flourished an association known as Comprachicos—"child-buyers"—which traded in children. The Comprachicos bought little human beings and disfigured their features, distorted their bodies, fashioned them into ludicrous, grotesque, or hideous monstrosities for king and populace to laugh at, and then resold them. Soft, immature faces were made into animal likenesses; tender, unformed bodies were put into wicker forms or porcelain vases and allowed to grow; then when they had become things of compressed flesh and twisted bone, the wicker was cut, the vase was broken, leaving a man in the shape of a bottle or a mug.

That is precisely what environment does.

In the case of Allegheny Briskow, poverty, the drought, the grinding hardships of these hard-scrabble Texas counties, had dwarfed the intellect, the very soul of a splendid young animal. Or so, at least, Gray told himself. It was a thought that evoked profound consideration.

Now that the girl was beginning to lose her painful embarrassment, she showed to somewhat better advantage and no longer impressed him, as bovine, stolid, almost stupid; he could not but note again her full young figure, her well-shaped, well-poised head, and her regular features, and the pity of it seemed all the greater by reason thereof. He tried to visualize her perfectly groomed, clad in a smart gown molded over a well-fitting corset, with her feet properly shod and her hair dressed—but the task was beyond him. Probably she had never worn a corset, never seen a pair of silk stockings. He thought, too, of what was in store for her and wondered how she would fit into the new world she was about to enter. Not very well, he feared. Might not this prove to be the happiest period of all her new life, he asked himself. As yet the wonder and the glory of the new estate left room in her imagination for little else; the mold was broken, but the child was not conscious of its bottle shape. Nevertheless the shape was there. When that child learned the truth, when it heard the laughter and felt the ridicule, what then? He could not bring himself to envy Allegheny Briskow.

"First off, Ma and me are goin' over to Dallas to do some tradin'," the girl was saying. "After that we're goin' to the mountains."

"Your mother mentioned mountains."

"Yep. Her and Pa have allus been crazy about mountains, but they never seen 'em. That's the first thing Ma said when Number One blowed in. When we saw that oil go over the crown block, and when they told us that black stuff was really oil, Ma busted out cryin' and said she'd see the mountains, after all—then she wouldn't mind if she died. Pa he cried, too, we'd allus been so pore—You see, Ma's kind of marked about mountains—been that way since she was a girl. She cuts out stories and pictures of 'em. And that's how me and Buddy came to be named Allegheny and Ozark. But we never expected to *see* 'em. The drought burned us out too often."

Allegheny and Ozark. Quaint names. "Times must have been hard." The remark was intended only as a spur.

"*Hard!*" There was a pause; slowly the girl's eyes began to smolder, and as she went on in her deliberate way, memory set a tragic shadow over her face. "I'll say they was hard! Nobody but us nesters knows what hard times is. Out west of here they went three years without rain, and all around here people was starvin'. Grown folks was thin and tired, and children was sickly—they was too peaked to play. Why, we took in a hull family—wagon-folks. Their hosses died and they couldn't go on, so we kep' 'em—'til *we* burned out. I don't know how we managed to get by except that Pa and Buddy are rustlers and I can do more 'n a hired man. We *never* had enough to eat. Stuff just wouldn't grow. The stock got bonier and bonier and finally died, 'count of no grass and the tanks dryin' out. And all the time the sun was a-blazin' and the dust was a-blowin and the clouds would roll up and then drift away and the sun would come out hotter 'n ever. Day after day, month after month, we waited—eighteen, I think it was. People got so they wouldn't pray no more, and the preachers moved away. I guess we was as bad off as them pore folks in Beljum. Why, even the rattlesnakes pulled out of the country! Somehow the papers got hold of it and bime-by some grub was shipped in and give around, but—us Briskows didn't get none. Pa'd die before he'd beg."

The girl was herself now; she was talking naturally, feelingly, and her voice was both deep and pleasing.

"The thinner Ma got, the more she talked about the mountains, where there was water—cool, clear water in the criks. And timber on the hills—timber with green leaves on it. And grass that you could lay down in and smell. I guess Ma was kind of feverish. We was drier 'n a lime-burner's boot when the rain did come. I'll never forget—we all stood out in it and soaked it up. It was wonderful, to get all wet and soaky, and not with sweat."

"Then on top of that the oil came, too. It *must* have been wonderful."

"Yep. Now we're rich. And buyin' di'mon's and pianos and goin' to Dallas for pretty fixin's. Seems kinda dreamy." Allegheny Briskow closed her eyes, her massive crown of damp, disordered hair drooped backward and for a moment Gray was able, unobserved, to study her.

She had revealed herself to him, suddenly, in the space of a few moments, and the revelation added such poignancy to his previous thoughts that he regarded her with a wholly new sympathy. There was nothing dull about this girl. On the contrary, she had intelligence and feeling. There had been a rich vibrance in her voice as she told of that frightful ordeal; a dimness had come into her eyes as she spoke of her mother gabbling feverishly of the green hills and babbling brooks; she had yearned maternally at mention of those wretched little children. No, there was a sincere emotional quality concealed in this young giantess, and a sensitiveness quite unexpected.

Gray remained silent until she opened her eyes; then he said: "When you and your mother come to Dallas to do your shopping, won't you let me take you around to the right shops and see that you get the right things?" Then, prompted by the girl's quick resentment, he added, hastily,"—at the right prices?"

Allie's face cleared. "Why, that's right nice of you!" she declared. "I—I reckon we'd be glad to."

Gus Briskow was a sandy, angular man; a ring of air holes cut in the crown of his faded felt hat showed a head of hair faded to match the color of his headgear; his greasy overalls were tucked into boots, and a ragged Joseph's coat covered his flannel shirt. Both the man and his makeup were thoroughly typical of this part of the country, except in one particular—Pa Briskow possessed the brightest, the shrewdest pair of blue eyes that Calvin Gray had ever seen, and they were surrounded by a network of prepossessing wrinkles.

He came directly in to greet his visitor, then said: "I never expected you'd come 'way out here an' bring your plunder with you. Ma says you got a hull gripful o' di'mon's."

"I have, indeed." Gray pointed to the glittering display still spread out upon the varicolored counterpane.

Briskow approached the bed and gazed curiously, silently down at the treasure, then his face broke into a sunshiny smile. He wiped his hands upon his trousers legs and picked up a ring. But instead of examining the jewel, he looked at the price mark, after which his smile broadened.

Ozark had entered behind his father, and his sister introduced him now. He was a year or two younger than Allegheny, but cast in the same heroic mold. They formed a massive pair of children indeed, and, as in her case, a sullen distrust of strangers was inherent in him. He stared coldly, resentfully, at Gray, mumbled an unintelligible greeting, then rudely turned his back upon the visitor and joined his father.

The elder Briskow spoke first, and it was evident that he feared to betray lack of conservatism, for he said, with admirable restraint:

"Likely-lookin' lot of trinkets, eh, Bud?"

Bud grunted. After a moment he inquired of Gray, "How much is that hull lot wuth, Mister?"

"Close to a hundred thousand dollars."

Brother and sister exchanged glances; the father considered briefly, smilingly, then he said, "With oil at three an' a quarter, it wouldn't take long for a twelve-hundred bar'ler to get the hull caboodle, would it?" "Is your well producing twelve hundred barrels a day?"

"Huh!" Briskow, junior, grinned at his sister, exposing a mouth full of teeth as white and as sound as railroad crockery, but his next words were directed at Gray: "We got *four* wells and the p'orest one is makin' twelve hundred bar'l."

The guests' mental calculations as to the Briskow royalties were interrupted by an announcement that dinner was ready, whereupon the father announced:

"Mister, it looks like you'd have to stay overnight with us, 'cause I got important business after dinner an' I wouldn't trust Ma to pick out no jewelry by herself—them prices would skeer her to death. We're ignorant people and we ain't used to spendin' money, so it'll take time for us to make up our minds. Kin you wait?"

"I'll stay as long as you'll keep me," Gray declared, heartily.

A moment later, having learned that a place at the table had been set for his driver as well as himself, Gray stepped out to summon the man and to effect the necessary change in his arrangements. He was not surprised to find the chauffeur with nose flattened against a pane of the front-room window, his hands cupped over his eyes. Ignoring the fellow's confusion at being discovered, Gray told him of his change of plan and instructed him to drive back to Ranger and to return late the following afternoon. Then he led the way toward the kitchen.

That stay at the Briskows' turned out to be less irksome than the visitor had anticipated, for the afternoon was spent with Buddy examining the Briskow wells and others near by. It was an interesting experience, and Gray obtained a deal of first-hand information that he believed would come in handy. Buddy's first mistrust was not long in passing, and, once Gray had penetrated his guard, the boy was won completely, the pendulum swung to the opposite extreme, and erelong suspicion changed to liking, then to approval, and at last to open, extravagant admiration.

And Gray liked the youthful giant, too, once the latter had dropped his hostility and had become his natural self, for Ozark was a lad with temper and with temperament. They got along together swimmingly; in fact, they grew thicker than thieves in the course of time. The elder man soon became conscious of the fact that he was being studied, analyzed, even copied—the sincerest form of flattery—and it pleased his vanity. Buddy's mind was thirsty, his curiosity was boundless, questions popped out of him at every step, and every answer, every bit of information or of philosophy that fell from the visitor's lips he pounced upon, avidly examined, then carefully put away for future use. He was like a magpie filling its nest. Gray's personal habits, mannerisms, tricks—all were grist for Buddy's mill. The stranger's suit, for instance, was a curiosity to the boy, who could not understand wherein it was so different from any other he had ever seen; young Briskow attributed that difference to the fact that it had probably come from a bigger store than any he had known. It amazed him to learn, in answer to a pointed question, that it had been cut and fitted to the wearer by expert workmen. It disappointed him bitterly to be informed that there was not another one exactly like it which he could buy.

And the visitor's silk shirt, with double cuffs and a monogram on the sleeve! Fancy "fixin's" like this, Buddy confessed, he had always associated with womenfolks, but if Gray wore them there could be nothing disgraceful, nothing effeminate about the practice. There was a decided thrill in the prospect of possessing such finery, all initialed with huge, silken O. B's. Life was presenting wholly novel and exciting possibilities to the youth.

When Gray offered him a cigarette, Buddy rudely took the gold case out of his hand and examined it, then he laughed in raucous delight.

"Gosh! I never knew men had *purty* things. I—I'm goin' to get me one like that."

"Do you like it?" "Gee! It's *swell*!"

"Good! I'll make you a present of it."

Buddy stared at the speaker in speechless surprise. "What—what for?" he finally stammered.

"Because you admire it."

"Why—it's solid gold, ain't it?"

"To be sure."

"How much d'it cost?"

"My dear fellow," Gray protested, "you shouldn't ask questions like that. You embarrass me."

Buddy examined the object anew, then he inquired, "Say, why'd you offer to gimme this?"

"I've just told you." Gray was becoming impatient. "It is a custom in some countries to present an object to one who is polite enough to admire it."

"Nobody never give *me* a present," Buddy said. "Not one that I wanted. I never had *nothing* that I didn't have to have and couldn't get along without. This cigareet case is worth more 'n all the stuff I ever owned, an' I'm sure obliged to you." He replaced the article in Gray's hand.

"Eh? Won't you accept it? Why not?"

"I—Oh, I dunno."

Gray pondered this refusal for a moment before saying, "Perhaps you think I'm—trying to make a good impression on you, so you'll buy some diamonds?"

"Mebbe." Buddy averted his eyes. He was in real distress.

"Um-m! I ought to punch your head." Gray slipped the case into young Briskow's pocket. "I don't have to bribe people. Some day you'll realize that I like you."

"*Honest?*"

"Cross my heart."

The boy laughed in frank delight, his brown cheeks colored, his eyes sparkled. "Gosh!" said he. "I—like *you!*" For some time thereafter he remained red and silent, but he kept one big hand in the pocket where lay the gold cigarette case. There was a wordless song in Buddy Briskow's heart, for—he had made a friend. And such a friend!

The Briskow children possessed each other's fullest confidence, hence Ozark took the first occasion to show his gift to Allegheny, and to tell her in breathless excitement all about that wonderful afternoon.

"He said he'd a mind to lick me, an' I bet he could 'a' done it, too," the boy concluded.

"Lick you? Hunh!"

"Oh, he's hard-boiled! That's why I like him. He's been 'round the world and speaks furrin language like a natif. That suit of clo's was *made* for him, an' he's got thirty others, all better 'n this one. Shoes, too! Made special, in New York. Forty dollars a pair!"

"What's he doin' here if he's so rich?" It was the doubting female of the species speaking. "Drummers is terrible liars."

Buddy flew to the defense of his hero. "He's doin' this to he'p a friend. Told me all about it. I'm goin' to have thirty suits—"

"Shoes don't cost forty dollars. *Clo's* don't cost that much." Allie regarded her brother keenly, understandingly, then she said, somberly, "It ain't no use, Buddy."

"What ain't?"

"It ain't no use to wish. Mebbe you can have thirty suits—if the wells hold out, but they won't look like his. And me, too. We're too big, Buddy, an' the more money we got, the more clo's we put on, the more folks is goin' to laugh at us. It shames me to go places with anybody but you."

"*He* wouldn't laugh. He's been all over the world," the boy asserted. Then, after some deliberation, "I bet he's seen bigger people than us."

As a matter of fact, Allegheny's sensitiveness about her size had been quickly apparent to Gray, and during that day he did his utmost to overcome it, but with what success he could not know. Buddy was his, body and soul, that much was certain; he made the conquest doubly secure by engaging the young Behemoth in a scuffle and playfully putting him on his back.

Defeat, at other hands than Gray's, would have enraged Ozark to the point of frenzy, it would have been considered by him an indignity and a disgrace. Now, however, he looked upon it as a natural and wholly satisfactory demonstration of his idol's supreme prowess, and he roared with delight at being bested. Gray promptly taught him the wrestling trick by which he had accomplished the feat, and flattered the boy immensely by refusing to again try his skill. The older man, when he really played, could enter into sport with tremendous zest and he did so now; he taught Buddy trick after trick; they matched each other in feats of strength and agility. They wound up finally on opposite sides of the Briskow kitchen table, elbows planted, fingers interlocked, straining furiously in that muscle-racking, joint-cracking pastime of the lumber camps known as "twisting arms." Here again Gray was victorious, until he showed Buddy how to gain greater leverage by changing the position of his wrist and by slightly altering his grip, where-upon the boy's superior strength told. They were red in the face, out of breath, and soaked with perspiration, when Pa Briskow drove up in his expensive new touring car.

By this time Buddy's admiration had turned to adulation; he had passed under the yoke and he gloried shamelessly in his captive state. At supper time he appeared with his hair wetly combed in imitation of Gray's. He wore a necktie, too, and into it he had fastened a cheap brass stickpin, much as Gray wore his. During the meal he watched how the guest used his knife and fork and made awkward attempts to do likewise, but a table fork was an instrument which, heretofore, Buddy had looked upon as a weapon of pure offense, like a whaler's harpoon, and conveniently designed either for spearing edibles beyond his reach or for retrieving fragments of meat lurking between his back teeth. He even did some hasty manicuring under the edge of the table with his jack-knife.

Pa Briskow was scarcely less observant than his son. He watched Gray's every move; he sounded him out adroitly; he pondered his lightest word. After the supper things had been cleared away and the dishes washed, the entire family adjourned to the front room and again examined the jewelry. It was an absorbing task, they did not hurry it. Not until the following afternoon, in fact, did they finally make their selections, and then they were guided almost wholly by the good taste of their guest. Gray did not exploit them. On the contrary, his effort was to limit their extravagance; but in this he had little success, for Pa Briskow had decided to indulge his generous impulses to the full and insisted upon so doing. The check he finally wrote was one of five figures.

By this time the visitor had become aware of arousing a queer reaction in Allegheny Briskow. He had overcome her diffidence early enough; he had unsealed her lips; he had obtained an insight into her character; but once that was done, the girl retired within herself again and he could get nothing more out of her. He would have believed that she actually disliked him, had it not been for the fact that whatever he said, she took as gospel, that wherever he chanced to be there she was, her ears open, her somber, meditative eyes fixed upon him. Evidently she did not actually dislike him; he decided finally that she was studying him, striving to analyze and to weigh him to her own complete satisfaction before trusting him further than she had.

When it drew near the time for him to leave, and he announced that the driver of his hired car had been instructed to return for him, there was protest, loud and earnest, from the Briskows, father and son. Buddy actually sulked at being denied the pleasure of driving his hero to town in the new car, and told about a smooth place on a certain detour where he could "get her up to sixty mile an hour." "If it was longer, she'd do a hundred," he declared.

Pa Briskow was worried for the security of the diamonds, and assured Gray that it was unsafe to trust those service-car drivers.

But the latter, seeing a threat to his carefully matured plans, refused to listen. "There's one thing you can do for me," he told them. "You can give me a pint of cream."

"Cream? What for?" The family regarded him with amazement.

"I'm fond of it. If you have no cream, milk will do."

"Pshaw! I'll put up a hull basket of lunch for you," Mrs. Briskow declared. "Buddy, go kill a rooster, an' you, Allie, get them eggs out of the nest in the garden, an' a jar of them peach preserves, while I make up a pan of biscuits."

Protest was unavailing.

When the others had hurried away, Pa Briskow said: "I been studyin' you, Mister Gray, and I got you down as a first-class man. When Ma and Allie come over to Dallas to get rigged out, I'd like you to help 'em. They 'ain't never been fu'ther from home than Cisco—that's thirty mile. I'll pay you for your time."

Gray's hearty acceptance of the first and his prompt refusal of the second proposal pleased the speaker.

"Bein' rich is mighty fine, but—" Gus Briskow shook his head doubtfully. "It takes a lot of thinkin', and I ain't used to thinkin'. Some day, mebbe, I'll get you to give *me* a hand in figgerin' out some worries."

"Business worries?"

"No. I got enough of them, an' more comin', but it ain't that. We're goin' to have a heap of money, and"—he looked up with straightforward eyes—"we ain't goin' to lose it, if I have my way. We've rubbed along, half starved, all our lives, an' done without things till we're—Well, look at us! I reckon we've made you laugh. Oh, I bet we have! Ma an' me can stand it, but, mister, I don't want folks to laugh at my children, and there's other things I don't want to happen to 'em. Buddy's a wild hoss and he's got a streak of the Old Nick in him. And Allie ain't broke no better 'n him. I got a feelin' there may be trouble ahead, an'—sometimes I 'most wish we'd never had no oil in Texas."

CHAPTER VI

"Well, did you land them hicks?" It was Gray's driver speaking. Through the gloom of early evening he was guiding his car back toward Ranger. The road was the same they had come, but darkness had invested it with unfamiliar perils, or so it seemed, for the headlights threw every rock and ridge into bold relief and left the holes filled with mysterious shadows; the vehicle strained, its motor raced, its gears clashed noisily as it rocked along like a dory in a boisterous tide rip. Only now and then did a few rods of smooth going permit the chauffeur to take his attention from the streak of illumination ahead long enough to light another cigarette, a swift maneuver, the dexterity of which bespoke long practice.

"Yes. And I made a good sale," the passenger declared. With pride he announced the size of the Briskow check.

"J'ever see a dame the size of that gal?" A short laugh issued from the driver. "She'd clean up in vaudeville, wouldn't she? Why, she could lift a ton, in harness. And hoein' the garden, with their coin! It's like a woman I heard of: they got a big well on their farm and she came to town to do some shoppin'; somebody told her she'd ought to buy a present for her old man, so she got him a new handle for the ax. *Gawd!*"

A few miles farther on the fellow confessed: "I wasn't crazy about comin' for you to-night. Not after I got a flash at what's in that valise."

"No?"

"You're takin' a chance, stranger."

"Nothing new about that." Gray remained unperturbed. His left arm was behind the driver; with it he clung rigidly to the back of the seat as the car plunged and rolled. "Frequently we are in danger when we least suspect it. Now you, for instance."

"Me?" The man at the wheel shot a quick glance at his fare.

"You probably take more chances than you dream of."

"How so?"

"Um-m! These roads are a menace to life and limb; the country is infested with robbers—"

"Oh, sure! That's what I had in mind. Joy-ridin' at night with a hatful of diamonds is my idea of a sucker's amusement. Of course, we won't 'get it'—"

"Of course! One never does."

"Sure! But if we should, there's just one thing to do."

"Indeed?" Gray was pleasantly inquisitive, but it was plain that he suffered no apprehensions. "And that is—?"

"Sit tight and take your medicine."

"I never take medicine."

The chauffeur shrugged his shoulders. "Well, I do, when it's put down my throat. I *been* stuck up."

"Really!"

"Twice. Tame as a house cat, me—both times. I s'pose I'll get nicked again sometime."

"And you won't offer any resistance?"

"Not a one, cull."

"I'm relieved to be assured of that."

For a second time the driver flashed a glance at his companion. It was a peculiar remark and voiced in a queer tone. "Yes? Why?"

"Because—" Gray slightly shifted his position, there was a movement of his right hand—the one farthest away from the man at the wheel—and simultaneously his left arm slipped from the back of the seat and tightly encircled the latter's waist. He finished in a wholly unfamiliar voice, "Because, my good man, you are now held up for the third time, and it would distress me to have to kill you."

The driver uttered a loud grunt, for something sharp and hard had been thrust deeply into that soft, sensitive region overlying his liver, and now it was held there. It was unnecessary for Gray to order the car stopped; its brakes squealed, it ceased its progress as abruptly as if its front wheels had fetched up against a stone wall.

"Hey! What the—?"

"Don't try to 'heel' me with your elbow," Gray warned, sharply. "Now, up with 'em—you know. That's nice."

The faces of the men were close together. Gray's was blazing, the driver's was stiff with amazement and stamped with an incredulous grimace. Paralyzed for the moment with astonishment, he made no resistance, not even when he felt that long muscular left arm relax and the hand at the end of it go searching over his pockets.

Gray was grim, mocking; some vibrant, evil quality to his voice suggested extreme malignity at full cock, like that unseen weapon the muzzle of which was buried beneath the driver's short ribs. "Ah! You go armed, I see. A shoulder holster, as I suspected. I knew you had nothing on this side." Seizing his victim's upstretched right hand with his own left, he gave it a sudden fierce wrench that all but snapped the wrist, and at the same instant he reached across and snatched the concealed weapon from its resting place. He flung the chauffeur's body away from him; there was a sharp click as he swiftly jammed the barrel of the automatic back and let it fly into place.

The entire maneuver had been deftly executed, even yet the object of the assault was speechless.

"Now then"—the passenger faced about in his seat and showed his teeth in a smile—"it is customary to permit the condemned to enjoy the last word. What have you to say for yourself?"

"I—got this to say. It's a hell of a joke—" the man exploded.

"Do I act as if I were joking?"

"If you think it's funny to jab a gun in a man's belly when he ain't lookin'—" "A gun? My simple friend, you have—or had—the only gun in this party, and you may thank whatever gods you worship that you didn't try to use it, for—I would have been rough with you. Oh, very rough! I might even have made you eat it. Now, inasmuch as you may be tempted to embellish this story with some highly imaginary details, I prefer that you know the truth. This is the 'gun' I used to stick you up." With a rigidly outthrust thumb Gray prodded the driver in the side. "Simple, isn't it? And no chance for accidents." The speaker's shoulders were shaking.

"Well, I'll be damned!"

"Not a doubt of it!" chuckled the other. "Especially if you

follow in the course you have chosen. And a similar fate will overtake your pal, Mallow. By the way, is that his right name?... Never mind, I know him as Mallow. A shallow, trusting man, and, I hope, a better judge of diamonds than of character. As for me, I look deeper than the surface and am seldom deceived in people—witness your case, for example. I knew you at once for a crook. It might save you several miles of bad walking to tell me where Mallow is waiting to high-jack me.... No?"

"I dunno what you're ravin' about," growled the unhappy owner of the automobile. "But, believe me, I'll have you pinched for this."

"How sharper than a serpent's tooth is ingratitude! And what bad taste to prattle of prosecution. I sha'n't steal your car, it needs too much overhauling. And I abominate cheap machines. It is true that I'm one pistol to the good, but in view of the law against carrying lethal weapons, surely you won't prefer charges against me for removing it from your person. Oh, not that! It seems to me that I'm treating you handsomely, for I shall even pay you the agreed price for this trip, provided only you tell me where you expect to meet Mr. Mallow."

"Go to hell!" "Very well. Oblige me now by getting out.... And make it snappy!"

The driver did as directed. Gray pocketed the automatic, slipped in behind the steering wheel, and drove away into the night, followed by loud and earnest objurgations.

He was still smiling cheerfully when, a mile farther on, he brought the car to a stop and clambered out. Passing forward into the illumination of the headlights, he busied himself there for several moments before resuming his journey.

For the first time in a long while Calvin Gray was thoroughly enjoying himself. Here was an enterprise with all the possibilities of a first-class adventure, and of the sort, moreover, that he was peculiarly qualified to cope with. It possessed enough hazard to lend it the requisite zest, it was sufficiently unusual to awaken his keenest interest; he experienced an agreeable exaltation of spirit, but no misgivings whatever as to the outcome, for he held the commanding cards. Little remained, it seemed to him, except to play them carefully and to take the tricks as they fell. He had not the slightest notion of permitting Mallow to lay hands upon that case of jewels.

There was no mistaking the road, but Gray did not bother to stick to the main-traveled course when detours or short cuts promised better going, for he knew full well that Mallow would be waiting, if at all, in some place he was bound to pass. It was an ideal country for a holdup; lonely and lawless. Derrick lights twinkled over the mesquite tops, and occasionally the flaming red mouth of some boiler gaped at him, or the foliage was illuminated by the glare of gas flambeaux—vertical iron pipes at the ends of which the surplus from neighboring wells was consumed in what seemed a reckless wastage. Occasionally, too, a belated truck thundered past, but the traffic was pretty thin.

At last, however, he beheld some distance ahead the white glare of two stationary lights. The road was narrow and sandy here, and shut in by banks of underbrush; as he drew nearer a figure stepped out and stood in silhouette until his own lights picked it up. The figure waved its arms, and called attention to the car behind—evidently broken down. Here, then, the drama was to be played.

Gray brought his machine on at such a pace and so close to the man in the road that the latter was forced to step aside, then he swung it far to the right, brought it back with a quick twist of the steering wheel, and killed his motor. He was now in the ditch and outside the blinding glare of the opposing headlights; the stalled machine was in the full illumination of his own lamps.

Contrary to Gray's expectations, the car in the road was empty and the man who had hailed him was a stranger. As the latter approached, he inquired:

"What's wrong?"

"Out of gas, I guess. Anyhow—I—" The speaker noted that there was but one new arrival, where he had expected two, and the discovery appeared to nonplus him momentarily. He stammered, involuntarily he turned his head.

Gray looked in the same direction, but without changing his position, and out of the corner of his eye he glimpsed a new figure emerging from the shadows behind him. Very clever! But, at least, his unexpected maneuver with his own car had made it necessary for both men to approach him from the same side.

While the first stranger continued to mumble, Gray sat motionless, keenly conscious, meanwhile, of that other presence closing in upon him from the rear. He simulated a violent start when a second voice cried:

"Don't move. I've got you covered."

"My God!" Gray twisted about in his seat and exposed a startled countenance. A masked man was standing close to the left running board, and he held a revolver near Gray's head; the apparition appeared to paralyze the unhappy traveler, for he still tightly clutched the steering wheel with both hands.

"Just sit still." The cloth of the mask blew outward as the words issued; through the slits two malevolent eyes gleamed. "Act pretty, and you won't get hurt."

"Why! It's—it's Mr. *Mallow!*" Gray hitched himself farther around in his seat and leaned forward in justifiable amazement. "As I live it's you, Mallow!" Both highwaymen were in front of him, now, and shoulder to shoulder; he made sure there were no others behind them.

"Shut up!" Mallow snapped. "Frisk him, Tony, and—"

The command was cut short by a startled, throaty cry—a hoarse sound of astonishment and rage—and simultaneously a strange, a phenomenal thing occurred. An unseen hand appeared to strike down both Mallow and his accomplice where they stood, and it smote them, moreover, with appalling force and terrifying effect. One moment they were in complete mastery of the situation, the next they were groveling in the road, coughing, sneezing, barking, retching, blaspheming poisonously. Baffled fury followed their first surprise. Mallow tore the mask from his face and groped blindly for the weapon he had dropped, but before he could recover it, pain mastered him and he fell back, clawing at himself, rubbing at his eyes that had been stricken sightless. He yelled. Tony yelled. Then upon the startled night there burst a duet of squeals and curses, a hideous medley of mingled pain and fright, at once terrifying and unnatural. Both bandits appeared to be in paroxysms of agony; from Tony issued sounds that might have issued from the throat of a woman in deadly fear and excruciating torment; Mallow's face had been partially protected, hence he was the lesser sufferer; nevertheless, his eyes were boiling in their sockets, his lungs were ablaze, ungovernable convulsions ran over him.

The men understood vaguely what had afflicted them, for they had seen Gray lift one hand from the wheel, and out of that hand they had seen a stream of liquid, or a jet of aqueous vapor, leap. It was too close to dodge. It had sprung directly into their faces, vaporizing as it came, and at its touch, at the first scent of its fumes, their legs had collapsed, their eyes had tightly closed, and every cell in their outraged bodies had rebelled. It was as if acid had been dashed upon them, destroying in one blinding instant all power for evil. With every breath, now, a new misery smote them. But worse than this torture was the monstrous nature of their afflictions. It was mysterious, horrible; they believed themselves to be dying and screamed in abysmal terror of the unknown.

Gray squeezed again the rubber bulb that he had carried in his hand these last several miles, ejecting from it the last few drops of its contents, then he opened the car door, stepped out of it and stood over his strangling victims. He kicked Mallow's revolver off the road, and, holding his breath, relieved the other high-jacker of his weapon. This he flung after the first, then he withdrew himself a few paces and lighted a cigarette, for a raw, pungent odor offended his nostrils. Both of the bawling bandits reeked of it, but their plight left him indifferent. They reminded him of a pair of horses he had seen disemboweled by a bursting shell, but he felt much less pity for them.

His lack of concern made itself felt finally. Mallow, who was the first to show signs of recovery, struggled to his feet and clawed blindly toward the automobile. He clung to it, sick and shaking; profanely he appealed for aid.

"So! It *is* Mr. Mallow," Gray said. "Fancy meeting you here!"

A stream of incoherencies issued from the wretched object of this mockery. Tony, the other man, stifled his groans, rose to his knees, and, with his hands clasped over his eyes, shuffled slowly away, as if to escape the sound of Gray's voice.

"Better quiet down and let me do something at once, if you wish to save your sight," the latter suggested. "Otherwise I won't answer for the result. And you needn't tell me how it hurts. I know." This proffer of aid appeared to throw the sufferers into new depths of dismay. They called to him in the name of God. They were harmless, now, and anyhow they had intended to do him no bodily harm. They implored him to lend succor or to put them out of their distress.

Gray fell to work promptly. The bottle of cream he had begged from Ma Briskow he now put to use. With this soothing liquid he first washed out their eyes, the membranes of which were raw and spongy, and excruciatingly sensitive to light, then he bandaged them as best he could with compresses, wet in it.

"You'll breathe easier as time goes on," he announced. "You'll cough a good deal for a few days, but where you are going that won't disturb anybody. Your eyes will get well, too, if you take care of them as I direct. But, meanwhile, let me warn you against lifting those bandages. Advise me as they dry out and I'll wet them again."

A blessed relief stole over the unfortunate pair; they were still sick and weak, but in a short time the acuteness of their suffering had diminished sufficiently for Gray to help them into the back seat of his car and resume his journey.

Sarcastically he referred to the sample case on the tonneau floor. "If those diamonds are in your way, I'll take them in front with me. If not, I'll ask you to keep an eye on them—or, let us say, keep a foot on them. If you should be foolish enough to heave them overboard or try to renew your assault upon me, I would be tempted to break this milk bottle. In that event, my dear Mallow, you'd go through life with a tin cup in your hand and a dog on a string."

Tony groaned in abject misery of body and soul. Mallow cursed feebly.

"What—is that devilish stuff?" the latter queried. It was plain from his voice that he meditated no treachery. "Oh! I was going to tell you. It is a product of German ingenuity, designed, I believe, for the purpose of quelling riotous and insurrectionary prisoners. It was efficacious, also, in taking pill boxes and clearing out dug-outs and the like. With some care one is safe in using it in an ordinary ammonia gun—the sort policemen use on mad dogs. Forgive me, if I say that you have demonstrated its utility in peace as well as in war. If there were more high-jackers in the world the device might be commercialized at some profit; but, alas, my good Mallow, your profession is not a common one."

"Cut out the kidding," Mallow growled, then he fell into a new convulsion of coughing. The car proceeded for some time to the tune of smothered complaints from the miserable figures bouncing upon the rear seat before Gray said: "I fear you are a selfish pair of rascals. Have you no concern regarding the fate of the third member of your treasure-hunting trio?" Evidently they had none. "Too bad! It's a good story."

Whatever their indifference to the welfare of the chauffeur, they still had some curiosity as to their own, for Mallow asked:

"What are you going to do with us?"

"What would you do, if you were in my place?"

"I'd—listen to reason."

"Meaning—?"

"Hell! You know what he means," Tony cried, feebly.

"So! You do me the honor to offer a bribe." Gray laughed. "Pardon my amusement. It sounds callous, I know, but, frankly, your unhappy condition fails to distress me. Well, how much do you offer?"

"All we got. A coupla thousand."

"A temptation, truly."

Mallow addressed his companion irritably. "Have a little sense. He don't need money."

Calvin Gray had never been more pleased with himself than now, for matters had worked out almost exactly according to plan, a compliment indeed to his foresight and to his executive ability. He loved excitement, he lived upon it, and much of his life had been devoted to the stage-management of sensational exploits like this one. As a boy plays with a toy, so did Gray amuse himself with adventure, and now he was determined to exact from this one the last particle of enjoyment and whatever profit it afforded.

Within a few minutes of his arrival at Ranger, the town was noisy with the story, for he drove down the brightly lighted main street and stopped in front of the most populous cafe. There he called loudly for a policeman, and when the latter elbowed his way through the crowd, Gray told him, in plain hearing of all, enough of his experience to electrify everybody. He told the story well; he even made known the value of his diamond stock; mercilessly he pilloried the two blindfolded bandits. When he drove to the jail the running boards of his car were jammed with inquisitive citizens, and those who could not find footing thereon followed at a run, laughing, shouting, acclaiming him and jeering at his prisoners.

Having surrendered custody of the latter, he dressed their eyes once more and explained the sort of care they required, then he made an appeal from the front steps of the jail, adjuring the mob to disperse quietly and permit the law to take its course.

Nothing like this had occurred during the brief, busy life of the town. It was a dramatic incident, but the manner in which this capable stranger had handled it and the discomfiture he had brought upon his assailants appealed more to the risibilities than to the anger of Ranger. Admiration for him displaced indignation at the high-jackers; cries for vengeance upon them were drowned in noisy appreciation of their captor. Gray became a popular character; men clamored to shake his hand, and complimented him upon his nerve. The editor of the local newspaper dragged him, protesting, to the office and there interviewed him. Gray was covered with confusion. Reluctantly he made known his identity, and retold the whole story of his trip, this time beginning at his meeting with Coverly in Dallas. He displayed the bewildering contents of his sample case, now guarded by a uniformed arm of the law, and explained how he had volunteered his services out of pure love of adventure, then how he had played into Mallow's hands

Rex Beach

while aware of his malign purpose at all times.

This was more than a local story; it was big enough for the wire. Gray sat at the editor's elbow while that enthusiastic gentleman called Dallas and gave it to the papers there.

He was escorted to the railroad station by an admiring crowd; he was cheered as he passed, smiling, into his Pullman car.

CHAPTER VII

Coverly was at the station when Gray's train arrived at Dallas the next morning. He was suffering intense excitement, and he deluged his friend with a flood of questions, meanwhile flourishing the morning papers, all of which appeared to have devoted much space to the Ranger episode. He hugged Gray, and he pumped his hand; he laughed and he chattered; he insisted upon hearing the whole story without delay. On their way uptown, the returning hero gave it to him, together with Gus Briskow's check.

At the size of the latter Coverly gasped. "Didn't I say you were a good salesman? And Mallow! You got him, didn't you? I *told* you he was a crook. Just the same, old man, you ran a terrible risk and I feel mighty guilty. Why, those fellows would have killed you."

"Probably."

"Why didn't you take along a policeman or somebody?"

"And miss all the fun? Miss my pay for the trip? I agreed to take my commission in thrills."

The jeweler was frankly curious. "Weren't you frightened?"

"Frightened? No." Gray shook his head. "I've never been really afraid of anything or anybody, so far as I recall. I've never been able to understand the necessity of being frightened. I dare say the capacity for enjoying that particular emotion was omitted from my make-up—the result of some peculiar prenatal influence, probably. I'm sorry, too, for fear must have a fascination and I like unusual sensations."

"Speaking of your commissions, how am I going to pay you— not for the sale you made, although I wouldn't have done as well, but for the loss you saved the firm and for the risk you ran?"

Gray felt a momentary desire to have done with pretense, to confess his true condition and to beg not only a suitable reward for his services, but also as large a loan as Coverly could spare. It is hard to maintain an attitude of opulence on less than nothing; it would be so much easier to have done with this counterfeit gesture and trust to a straightforward appeal. But he dared not yield to the impulse.

"You may give me anything you see fit," he declared, "and I sha'n't embarrass you by refusing. On the contrary, go as strongly as you possibly can."

Coverly actually appeared to be relieved at this statement, but he inquired, curiously: "What have you got up your sleeve? You don't need money."

"Obviously not. But I know a needy object of charity; a worthy case, I assure you. I can scarcely call him a friend, but I used to admire him greatly, and he is still an agreeable companion—a man at once capable, extravagant, entertaining, dissipated. He is in a bad way, temporarily, and can scarcely afford even the bare necessities of life. It is only with my help, in fact, that he maintains its luxuries. Your money shall go to him, and with every dollar of it that he squanders, there shall arise an earnest orison to you."

The jeweler was delighted. "Good!" he cried. "I detest the deserving poor as heartily as you do. And now I'd like to open a bottle of champagne with our breakfast."

On the very day that the new sign, "Tom and Bob Parker," went up over the door of the insurance office at Wichita Falls, the junior partner announced:

"Well, dad, the firm gets busy at once. I'm off for Dallas to-night."

"What for?" Tom was dismayed by such a prompt manifestation of energy. "I'll have to tell you—" Barbara perched herself upon her father's desk and began speaking with a note of excitement in her voice. "I heard Henry Nelson was in town, so I went to the bank this morning to see him. He's such a big man in the oil business I thought he might help me. He was there, but in conference with his father and another man. There were several people waiting, so I sat down. When the man they were talking to came out, it was Pete, that driller who put down the first well for us. He was glad to see me, and we had quite a talk, but I noticed he was fidgety. He said he was running a rig over near 'Burk,' and had a fishing job on his hands. With all the excitement and everybody running double 'towers' and trying to beat the other fellow down to the sand, it struck me as queer that a contract driller like Pete would be here in Wichita in conference with Bell and Henry Nelson, when he ought to be out on the lease fishing for a lost bit. It didn't sound right. The more I got out of him, the queerer it sounded, for he had all the fishing tools he needed, so I accused him of being a fraud. I told him I'd bet he had a showing of oil and was trying to borrow money to buy the offset or to get the Nelsons to buy it and carry him for an interest."

"Where'd you pick up this lingo?" Tom inquired. "You talk like them wild men at the Westland Hotel."

Barbara laughed delightedly. "Didn't I put down all our shallow wells? If I didn't, I thought I did. Anyhow, I spent most of my time around the rigs and Pete used to call me his boss. Well, that wretched man turned all colors when I accused him, and tried to 'shush' me. He said I mustn't talk about things I knew nothing about—somebody might overhear me. He declared the outfit he was working for were no good and wouldn't pay a driller a bonus if he made a well for them. He was sick of making other people rich and getting nothing for himself.... It was time the drilling crews shared in the profits.... He'd see that nobody froze him out again if he had to spoil the hole. He wound up by denying everything, and I pretended to swallow it, but when he had gone I went over my maps and located the lease where he's drilling. Three of the adjoining tracts are owned by the big companies, so that eliminated them, but the twenty to the west belongs to Knute Hoaglund. Henry was glad to see me when my turn came to go in, and—"

"I bet he was glad," Tom declared.

Barbara's smooth cheeks flushed faintly. "He is too busy and too rich to—think about girls."

"He wasn't too busy and too rich to inquire about you 'most every day since he got back from the war."

"I didn't forget to call him 'Colonel,' and that pleased both him and Bell. Then I told them that I proposed to become a rich and successful oil operator and wanted their advice how to begin. Old Bell was amused, but Henry—I beg pardon, *Colonel*—Nelson was shocked. He couldn't bear to think of women, and of me especially, in business. He might have become disagreeably personal if his father hadn't been there."

"Dunno's I care much for Henry," Tom said, mildly.

"Oh, he's all right, but—I *hate* Bell! It makes anybody mad to be laughed at. Henry was more diplomatic. He tried to convince me that the oil game is altogether a man's business and that no woman could succeed at it. 'It is a contest of wits,' he explained. 'You've got to outguess the other fellow. You've got to know everything he's doing and keep him from knowing anything you're doing. The minute he knows as much as you do, he's got it on you.' That seemed to prove to

Henry that no woman could win at it, for men are such superior creatures. They know so much more than a woman can possibly learn; their wits are so much keener!

"I was duly impressed. I asked him to call this evening, for I did so wish to have him teach me what little I was capable of learning. But he couldn't come, because he had been called to Dallas, unexpectedly. That was my cue. In my most sweetly girlish manner I said: 'Oh, indeed! Do you expect to see Knute Hoaglund while you're there?'"

Two hectic spots had come into "Bob's" cheeks during this recital; she was teetering upon the desk now like a nodding Japanese doll, and her blue eyes were dancing.

"I heard Old Bell's chair creak and I saw him shoot a quick glance at Henry. Henry admitted, casually, that he might drop in on Knute. Why?"

"'You'll be wasting time,' I told him, even more sweetly, 'for dad and I have that twenty west of Burkburnett.'"

"*Well!* You'd have thought I had stuck a hatpin into Bell. And Henry's mouth actually dropped open. Think of it: Colonel Henry Nelson, the hero of Whatever-it-is, with his imperial mouth open and nothing coming out of it—not even the imperial breath!"

"Bob" rocked backward and kicked up her neatly shod feet; she hugged herself and snickered with a malicious enjoyment not wholly Christian-like.

"But—we 'ain't even got an option! It takes *money* to lease close-in stuff." Tom was bewildered.

"Of course. And they realized that, or Bell did, as soon as he'd had time to collect himself. But it was too late then; he had betrayed himself and he knew it. Oh, he was sore! He'd have flung me out if I'd been a man. I got mad, too, and I told him it made no real difference whether I was bluffing or not; the jig was up, so far as he was concerned. I reminded him of what Henry had just said—that the oil business is a game of wits, and that when you know what the other fellow is doing you have him licked. I admitted that he could probably keep me from getting the lease, but I could also keep him from getting it. Bell nearly had a stroke at that threat. Henry behaved very decently throughout. I think it must have pleased him to find that somebody in Wichita, besides him, had the courage to defy his father; anyhow, he said, '"Bob" has beaten us at our own game. She knows enough now to place that lease in half an hour, and I think we'd better take her in. Otherwise she'll wire Knute, and he'll probably protect her for an interest.'

"That made me feel awfully fraudulent, but his smarty remarks about women in the oil business still rankled, so I just sat pretty and blinked like a little owl. Bell swore. In his best and most horrible manner, he swore, but—he gave in." "Bob" laughed again, a bit hysterically. "That's about all, dad. They agreed to put up the money and carry me—us, I mean—for a quarter interest if I can get the lease from Knute Hoaglund. So, I'm leaving on the night train."

"Son! I—I'm darned if I don't believe we'll make a go of this business," Tom Parker declared.

With a little cry Barbara flung herself into his arms.

* * * * *

The publicity Calvin Gray received from his exploit at Ranger could be nothing except agreeable to one of his temperament. Gratefully he basked in his notoriety, meanwhile continuing assiduously to cultivate the moneyed men of Dallas. His sudden leap into prominence aroused curiosity among the wives and families of the latter, and he became the recipient of some social attentions. He accepted every invitation, and so well did he carry himself in company, so ornamental and engaging was he as a dinner guest, that he was soon in great demand. He possessed accomplishments, too, that increased the respect of his masculine acquaintances. For instance, he displayed a proficiency at golf quite unusual in men of athletic training, and they argued that any man who could do par whenever he felt like it must be either a professional or a person of limitless leisure. And limitless leisure means limitless funds.

Gray studiously maintained his air of financial mystery; he was in and out of offices, always purposeful, always in a hurry, but always with sufficient time to observe the strictest niceties of polite behavior. It was a part of his plan to create an atmosphere of his own, to emphasize his knack for quick, decisive, well-calculated action. The money he received from Coverly enabled him to maintain the posture he had assumed; he spent it with his usual prodigality, receiving little direct benefit, but making each dollar look like four. Extravagance with him was an art, money ran out of his pockets like water, but although he was already in a position to borrow, he did not do so. He merely marked time, deriving a grim amusement at the way his popularity grew as his currency dwindled. It was a game, enjoyable so long as it lasted. Egotistical he knew himself to be, but it was a conscious fault; to tickle his own vanity filled him with the same satisfaction a cat feels at having its back rubbed, and he excused himself by reasoning that his deceit harmed nobody. Meanwhile, with feline alertness he waited for a mouse to appear.

He was relieved one day to receive a telegram from Gus Briskow asking him to meet Ma and Allie at the evening train and "get them a hotel." He managed to secure a good suite at the Ajax, and it was with genuinely pleasurable anticipation that he drove to the station.

Dismay smote him, however, at first sight of the new arrivals. Ma Briskow resembled nothing so much as one of those hideous "crayon enlargements" he had seen in farmhouses— atrocities of an art long dead—for she was clad in an old-fashioned basque and skirt of some stiff, near-silk material, and her waist, which buttoned far down the front and terminated in deep points, served merely to roof over but not to conceal a peculiarity of figure which her farm dress had mercifully hidden. Gray discovered that Ma's body, alas! bore a quaint resemblance in outline to a gourd. A tiny black bonnet, with a wide surcingle of ribbon tied under her chin, was ornamented with a sort of centerpiece built of rigid artificial fruit and flowers. Her hair, in brave defiance of current styles, was rolled into a high pompadour. Beneath that pompadour, however, her face was aglow with interest and her eyes gleamed almost as brightly as did the brand-new lavalliere and the bar pin with its huge six-carat center diamond.

If the mother's appearance was unusual, the daughter's was startling, what with her size and the barbaric latitude of color she had indulged herself in. Allegheny's get-up screamed. In the general store at Cisco, whence it had originated, it had doubtless been considered a sport costume, for there was a skirt of huge blue and white checks, a crepe waist of burnt orange, and over that a vegetable-silk sweater, with the broadest, greenest stripes Gray had ever seen. A violent, offensive green, it was; and the sweater was too tight. Her hat was large and floppy and adorned with preposterous purple blooms; one of her hands was gloved, but upon the other she wore her splendid solitaire. She "shone" it, as a watchman shines his flashlight.

They were enough to daunt a stronger man than Calvin Gray, these two. He could well imagine the sensation he and they would create in the lobby of the modish Ajax. But his first surprise was succeeded by a gentle pity, for Ma Briskow greeted him rapturously, and in Allegheny's somber eyes he detected a look of mingled suffering and defiance. She knew, somehow or other, that she was conspicuous, grotesque, and her soul was in agony at the knowledge. Before he had spoken a half dozen words to her, Gray realized that this girl was in torture, and that it had required a magnificent courage on her part to meet him as bravely as she did. He was ashamed of himself; amusement at their expense did him no credit, and he determined to relieve her pain and to help her attain the likeness of other women if it was in his power to do so. It was a tribute to his inherent chivalry that he rose to the occasion and welcomed the women with a cordiality that warmed their hearts. Enthusiastically he took charge of Ma's lunch basket; against Allie's muttered protest he despoiled her of her bilious, near-leather suitcase; he complimented them upon their appearance and showed such pleasure at seeing them again that they surrendered gratefully to him. By the time he had them in a taxicab they were as talkative as a pair of magpies.

Of course, they had to know all about the holdup, and his manner of telling the story made them feel that they had played an important part in it. Arrived at the hotel, he swept them along with him so swiftly that they had no time in which to become dismayed or self-conscious, and finally he deposited them in their rooms quite out of breath and quite delighted. He left them palpitating with excitement at the wonders he proposed unfolding for them on the morrow.

Allie answered his phone call about eight o'clock the next morning.

"Ready for breakfast?" he inquired.

"Why, we et at daylight," she told him, in some astonishment. "I been ridin' since then."

"Indeed! Putting roses in your cheeks, eh? With whom did you go?"

"Oh, one of the elevator men."

"B—but—" Gray sputtered, deeply shocked. "Why, Miss Briskow, they're *negroes!* Riding with a nigger! My heavens! Where did you go?"

"Nowhere. Just up and down."

It was a moment before the man could speak, then he said, in a queerly repressed voice: "That—is quite different. I'll run down and get a bite and join you in no time."

"Seems awful funny not to have any housework to do in the morning," Ma Briskow confessed, as they left the Ajax. "A hotel would spoil me in no time."

"I couldn't keep her from makin' up the beds," Allie announced.

Gray took the elder woman's hand in his and scolded her gently. Smilingly, he lectured her on the art of doing nothing, and voiced some elemental truths about living.

"Mr. Briskow has but one idea, and that is to surround you two, and Buddy, with the advantages and luxuries you have been denied," he reminded her. "You owe it to him to get the most out of your money, and you mustn't begin by making hotel beds and robbing some poor woman of her livelihood. Not one person in ten really knows how to live, for it isn't an easy task, and the saddest thing about the newly rich is that they won't learn. They refuse to enjoy their wealth. I propose to help you good people get started, if you'll permit me. It is not with contrition, but with pride, that I recommend myself to you as one of the greatest living authorities upon extravagance, idleness, and the minor vices of the prosperous."

The mother nodded, a bit vaguely. "That's kind of like Pa talks. He sent you this, and says to tell you it's our first spendin' spree and act accordin'." From her pocket she drew a folded check, made out in blank to Calvin Gray and signed by Gus Briskow.

"So! I assume that I'm to pay the bills. Very well. The sky is the limit, eh?"

"That's it. Of course, I don't need anything for myself—this dress and bunnit are good enough—but Allie's got to have new fixin's, from the inside out. I s'pose her things'll eat up the best part of a hundred dollars, won't they?" The speaker's look of worried inquiry bespoke a lifetime of habitual economy.

"We're not going to buy what you *need*, but what you want. You're going to have just as many pretty things as Allie."

Ma was panic-stricken at this suggestion. When Gray insisted she demurred; when he told her that one nice dress would cost at least a hundred dollars, she confessed:

"Why, I don't s'pose all the clo's I've had since I was married cost much more 'n that."

"I'll spend at least a thousand on you before noon," he laughed.

Mrs. Briskow gasped, she rolled her eyes and fanned herself; she appealed to Allegheny, but it was evident that the latter had kept her eyes open and had done some thinking, for she broke out, passionately: "You make me sick, Ma! It'll take all Pa can afford, and then some, to make us look like other people. I never knew how plumb ridic'lous we are till—"

"Not that," Gray protested.

"You *know* we're ridic'lous," she cried, fiercely. "We're a couple of sow's ears and all Pa's royalties can't make us into silk purses. But—mebbe we can manage to look like silk, if we spend enough."

Gray determined that the girl should not be disappointed if he could help it, so he went directly to the head saleswoman of the first store, and asked her to assume the role of counselor where circumstance compelled him to relinquish it, explaining that in addition to hats, gowns, shoes, and the like, both Ma and Allie needed a variety of confidential apparel with which he had only the vaguest acquaintance. Although the woman agreed to his request, he found before long that his trust in her had been misplaced. Not only did she threaten to take advantage of her customers' ignorance, but also, to Gray's anger, she displayed a poorly veiled contempt for and amusement at his charges.

Allegheny was not long in feeling this. She had entered the establishment aquiver with hope and anticipation. This was her great adventure. She was like a timid child, enraptured at sight of its first tinseled Christmas tree; to have that ecstacy spoiled, to see the girl's tenderest sensibilities wounded by a haughty clerk, enraged the man who played Santa Claus. Abruptly he resumed charge of the Briskow purchases, and it gave him a pang to note how Allegheny ran to him with her hurt, as it were.

But matters did not progress as well as he had expected. Allie's disappointment at the death of her dream she hid under an assumption of indifference; she merely pawed over the pretty things shown her and pretended to ignore the ridicule she and her mother excited. But her face was stony, her eyes were hopeless, miserable.

For once in his life Calvin Gray was at a loss, and knowledge of that fact caused him to chew savagely at his cigar. To his bewildered companions he remained enthusiastic, effervescent, but behind their backs he glowered at the well-groomed customers and cursed the snickering models who paraded their wares. Engaged thus, he became aware of a stranger who looked on at the pitiful little comedy without amusement. She was a pretty thing. Gray stared at her openly and his scowl vanished. When she moved away, he made a sudden decision, excused himself, and followed her.

He was gratified at the manner in which she accepted his breathless apology for speaking to her, at the poise with which she listened while he made himself and his companions known to her and explained the plight in which he found himself.

"You can save the reason of a distracted man and add to the

happiness of two poor, bewildered women, if you will," he concluded, earnestly. "It isn't a funny situation; it's tragic."

"What do you wish me to do?" the girl inquired.

"It's a lot to ask, I know, but won't you help them buy the things they need and save them from further humiliation at the hands of these highbrow clerks and lowbrow customers? I—I want to punch somebody in the nose."

"I was sure you did. That is what attracted my attention."

"You are a person of taste, if you will pardon a perfectly obvious compliment from a total stranger, and they need such a woman's guidance. But they need, even more, a little bit of feminine tact and sympathy. Look!" He showed Gus Briskow's blank check. "The whole store is theirs, if they wish it. Think what that ought to mean to two poor starved creatures who have never owned enough clothing to wad a shotgun."

"The girl is stunning. All she needs is the right sort of things —"

Impulsively Gray seized the speaker's hand. "I *knew* it!" he cried. "I can choose gowns for her, but how can I tell her the sort of—well, corsets she ought to wear? How can I select for her things a bachelor is presumed to know nothing about? Haven't you an hour or two in which to play Fairy Godmother?"

"I have all day," the young woman confessed. "I merely came in to yearn over the pretty things."

"O messenger from Heaven!" he cried, more hopefully. "Would it appear presumptuous if I asked you, in return for this favor, to select the very prettiest gown in this shop for your very own?"

The offer was refused pleasantly, but firmly. "I'd be paid ten times over by the fun of spending oodles of money even if it were not my own. But would they consent to have a stranger—?"

"If you will permit a tiny deceit, I'm sure they will. I shall burden my conscience with a white lie and pretend that you are a friend to whose judgment I have appealed. My poor conscience is scandalously overburdened, but—that girl is suffering!"

"I thought they must have struck oil. I've seen others like them."

Without further ado, Gray hurried his new acquaintance back to the dress department, then, in his easiest manner, introduced her to the Briskows. She flashed him a look of amusement as he glibly made her known as "Miss Good." He had invited Miss Good to join their picnic immediately upon hearing that Ma and Allie were coming to Dallas, and she had been overjoyed. Miss Good, as they could see, possessed unerring good taste, but what was more, she had a real genius for finding bargains. As a bargain hunter Miss Good was positively unique.

Ma Briskow pricked up her ears at this, soon she and the newcomer had their heads together, and within a few minutes Gray realized that his experiment was a success. The stranger possessed enthusiasm, but it was coupled with common sense, and before her sunshiny smile even Allegheny's sullen distrust slowly began to thaw. She drew Gray aside finally, and said: "It's all right. They're perfect dears, and, now, the best thing you can do is to take yourself off."

He agreed promptly, but cautioned her against economy. "That bargain-hunting remark was only a bait. Remember, Gus Briskow wants them to have everything, and be everything they should be, regardless of expense. Why, both he and I would like nothing better than to have Allegheny look like you, if that were possible."

Miss Good eyed the speaker curiously. "Who are you?" she inquired. "What are these nesters to you?"

"I am nobody. They were kind to me and I'm interested in their future."

"Are you a fortune hunter, Mr. Gray?"

"I am." Gray's face instantly lighted. "I am the most conscienceless fortune hunter you ever met, but—I am hunting my own fortune, not Allie Briskow's."

"You needn't laugh. She's very—unusual and—But I dare say you wouldn't tell me, anyhow."

"If I have excited your curiosity, I am delighted," Gray declared. "Please let me return at lunch time and gratify it. I promise to talk upon that subject which every man can discuss to best advantage—himself—and I pledge myself not to ask one single question about you, Miss Good. Not one—" He bowed ceremoniously over her hand. "Although, as you can imagine, I'm dying to ask a thousand."

CHAPTER VIII

The luncheon hour was long in arriving, and when it did come around Calvin Gray regretted that he had elected to play a game of make-believe with "Miss Good," for she rigidly held him to his promise, and however adroitly he undertook to ascertain who or what she was, she foiled him. It gave her a mischievous pleasure to evade his carefully laid conversational traps, and what little he learned came from Ma Briskow. Briefly, it amounted to this: Miss Good was what the elder woman called "home folks," but she had been schooled in the East. Moreover, she was in the oil business. This last bit of intelligence naturally intrigued the man, and he undertook to gain further illumination, but only to have the girl pretend that he knew all about it. He accepted this checkmate with the best possible grace, but revenged himself by assuming the airs and privileges of a friend more intimate even than Miss Good had implied, a pretense that confused and even annoyed her. For some reason this counterfeit pleased him; it was extremely agreeable even to pretend a close acquaintance with this girl.

The luncheon went off gaily enough, then Gray was again banished with instructions to return at closing time.

"You took a mean, a malicious advantage of an offer intended only to spare your feelings. And you haven't any," he told Miss Good when they had a chance for a word alone.

"I have no feelings?"

"None. Or you'd see that I'm perishing of curiosity."

She shook her head, and her blue eyes laughed at him provokingly. "Curiosity is fatal only to cats. It is good for people."

"I shall find out all about you."

"How?"

"By cross-examining the Briskows, perhaps."

"But they're waiting to have you tell them what you know. I've seen to that."

"If they ask any questions, I'll invent a story. I'll act confused, self-conscious. I'll make them think you are a much dearer friend than I have pretended, so far; dearer, even, than I can hope you ever will be."

"That wouldn't be fair."

"There are occasions when everything is fair. Perhaps these store people know something—"

"Nothing whatever."

"Then, for Heaven's sake, release me from my pledge!" Gray spoke desperately. "When I return, permit me to ask those thousand questions, and what others occur to me. Won't you?"

The girl pondered this request briefly, then smiled. "Very well. If you are still curious, when you see me, I'll tell you who I am."

"A bargain! I'll be back early." More seriously, Gray declared: "I must tell you right now how perfectly splendid I think you are. You have completely renewed my belief in human kindness, and I'm sure your name must be Miss Good."

But a disappointment awaited Calvin Gray when, late that
afternoon, he returned to the store. Miss Good had gone. At
first he refused to believe Ma Briskow's statement, but it was
true: she had disappeared as quietly and as unobtrusively as she
had appeared, and, what was more annoying, she had left no
word whatever for him. This was practical joking, for a
certainty, and Gray told himself that he abhorred practical
jokes. It was a jolt to his pride to have his attentions thus
ignored, but what irked him most was the fact that he was
stopped, by reason of his deceit, from making any direct
inquiries that might lead to a further acquaintance with the
girl.

Mrs. Briskow, however, was in no condition either to note his
dismay or to volunteer information upon any except one
subject; to wit, corns. Human hearts were of less concern to
her, for the time being, than human feet, and hers were killing
her. She began a recital of her sufferings, as intimate, as
agonizing, and as confidential as if Gray were a practicing
chiropodist. What she had to say about tight shoes was bitter
in the extreme; she voiced a gloomy conviction that the
alarming increase in suicides was due to bunions. The good
woman confessed that she dearly loved finery and had bought
right and left with reckless extravagance, but all the merchandise in this department store was not worth the anguish she
had endured this day. With her stiff little bonnet tilted
carelessly over her wrinkled forehead, she declared emphati-
cally that she would gladly swap all her purchases at this
moment for a tub of hot water.

"Where is Allie?" Gray inquired.

"Lord knows! She's som'eres around bein' worked over by a
couple of women. Gettin' her hair washed an' her finger nails
cured an' I dunno what not. Mercy me! The things Miss Good
had 'em do to her! An' the money we've spent! Allie's gone hog
wild." The complaint ended in a stifled moan induced perhaps

by some darting pain, then without further ado Ma Briskow unbuttoned one shoe and removed it. "Whew!" She leaned back in her chair, wiggled her stockinged toes, and feebly fanned herself. "But wait till you see her. I can't scarcely reco'nize my own flesh an' blood. I never seen such a change in a human person."

Gray pretended to listen as the good woman babbled on, but he was thinking about the girl who had disappeared. He was surprised at the keenness of his chagrin. He had seen Miss Good but a short time, and she had made no effort whatever to excite his interest; nevertheless, she remained a tantalizingly vivid picture in his mind. It was extraordinary.

So engrossed was he in his thoughts that he did not notice Allegheny Briskow until she stood close beside him. Then, indeed, he experienced a shock, for it was difficult to recognize in this handsome, modish young woman the awkward, ill-dressed country girl he had seen at noon. Allie was positively stunning. She was completely transformed from the soles of her well-shod feet to the tip of her French coiffure, and what was more astonishing, she had lost much of her self-consciousness and carried herself with a native grace that became her well.

"Why, *Allie!*" Gray exclaimed. "You're wonderful! Let me see you." He stood off and gazed at her while she revolved before him.

"Sakes alive! Who'd ever s'pose you'd look like *that!*" the mother exclaimed.

"Miss Good told me I'd look nice, but I didn't believe her. Do I?"

"You're wonderful, Allie." Gray said it with conviction.

"Honest? You ain't laughin' at me?" The amazon's voice quavered.

"Can't you see? Look at yourself. I'm proud of you."

"I—She said—" Allegheny twisted her hands, she cast an appealing glance at her mother, but the latter was staring at her in open amazement, slowly nodding her head and clucking.

"Tse! Tse! Tse!" It was an approving cluck, and it had a peculiar effect upon the girl. Allegheny's tears started, she turned suddenly and hid her face in her hands.

Gray crossed quickly to her side, saying: "There! We've overdone it the first day, and you're tired."

"I *ain't* tired." His sympathy brought audible sobs; the girl's shoulders began to heave.

"Well, *I* am," the mother complained. "I'm wore to the bone. Allie! You dry up an' stop that snivelin' so we kin go home and I kin let my feet swell, an' scream."

"You're not too tired, I hope, to have dinner with Allie and me in the big dining room at the Ajax?" Gray said, gayly. "You'll be all right after an hour's rest, and—'I want to show her off, if her nose isn't too red."

"I 'ain't seen that girl cry in ten years," Ma declared, in mingled wonderment and irritation. "Why, she didn't cry when Number One blowed in."

Allie spoke between her sobs. "There wasn't nothin' to cry for, then. But—Miss Good said I—I'd look jest as purty as other folks when I got fixed up. An' *he* says—I do."

Gray decided that all women are vain. Nevertheless, it surprised him to discover the trait so early in Allegheny Briskow.

It was on the second day thereafter that Gus Briskow appeared at the hotel. He came unexpectedly, and he still wore his rough ranch clothes. After an hour or more spent with his wife and daughter, he went down to Gray's room and thanked him for the assistance he had rendered the two women.

Followed a few moments of desultory conversation, then he put an abrupt question: "Mr. Gray, you're a rich man, ain't you?"

"I—am so considered."

"Um-m! Dunno's I'm glad or sorry."

"Indeed! What difference can it make to you?"

"A lot. It's like this: my boy Buddy has took a turrible shine to you, an' he can't talk about nothin' else. I was sort of hopin'—"

"Yes?"

"Buddy's ignerunt. He can read an' write an' figger some, but he's got about the same company manners as a steer, an' he's skeered of crowds. When he sees strangers he's liable to charge 'em or else throw up his head an' his tail an' run plumb over a cliff. He'd ought to go to school, but he says he's too big, an' he'd have to set with a lot of little children. Him an' Allie's alike, that way—it r'ars 'em up on their hind feet to be laughed at."

"Get a tutor for them."

"A what?" When Gray had explained the meaning of the word, Mr. Briskow's face cleared. "That's what I figgered on, but I didn't know what you called 'em. That's why I'm sorry you're so well off. Y' see I'd of paid you anything—I'd of doubled whatever you're gettin'—" The speaker raised a hopeful gaze; he paused as if to make sure that his hearer was beyond temptation. "I thought mebbe him and you'd like to travel some—go to furrin places—see the hull world. I kin afford it."

"Thank you for the compliment, but—"

"I got some big deals on, an' Buddy's got to learn enough so's to hang onto what's comin' to him an' Allie. He needs a man like you to learn him, an' be an example. It would be a payin' job, Mister Gray."

It was in a voice graver than usual that the younger man spoke: "Briskow, you're sensible enough to understand plain talk. I'm not a fit man to teach Buddy what he ought to know. In fact, I'm about the worst person you could select."

"How so?"

"Because I'm a good deal of a—rotter. I couldn't permit Buddy to make a mess of his life, such as I've made of mine."

The father sighed. "I s'pose you know, but—Well, I'm disapp'inted. But it wasn't hully on that account I come to Dallas. Ma told me over the telephone how nice you been an' what you done for her 'n' Allie, so I says to myself I'll square things by givin' him a chance to make some money."

Gray stirred slightly in his chair and regarded the speaker more keenly.

"When oil come in at Ranger, nobody thought it would get out our way, but Ma had a dream—a lot of dreams—about oil on our farm, so I got an outfit to come there an' drill. Folks thought we was crazy, and we didn't expect they'd find much, ourselves—a few bar'l a day would of looked big—but I allus had ambitions to be good an' rich, so I got options on quite a bit of acreage. It didn't take no money at the time, 'cause land was what people had most of. Along with the rest, there's a hundred an' sixty right next to ours—hill stuff that wouldn't feed a goat. It's wuth a lot of money now, but the option's 'most run out."

"When does it expire?"

"Saturday."

"That's to-morrow."

Gus Briskow nodded. "It's cheap at a thousand dollars an acre, an' it costs two hundred."

"Of course you'll take it."

"Nope."

"Why not?"

"Per one thing, I got a lot of other land just as good an' mebbe better, an' I been takin' it up out of the royalties that come in. We got enough sure money in sight to do us, but I promised Ma to play safe, an'—we can't take everything. You kin have that option, Mister Gray, for nothin'. You kin sell the lease inside of a week an' make fifty thousand dollars, or you kin hold it an' make mebbe a million. All it'll cost you is thirty-two thousand dollars. I don't make a cent out of it."

"Thirty-two thousand dollars! Not much, is it?"

"It ain't nothin' to a man like you."

Gray nodded and smiled queerly as he thanked the nester, then from his pockets he removed several crumpled wads of currency and a handful of silver. These he counted before saying: "What capital I have is entirely liquid—it's all in cash. There is eighty-seven dollars and forty-three cents. It is every dollar in the world that I possess."

"Huh?" Gus Briskow's bright eyes searched the smiling countenance before him. "You're—jokin'. I thought you said you was rich."

"I am rich. I don't owe a nickel, and won't, until my hotel bill is due, day after to-morrow. I'm in full possession of all my faculties. I'm perfectly healthy and cheerful. I know men who would pay a million dollars for my health alone, and another million to enjoy my frame of mind. That's two million—"

"Well—doggone *me*!" There was a pause, then the speaker brightened. "Mebbe you'll take Buddy, after all? You kin set your own wages."

Gray shook his head. "There are two good reasons why I couldn't accept, even if I wished. I've told you one; I'm too fond of you Briskows to risk ruining Buddy."

"What's the other one?"

"A purely personal reason. I have a definite something to do here in Texas. Before I can accomplish it, I shall have to make a lot of money, but that I shall do easily. I make money rapidly when I start."

"You gotta git goin' afore long." Briskow allowed his eyes to rove about the spacious Governor's suite. "'Specially with only eighty-seven forty—"

"That is nearly eighty-seven dollars more than I had when I arrived. Three weeks ago I was an utter stranger here; to-day I know everybody worth knowing in a business way, and some of them are my friends."

"If you could learn Buddy to make friends like that—"

But Gray raised his hand. "I derive a certain amusement from my own peculiar characteristics and capabilities, but I should detest them in another."

"Well, you sure need money, and—I kin he'p you out."

"Thank you, but I sha'n't borrow. If the time were not so short, I could probably turn this lease you so kindly offered me. But something else will happen along."

Briskow sighed. "I could of sold it myself—thought I had it sold to a bunch from Wichita, but they tricked me. I offered it the day you was at our house for eighty thousand and Nelson more 'n half agreed to—"

"*Who?*"

Briskow looked up at the tone of this inquiry. "One of the fellers from Wichita Falls. I s'pose he knowed the option was about run out; anyhow, he's been holdin' me off from day to day till it's too late now fer me to—"

"What is his name?" Gray broke in, sharply. "Name's Nelson. Bell Nelson's son. Bell's hard-boiled, but—"

"Henry Nelson?"

"That's him."

Gray rose from his chair and strode swiftly to the window. He stood there staring down into the street for a moment before saying, curtly, "Go on!"

"You know them Nelsons?"

"I know—Henry."

"He's hard-boilder 'n his old man. They got a lot o' money behind 'em—too much money to act like he done with me. I sure hate to see him git that Evans lease for next to nothin', after the way he done. I'd call it cheat-in', but—well, I can't han'le it."

The man at the window wheeled suddenly and his face was white, his brows were drawn down. "By God!" he cried, tensely. "He *won't* get it. Where's that option?"

"I got it right here." Briskow handed over a paper. "An' I got the hull title abstrack, too. Had it all ready for Nelson."

When he had swiftly scanned the document, Gray said: "This deal means little to you, Briskow, but it means much to me, and I'll make it worth something to both of us. At first I thought the time was too short, but—I work best when I work fast. You've had your chance and failed. Now then, step aside and let a man run who knows how."

Mr. Roswell, president of the bank where Gray had first made himself known, was a shrewd, forceful man who had attained a position in business and arrived at a time of life when he could well afford to indulge his likes and his dislikes. Those likes and dislikes were strong, for his was a positive character. As is the case with most successful men who pride themselves upon their cold caution and business acumen—and Mr. Roswell did so pride himself—he really was a person of impulse, and intuition played a much larger part in his conduct of affairs than he would have acknowledged. Such people make mistakes, but they also make friends; occasionally they read character wrong, but they inspire loyalty, and big institutions are founded upon friendship and loyalty as well as upon stability and fair dealing.

Roswell had liked Gray upon their first meeting, and that liking had deepened. Owing to that fact, he had neglected to secure a report upon him, assuring himself that there was always time for such formalities. He was cordial to-day when Gray strode into his office bringing Gus Briskow with him.

The banker listened with interest to what he was told, then he studied the map that Briskow spread upon his desk showing the location of his own and other near-by wells.

"That looks like a sure thing," Roswell said, finally. "As sure as anything in oil can be. What is on your mind?"

"I'd like to get the opinion of the bank's oil expert," Gray told him.

This was a matter easily disposed of; the expert was summoned and he rendered a prompt opinion. He knew the property; he considered it a cheap lease at a thousand dollars an acre. It was proven stuff and within thirty days it would probably treble in value. When he had gone, the banker smiled.

"Well, Gray," said he, "I knew you'd land something good. You're a hustler. You'll make a fortune out of that land."

Gray handed him Gus Briskow's option, and the assignment thereof, the ink upon which was scarcely dry. "There's the joker. It expires to-morrow night and—it will go to the Nelsons. They've double-crossed Mr. Briskow."

"Then don't let them get away with it. Take it yourself."

"It is now three o'clock and this is the golfing season in New York," Gray told him. "I couldn't reach my—associates and get any action before Monday." "No funds of your own available?"

"Not enough, at such short notice."

"Well?"

"That lease is worth one hundred and sixty thousand dollars, isn't it?" The banker nodded. "I'm going to sell it before six o'clock for—eighty thousand. I know people here who will take it, but I've come first to you. Get together a little syndicate right here in the bank, and buy it. I'll agree to take it off your hands within thirty days at one hundred and sixty thousand dollars. In other words, it is worth to me eighty thousand dollars to have you carry it for a month."

"Is your guaranty any good?"

"That is for you to determine. Assume that it is not, and I'll better my first offer. I'll undertake to sell off the land in twenties right here in Dallas, double your money, and divide the profits thereafter with you. It is a safe speculation and a quick one. You know I can put it through."

Mr. Roswell considered briefly before replying. "There's no use denying that we've made money on deals like this—everybody has. So it's nothing new. There's a big play on Ranger stuff and we couldn't lose. But I know nothing about you except the little you've told me. When I go into a deal I put my trust more in the man than the proposition."

"And I trust my own judgment of human character more than that of strangers," Gray said, quickly. "So do you. Thirty days is a long time with me, and the oil business is just my speed. Permit me to remind you that time is flying and that I have given myself only three hours in which to turn this property. I intend to beat Nelson, and apply that beating on account of an old score. This is more than a mere business deal."

"I like your energy," the banker confessed, "and I'm inclined to bet some of my own money on you. Now"—he pushed a button on his desk—"let's see if there are any others here who feel as I do." It was early evening when Gus Briskow returned to his wife's and his daughter's rooms at the Ajax. He slipped in quietly and sank into a chair.

"Mercy me! I thought you was run over," Ma Briskow exclaimed.

"I feel like I was," the nester declared, with a grin. "Say! Mister Gray sold the Evans lease an'—we got more money than ever."

"Then mebbe you can afford a new suit," Allie told him. "You look like sin."

Her father nodded, but his mind was full of the incidents of that afternoon and he began at once to recount them. He told the story badly, but in a language that the women understood. He had not gone far, however, when the girl interrupted him to exclaim:

"Wait! Why, Pa! You mean to say Mister Gray 'ain't got no money?"

"He had less 'n a hundred dollars. An' him livin' here like a king with everybody bowin' an' scrapin'!"

Ignoring the effect upon Allie of this intelligence, he continued his recital. "All I done was set around while him an' them bank people talked it over," he said, finally. "Then they got their lawyer in an' he examined the title papers. Seemed like he'd never git through, but he did, an' they signed some things an' we come out, an' Mister Gray told me I'd made forty-eight thousand dollars."

"Goodness me!" Ma Briskow's eyes widened. "Why, that Evans place ain't wuth the taxes."

"It's more 'n likely wuth a million. But think! Him tellin' me *I'd* made forty-eight thousand dollars! It give me a jolt, an' I says *I* didn't make it. I told him I'd fell down an' turned the hull thing over to him. 'It's *you* that's made forty-eight thousand,' I says."

"*What?*" Allie inquired, sharply. Then when her father had repeated himself, she asked with even greater intensity: "Wha'd he say to that? He didn't take it, did he?"

"He laughed kinda queer an' says all I got to do to give him a good night's rest is to wire Henry Nelson the deal's closed. An' him with less 'n a hundred dollars!"

Allie spoke again in great relief. "Lord! You give me a turn." Her expression altered, her lips parted in a slow smile. "So! He's pore, eh? Pore as we was. Well, I declare!" She rose and turned her back upon her father.

"No, he ain't pore," Briskow said, irritably. "Not now he ain't. I says it's his deal an' his money, an' we got plenty. An' I stuck to it."

Allie wheeled suddenly at this announcement. She uttered a cry of protest; then, "What are you talkin' about?" she roughly demanded.

"We had some argyment an' I got kinda r'iled. Finally he says if I feel that way we'll go pardners. He wouldn't listen to nothin' else, an'—that's how it stands. He made twenty-four thousand an' I—"

"You—You *fool!*"

Gus Briskow looked up with a start to find his daughter standing over him, her face ablaze, her deep bosom heaving. He stared at her in frank amazement, doubting his senses. Never had Allegheny used toward him a word, a tone like this, never had he seen her look as she did at this moment. He could not believe his eyes, for the girl had become a scowling fury, and she seemed upon the verge of destroying him with her strong hands, a task she was amply able to accomplish.

"Allie-*Allie!*" the mother gasped. She, too, was aghast. "You—you're talkin' to your pa!"

"You give him twenty-four thousan' dollars? *Give* it to him? Wha'd you do it for? Wha'd you—?" Allie's voice failed her completely, she groped at her throat, uttering unintelligible, animal-like sounds.

"Why, Allie, you're *mad!* And after all he done for me an' you," Mrs. Briskow cried, accusingly. "You oughter be ashamed."

"Sure! Didn't he make us twenty-four thousan' dollars, where we wouldn't of got nothin'? An' us rich as we are, an' him broke? I'm supprised at you." A harsh exclamation burst from the girl—to the astonished parents it sounded like an oath, but it could not have been—then she swung herself heavily about and rushed blindly into the next room, slamming the stout metal door behind her with a crash that threatened to unhinge it.

"Well, I be—darned!" Gus Briskow turned a slack, empty face upon the partner of his joys. "I—I never s'posed that girl would turn out—*greedy*."

The mother's countenance slowly wrinkled into lines of grief and worry, she wrung her hands and rocked from side to side. "I dunno what's come over the child," she moaned, tearfully. "She behaves so queer over them silk stockin's an' corsets an' lingeries an' things that she skeers me. Sometimes I'm afeerd she's goin' crazy—or something."

CHAPTER IX

No industry can boast a history more dramatic, more exciting, than that of oil. From the discovery of petroleum, on through the development of its usefulness and the vast expansion of its production, the story is one of intense human interest, and not even the story of mining has chapters more stirring or more spectacular.

The average man has never stopped to consider how close he is to the oil business or how dependent he is upon it; from babyhood, when his nose is greased with vaseline, to the occasion when a motor hearse carries him on his last journey, there is not often a day when he fails to make use of mineral oil or some of its by-products. Ocean liners and farmers' plows are driven by it; it takes the rich man to his office and it cleans the shopgirl's gloves; it gives us dominion over the air and beneath the waters of the sea. We live in a mechanical age, and without oil our bearings would run hot and civilization, as we know it, would stop. It is the very blood of the earth.

Oil production is a highly specialized industry, and it has developed a type of man with a type of mind quite as characteristic as the type of machinery employed in the drilling of wells. The latter, for instance, appears at first glance to be crude and awkward, but as a matter of fact it is amazingly ingenious and extremely efficient, and your oil-field operator is pretty much the same. Nor is there any business in which practical experience is more valuable. As a result, most of the big oil men, especially those engaged in production, are graduates of the school of hard knocks; they are big-fisted, harsh-handed fellows who are as thoroughly at home on the "thribble board" of a derrick as at a desk or a directors' table, and they are quite as colorful as the oil fields themselves. Their lives are full and vigorous.

Of all the oil excitements, that which occurred in North Texas was perhaps the most remarkable; at any rate, the world has never witnessed such scenes as were enacted there. The California gold rush, the great Alaskan stampede, the diamond frenzies of South Africa and of Australia, all were epic in their way, but none bred a wilder insanity than did the discovery of oil in the Red River district.

For one thing, the time was ripe and conditions were propitious for the staging of an unprecedented drama. The enormous wastage of a world's war, resulting in a cry for more production, a new level of high prices for crude, rumors of an alarming shortage of supply, the success of independent producers, large and small—all these, and other reasons, too, caused many people hitherto uninterested to turn their serious attention to petroleum. The country was prosperous, banks were bulging with money, pockets were stuffed with profits; poor men had the means with which to gamble and rich men were looking for quicker gains. Inasmuch as the world had lived for four years upon a steady diet of excitement, it was indeed the psychological moment for a spectacular boom.

The strike at Ranger lit the fuse, the explosion came with the first gush of inflammable liquid from the Fowler farm at Burkburnett. Then, indeed, a conflagration occurred, the comprehensive story of which can never be written, owing to the fact that no human mind could follow the swift events of the next few tumultuous months, no brain could record it. Chaos came. Life in the oil fields became a phantasmagoria of ceaseless action and excitement—a fantastic stereopticon that changed hourly.

"Burk" was a sleepy little town, dozing amid parched wheat

fields. The paint was off it; nothing much more exciting than a crop failure ever happened there. The main topic of conversation was the weather and, as Mark Twain said, everybody talked about it, but nothing was done. Within sixty days this soporific village became a roaring bedlam; every town lot was leased, derricks rose out of chicken runs, boilers panted in front yards, mobs of strangers surged through the streets and the air grew shrill with their bickerings. From a distance, the sky line of the town looked like a thick nest of lattice battle masts, and at night it blazed like Coney Island.

The black-lime territory farther south had proven too expensive for individual operators and small companies to handle, but here the oil was closer to the surface and the ground was easily drilled, hence it quickly became known as a poor man's pool. Then, too, experienced oil men and the large companies who had seen town-site booms in other states, kept away, surrendering the place to tenderfeet and to promoters. Of these, thousands came, and never was there a harvest so ripe for their gleaning.

Naturally a little country town like this could not hold the newcomers, therefore Wichita Falls became their headquarters. Here there were at least a few hotels and some sort of office quarters—sheds beneath which the shearing could take place —and there the herd assembled.

Of course, the cougars followed, and, oh, the easy pickings for them! A fresh kill daily. Warm meat with every meal. Such hunting they had never known, hence they gorged themselves openly, seldom quarreling among themselves nor even bothering to conceal the carcasses of their prey. It was easier to pull down a new victim than to return to the one of the day before.

Rooming houses slept their guests in relays, canvas dormitories sprang up on vacant lots, the lobbies of the hotels were packed with shouldering maniacs until they resembled wheat pits, the streets were clogged with motor cars, and the sidewalks were jammed like subway platforms. Store fronts were knocked out and the floor space was railed off into rows of tiny bull-pen brokers' offices, and in these companies by the hundred were promoted. Stock in them was sold on the sidewalks by bally-hoo men with megaphone voices. It seldom required more than a few hours to dispose of an entire issue, for this was a credulous and an elated mob, and its daily fare was exaggeration. Stock exchanges were opened up where, amid frenzied shoutings, went on a feverish commerce in wildcat securities; shopgirls, matrons, housemaids gambled in shares quite as wildly as did the unkempt disreputables from the oil fields or the newcomers spilled out of every train. People trafficked not in oil, but in stocks and in leases, the values of which were entirely chimerical.

But this speculative frenzy was by no means local. Burkburnett became a name to conjure with and there was no lack of conjurers. These latter spread to the four points of the compass, and the printing presses ran hot to meet their demands. A flood of money flowed into their pockets. While this boom was at its height a new pool, vaster and richer, was penetrated and the world heard of the Northwest Extension of the Burkburnett field, a veritable lake—an ocean—of oil. Then a wilder madness reigned. Daily came reports of new wells in the Extension with a flush production running up into the thousands of barrels. There appeared to be no limit to the size of this deposit, and now the old-line operators who had shunned the town-site boom bid feverishly against the promoters and the tenderfeet for acreage. Farms and ranches previously all but worthless were cut up into small tracts and drilling sites, and these were sold for unheard-of prices. Up leaped another forest of skeleton towers some ten miles long and half as wide.

But this was the open range with nothing except the sky for shelter, so towns were knocked together—queer, greasy, ramshackle settlements of flimsy shacks—and so quickly were they built that they outran the law, which is ever deliberate. The camps of the black-lime district, which had been considered hell holes, were in reality models of order compared with these mushroom cities of raw boards, tar paper, and tin. Gambling joints, dance halls, and dens more vicious flourished openly, and around them gathered the scum and the flotsam that crests a rising tide.

Winter brought the rains, and existence in the new fields became an ugly and a troublesome thing. Roads there were none, and supplies became difficult to secure. The surface of the land melted and spinning wheels churned it; traffic halted, vehicles sank, horses drowned. Between rains the sun dried the mud, the wind whirled it into suffocating clouds. Sandstorms swept over the miserable inhabitants; tornadoes, thick with a burden of cutting particles, harried them until they cursed the fate that had brought them thither.

But in Wichita Falls, where there was shelter overhead and pavements underfoot, the sheep shearing proceeded gayly.

Of the men engaged in this shearing business, none, perhaps, had gathered more wool in the same length of time than the two members of the firm of McWade & Stoner. Mr. Billy McWade, junior partner, was a man of wide experience and some accomplishments, but until his arrival at Wichita Falls he had never made a conspicuous success of any business enterprise. The unforeseen invariably had intervened to prevent a killing. Either a pal had squealed, or the postal authorities had investigated, or a horse had fallen—anyhow, whenever victory had perched upon his banner something always had happened to frighten the bird before its wings were fairly folded.

Mr. McWade had finally determined to wipe off the slate and commence all over. Accordingly, he had selected a new field, and, in order to make it a real standing start, he had likewise chosen a new name. He had arrived at Wichita Falls with one suit of clothes and nothing more, except an assortment of contusions ranging in color from angry red to black-and-blue, these same being the direct result of repeated altercations with roughshod members of a train crew. These collisions McWade had not sought. On the contrary, when, for instance, outside the yards at Fort Worth his unobtrusive presence on the blind baggage had been discovered, he had done his best to avoid trouble. He had explained earnestly that he simply must leave the city by that particular train. The circumstances were such that no other train would do at all, so he declared. When he had been booted off he swung under and rode the trucks to the next stop. There a man with a lantern had searched him out, much as a nigger shines the eyes of a possum, and had dragged him forth. He was dragged forth at the second stop, and again at the third. Finally, the train was halted far out on a lonely prairie and a large brakeman with gold teeth and corns on his palms held a knee upon Mr. McWade's chest until the train started. Ignoring the hoarse warning breathed into his dusty countenance, along with the odor of young onions, the traveler argued volubly, but with no heat, that it was vitally necessary to his affairs that he continue this journey without interruption; then, when the brakeman rose and raced after the departing train, he sprang to his feet and outran him. McWade was lithe and nervous and fleet; he managed to swing under the last Pullman at the same instant his captor reached its rear platform.

It is probable that a blithe determination even such as this would have eventually succumbed to repeated discouragements, but at the next stop, a watering tank, aid came from an unexpected quarter. From the roof of the car another knight of the road signaled, and thither McWade clambered, kicking off the clutching hand of his former enemy.

The second traveler was a robust man, deliberate but sure of movement, and his pockets were filled with nuts and bolts. This ammunition he divided with his companion, and such was their unerring aim that they maintained their sanctuary for the remainder of the journey.

On the way in to Wichita Falls the stranger introduced himself as Brick Stoner. He was a practical oil man, a driller and a sort of promoter, too. It was his last pro motion, he confided, that had made it necessary for him to travel in this fashion. He had many practical ideas, had Mr. Stoner, as, for instance, the use to be made of a stick with a crook in it or a lath with a nail in the end. Armed thus, he declared, it was possible for a man on the roof of a sleeping car to pick up a completely new wardrobe in the course of a night's ride, provided the upper berths were occupied and the ventilators were open. Mr. Stoner deeply regretted the lack of such a simple aid, but agreed that it was better to leave well enough alone.

McWade warmed to his traveling companion, and they talked of many things, such as money and finance, sudden riches, and ways and means. This led them back naturally to a discussion of Stoner's latest promotion; he called it the Lost Bull well, and the circumstances connected therewith he related with a subtlety of humor rare in a man of his sorts. The nature of the story appealed keenly to McWade, and it ran like this: Stoner had been working in the Louisiana gas fields near the scene of a railroad accident—three bulls had strayed upon the right of way with results disastrous to a freight train and fatal to themselves. After the wreckage had been cleared away, the claim agent settled with the owner of the bulls and the carcasses were buried in an adjoining field. This had occurred some time prior to Stoner's arrival; in fact, it was only by chance that he heard of it.

One day in passing the spot Stoner noticed a slight depression in the ground, filled with water through which occasional bubbles of gas rose. Being of an inquisitive turn of mind, he had amused himself with some experiments and found that the gas was inflammable. Moreover, it gave off an odor not unlike that of natural gas. It was a phenomenon of decomposition new to the driller, and it gave him a great idea. He went to town and very cautiously told of his discovery—a gas seepage, with traces of oil. His story caused a sensation, and he led several of the wealthiest citizens to the spot, then watched them in all gravity while they ignited the gas, smelled it, tasted the soil. They were convinced. They appointed Stoner their agent to buy the farm, under cover, which he did at a nice profit—to himself. This profit he spent in riotous living while a rig was being moved upon the ground. Not until the derrick was up and the crew, in the presence of the excited stockholders, came to "spud in," was the true source of that gas discovered—then the enterprise assumed such a bad odor that bystanders fled and Mr. Stoner was forced to leave the state without his baggage.

This had been the nature of McWade's and Stoner's meeting; on the roof of that swaying Pullman they laid the corner stone of their partnership.

Arrived at Wichita Falls, Stoner went into the field and McWade obtained employment in a restaurant. It was a position of trust, for upon him developed the entire responsibility of removing the traces of food from the used dishes, and drying them without a too great percentage of breakage. It kept McWade upon his feet, but, anyhow, he could not sit with comfort, and it enabled him, in the course of a week, to purchase a change of linen and to have his suit sponged and pressed. This done, he resigned and went to the leading bank, where he opened an account by depositing a check drawn upon a Chicago institution for fifty thousand dollars. McWade made it a practice always to have a few blank checks on hand. Airily, but in all earnestness, he invited the Texas bank to verify the check at its convenience.

So many were the strangers in Wichita Falls, so great the rush of new customers, that the banks had no means of investigating their accounts except by wiring at their own expense. This was Saturday afternoon, which gave McWade two days of grace, so he pocketed his new pass and check books, then mingled with the crowd at the Westland Hotel. He bought leases and drilling sites, issuing local checks in payment thereof—nobody could question the validity of those checks with the evidence of fifty thousand dollars deposited that very day—and on Sunday he sold them. By the time the Wichita Falls bank opened its doors on Monday morning he had turned his last lease and had made ten thousand dollars.

A few days later he and Stoner incorporated their first company. This was at the height of the town-site boom, and within a few hours McWade had sold the stock. Thereafter prosperity dogged the pair, and before long they had made reputations for themselves as the only sure-fire wildcat promoters in town. McWade possessed the gift of sidewalk oratory; Stoner posed as the practical field man whose word upon prospects was final. He it was who did the investigating, the "experting"; his partner was the bally-hoo.

But competition grew steadily keener, other promoters followed their lead, and it became necessary to introduce new and original methods of gathering an audience. Mere vocal persuasiveness did not serve to arrest the flow of pedestrians, and so McWade's ingenuity was taxed. But he was equal to the task; seldom did he fail of ideas, and, once he had the attention of a crowd, the rest was easy.

One morning he and his partner provided themselves with some dice and several hundred dollars in gold coin. With these they began shooting craps on the sidewalk in front of their office. Now gambling was taboo, hence the spectacle of two expensively dressed, eminently prosperous men squatting upon their heels with a stack of double eagles before them caused a sensation, and people halted to witness their impending arrest. Soon traffic was blocked.

The gamblers remained engrossed in their pastime, as well they could, having thoughtfully arranged the matter with the policeman on duty; gravely they breathed upon the cubes; earnestly they called upon "Little Joe," "Long Liz," "Ada," and the rest; silently they exchanged their stacks of gold pieces as they won or lost.

Calvin Gray, but just arrived from Dallas, looked on at the game with some curiosity, not divining its purpose, until McWade pocketed the dice, then mounted a box at the curb and began, loudly:

"Now, gentlemen, that is one way of making money, but it is a foolish and a hazardous way. There is a much saner, safer method, and I'm going to tell you about it. Don't pass on until you hear me, for I have a most incredible story to relate, and you'll be sorry you missed it."

There was a ripple of appreciative laughter, but the crowd pressed closer as the orator continued:

"You've all heard about these 'doodlebugs' who go around locating oil with a divining rod, haven't you? And you don't believe in them. Of course you don't. Neither do I. I can't put any trust in willow twigs, but—we'll all admit that there are forces of nature that we don't understand. Who can explain the principle of magnetic attraction, for instance? What causes the glowing splendor of the Aurora Borealis? What force holds the compass needle to the north? What makes a carpet tack jump onto a magnet like"—the speaker paused and stared hard at a member of his audience who had passed a humorous remark at his expense—"just like I'll jump you, stranger, if you don't keep your trap closed. I say who can read those secrets, who can harness those forces? The man who can has got the world by the tail and a downhill pull. Now then, for the plot of my story, and it will pay you to do a week of listening in the next five minutes. Awhile ago an eminent scientist, unknown to me or to my partner, Mr. Stoner, came into our office, which is at your backs, one flight up, second door to the right, and showed us an electrical device he has been working on for the last eight years. He claimed he had it perfected and that it would indicate the presence of oil on the same principle that one mineral attracts another. 'Oil is a mineral,' said he, 'and I think I've got its magnetic complement. I believe my invention will work.'

"'I'll bet a thousand dollars it won't,' I told him. But what do you think that pilgrim did? He took me up. Then he bet Stoner another thousand that I'd made a bad bet." McWade grinned in sympathy with the general amusement. "We arranged a thorough test. We took him, blindfolded, through the field, and, believe me or not, he called the turn on forty-three wells straight and never missed it once. Call it a miracle if you choose, but it cost Brick and me two thousand iron men, and I've got ten thousand more that says he can do the trick for you. I'll let a committee of responsible citizens take a dozen five-gallon cans and fill one with oil and the rest with water and set them in a row behind a brick wall. My ten, or any part of it, says his electric wiggle stick will point to the one with the oil. What do you say to that? Here's a chance for a quick clean-up. Who cares to take me on?"

From the edge of the crowd Gray watched the effect of this offer. Divining rods, he well knew, were as old as the oil industry, but he was surprised to see that fully half of this audience appeared to put faith in the claim, and the other half were not entirely skeptical. A man at his side began reciting an experience of his own.

McWade now introduced the miracle worker himself, and Gray rose on tiptoe to see him. A moment, then he smiled widely, for the eminent scientist was none other than Mr. Mallow—Mallow, a bit pallid and pasty, as if from confinement, and with eyes hidden behind dark goggles. With a show of some embarrassment, the inventor displayed his tester, a sufficiently impressive device with rubber handles and a resistance coil attached to a dry battery, which he carried in his pocket.

Gray looked on as the comedy was played out. It transpired that Professor Mallow had tested, among other properties, the newest McWade-Stoner lease, a company to drill which had just been formed under the title of "The Desert Scorpion," and he really judged from the behavior of his machine that a remarkable pool underlaid the tract. He was willing to risk his reputation upon the guaranty that the first well would produce not less than three thousand barrels a day. He was interested in the out-come only from a scientific standpoint; he owned not one single share of stock. Then McWade resumed his sway over the crowd, and soon shares in "The Desert Scorpion" were selling rapidly.

Shortly after lunch, Mallow and the two partners were seated in the office upstairs, their work done for the day. Another successful promotion had gone to the credit of McWade and Stoner; all three were in a triumphal mood. Mallow was recounting a story that had just come to his ears.

"Remember that old silver tip that took a stand in front of the Owl Drug Store a few days back? He called his company 'The Star of Hope.'"

Stoner nodded. "He had a good piece of ground, right adjoining the Moon Petroleum tract—three wells down to the sand. I wondered how he ever got hold of it."

"He didn't. That's the big laugh. He didn't own that land at all. He just had himself a map drawn, with the numbers changed. His ground was a mile away. He sold his stock in two days, thirty-five thousand shares, then he blew. Some Coal-oil John, who had plunged for about three shares, got to studying his own map, found there was something wrong and let up a squawk. But Silver Tip had faded like the mists of early morn—thirty-five stronger than he was. Snappy work, eh?"

McWade frowned his disapproval. "Something ought to be done to stop those crooks or they'll kill us legitimate promoters. You can't sting a crowd too often in the same spot."

There came a knock at the door, and in answer to an invitation to enter it opened. The next instant both McWade and Stoner sat erect in their chairs, with eyes alert and questioning, for at sight of the stranger Mallow had leaped to his feet with a smothered exclamation, and now stood with his back to the desk and with his head outthrust in a peculiar attitude of strained intensity.

CHAPTER X

"Well, well, Mallow!" The caller's face broke into an engaging smile as he crossed the threshold. "Still wearing dark glasses, eh? I'm afraid you didn't heed my instructions."

Mallow spoke huskily, "What the hell you doing here?"

"Following the excitement, merely. I shall open an office and spend a good deal of my time in Wichita Falls. I hoped I'd find you here, for this morning I heard you describe your invention and—admiration overcame me. I felt constrained to congratulate you upon your scientific attainments. Marvelous, my dear Doctor! Or is it Professor Mallow?" The speaker laughed heartily. "Won't you introduce me to these—let us say magnetic forces of nature that you have discovered?" He indicated the two partners.

"What do you want?" Mallow barked.

"Momentary agitation has robbed our Professor of his habitual politeness—a not unusual phenomenon of the preoccupied scientific mind." These words were directed at McWade and Stoner. "My name is Gray. Perhaps Doctor Mallow has made mention of me."

"So you're the lad that threw pepper in his eyes?" Brick Stoner stared at the newcomer with undisguised interest. He rose, as did McWade. "I'll say we've heard of you. Your name's getting as common as safety-razor blades. You've been cleaning up, haven't you?"

"Um-m, moderately." Calvin Gray shook hands with the promoters, then to the agitated Mallow, who still peered at him apprehensively, he said: "Come, come! Let down your hammer! Uncoil!"

"Listen, you!" the other burst forth. "I beat that thing out. I'm clean and I don't intend to go back. You're a strong guy and you got a bunch of kale, and you're a getter, but the taller they come the harder they fall. You can be had." The speaker was desperate; his face was flushed with anger, the tone of his voice was defiant and threatening.

Gray helped himself to a chair, crossed his legs, and lit a cigar. McWade and Stoner neither moved nor spoke.

"My dear Mallow, you wrong me." In the newcomer's voice there was no longer any mockery. "I gave you credit for more intelligence. We played our little farce and it is done—the episode is closed, so far as I am concerned. I supposed you understood that much. I helped you and I came here to enlist your help."

"You helped *me*?" Mallow showed his teeth in a snarl.

"Precisely. Think a moment. Was it not odd that I failed to appear against you? That the case was never pressed, the prosecution dropped?"

"I s'pose you were afraid to go through. Thought I'd get you."

Gray shook his head impatiently. "Afraid? Of you? Oh, Mallow! Had I feared your majestic wrath, do you think I would have arranged for that doctor to see you every day? And paid his bill? Who, pray, sent in those good things for you to eat?"

There was a pause.

"Did you?"

"I did."

Again there was silence.

"Why?"

"For one thing, I was sorry for you. I really was. I had caused you and Tony a great deal of suffering, and I cannot bring myself to inflict actual suffering upon anyone without doing my best to alleviate it. Then again, I had nothing against you personally. We merely clashed in the course of—business." Mallow allowed himself to sink back upon the desk; he turned his dark goggles upon his friends in a blind stare of bewilderment.

"Well, I'll be damned!" he said, finally.

"Mallow thought *we* had helped to spring him." It was McWade speaking. "That's why he beat it up here and that's how we happened to put him to work."

"I don't get you yet," the man in glasses muttered. "I can't understand why—"

"What's the odds why he done it?" Stoner inquired, sharply. "Any man that can squirt my eyes full of tobasco, and me with a six gun on him, is all right. And him with a bottle of milk duly made and provided!" The field member of the firm slapped his thigh and laughed loudly. "Then to forget the whole fracas and shake hands on it! That's handsome! Mr. Gray, I'm here to say there's a lot of boys going to lay off you like you was a cactus."

The object of this commendation was pleased. "Gratitude is rare," he murmured. "I thank you. Now then, I was thinking of making friend Mallow a business proposition, but—perhaps I can interest you, also, in doing something for me. I'll pay well."

"We're live ones," Stoner asserted.

"It is business of a confidential nature."

"All the talking we do is on the street. We're promoting wildcats, but I guess we know as much about the good wells as the big companies themselves, and when it comes to actual drilling, I've forgotten more than all these boll weevils will ever learn. What can we do for you?"

"For one thing, I wish to hire the brightest oil scout in the district, but I don't want him, nor anyone else, for the time being, to suspect that he's working for me. I will double his salary to watch one operator. Perhaps he could appear to be in your employ? Furthermore, I intend to do considerable secret buying and selling, and I will need several dummies—moral character unimportant. All I insist upon is absolute loyalty and obedience to my orders."

During the silence that followed, Gray felt the three men staring at him curiously.

"You're after big game, I take it?" McWade inquired, mildly.

"The biggest in these woods."

"One man, did you say?"

"One man."

"Some—grudge, perhaps?"

"Perhaps."

"A yacht is too expensive for most men, but they don't burn money as fast as a grudge."

"This one will take his last dollar—or mine."

"We're a legitimate firm, you know—"

Gray's eyes twinkled as he exclaimed: "Exactly! If I have caused you to infer that I shall employ anything except legitimate means to effect my purpose, it is my error. At the same time, my proposition is not one that I could well afford to take to the ordinary, conservative type of broker. Now then, how about you, Mallow? Would you care to work for me?"

The latter's pale face broke into a grin. "I am working for you," he declared. "I've been on your pay roll now for five minutes. What's more, if it'll save money to croak this certain party and be done with it, why, maybe that can be arranged, too. My new wiggle stick may not find oil every crack, but I bet I can make it point to half a dozen men who—"

Gray lifted an admonitory hand. "Patience! It may come to something like that, but I intend to break him first. Can I arrive at terms with you gentlemen?"

"Write your own ticket," McWade declared, and Mr. Stoner echoed this statement with enthusiasm.

"Very well! Details later. Now, I shall give myself the pleasure of calling upon my man and telling him exactly what I intend doing." The speaker rose and shook hands with the three precious scoundrels. When the door had closed behind him McWade inquired: "Now what do you make of that? Going to serve notice on his bird!"

"Say! He's the hardest guy I ever saw," Stoner declared, admiringly. Mallow spoke last, but he spoke with conviction. "You said it, Brick. I had his number from the start. He's a master crook, and—it'll pay us all to string with him."

Henry Nelson's activities in the oil fields did not leave him much time in which to attend to his duties as vice-president of his father's bank, for what success he and Old Bell Nelson had had since the boom started was the direct result of the younger man's personal attention to their joint operations. That attention was close; their success, already considerable, promised to be enormous.

But of late things had not been going well. The turn had come with the loss of the Evans lease, and that misfortune had been followed by others. Contrary to custom, it was Henry, and not Bell, who had flown into a rage at receipt of Gus Briskow's telegram announcing a slip-up in the deal—a sale to Calvin Gray; that message, in fact, had affected the son in a most peculiar manner. For days thereafter he had been nervous, almost apprehensive, and his nervousness had increased when he secured the back files of the Dallas papers and read those issues which he had missed while out of town. Since that time he had made excuses to avoid trips into the Ranger field and had conducted much of his work over the telephone. Perhaps for that reason it was that trouble with drilling crews had arisen, and that one well had been "jimmed"; perhaps that explained why a deal as good as closed had gotten away, why a certain lease had cost fully double what it should have cost, and why the sale of another tract had not gone through.

Be that as it may, it was this generally unsatisfactory state of affairs that accounted for the junior Nelson's presence in Wichita Falls at this time. He and Bell had spent a stormy forenoon together; he was in an irritable mood when, early in the afternoon, a card was brought into his office.

Nelson could not restrain a start at sight of the name engraved thereon; his impulse was to leap to his feet. But the partition separating him from the bank lobby was of glass, and he knew his every action to be visible. He allowed himself a moment in which to collect his wits, then he opened slightly the desk drawer in which he kept his revolver and gave instructions to admit the caller.

Nelson revolved slowly in his chair; he stared curiously at the newcomer, and his voice was cold, unfriendly, as he said:

"This is quite a surprise, Gray."

"Not wholly unexpected, I hope."

"Entirely! I knew you were in Texas, but I hardly expected you to present yourself here."

Gray seated himself. For a moment the two men eyed each other, the one stony, forbidding, suspicious, the other smiling, suave, apparently frank.

"To what am I indebted for this—*honor?*" Nelson inquired, with a lift of his lip.

"My dear Colonel, would you expect me to come to Wichita Falls without paying my respects to my ranking officer, my immediate superior?"

"Bosh! All that is over, forgotten."

"Forgotten?" The caller's brows arched incredulously. "You are a busy and a successful man; the late war lives in your mind only as a disagreeable memory to be banished as quickly as possible, but—"

Henry Nelson stirred impatiently. "Come! Come! Don't let's waste time."

"—but I retain distinct recollections of our Great Adventure, and always shall."

"That means, I infer, that you refuse to close the chapter?"

As if he had not heard this last remark, Gray continued easily: "It is a selfish motive that brings me here. I come to crow. It is my peculiar weakness that I demand an audience for what I do; I must share my triumphs with some one, else they taste flat, and since you are perhaps the one man in Texas who knows me best, or has the slightest interest in my doings, it is natural that I come to you."

This guileless confession evoked a positive scowl. "What have you done," the banker sneered, "except get your name in the papers?"

"I have made a large amount of money, for one thing, and I am having a glorious time. Now that Evans lease, for instance—"

"Oh! You've come to crow about that."

"Not loudly, but a little. I turned the greater part of that land for as much as five thousand dollars an acre. Odd that we should have come into competition with each other on my very first undertaking, isn't it? Fascinating business, this oil. All one needs, to succeed, is experience and capital."

"What do you know about the business?"

"Nothing. Absolutely nothing. But I am learning. Luck, I find, is a good substitute for experience, and I certainly am lucky. As for capital—of course I was blessed in having unlimited money with which to operate. You inferred as much, I take it. Of course! Yes, Colonel, I have the money touch and everything I have put my hand to has turned out well."

Nelson burst forth in sudden irritation. "What are you getting at? You know I don't care a damn what you're doing, how much money you're making—"

"Strange! Inasmuch as practically every dollar I have made has come out of you, indirectly."

For a moment Nelson said nothing; then, "Just what do you mean by that?"

Rex Beach

"Exactly what I said. I've cut under you wherever possible. When you wanted acreage, I bid against you and ran the price up until you paid more than it was worth. That which I secured I managed—"

"*You!* So—*you're* the one back of that!" Nelson's amazement destroyed the insecure hold he had thus far maintained upon himself. Furiously he cried: "You're out to get me! That's it, eh?"

"I am, indeed. And half my satisfaction in doing so will be in knowing that you know what I'm up to. One needs steady nerves and a sure touch in any speculative enterprise; he daren't wabble. I'm going to get your nerve, Nelson. I'm going to make you wabble. You're going to think twice and doubt your own hunches, and make mistakes, and I—I shall take advantage of them. Of course I shall do more than merely—"

"Well, by God! I knew you had the gall of the devil, but—See here, Gray, don't you understand what I can do to you? I don't want any trouble with you, but one word from me and—"

"Of course you want no trouble with me; but, alas! my dear Colonel, you are going to have it. Oh, a great deal of trouble. More trouble than you ever had in all your life. Either you are going broke, or I am. You see, I have all the advantage in this little game, for I will pay a dollar for every dollar I can cause you to lose, and that is too high a price for you to meet. If I should go bankrupt, which of course I sha'n't, it would mean nothing to me, while to you—" The speaker shrugged. "You haven't my temperament. No, the advantage is all mine." Gray's tone changed abruptly. "For your own good remove your hand from the neighborhood of that drawer. I am too close to you for a gun-play. Good! Now about that one word from you. You won't speak it, for that would force me to utter nasty truths about you, and you would suffer more than I, this being your home town where you are respected. And the truth is nasty, isn't it?"

Colonel Nelson had grown very white during this long speech. He rose to his feet and laid one shaking hand upon his desk as if to steady himself; his tongue was thick in his mouth as he said, hoarsely:

"I'd like to think you are crazy, but—you're not."

"Almost a compliment, coming from you!"

"You think you can beat me—Want to make it a money fight, do you? Well, I'll give you a bellyful. Every dollar I've got will go to smash you—smash you!"

"Splendid!" Gray was on his feet now and he was smiling icily. "One or the other of us will be ruined, and then perhaps we can resort to those methods which both of us would enjoy using. Of the two, I believe I am the more primitive, for the mere act of killing does not satisfy me. I've come a long way to sink my teeth into you. Now that they're in, they'll stay. So long as you're willing to fight clean, I'll—"

"Are you gentlemen going to talk forever?" The inquiry came in a woman's voice. Both Nelson and Gray turned to behold a smiling, animated face framed in a crack of the door.

"Miss Good!" Calvin Gray strode forward, took the girl's hands in his and drew her over the threshold. "My dear Miss Good, I have rummaged half the state, looking for you."

"I hope I'm not interrupting.—I recognized you and—" The girl turned her eyes to Henry Nelson, but at sight of his face her smile vanished. "Oh, I'm sorry!" she cried. "Let me run out—"

Gray held her hands more firmly. "Never. Do you think I shall risk losing you again? Colonel Nelson and I had finished our chat and were merely exchanging pleasantries."

"Cross your heart?"

"Cross my heart and hope to die." Gray laughed joyously and again shook the girl's hands.

"Yes. Colonel Gray was just leaving," Nelson managed to say.

"Colonel? Are you a colonel, too?" the girl inquired, and Gray bowed.

"I was."

"And you knew each other abroad?"

"We came to know each other very well. We were, in fact, commissioned at the same time and place, but Colonel Nelson received his a moment earlier than I received mine, therefore he outranked me. Now then, permit me to retire while you and he—"

"Oh, there's nothing confidential about what I have to say. It's good news for my partner, and I'm sure he'd love to share it." To Nelson she announced, "Pete has a showing of oil!"

The vice-president of the bank murmured something which was lost in Gray's quick inquiry: "Partner? Are you a partner of Colonel Nelson's?"

"After a fashion. We own a twenty-acre lease west of 'Burk'— that is, I have a quarter interest and Henry is putting down a well. I drove out there, and his driller told me it is looking good."

Gray turned a keenly inquisitive gaze upon his enemy, and what he saw, or fancied he saw, gave him the thrill of a new discovery. It may have been no more than intuition on his part, but something convinced him that his acquaintance with Miss Good deeply displeased the man. If he knew Henry Nelson as well as he believed he did, it was more than disapproval, more than mere personal dislike, that smoldered in the latter's eyes. This was luck!

In his warmest tone he cried: "Congratulations, my dear Colonel. However badly you have fared in the Ranger district, fortune favors you here. But why only a quarter interest? You put too low a price upon your blessings. I'll better that arrangement. Why, I was ready to offer Miss Good a full half of all I have, when she played a heartless jest upon me. Ran away! Disappeared! I'll admit I was piqued. I was deeply resentful, but—"

Nelson interrupted this flow of extravagance. "'Miss Good'?" he said, curiously. "Why does he call you that, 'Bob'?"

"A secret! A little game of pretense," Gray declared, nastily. "For the sake of our friendship, Colonel, don't tell me her real name and rob me of the pleasure of hearing it from her own lips. Come, Miss Good! Enough of money making and oil wells and stupid business affairs. I am going to bear you away upon my arm, even at the risk of displeasing my superior officer. Ha! Lucky the war is over. Now then, your promise."

Gray's impetuosity, his buoyancy, robbed his speech of boldness, nevertheless Barbara Parker flushed faintly. She was ill at ease; she felt sure she had erred in interrupting these two men; she was glad of an excuse to leave.

Gray lingered a moment, long enough for his eyes to meet those of the banker. In his there was a light of triumph, of mockery, as he said:

"A pleasant interview, wasn't it, Colonel? And now we understand each other perfectly. A fair fight and no quarter asked."

Henry Nelson stood motionless as he watched his two callers leave the bank together, then slowly he clenched his muscular hands, and from his lips there issued an oath better left unwritten.

CHAPTER XI

It was several moments after they had left the bank before "Bob" Parker could manage to slip a word in edgewise, so rapid, so eager was Gray's flow of conversation, so genuine was his pleasure at again seeing her. Finally, however, she inquired, curiously:

"What was it you said to Henry Nelson as I came out? 'No quarter asked'?"

Her escort stared down at her, his brows lifted, his tone betrayed blank astonishment. "'No quarter asked'? Bless me! What are you talking about?" Then his face cleared. "Now I remember—I said I had found quarters at last. The town is so crowded, you know; I didn't want him to feel bound to put me up. I abhor visiting. Don't you?"

"Are you really good friends? I felt very queer, the instant after I had walked in. But—I was bursting with good news and I couldn't see Henry's face until too late. Then, it seemed to me—"

"Nelson and I are scarcely 'good' friends—we never were chummy—but we were thrown together in France and saw a lot of each other. At first, my respect for him was not great, for he is a—difficult person to understand; but as my understanding grew, so did my respect. He is a remarkably capable man and a determined fighter. Admirable qualities in a soldier. My call to-day was in the nature of a ceremonial."

"Um-m! There's a ceremony before every duel—the salute. I thought I could hear the ring of steel."

Gray laughed off the suggestion. "Merely the jingle of officers' spurs, I assure you. We amateurs cling to the Regular Army pomp and practice. Frankly, I love it; I admire the military method—a rule for every occasion, a rigid adherence to form, no price too high for a necessary objective. And the army code! Ironclad and exacting! Honors difficult and disgrace easy. One learns to set great store by both. You've no idea, Miss Good, how precious is the one and how-hideous is the other."

"You mustn't call me Miss Good any longer," the girl told him. "My name is Barbara Parker."

"Oh, I like that!"

"I'm more generally known as 'Bob.'"

"Even better! It sounds tomboyish."

"It's not. It is Tom Parkerish. Father insisted on calling me that and—it stuck. He's a man's man and my being a girl was a total surprise to him. It completely upset his plans. So I did my best to remedy the mistake and learn to do and to take an interest in the things he was interested in."

"Those were—?"

Miss Parker looked up from beneath her trim velvet hat and her blue eyes were defiant. "All that people like you disapprove of; all that you probably consider undignified and unladylike, such as riding, roping, shooting—"

"Riding—unladylike? It's very smart. And why do you say people 'like me'? There are no people like me."

"You know what I mean. You're not a Westerner. You are what a cowpuncher would call a swell Easterner." Ignoring

Gray's grimace of dislike she went on, deliberately exaggerating her musical Texas drawl. "You are a person of education and culture; you speak languages; you have the broad 'a,' and if you had to go unshaven it would be a living death. You are rich, too, and probably play the piano. People like that don't admire cow-girls."

The man laughed heartily. "In spite of my broad 'a' and my safety razor, I'm as much of a man's man as your father. Frankly, I don't admire cowgirls, but I do admire you and everything you say about yourself adds to that admiration. If your father is Tom Parker—well. I congratulate you upon an admirable taste in the selection of parents."

"Do you know him?" Barbara eagerly inquired.

"No. But I know of him and I know what he stands for. I think we have many things in common, and I venture to say that he is going to like me."

Barbara smiled. This vibrant stranger had an air about him and an irresistible magnetism. It was flattering to receive marked attentions from a person of his age and consequence—the girl felt an access of importance—and the tone of his voice, his every look, assured her that she had indeed challenged his deepest interest. She colored faintly as he ran on:

"So you're a partner of Henry Nelson's! He doesn't deserve it and—our friendship ceases. I shall now hate him. Yes, henceforth he and I shall be enemies."

"I love to be flattered, but please don't become Henry's enemy. The most dreadful things happen to them."

"He pretends to be a friend, but in reality he is a suitor—a detestable suitor—and the ties of business bind you closer! I see it all. I—I consider it abominable." Gray's tone was as gay as his demeanor had been thus far, nevertheless he was probing deliberately, and the result appeared to verify his earlier suspicions. Calm as he had appeared to be during that interview in the bank, in reality he had been, and still was, in a state of intense nervous excitement; his mind was galloping; the effect of that clash had been to rouse in him a keen exaltation and a sense of resistless power. If Henry Nelson was seriously interested in this girl, he reasoned, here then was another weapon ready shaped—a rapier aimed at his enemy's breast—and all he had to do was grasp it. That promised to be a pleasant undertaking. Nor had he any doubt of success, for Barbara Parker had aroused his liking so promptly that reason—and experience—told him they must be in close sentimental accord. Even had she proven less responsive, he would still have been confident of himself, for few women remained long indifferent to his zeal, once he deliberately set about winning them. To build upon that subtle, involuntary attraction, therefore, and to profit by it, appeared advisable, nay, necessary, for henceforth all must be grist that came to his mill. In view of his declaration of war, he could afford to scorn no advantage, however direct or indirect its bearing.

"Tell me about the Briskows," Barbara demanded.

"Of course! I'm dying to do so, but"—Gray looked at his watch—"even the good must lunch. No doubt you abhor the public eating places, but, alas—"

"I do. So does everybody who tries them. But our cook has been speculating in shares, and yesterday she stalked majestically from the kitchen. She was a wretched cook, anyhow; but we couldn't afford a better one. We're very poor, dad and I."

"Were poor. Not poor any longer, I hope."

"Oh, that well! It is exciting, isn't it? Dad has gone out there to see it, so—Yes, I'll lunch with you and be duly grateful."

"Where shall we go?"

Barbara's brows drew together in a frown of consideration, and

Gray told himself that she was even more charming when serious than when smiling. "Wherever we go, we'll be sorry we didn't go somewhere else. We might try the Professor's place. He's a Greek scholar—left his university to get rich quick in the oil fields, but failed. He started a sandwich and pie counter—a good one—and it pays better than a pumper. But we'd have to sit on high stools and be scowled at if we didn't gobble our food and make room for others. Then there is Ptomaine Tommy's. Cafes are good and bad by comparison. After you've been here a few days you'll enjoy Tommy's."

"Then I vote for his poison palace. The very name has a thrill to it."

On their way to the restaurant, Gray said: "Pa and Ma and Allie Briskow and the tutoress have gone to the mountains—Ma's beloved mountains—and they appear to be living up to her expectations. The mountains, I mean. The old dear writes me every week, and her letters are wonderful, even outside of the spelling. She hasn't lost a single illusion. She has a soul for adventure, has Ma; she's hunting for caves now—keeps her ears open to hear if the ground sounds hollow; wants to find a mysterious cavern and explore it, with her heart in her mouth. She revels in the clean, green foliage and the spring brooks. She says the trees are awful crowded in places and there's no dust on them."

"And Allie has a tutor!"

"The best money could secure. And, by the way, you wouldn't have known the girl after you got through with her that day. That was only the beginning, too. She fills the eye now, and she's growing."

"*Growing?*"

Gray chuckled. "Not physically, but mentally, psychologically, intellectually."

"I said she had possibilities."

"Yes. More than I gave her credit for, but what they are, where they will lead her, I don't know. I'm a foolish person, Miss Parker, for I take an intense interest in the affairs of other people, especially my friends. My favorite dissipation is to share the troubles of those whom I like, and right now I'm quite as worried over Allie as her father is. You see, she has outdistanced her parents already; the dream part is wearing off and her new life is a reality. She is confronted with the grim and appalling necessity of adapting herself to a completely new and bewildering set of conditions. I'm not sure that she will be equal to it."

"I presume you mean that she is sensitive."

"Supersensitive! And ambitious! That's the trouble. If she were dull and conceited she could be both happy and contented. But she's bright, and she lacks egotism, so she'll never be either. Adversity would temper a girl like her; prosperity may—spoil her."

"There is a boy, too, isn't there?"

"Oh, Buddy! He's away at school. He'll make a hand, or— well, if he doesn't, I'll beat the foolishness out of him. I've assumed complete responsibility for Buddy, and he'll be a credit to me."

There was a tone in Gray's voice when he spoke of the Briskows that gave Barbara Parker a wholly new insight into his character; it was with a feeling that she knew him and liked him better that she said:

"You think a lot of those nesters, don't you?"

"More than they believe, and more than I would have thought possible," he readily declared. "I'm a lonesome institution. There's nobody dependent upon me; I owe no bills, no gratitude, and I've canceled the obligations that others owe me. You've no idea how unnecessary I am. It gives me a pleasing sense of importance, therefore, to feel that I fill a place in somebody's affairs."

Wichita Falls's facilities for public entertainment reflected perhaps as correctly as anything else the general chaos consequent upon its swift expansion into a city. Such hotels as had been capable of caring for the transient trade of pre-petroleum days were full and carried waiting lists like exclusive clubs; rooming houses and private dwellings were crowded. A new and modern fireproof hotel was stretching skeleton fingers of steel skyward, but meanwhile the task of sheltering, and especially of feeding three times a day, the hungry hordes that bulged the sides of the little city was a difficult one. To wrest possession of a cafe table for two at the rush hour was an undertaking almost as hazardous as jumping a mining claim, but Calvin Gray succeeded and eventually he and "Bob" found themselves facing each other over a discolored tablecloth, reading a soiled menu card to a perspiring waiter. It was in some ways an ideal retreat for a tete-a-tete, for the bellowed orders, the rattle of crockery, the voice of the hungry food battlers, and the clash of their steel made intimate conversation easy. Gray noted with approval the ease with which his dainty companion adapted herself to the surroundings and remarked upon it.

"After four years in the East it took me a little while to get used to it," she confessed. "The Wichita I left was a quiet town; the one I came home to was a madhouse. At first the excitement frightened me, for I felt as if I were being run over, tossed aside. But now that I've fallen in with the chase, why—I think it is splendid."

"Just what are you doing and how do you do it?" Gray wanted to know.

Barbara was glad to tell him about her brief but eventful experience since that morning at the Nelson bank when she had executed her coup, and she recited the story with enthusiasm.

"Having no capital to go on," she explained, "I've merely bought and sold on commission so far, but I'm not always going to be a broker. I'm making good, and some day dad and I will be big operators. I've been able to buy a car, and most of my time I'm out in the field. They tell me I'm as good an oil scout as some of the' men working for the big companies; but, of course, I'm not. I merely have an advantage; drillers tell me more than they'd tell a man."

"Of course, with your father along you're safe in going anywhere, but to go through the fields alone—"

"Oh, dad doesn't go!"

"What?" Gray looked up incredulously, but "Bob" nodded her head vigorously.

"Dad hates automobiles; they frighten him. So I go out alone while he runs the office."

"Extraordinary! But, my dear girl, it's dangerous."

"Naturally, I avoid 'Burk' and the Northwest Extension after dark—even the scouts do that. But it wouldn't pay anybody to high-jack me. No. I go right in on the derrick floors and hobnob with the drillers, talk about their wives and their families, discuss croup and fishing jobs; sometimes they let me taste the sand and even show me the logs of their wells. It amused them at first to think of a girl playing the game single-handed—most men, however rough, have a sense of chivalry, you know, and are better sports than they realize. Now—well, they're beginning to respect my business ability. They have learned that I keep my mouth closed and that I'll treat them squarely. Some of them would fight for me. I tell you it is the greatest experience, the most thrilling adventure, a girl ever had."

"You are a brave child, and I admire your courage," Gray declared.

"But I'm not. I'm afraid of everything that other girls are afraid of." Leaning forward confidentially, the girl continued: "I'm a hollow sham, Mr. Gray, but dad doesn't know it. After I learned how badly he wanted me to be a boy, and how he had set his heart on teaching me the things he thought a son of his should know, I had a secret meeting with myself and I voted unanimously to fill the specifications if it killed me. So I began a fraudulent life. I'm in earnest. For instance, I abhor guns, but I learned to shoot with either hand until—well, I'm pretty expert. And roping! I can build a loop, jump through it, do straight and fancy catches like a cowboy. I worked at it for months, years it seemed to me. I knew very well it was a ridiculous waste of time, but I'll never forget how proud dad was when I learned the 'butterfly.' That was my reward. Horses used to frighten me blue, but I learned to ride well enough. In fact, it has been a keen disappointment to him that I won't enter the Frontier Day contests. He'd like nothing better than to see me win the bucking-horse match. Think of it! And I'm so timid I can't look an oat in the face!" Barbara attempted a shy laugh, but there was a quaver to her voice, and when Gray continued to stare at her gravely, sympathetically, her face quickly sobered. "Now you understand why my father doesn't think it necessary to go along on my trips through the oil fields. It has never occurred to him that I'm anything but 'Bob' Parker, his boy. Mind you, he is lost in admiration of me and I rule him like a slave. I think he is great, too, and he *is*. He is the dearest, gentlest, sweetest father in the world, and I wouldn't have him learn the hideous truth about me for anything."

For a moment Barbara's listener studied her thoughtfully, then he said: "I'm immensely flattered that you like me well enough to make me your confessor. Now I'm going to confess to you that I also am an arrant coward."

"Please don't joke. You have become quite a famous character, and if the stories I hear are true—"

"The stories one hears are never true. I have my share of physical courage, perhaps; that's a common, elementary virtue, like generosity, gratitude, sympathy. The most mediocre people are blessed that way."

"Oh! Generosity and gratitude are divine qualities!"

Gray shook his head positively. "Impulses! Heart impulses, not brain impulses. They have nothing to do with character. Now I'm deathly afraid of one thing."

"What, pray?"

"Ridicule! You see, I'm egotistical and ostentatious. Oh, very! Disgustingly vain, in fact. If I were unconscious of it, I'd be unbearable, but—it amuses me as much as it amuses others, and that takes the curse off of it. I am delighted at some of my own antics. I love to swagger and I adore an audience, but to be laughed at by others would kill me. Ridicule! Scorn! I'm insensible to anything except those."

"You're a queer man."

Gray's gaze became fixed; there was a peculiar light—almost a glitter—in his eyes; he talked on as if voicing some engrossing thought. "Of course, I'm vindictive—that's a part of the swashbuckling character; it goes with the ruffles, the jack boots, and the swagger. It is a luxury of which I am extremely jealous." Bringing his attention back to the girl, he smiled and his manner changed abruptly. "There! I've proved it all by talking about myself when I'm interested only in you. However, it is sometimes easier to sell a thing by frankly decrying it than by covering up its bad points, and I'm trying desperately to make a good impression upon you. Now then, I'm tremendously interested in what you have told me about yourself, and I'm sure you are a better oil man—oil girl—than you have led me to suppose. But these are no times for social pleasantries. We are living in bedlam. There is nothing in the air but business—oil—profits. You are a business woman, and if we are to become as well acquainted as I hope we will, it must be the result of a common business interest. So, then, for a bargain. I am going to enter this field in a large way; if you will take me for a client, I will buy and sell through you whenever possible. Perhaps we can even speculate together now and then. I'll guarantee you against loss. What do you say?"

"Why—it's a splendid opportunity for me. And I know of some good things; I'm overflowing with information, in fact. For instance—" Barbara hurriedly produced her oil map and, shoving aside the dishes in front of her, she spread it upon the table. "There is a wildcat going down out here that looks awfully good." As she indicated a tiny circle marked into the corner of one square, Gray noted that there was a dimple at the base of her finger. "The scouts don't think much of it, but I happen to know it is on a structure and has a good showing of oil. The driller is a friend of mine, and he has told me that his casing is set. He'll tip me off when he intends to drill through, and if you like we'll go out there and see what happens. If it comes in, it will mean a big play on surrounding property; prices will double, treble. My theory is this—"

Gray's head was close to the speaker's, but, although he pretended to listen to her words and to follow the tracings of her finger with studious consideration, in reality his attention was fixed upon the tantalizing curve of her smooth cheek and throat. In some perplexity of spirit he asked himself why it was that mere proximity to this wholly sensible and matter-of-fact young creature filled him with such a vague yet pleasurable excitement. He realized that he was not easily thrilled; feminine beauty, feminine charm were nothing new, neverthe-less at this moment he experienced an intense elation, an eagerness of spirit, such as he had not felt since he was in the first resistless vigor of youth, and his voice, when he spoke, carried an unconscious quality strange to his ears.

It was the more bewildering because nothing had happened to awaken such feelings. He had met this unworldly, inexperienced prairie girl but twice, and on her part she had betrayed no particular attraction for him. As a matter of fact, she probably considered him an old man—young girls were like that. Of course, that was absurd. He was right in his prime, youth sang through his veins at this moment, and yet—she must like him, he must have somehow impressed her. That was fortunate, in view of her relations with Henry Nelson; luck was coming his way, and she would undoubtedly prove useful. The last thing Calvin Gray contemplated was a sentimental woman complication, but on account of this girl's peculiar knowledge it seemed to him the part of wisdom to cultivate her—to see as much of her as possible.

"If you will come over to the office, I'll show you how I think that pool lies," Barbara was saying, and Gray came to with a start.

It was midafternoon when he left the Parker office—at least he thought it must be midafternoon until he consulted his watch and discovered that, to all intents and purposes, he had completely lost two hours. An amazing loss, truly. There was no lack of youthful vigor in Calvin Gray's movements at any time, but now there was an unusual lightness to his tread and his lips puckered into a joyous whistle. It had been a great day, a day of the widest extremes, a day of adventure and romance. And that is what every day should be.

CHAPTER XII

If Gray cherished any lingering doubts as to the loyalty of
Mallow, erstwhile victim of his ruthlessness, or of McWade
and Stoner, the wildcat promoters, those doubts vanished
during the next day or two. As a matter of fact, the readiness,
nay, the enthusiasm with which they fell in with his schemes
convinced him that he had acted wisely in yielding to an
impulse to trust them. At first, when he divulged his enemy's
identity, they were thunderstruck; mere mention of Henry
Nelson's name rendered them speechless and caused them to
regard their employer as a harmless madman, but as he
unfolded his plans in greater detail they listened with growing
respect. The idea seized them finally. In the first place, it was
sufficiently fantastic to appeal to their imaginations, for they
saw in Gray a lone wolf with the courage and the ferocity to
single out and pull down the leader of the herd, and, what was
more, they scented profit to themselves in trailing with him.
Then, too, the enterprise promised to afford free scope for
their ingenuity, their cunning, their devious business methods,
and that could be nothing less than pleasing to men of their
type.

But early enough he made it plain that he intended and would
tolerate no actual dishonesty; crooked methods were both
dangerous and unsatisfactory, he told them, hence the fight
must be fair even though merciless. To annoy, to harass, to
injure, and if possible actually to ruin the banker, that was his
intention; to accomplish those ends he was willing to employ
any legitimate device, however shrewd, however smart. His

entire fortune—and his associates, of course, greatly exaggerated its size—would be available for the purpose, and when he sketched out the measures he had in mind the trio of rogues realized that here indeed was a field wide enough for the exercise of their peculiar gifts. They acknowledged, too, a certain pleasure in the comfortable assurance that they would involve themselves in no illegal consequences.

At their first council of war Gray gave each of them a number of definite things to do or to have done, the while he sought certain facts; when they assembled for a second time, it was to compare, to tabulate, and to consider an amount of information concerning the activities of Henry Nelson that would have greatly surprised that gentleman had he been present to hear it.

For one thing, there had been prepared a comprehensive list of the Nelson holdings, together with maps showing their acreage and production, the location of drilling wells, the ownership of adjoining properties, and the like. There was also a considerable amount of data concerning the terms of the Nelson leases, renewal dates, and such matters. Gray was forced reluctantly to admit that his enemy was more strongly intrenched than he had supposed; careful study of the data showed that the Nelson acreage had been well selected and that it was scientifically "checkerboarded" throughout the various fields. What was more significant was the amount of proven or semiproven stuff.

"It took work and money to get together that group of leases," Brick Stoner declared, after he had checked them off. "That's one of the best layouts in Texas, and they're shaped up to put over a big deal if they want to."

"They lack production," said Gray.

"Sure! But they'll have it before long. Lookit the wells they're putting down and that's going down around 'em."

The former speaker chewed his cigar thoughtfully for a while, then: "I don't believe they contemplate a big deal. They're not that sort. Henry Nelson is selfish and suspicious, and I'm told that Bell wouldn't trust anybody. I'm informed also that every dollar they have made has gone back into new leases and wells and that they intend to hold everything for themselves. It is rumored, quietly, that they are overextended."

"I wouldn't care how thin I was stretched if I had their gamble," McWade asserted. "All they have to do is to sit tight. The law of average will pull them out. What do you intend to do?"

"To begin with, I intend to stretch them even thinner—so thin they'll break, if that is possible."

"You can't load them up with more property."

"Certainly not, but I can make them drill more wells."

"Offsets, eh?" Stoner studied the map a bit doubtfully. "You can't make 'em offset dry holes, and if they strike oil in their wells the other fellers will have to do the offsetting."

"True. I can, of course, prevent them from extending their renewals. I can cost them a pretty penny just by forcing them to a rigid adherence to the terms of their leases and agreements and—"

"What do you mean, 'offsets'?" Mallow inquired. "How you going to break a man by bringing in wells alongside of his property? That'll make him rich."

"Can you beat that?" Stoner inquired. "Mallow's been selling oil stock and experting wells for us with the Marvelous Magnetic Finder and he don't know an offset from a headache post."

"Certainly, I know—"

"Why, Professor! Is it possible we have been deceived in you? An offset is the thing that sets off to one side of the crown block and it's a light blue, the same as a formation. It's the shape of a syncline, only bigger."

"Don't get funny. You drill an offset well to keep a man from sucking all the oil out from under your land."

"Right!" said Gray. "Wells, as you know, are drilled as close to the side lines as the law allows. When oil is found, the adjoining landowner can compel his lessee to put down a well to offset every one that threatens to draw oil from beneath his property." "That's what I've just been telling you."

"Many an operator has gone broke offsetting wells in order to protect his leases, especially if he has a number of neighbors who all start drilling promptly. That is one of the many production troubles—and there's a saying that trouble begins when the oil starts."

"You said it. But to offset the Nelsons so's to cripple 'em—" Brick Stoner shook his head. "It ain't hard to borrow money for good offsets. "Most any bank will lend."

"It is hard for anybody who is overextended to borrow. Possibly my plan won't work, but to annoy, to harass, to embarrass, to stretch them thin—it's all a part of the game. People are never as well off as we think they are. The Nelsons are close to the sand in a number of places. I want to procure the adjoining acreage. For every well they make, I'll force them to drill six more. The day they strike oil I'll have a string of derricks every two hundred feet along their side lines."

It was Mallow who spoke next. "That will cost you dollar for dollar, boss. Have you got chips enough to match their stack?"

"I don't have to invest dollar for dollar. My money will go for leases, and I'll let drilling contracts, fifty-fifty, sixty-forty, seventy-thirty—anything to get quick action. Other people's money will do the work for me. Remember, I'm not after oil, I'm after a man."

"I'll say you are!" Stoner looked up from a frowning contemplation of the maps. "And if you'll take a chance I'll show you how you can drill one well and cost them three—that is, provided you hit." As the others leaned over his shoulder he explained: "Here's a square block of four twenties—separate leases, all of 'em—and the Nelsons own three. You can cop the fourth twenty, drill right at the inside corner, where all the lines cross. If you pull a duster, you'll be out and injured, maybe twenty-five thousand, but if it comes wet they'll have to protect those three leases with three offsets. It ain't a bad-looking piece of ground; you'll have about a one-to-three chance of making a well."

"How many companies have you gentlemen promoted?" Gray inquired.

"Twenty-two. And from a shoestring. Every well went down, or is going down, and every dollar we got right here on the street."

"And all of them are dry, are they not?"

McWade spoke up, defensively: "Sure. They were all wildcats of the wildest kind. But we don't deal in oil, we sell stock. Every issue we've put out has gone above par at some time or other, and that's playing the game square with our customers, ain't it? We see that they have a chance to get out with a profit; if they hang on it's their own fault. That's how we've built up a clienteel."

"It wouldn't hurt your reputation to bring in a wet well for a change, would it?" Both partners agreed that it would not. "I'll buy this twenty-acre lease, and you can promote a company to drill ten of it, Stoner says it's a one-to-three shot."

McWade blazed with enthusiasm at the suggestion. "Take a

piece of the stock yourself, Mr. Gray, and we'll put it over in a day. With your name at the top of the list it will bally-hoo itself."

"Not a share. Your amiable proposition brings me directly to another point which has a bearing upon our main campaign. Law is a dry subject, but I must bore you with a brief disser-tation upon a provision of one statute which has doubtless escaped your notice. It has escaped the notice of most people, even of Henry Nelson, I believe. You realize that all but a few Texas oil companies are not organized as corporations, but as joint stock associations—in effect declarations of trust."

"We oughta know it," Stoner said. "It saves paying a big corporation tax and lets you sell all the full-paid, nonassessable stock you want to issue, regardless of what the property is worth. Oh, we got wise to that, *muy pronto!* Why, these here Texas laws are the bunk! Them fellows at Austin, if they had their way, would make it impossible to promote a legitimate enterprise—on a paying basis. They'd make you turn in cash or property the equivocal thereto every time you organized. Wouldn't that be sweet? This joint-stock arrange-ment is the only way to beat the game. It's a shrewd device, and my hat's off to the guy that invented it."

"Very true. Very well expressed. But in the statute governing the procedure there is wrapped up a bundle of bad news, for it is provided that any officer or stockholder may become personally liable for the entire debt of the association. There is going to be a lot of sleep lost over that fact when the truth becomes known."

"You mean if I got stock in a company that's blowed up, and I'm living in Oshkosh, all pretty, that I can be hooked for the debts some crook runs up here in Texas?"

"Precisely."

This intelligence brought no consternation to the partners; on the contrary, McWade, the optimist, grinned widely. "Goes to show you we have been playing the game along safe and legitimate lines," said he. "We don't own a share in any of our own enterprises, and if we have to pick up a few now and then to boost the market, we drop them again as if they were hot. It's a pretty thought, though. Why, I can see years of activity ahead of Brick and me, buying up the debts of defunct oil companies and collecting in full from prosperous strangers hither and yon. For Heaven's sake, don't let it get out!"

"I won't, at least until after I have accumulated a number of potential judgments against Henry Nelson. He has had his share of cats and dogs, of course, and some day I hope to lead them back to his doorstep. If they return at the right moment, they may prove an embarrassment. Who knows?"

"Got anything else up your sleeve?" Behind Mallow's dark glasses his eyes could be dimly seen, and they were active with curiosity.

"Plenty. But we have enough here to start on. First, I want these various leases, then I want a company promoted and a well started on that twenty we talked about."

For some time longer the conspirators busied themselves over the details of their plans, and Gray was beginning to feel some satisfaction at his rate of progress when an interruption occurred that threatened to delay action and even to rob him of the services of the two partners. That interruption took the form of a call from a group of highly excited and indignant purchasers of stock in the Desert Scorpion Company, that promotion in which Professor Mallow had assisted on the morning of Gray's arrival. These stockholders swarmed into the office, bringing with them an air of angry menace; they were noisy; they all talked at once.

From out of the confusion it soon became apparent that they had a real grievance, and one which called for immediate satisfaction; moreover, it was made plain that the callers cared little what form that satisfaction took, whether tar and feathers or a rope and a lamp-post. They had been sold, victimized, flimflammed, skinned; the scorpion had stung them and the poison was boiling in their veins. Briefly, the swindle was this: investigation had shown that the land owned by the Desert Scorpion was not where it had been represented to be, but more than a mile distant therefrom. Chance alone had brought forth the truth; the hour of vengeance had struck.

Calvin Gray withdrew quietly from the hubbub and asked Mallow, "Can that be true?"

The eminent scientist shrugged; out of the corner of his mouth he murmured: "Why not? It all looks alike."

Me Wade and Stoner were not in the least dismayed by this amazing intelligence; as a matter of fact, the former assumed an air of even greater geniality than usual and nodded a careless agreement to every accusation hurled against him. "Right you are, men! Absolutely right. We were victimized, but we're tickled to death to rectify the error. Mighty fortunate mistake, as a matter of fact. Brick, out with the old check book and give these birds back their money." With alacrity Mr. Stoner cleared off his desk and seated himself, pen in hand. "Step up and get a dollar a share—just what you paid. Fair enough, I calls it. The banks are open and the checks are good."

Immediately the repurchase of stock began, but anger and suspicion still smoldered; there were dissatisfied mutterings. One investor, a field man in greasy overalls, spoke out:

"We'll get ours, all right. Don't worry. But how about the other suckers? There's fifty thousand shares out. What you going to do about that?"

"Buy it back. Know where you can get any more?"

"Maybe."

"We'll pay a dollar and a half a share for all you can get, to-morrow."

"What?"

"You heard me. Breast up, boys, and get your money back. Our offer stands—a dollar a share to-day, a dollar and a half to-morrow."

There was a stir among the indignant speculators; the man for whom Stoner was writing a check inquired: "What's the idea? Why not a dollar and a half now?"

Stoner and McWade exchanged a meaning glance—it was not lost upon their attentive audience—but the latter shrugged and smiled provocatively. "That's our business," he declared, lightly. "You ghost dancers want your money back and we're giving it to you. You're letting up a holler that you were robbed, so come and get it. The faster you come the better it'll suit us. Scorpion stock will close at a dollar and a half or better to-morrow night."

"Bluff!" somebody growled.

Stoner finished his signature with a nourish, blotted it, then he hesitated. He flung down his pen and turned defiantly upon his partner, crying:

"This ain't fair to these men, Mac. They're customers of ours and we owe 'em the chance to make a killing. It's up to us to tell 'em the truth."

McWade was angry. His indignation flamed. Vigorously he denied the charge of unfairness. A spirited argument ensued, with Stoner asserting that the firm was morally obligated to protect its clients to a greater extent than merely by returning their money, and with McWade as stoutly maintaining that all obligations, moral and legal, were canceled with the repurchase of the stock.

Meanwhile it became evident that the alarming rumor about Desert Scorpion was rapidly spreading, for other investors were climbing the stairs now, and the office was becoming crowded. The later arrivals were in time to witness McWade finally defer to his partner and to hear him announce that a rare stroke of fortune had favored purchasers of this particular issue of stock, for the land which really belonged to the company had turned out to be much better than that which it owned. Certain information from the field had arrived that very day which was bound to send the stock to two dollars. If anybody wanted to sell, the promoters would be glad to buy, and they would advance their price on the morrow, as McWade had promised, so here was a chance for those present to turn a pretty penny by getting busy at once. Frankly, however, he advised his hearers to hang on and make a real clean-up. The information, which was not yet public, had nothing to do with the fact that Doctor Mallow had experted both properties with his scientific device and pronounced the new acreage much richer than the old—this latter was merely corroborative evidence, and in view of the fact that some people put no credence in so-called "doodle bugs," he merely offered the record of the tester for what it was worth. His original bet of ten to one still held, by the way, and once again he repeated that those who wished to sell out would be accommodated with the greatest alacrity. Only they mustn't return later and squawk.

McWade confessed that he was neither angry nor offended at the recent attitude of suspicion—he was merely amused. It made him laugh. The idea of his firm turning a crooked trick, when it was an established institution as strong as Gibraltar and as conservative as a national bank, was ridiculous. He and Stoner could point with pride to an unbroken record of successes and to a list of satisfied investors as long as a Santa Fe time-table. Desert Scorpion stock would go to two dollars, and five would get you ten if you didn't think so. Now then, step lively!

The refunding of money halted; there was a deal of noisy argument. Some of the disgruntled investors still insisted upon selling out; others decided to hold on; even a few asked to repurchase the stock they had turned in, and this they were reluctantly permitted to do at an advance of fifty per cent.

When the last caller had disappeared, Gray inquired, curiously: "How are you going to make good on your assertion that the stock will rise?"

"Easy!" said Stoner. "I'll change into my old clothes, put four mud chains on my car, and drive up, to the exchange in a hurry, then give some gabby guy a tip to grab Desert Scorpion for me at a dollar and a half—all he can get. After that I'll shoot out of town on high, with the cut-out open. There will be a string of cars after me inside of half an hour, and the stock will be up before I can get back."

"We'll make good, all right," McWade asserted. "Those customers are in luck dealing with a house like us. All they expect is a chance to get out with a profit and sting the next fellow. They don't want oil; they want a run for their money and a quick turn. We give it to them."

"And do they always buy your issues?"

"I ain't saying they do. Sometimes they're cold until you put on the Indian sign. But all you have to do when stock don't sell is to raise the price. Oh, if you know how, it ain't hard to make an honest dollar in the oil business!" Mr. McWade smiled with conscious satisfaction.

"I'm sure of it," Gray said, heartily. "There is so little competition."

CHAPTER XIII

Ma Briskow always had been known as a woman without guile, but of late she had developed rare powers of dissimulation. She was, in fact, leading a double life, and neither her husband nor her daughter suspected the extent of her deception. To the patrons of the Burlington Notch Hotel she was merely a drab, indistinct, washed-out old woman, unmarked except by a choice of clashing colors in dress; to her family she remained what she always had been; nobody dreamed that she was in reality a bandit queen, the leader of a wild, unfettered band of mountaineers. But that is what she was. And worse at times.

Yes, Ma had slipped the leash. She was a robber baroness; she dwelt in a rocky "fastness"—whatever that was—surrounded by a crew of outlaws as desperate as any that ever drew cutlass and dagger, and she ruled them not only by native strength of character, but also by the aid of other forces, for she was on friendly terms with the more prominent wood sprites, fairies, and the like, and they brought her wisdom. Moreover, she had learned the language of dumb animals and could talk to squirrels, beetles, porcupines, frogs.

All this, as may be surmised, had come about as the result of Ma's early reading: a haphazard choice of story books, in which were tales of treasure trove, of pirates, of wronged maidens and gallant squires—romantic stories peculiarly designed to stir a cramped imagination like hers. It was from them that she had gained her ideas of the world, her notions of manners, even her love of the mountains, and that unquenchable desire to see them that she had confided to Calvin Gray.

He it was, by the way, who had selected the Notch for these Texas nesters. It had proved a happy choice, for the hotel sat upon the top of the world, and beneath it lay outspread the whole green and purple vastness of the earth. The Briskows were entranced, of course, and, once they had established themselves here, they never thought of moving, nor did it occur to them that there might—be other mountains than these, other hotels as good as this. To them Burlington Notch became merely a colloquial name for Paradise, and life in the great hotel itself a beautiful dream.

The place was famous the country over as a health resort, and, indeed, it must have possessed miraculous curative properties, otherwise Gus Briskow, strong and vigorous as he was, could never have survived the shock of receiving his first week's bill. It was with conflicting emotions that he had divided the sum at the foot of the statement into seven parts and realized the daily ransom in which he and his family were held; it had given him a feeling of tremendous importance and extreme insignificance. He spoke feelingly that night about the high cost of loafing, but Ma showed such dismay at the mere suggestion of leaving that he had resigned himself, and thereafter the sight of his weekly bill evoked nothing more than a shudder and a prayer—a prayer that none of his wells would go dry overnight.

But lifelong habits of prudence are not easily broken. The Notch Hotel was altogether too rich for Gus Briskow's blood, so he sought a more congenial environment. He found it in the village, in a livery stable; there, amid familiar odors and surroundings both agreeable and economical, he spent most of his time, leaving Ma to amuse herself and Allie to pursue the routine of studies laid down by her tutoress.

Now Ma had not gone wild all at once; her atavism had been

gradual—the result of her persistent explorations. She had never seen a real waterfall, for instance, and the first one proved so amazing that she was impelled to seek more, after which she became interested in caves, and before long her ramblings had taken her up every watercourse and into every ravine in the neighborhood. This sense of treading untrodden ground roused in Ma a venturesome spirit of independence, an unsuspected capacity for adventure, and when the wealth of her discoveries failed to awaken interest in her family she ceased reporting them and became more solitary than ever in her habits. Every morning she slipped out of the hotel, meandered through the grounds apparently without purpose, but in reality pursuing a circuitous route and taking sudden twistings and turnings to throw pursuers off the scent. Ever deeper into the wilderness she penetrated, but with the sly caution of an old fox returning to its lair, for she was always being followed by wicked people, such, for instance, as minions of the law, members of the Black Hand, foreign spies, gen-darmys, and detectifs. Having baffled them all, she laughed scornfully, flung deceit to the winds, then hurried straight to the "fastness," and there uttered the tribal call. At the sound her gypsy band came bounding forth to meet her, and she gave them her royal hand to kiss, raising them graciously when they knelt, giving a kind word here or a sharp reprimand there.

They were the fiercest gypsies in the world, and quarrelsome, too. They were forever fighting among themselves and crying: "Curse you, Jack Dalton! Take that!" and plunging swords into one another, but they had good hearts and they loved Ma and were devoted to her lost cause. She could handle them where others would have failed.

Having accepted their homage and heard the details of their latest raids against her enemy, the false Duke of Dallas—he whose treachery had made her what she was—she assumed her throne and held formal court.

The throne was a low, flat rock beside a stream, and usually

Ma removed her shoes and stockings and paddled her feet in the water while she gave audience to visiting potentates. Those enlarged joints never seemed to ac commodate themselves wholly to the sort of shoes Allie made her wear. Court "let out" when Ma's feet had become rested, after which there were less formal affairs of state to settle. These out of the way, it was time for the queen's recreations, which took the form of singing, dancing, conversations with animals, visits with the invisible fairy folk who lived in flowers arid gave them their pretty smells.

Ma never had any trouble putting in the whole day in some such manner as this; evening came all too soon, as a matter of fact. Then it was that she bade good-by to her faithful subjects and prepared once more to fare forth and mingle, in the cunning guise of an old woman, with the followers of the false and lying Duke of Dallas. But courage! Patience! The day of reckoning was at hand when she would come into her own and the world would recognize her as the wronged but rightful Princess Pensacola.

Thus would Ma Briskow spend one morning. Another perhaps she would be an altogether different character, but always she was young and beautiful and full of grace, and only when it came time to go did she assume the disguise of an aged, wrinkled, bent old woman. Sometimes she ran miles and miles at a stretch, darting, springing like a fawn, rushing through the soft, green leaves, leaping rock and rill, her laughter echoing, her bare limbs flashing, her gold hair streaming, her scanty silken draperies whipped to shreds behind her by the very swiftness of her going. Oh, the ecstasy of that! The excitement!

Of course Ma did not actually run. Neither did her bare limbs flash—being incased in flannels. And her hair was not gold. It was gray, what little there was of it. No, she ambled a bit, perhaps, where the grass was short and the ground smooth, then she stood still, closed her eyes, and ran and leaped and swayed and darted—with her arms. Anybody can do it.

At other times she defied gravitation, a secret accomplishment all her own, which she manifested in this wise. She would begin to jump, higher and higher, and the higher she jumped the lighter she became, until finally she weighed no more than a thistledown, and the effort of leaping became a pure joy and an exhilaration. Having attained this perfect state of buoyancy, she would set out upon wonderful journeys, springing lightly as far as it pleased her to spring, soaring gracefully over obstacles, and deriving a delirious pleasure from the sensation. One cannot appreciate the enjoyment to be had from this method of locomotion without trying it.

And always when Ma came back to earth and opened her eyes there were the great smiling mountains, the clear, clean waters foaming over the rocks, and underfoot was the cool, green grass, not that hot, hard 'dobe clay she had always known. Trees, too! Beautiful whispering trees, with smooth leaves instead of burrs and spines and stickers. Nor was there the faintest choking smell of dust; no sand blowing up her nose and smarting her eyes.

Ma Briskow had never dreamed that the world was so clean. She blessed God for making oil to lie in the rocks of the earth, and she prayed that none of "them hotel people" would discover her retreat.

But, of course, somebody did discover it. Mr. Delamater, the dancing instructor, for one, stumbled upon it while Ma Briskow was in the midst of one of her imaginary games, and he reported his discovery to the day clerk.

"What ails that old dame, anyhow?" he inquired, after recounting Ma's peculiar behavior.

"Not a thing in the world except money," the clerk declared.

Doubtfully Mr. Delamater shook his handsome auburn head. "People with good sense don't act like that. She was doing an Isadora Duncan when I saw her. Dancing—if you care to call it that! Anyhow, her hair was hanging, she was flapping her arms and jiggling up and down." Delamater laughed at the memory. "There's a big, awkward bird—sort of a crane or buzzard of some kind—that dances. I never saw one, but she reminded me of it. And she *sang*! Gee! it was fierce!"

"Did she see you?"

"Scarcely. I don't mind being alone with Allie"—Delamater's teeth shone in a smile, then, seeing his reflection in a convenient mirror, he studied it with complacent favor. He tried the smile again, and, getting it to his better satisfaction, concluded—"don't mind it a bit, but a bosky dell with a mad woman is my idea of no place to be."

"Allie?" The clerk lifted his brows. "So—'*Allie*'! Has it gone as far as that, Del?"

"Oh, you know how it is! A lesson every day, soft music, arm around the waist, a kind word. The girl is human. I'm probably different to anything that ever came into her young life. Look at my wardrobe! She's not so bad to take, either, and yet—" The immaculate speaker frowned. "Father smells like a horse, and mother's a nut! Gee! It would take some coin to square that."

"That's one thing they've got," asserted the clerk. "Nothing but!"

Mr. Delamater debated further. "Think of marrying The Powerful Katrinka! I'll admit it has its points. If anything went wrong with the bank roll Allie could make a good living for both of us. Suppose, for instance, the old Statue of Liberty slipped and fell. Allie could jump over to Bedloe's Island and take a turn at holding the torch. Ifi they've got the coin you say they have, I think I'll have to see more of her."

"You won't see any more than you do. She's hitting on all four."

"What is she up to all day?"

"I don't know. Working, studying, exercising. Rehearsing for the movies, I guess. She has worn that companion of hers down to a frazzle. She has her own masseuse in the bath department, she rides a horse three days a week, and every morning she takes a long walk—"

"I've got it!" Mr. Delamater slapped his thigh. "Road work! She's getting ready to take on Dempsey." He laughed musically. "If she marries me her days of labor will be over; it will mean for her the dawn of a new life—provided, of course, those oil wells are what you say they are. Kidding aside, though, I don't dislike the girl and—I've a notion to give her a chance."

What the clerk said was true. Allie Briskow was indeed in training, both physical and mental, and the application, the energy she displayed had surprised not only her parents, who could but dimly understand the necessity of self-culture, but also Mrs. Ring, the instructress. Mrs. Ring, a handsome, middle-aged woman whose specialty was the finishing of wealthy young "ladies," had been induced to accept this position partly by reason of the attractive salary mentioned in Calvin Gray's telegram, and partly by reason of the fact that she needed a rest. She had met the Briskows in Dallas only a short time before their departure for the north, and although that first interview had been a good deal of a shock to her— almost as much of a shock as if she had been asked to tutor the offspring of a pair of chimpanzees—nevertheless she had nerved herself to the necessary sacrifice of dignity. After all, Allegheny was only an overgrown child in need of advanced kindergarten training, and in the meantime there was the prospect of a season at Burlington Notch. The latter was, in itself, a prospect alluring to one suffering from the wear and tear of a trying profession. After some hesitation, Mrs. Ring had accepted the position, feeling sure that it would rest her nerves.

But never had the good woman suffered such a disillusionment. Allie, she soon discovered, was anything but a child, or rather she was an amazing and contradictory combination of child and adult. What Mrs. Ring had taken to be mental apathy, inherent dullness, was in reality caution, diffidence, the shyness of some wild animal.

Nor was that the most bewildering of the teacher's surprises; Allie possessed character and will power. For some time she had accepted Mrs. Ring's tutorship without comment or question—Calvin Gray had recommended it, therefore she obeyed blindly—but one day, after they had become settled in the mountains, she came out with a forceful declaration.

She knew full well her own shortcomings, so she declared, and she was not content to learn a few things day by day. She demanded intensified training; education under forced draught.

"They took green country boys durin' the war—"

"During the war. Don't drop your g's, my dear."

"—during the war, and learned 'em—"

"Taught them!"

"—taught them to be soldiers in six months. Well, I'm strong as a horse, and I've got a brain, and I'm quick at pickin'—I mean I pick up things quick—"

"You pick them up quickly. Quickly is an adverb; quick is an—"

Allie's dark eyes grew darker. Imperiously she cried: "All right! But let me say this my own way. It won't be right or elegant, but you'll understand. And that's what we got to have first off—a good understanding. After I've said it, you can rub it down and curry it. I been watching you like a hawk, Miz'

Ring, and you're just what he said you was. You got everything I want, but—I can't go so slow; I got to get it quick—quickly. You been teaching me to read and talk, and how to laugh, and how to set—sit—but we been *playing*. We got to *work*! Oh, I know I'm forgetting everything for a minute. Miz' Ring, I gotta learn how to act pretty and talk pretty and *look* pretty. And I gotta learn how, *quick*."

"You are a fine-looking girl as it is, Allegheny."

"Oh, I guess I look *dressed up*, but I'm awkward. I'm stiff as a hired hand, and I fall over my feet. Look at 'em. Biggest live things in the world without lungs! I got to get slim and graceful—"

"I'll teach you a setting-up routine, if you wish, although it is scarcely in my line. Goodness knows you don't need physical culture."

"But I do," cried the girl.

"Very well. Riding is a smart accomplishment. Can you ride a horse?"

"Pshaw! I can carry a horse."

"You'd look well in a habit, and with baths, massage, dancing, and a little diet I dare say you can reduce."

"I'll starve," Allie asserted, fiercely. "But that ain't half enough. You gotta give me more studyin'. I got callouses on my hands and I'm used to work. We'll get up at daylight—"

"Good heavens!" Mrs. Ring exclaimed, faintly.

"You learn me how to do the sitting-up things first off, then I'll do 'em alone. Ride me hard, Miz' Ring. I'll remember. I'll work; you won't have to tell me twice. But I gotta make speed. I 'ain't got the time other girls have."

"My dear child, all this cannot be done in a day, a week, a month."

"How long you allow it will take?"

The elder woman shrugged. "Years, perhaps."

"Years?"

"Real culture, social accomplishments, are the results of generations of careful training. I'm not a miracle worker. But why this impatience?"

"I got—"

"I have."

"I have a reason. I can't take a generation; I'd be too late."

"Too late for what?"

But Allie refused to answer. "We'll start in to-day and we'll work double tower till one of us plays out. What d'you say?"

At first Mrs. Ring took this energetic declaration with some reserve, but before long she realized with consternation that Allie Briskow was in deep earnest and that this was not a soft berth. Instead of obtaining a rest she was being worked as never before. Allie was a thing of iron; she was indefatigable; and her thirst for knowledge was insatiate; it grew daily as she gained fuller understanding of her ignorance. There was a frantic eagerness to her efforts, almost pitiful. As time went on she began to hate herself for her stupidity and to blame her people for her condition. She was a harder taskmaster than her teacher. Most things she apprehended readily enough, but when she failed to learn, when mental or physical awkwardness halted progress, then she flew into a fury. Her temper appalled Mrs. Ring.

At such times Allie was more than disagreeable. Hate flamed in her eyes, she beat herself with her fists, she kicked the furniture, and she broke things. Once she even butted her head against the wall, uttering language meanwhile that all but caused her companion to swoon.

Mrs. Ring resigned after this final exhibition, but, lacking the courage to face Allie in a mood like that, she went to Gus Briskow.

"It is simply impossible to remain," she told him. "Already I'm a physical wreck, for I never get a moment's rest. The salary is attractive, but Allegheny is too much for me. She saps every ounce of vitality I have; she keeps me going every hour. And her terrific tempers are actually—dangerous."

"She don't ever get mad at you, does she?"

"Oh no! And she repents quickly enough. As a matter of fact, I am afraid she is overdoing her studies, but there's no holding her back."

"You're kinda worked up, Miz' Ring. Mebbe I can make it pleasanter for you."

"In what way, may I ask?"

"Well, by payin' you more."

"You are generous. The salary we agreed upon isn't low."

"Yes'm—No, ma'am!"

"I wouldn't feel right to accept more."

"Try it, ma'am, for a little while. Mebbe it won't bother you so much after you get used to it. Allie likes you."

"And I—I *am* interested in her. She is progressing, too; in fact,

I have never seen anyone learn more rapidly. But—she is so unusual. Still, perhaps I *am* the one—perhaps it is my duty, under the circumstances—"

With this disposition to compromise the father had little difficulty in dealing, so the daily routine was continued. Allie applied herself to the cultivation of the ordinary social niceties with the same zeal that she followed her studies and her physical exercises. Fortunately these exercises afforded outlet for the impatience and the scorn that she felt for herself. Otherwise there would have been no living with her. As it was she showed herself no mercy. Daylight found her stirring, her Swedish drill she took with a vigor that fairly shook the floor, and, having finished this, she donned sweater and boots and went for a swift walk over the hills. At this hour she had the roads to herself and was glad of it, for she felt ridiculous. At breakfast, although she had a ravenous appetite, she ate sparingly. The day was spent in reading aloud, in lessons in deportment, voice modulation, conversation, and the like; in learning how to enter and how to leave a room, how to behave at a tea or a reception, how to accept and how to make an introduction, how to walk, how to sit, how to rise. Allie did sums in arithmetic, she studied grammar and geography and penmanship—in short, she took an intensified common-school course. Here was where her tutoress had trouble, for when the girl's brain became weary or confused she relieved her baffled rage in her most natural way, the while Mrs. Ring stopped her ears and moaned. It was a regimen that no ordinary woman could have endured; it would have taxed the strength of an athlete.

Late in the afternoon Allie went riding, and here was one accomplishment in which she required no coaching. Frequently she vented her spite upon her horse, and more than once she brought it home with its mouth bleeding and its flanks white with lather. She rode with a magnificent reckless-ness that finally caused comment among the other guests.

Allie was sitting alone in her room one evening, fagged out

from a hard day. Some people were talking on the veranda outside her window, and she heard one say:

"The girl can look really stunning."

"Exactly. I don't understand where she gets her looks, for her parents are—impossible. Wouldn't you *know* what they were?"

Allie needed no clearer indication of who was under discussion. Instinctive resentment at the reference to her father and mother was followed by amazement, delight, at the compliment to herself—the first she had ever received. She leaned forward, straining to hear more. What mattered it how these contemptuous outsiders referred to her parents? They agreed that she was "stunning," which was their way of saying that she was pretty, nay, more—beautiful, perhaps.

"She's a glorious rider," the first speaker was saying. "She passed me the other day, going like sin, with her face blazing and that big, lively chestnut running flat. The way she took that curve above the Devil's Slide brought my heart into my mouth."

The breathless eavesdropper felt a hot wave of delight pour over her, her very flesh seemed to ripple like the fur of a cat when it is stroked.

"Oh, she's a picture, mounted! Seems to have complete confidence in herself; and the strength of a giantess, too. But— my God! when she's on her feet! And have you heard her talk?" Evidently the other speaker had, for there came the sound of low laughter, a sound that stabbed Allie Briskow like a bayonet and left her white and furious. She sat motionless for a long time, and something told her that as long as she lived she would never forget, never forgive, that laughter.

She was unusually silent and somber for the next three or four days; she went through her exercises without vim; at her studies she was both stupid and sullen. When Mrs. Ring's patience was exhausted and her frayed nerves finally gave out, Allie rounded upon her with a violence unparalleled. Those previous exhibitions of temper were tame as compared with this one; the girl spat scorn and bitterness and hatred; she became a volcano in active eruption.

In a panic Mrs. Ring sought out Gus Briskow and again resigned. By this time, however, the novelty of her resignation had largely worn off, for seldom did more than two weeks elapse without a hysterical threat to quit. But this one required more than the usual amount of persuasion, and it was not without long and patient pleading, coupled with the periodical raise, that the father induced her to change her mind. Gus told himself somberly that the price of Allegheny's education was mounting so rapidly that it might be the part of economy to take Mrs. Ring in as a full partner in the Briskow oil wells. He decided, after some consideration, to wire Calvin Gray and offer to pay his traveling expenses if he would come to Burlington Notch for a few days.

CHAPTER XIV

One accomplishment that Allegheny mastered with gratifying ease was dancing. It came naturally to her, for both she and Buddy were full of music. At first she had been extremely self-conscious; Professor Delamater had found her to be as heavy as stone and as awkward as a bear; but later, as her embarrassment became less painful, she relaxed. She regained her power of speech, also, and in time she voiced an eager desire to learn all there was to learn.

Having quickly schooled her in the simpler forms of ballroom dancing, Delamater suggested a course in the deeper intricacies of fancy dancing.

"You're getting on," he told her, one day. "That last was splendid—top hole, absolutely."

Delamater, who was quite thoroughly American, affected at times an English turn to his conversation, believing that it gave him an air. It went particularly well, he thought, with light trousers, spats, and an afternoon coat cut close at the waist.

"Don't fool me," panted the red-faced Juno. "You must have iron feet."

"My word! Spoof you, indeed! Not for worlds, if you know what I mean? I shall expect to see you in the ballroom every evening."

But Allie's confidence forsook her at this. "I'd—be scared stiff. Folks would laugh. They haven't got—haven't anything to do but laugh at other folks, and I don't like to be laughed at."

"Laugh at you! Fancy that! You're too modest." Delamater adopted the cooing note of a dove. "'Pon my word, you're too modest. If you could hear the things I hear—" He paused, not knowing exactly what to say he had heard, but his vagueness, the very eloquence of his hesitation, caused Allie's face to light up. This was the second compliment paid her since her arrival at the Notch, therefore when the phonograph resumed its melodious measures she yielded herself with abandon to the arms of her partner, and her red lips were parted, her somber eyes were shining. That day she began a course of exhibition dancing.

It was on that afternoon that Delamater had told the clerk of discovering Ma Briskow alone in the woods. There was an open golf tournament at the Notch, prominent amateurs and professionals were competing, and the hotel was crowded to its capacity with players, fashionable followers of the game and a small army of society reporters and sport writers. This being the height of the season, social doings at the resort were featured in all the large Eastern papers, for famous names were on the register and the hotel switch was jammed with private cars.

Allie Briskow was in one of her trying moods to-day, for the out-of-doors called to her. Sounds of laughter and gayety, strains of music, had distracted her from her studies, her monotonous routine had become hopelessly unbearable all at once. From her window she could see young people, hear young voices, and envy flamed in her soul. Those girls were her age; those men, easy, immaculate, different from anything she had ever seen—except Calvin Gray—they, too, were young and they courted those girls. Contemplation of the chattering throngs showed Allie more clearly than ever the chasm separating her from these people, and reawakened in her that black resentment which at times made her so difficult to manage. She was thankful that her mother had disappeared and that her father was at the livery stable; she hoped they would stay away all day. At least, they were safe from ridicule. She wondered if she might not induce them to dine in their rooms that evening, and thus spare herself the embarrassment she always suffered when she accompanied them into the public dining room.

It seemed to her that whenever they went to dinner—Gus in his baggy pepper-and-salt sack suit, his loose, lay-down collar, and his wide-toed shoes, Ma in one of her giddy, gaudy dinner dresses—it seemed as if the entire assemblage was stricken dumb and as if every eye was turned upon them in mockery and amusement. Even the waiters, Allie felt sure, noted the difference between the Briskows and the other guests, and only with difficulty concealed their contempt.

The occasional presence of Mrs. Ring, handsome, dignified, unruffled, intensified that contrast and fairly shouted the humiliating announcement that here were three nobodies who wanted to be somebodies, but never could.

Invariably when they went out in public together Mrs. Ring made Allie feel as if she belonged to a lower, cruder order of animal life; as if she were an inhabitant of another sphere. And yet, Mrs. Ring was poor; she worked for wages! Allie could not understand this phenomenon; thought of it now caused her resentment to kindle.

Of course it was the lot of the hapless tutoress to select such a moment as this in which to sweetly chide the girl for some lapse of form. Allie exploded. She reduced the elder woman to tears, then, ashamed of herself, she flung blindly out of the room, crashing the door to behind her. She decided to dance her anger away. It was some consolation to know that she could dance as well, or better, than those slim and pampered beauties outside her window. Some consolation, even though she never expected to have a chance of proving it.

Delamater was especially agreeable to-day, more than usually nattering. Not for some time did his scholar become conscious of the subtle change in his demeanor, and even then its significance awoke only a shadowy contentment. Allie hated herself too thoroughly to-day to believe that anybody could really approve of her. As for him, he entirely misconstrued the meaning of her silent acceptance of his flattery.

They had become well acquainted by now and were on a basis of easy familiarity, nevertheless it came as a shock to Allie to be called by her first name-such a shock that she missed a step and trod on Delamater's foot. They came to a pause.

The dancing master was tall and slim, his face was on a level with hers, and now he smiled into it, saying, "My mistake, my dear."

"I—reckon it was." The girl's eyes were glowing queerly, and the man was amused at her evident agitation. His first word had thrown the poor thing into a flurry.

They began to dance again, and, after a moment, with a gently rising inflection, Delamater murmured, "You heard what I called you?" He approved of the sachet that Allie used, and he became acutely conscious of the jewels resting in the palm of his left hand. The girl was rich and she was—different, unusual. Ever since she had learned to yield herself to his embrace, he had been conscious of her strong physical attraction, and now it got the better of him. "You don't care?" he said, with his lips close to her ear.

"Humph! I'm not caring for anything or anybody to-day."

"Somebody has hurt my little girl."

Allie threw back her head and stared at him with quick suspicion. "Your little girl?" she repeated.

It is the lot of any man in the heat of his desire to make

mistakes, and Delamater erred gravely at this moment. He kissed Allie. Without warning he kissed her full and fair upon her red, half-open lips.

For the briefest instant of amazement the two stood motionless in the middle of the polished floor while the phonograph brayed on; then Allie shook herself free of her partner, and in the same movement she smote him a mighty slap that sent him reeling. Delamater saw stars. The constellation of Orion gleamed in dazzling splendor within his tightly shut lids; he collided with a chair and went sprawling.

With a cry he scrambled to his feet. "What the hell—?" he growled, savagely.

Allie's face was chalky. Breathlessly, curiously she inquired, "Wha'd you do that for?"

"What did I *do* it for? Say! You ought to be complimented—tickled to death." Delamater rubbed his cheek and glared at her. "By God! I wish you were a man. Oh, don't worry, I won't touch you again! Who the hell would, after that?" Allie opened her lips to speak, but he ran on more angrily as the pain bit into him. "Thought I meant it, eh? Why, you lumbering ox—"

"Then you ain't—in love with me or—or anything?"

"*Love?*" The speaker uttered an unpleasant sound indicative of scorn. "Wake up, sister! What d'you take me for? Why, your mother talks bird talk, and your dad lives in a box stall and eats oats with his knife! Here I kid you along a little bit—slip you a little kiss, as I would any girl, and you—you—" Delamater stuttered impotently. "*Love?* I guess I'm the first regular fellow that ever gave you a chance."

Delamater was surprised when his pupil turned her back upon him, strode to the nearest window, and flung it open as if for air; his surprise deepened when she faced him again and moved in his direction. Her expression caused him to utter a profane warning, but she continued to bear down upon him, and when she reached out to seize him he struck at her as he would have struck at a man.

To those who are familiar with Burlington Notch, it will be remembered that the hotel is pitched upon a slope and that the rooms on the first floor of the east wing are raised a considerable distance above the lawn. The windows of these east rooms overlook the eighteenth green, and during tournaments they are favorite vantage points of golf widows and enthusiasts who are too old to follow the competitors around the course. To-day they were filled, for an international title was at issue and Herring, prince of amateurs, was playing off the final round of his match with the dour Scotch professional, McLeod.

A highly enthusiastic "gallery" accompanied the pair, a crowd composed not only of spectators, but also of officials, defeated players, newspaper writers, camera men, caddies, and the like. They streamed up the final fairway behind the gladiators and for the moment they were enveloped in gloom, for Herring had sliced off the seventeenth tee and a marvelous recovery, together with a good approach, had still left his ball on the edge of the green, while McLeod, man of iron, had laid his third shot within three feet of the flag. It meant a sure four for the latter, with not less than a five for Herring. One of those golfing miracles, a forty-foot putt, would halve the match, to be sure, but in tournament golf miracles have a way of occurring on any except the deciding hole.

Sympathy usually follows the amateur, therefore it was a silent throng that ranged itself about the gently undulating expanse of velvet sod in the shadow of the east wing. Herring had played a wonderful match; he stood for all that is clean and fine in golf. The end of the balcony was jammed; nearly every window framed eager faces; amid a breathless intensity of interest the youthful contender tested the turf with the head of his club and studied the run of the green. A moment, then he took his stance and swung his putter smoothly. The ball sped away, taking a curving course, and followed by five hundred pairs of eyes. It ran too swiftly! Herring, in desperation, had overplayed! But no—it lost momentum as it topped a rise, then gathered speed, all but died at the edge of the cup and—toppled in amid a salvo of handclaps and roar of "Bravo!"

That was nerve, courage, skill! That was golf! The miracle had happened! Another hole to decide the match.

Quickly the crowd became still again as McLeod, his teeth set upon the stem of his pipe, his stony face masking a murderous disappointment, stepped forward to run down his four.

The silence was broken by a cry. Out of the air overhead came the sound of a disturbance, and every face turned. A most amazing thing was in the way of happening, a phenomenon unique in the history of tournaments, for a man was being thrust forth from one of the hotel windows, perhaps twenty-five feet above the ground—a writhing, struggling, kicking man with fawn-colored spats. He was being ejected painlessly but firmly, and by a girl—a grim-faced young woman of splendid proportions. For a moment she allowed him to dangle; then she dropped him into a handsome Dorothy Perkins rosebush. He landed with a shriek. Briefly the amazon remained framed in the casement, staring with dark defiance down into the upturned faces; her deep bosom was heaving, her smoky hair was slightly disarranged; she allowed her eyes to rest upon the figure entangled among the thorns beneath her, then she closed the window.

Nothing like this had ever occurred in Scotland. The mighty McLeod missed his putt and took a five.

As Allie Briskow passed through the lobby with her head erect and her fists clenched, she heard the sound of a great shouting outside and she believed it was directed at her. She fled into her room and flung herself upon her bed, sobbing hoarsely.

Mrs. Ring was waiting on the veranda for Gus Briskow when he returned to the hotel about dark. He had learned to dread the sight of her on that veranda, for it was her favorite resigning place—what Gus called her "quitting spot," and it was evident to-night that she was in a quitting mood, a mood more hysterical than ever before. It was some time before he could get at the facts, and even then he could not fully appreciate the enormity of the disgrace that had overwhelmed Allie's instructress.

"She chucked the dancin' teacher out of a winder?" he repeated, blankly. "What for?"

"Goodness knows, Mr. Briskow! Something he said, or did—I couldn't make out precisely. I found her in a dreadful state, and I tried to comfort her, I did really, but—oh! If you could have *heard* her! Where she learned such language I don't know. My ears *burn*! But that isn't the worst; you should hear what—"

"He must of said something pretty low down." Briskow spoke quietly; his bright blue eyes were hard. "I reckon she'll tell me."

"You don't understand," chattered the woman. "She flung the man bodily out of the window and into a bed of thorns. It nearly killed him; he was painfully lacerated and bruised and— Right in the middle of a golf game! It did something dreadful—I don't know what—just as the world's champion caught the ball, or something."

"If he's crippled I'll get him that much easier," said Briskow, and at the purposeful expression upon his weather-beaten face Mrs. Ring uttered a faint bleat of terror. She pawed at him as he undertook to pass her.

"Oh, my heavens! What are you going to do?"

"Depends on what he said to Allie."

The woman wrung her hands. "What people! What—*savages*! You're—going to shoot him, I suppose, just because—"

"Yes'm!" the father nodded. "You got it right, motif an' all. 'Just because'!"

"You *can't*. I sha'n't permit it. I—I'll call the police."

"Don't do that, ma'am. I've stood a lot from you, in one way or another."

"But it's *murder*! You—you can't mean it." Moans issued from the speaker. "What *ever* possessed me to accept this position? It's unendurable, and I'll be involved—"

"I've saw your last raise, Miz' Ring."

"Do you think I'd stay, after this? It's bad enough to be made ridiculous—the whole hotel is in laughter; laughter at me, I dare say, as much as at her. Imagine! Hurling a full-grown man from a window—"

"I don't hear nobody laughing." Briskow swung his head slowly from side to side.

"But to contemplate murder—"

"What's more, I don't intend to hear nobody laugh. By God! Now I come to think about it, there ain't a-goin' to be no laughing at all around here." Gus continued slowly to swing his head, like a bear. "She's my kid!" He pushed past Mrs. Ring, still muttering, "My kid—there ain't a-goin' to be no laughing at all."

Going directly to the desk, he asked for the manager, then stood aside, hat in hand, until the latter made his appearance. The manager began a hasty and rather mixed apology on behalf of the hotel for what had occurred in the dancing room, but his tone of annoyance was an accusation in itself. It was plain that, to his mind, the catastrophe on the eighteenth green outweighed in importance whatever may have led up to it. That was something actually tragic, something frightful, appalling; it involved the good name of the hotel and affected the world's golf title.

"Very—unfortunate," he lamented. "We haven't heard the last of it, by any means. McLeod may file a protest. And there is something to be said on both sides; rather a nice question, in fact."

"Prob'ly so," the father agreed. "An' I got something to say about it, too. Get that dancin' perfessor off the place quick or I'll kill him."

The manager recoiled; his startled eyes searched Briskow's face incredulously. "I—beg pardon?"

"I 'ain't heard my kid's side of the story yet, but I'm goin' to see her now, so you better get word to that jumpin' jack in a hurry. That is, if you want to save him."

"He is discharged, of course, for we tolerate no rudeness on the part of our employees—or our guests, for that matter; but I believe he is suffering some effects from the shock. I couldn't well ask him to go before—"

"It'll take me prob'ly twenty minutes, talkin' to my girl. That'll give him time, if he moves fast. But I may get through in fifteen."

At the door to his suite Gus Briskow paused to wipe his countenance clean of the expression it had worn for the last few minutes, and when he entered it was with his usual friendly smile. Allie and her mother were waiting; they were white and silent. Gus kissed his daughter before saying:

"Don't worry, honey; he won't bother you no more."

Allie averted her face. Mrs. Briskow inquired, "Did you see the skunk?"

"No. I give him a few minutes to clear out."

"Hadn't we better leave, too?" ventured Allie.

"Oh-h!" In Ma's eyes was such bleak dismay, such a piteous appeal, that Gus shook his head.

"What fer? We got nice quarters and your ma likes it here—"

"They're laughing at me. I heard 'em hollering."

"They won't laugh long. No, you're learnin' fast, and we're all havin' a nice time. Only one thing—I'm kinda tired of that Miz' Ring. I let her go, but I'll get you another—"

"She quit, eh?"

"Um-m, not exactly. I—"

"I don't blame her. I've been mighty mean. But I couldn't help it, pa. When you put a wild horse in a pen, it don't do to prod him and throw things and—That's what they've done to me. I bite and kick like any bronc. When you're hurt, constant, you get spells when you've got to hurt back. I've been rotten to her, and now this coming on top of it—"

"Wha'd that dancin' dude do, anyhow?"

Allie related her experience with Professor Delamater; she told it all up to the burst of shouting that followed her through the lobby. "You should of heard 'em yelling, clapping their hands—! I"—she choked, her voice failed her, miserably she concluded—"I wish to God we'd never struck oil!"

"You're just wore out, dearie," her mother said, comfortingly, and Briskow agreed. He assured her that all would be well.

All was not well, however. The next morning when Gus Briskow was about to leave the hotel as usual—Professor Delamater having departed hurriedly the evening before with fully four minutes of his twenty to spare—he was stopped by the manager, who requested him to give up his rooms. The Texan was bewildered; he could not understand the reason for such a request.

"'Ain't I paid my bills?" he queried.

The manager assured him that he had; he was profoundly regretful, as a matter of fact; but it so happened that the Briskow suite had been reserved early in the season, and the party who had made the reservation had just wired that he was arriving that day. He was a gentleman of importance—it was indeed unfortunate—the management appreciated Mr. Briskow's patronage—they hoped he and his family would return to the Notch sometime.

"Mebbe you got some other rooms that would do us," Gus ventured.

It was too bad, but the hotel was overcrowded. Later, perhaps —Now at that very moment the lobby was filled with tournament golfers who were leaving on the morning train, and Briskow knew it. He studied the speaker with an expression that caused the latter extreme discomfort; it was much the same expression he had worn the night before when he had served warning upon Delamater.

"Lemme get this right," he said. "You can talk straight to me. Bein' ignerunt, I 'ain't got the same feelin's as these other folks got. I got a shell like a land turtle."

"It is quite customary, I assure you. No offense, my dear sir."

"That's how I figgered! Just bouncin' a low-down var mint ain't offense enough to be throwed out about, when you pay your bills—"

"You quite misapprehend—"

"Fired, eh? It 'll go hard with Ma. She's gainin' here, and she likes it. That's why I never told her you was chargin' us about double what you charge these rich folks."

The manager stiffened. "I regret exceedingly, sir, that you take it this way. But there is nothing more to be said, is there?"

It was with a heavy heart and a heavy tread that Briskow returned to his room. Ma took the announcement like a death blow, for it meant the end of all her dreams, all her joyous games of "pretend." Her mountains—those clean, green, friendly mountains that she loved with a passion so intense that she fairly ached—those and her caves, her waterfalls, her gypsy band, were to be taken from her. She was to be banished, exiled.

She did not weep a great deal, but she seemed suddenly to grow older and more bent. Listlessly, laboriously she began to pack, and her husband noticed with a pang that her hands shook wretchedly.

As for Allie, she told herself that this was the end. She had tried to make something of herself and had failed. She had crucified herself; she had bled her body and scourged her soul only to gain ridicule and disgrace. There was no use of trying further; Gray had been mistaken in her, and her misery, her shame at the realization was intolerable. There was no facing him, after this.

Allie decided to do away with herself.

CHAPTER XV

Gus Briskow was waiting at the cashier's desk for his bill when the bustle of incoming guests told him that the morning train had arrived. Probably it had brought that "gentleman of importance" to whom the manager had referred. "To hell with people like that manager!" the Texan muttered. He would take his family back home and chance no more humiliations like this. And to think that he had allowed that dancing monkey to escape when he could have shot him as well as not!

Briskow's chain of thought was broken by a slap on the back that nearly drove him through the cashier's window; then by a loud, cheery greeting. The next moment he found himself actually embraced by—Gus could not believe his eyes—by Calvin Gray!

The latter's affectionate greeting, his frank delight at seeing the Texan, caused people in the lobby to center amused attention upon them, and induced those behind the desk to regard Briskow with new respect.

"Gus! You precious pirate! My, but I'm glad to see you! Ma and Allie are well, I know; they couldn't be otherwise here. Great place, isn't it? Nothing in this country or Europe that compares with it, and I've sent dozens of my friends here. I came north on business and couldn't bear to go back without seeing you. Come! Give me a welcome, for I've traveled across three states to get here."

The two stood hand in hand. Gray beamed approvingly. Gus, too, was smiling, but earnestly he said, "I'm right glad to see you, Mr. Gray, for we're in trouble."

"Trouble? What sort? Not illness?"

"No. We're leavin'—been throwed out."

The younger man's face sobered. "Don't joke!" he cried, sharply.

"I ain't joking. Feller insulted Allie and she throwed him out of a window—"

"Exactly! It's in the morning paper."

"They don't seem to think it was reefined, so they—throwed *us* out."

"Nonsense! Why, it is a corking story, and Allie was splendid —she gave the championship to Herring, who deserved it, thereby delighting every golfer on this side of the Atlantic. Jove! that girl is developing and I'm going to hug her—if there's no window handy! Throw you out? Why, there's some mistake, surely!"

Briskow shook his head; in greater detail he made known the facts. When he had finished his halting recital Calvin Gray's face was flushed with anger, there was a dark frown between his eyes.

"We'll see!" he muttered. "Wait here—or go back and tell Ma to commence unpacking." Then he was gone.

For perhaps ten minutes Gus waited nervously; he was amazed finally to see Gray approaching arm in arm with the manager; both were laughing, the hotel man's face was radiant with good humor. To the departing guest he said, genially:

"You are not going to leave us, after all, Mr. Briskow. On the contrary, we are going to keep you at the Notch as long as you'll stay. Stupid misunderstanding on my part, and I apologize. I'm going to ask you to move, but into a better suite —the very best one we have. And the rate will be the same. Come! What do you say?" When he was met by a stammered protest, he insisted forcefully: "I sha'n't take 'no' for an answer, my dear sir; we simply refuse to let you leave. The best we have is yours, and I guarantee that you will be made comfortable."

"He offered to extend you the courtesies of the house—make you guests of the hotel," Gray added, "but I knew you wouldn't accept."

"Dunno's I want to stay at all," Gus murmured, angrily. "We ain't no better'n we was a half hour ago."

"To be sure, but I've made you better known. You are too shy; you didn't afford my friend here the pleasure of making your acquaintance, and I had to tell him the sort of person you really are. Serves you right, Gus, for being so exclusive. Gad! I think I'll give you a few lessons in democracy. Now then, come along! I'm dying to see Ma."

As the father trotted down the hall beside his swiftly striding deliverer, he gasped, "How'd you do it?"

"Nothing simpler. I merely showed Mr. What's-his-name that he was making an ass of himself. I've spent a fortune here; know the owners, too. Nice chap, that manager, but he has no businessrunning a hotel, and I so informed him. He'll probably annoy you to death with his attentions. He'll let you play 'shinny' in the halls if you want to. Now—wait!" The speaker laid a finger upon his lips; his eyes were dancing. He knocked sharply at the Briskow door and cried, "Baggage ready, ma'am?"

There was a stir from within, the door was slowly opened by a bent, pathetic figure of grief.

"Ma!" Gray cried, and he held out his arms.

Perhaps it was his virile personality radiating confidence, security, or perhaps it was Gus Briskow's shining face that told the story; whatever the fact, Ma Briskow uttered a thin, broken wail, then walked into those open arms and laid her head upon Gray's breast. She clung to him eagerly and the tears she had been blinking so hard to restrain flowed silently.

"Oh-n-h! We ain't goin'away!" she said. "We ain't—goin' away!"

"Of course not. Gus misunderstood. The manager merely wanted you to move—into a larger, finer suite, and he is positively distressed at the thought of your leaving. The poor man is dashing about collecting an armful of roses for you and Allie. He wants to come in person and apologize."

There was another sound and Gray looked up to see Allie standing in the doorway to her bedroom; with one hand she clutched the jamb, the other was pressed to her bosom; she was staring at him as at an apparition. The girl was quite colorless, there was a look almost of fright in her eyes, and when he came toward her she swayed weakly. Her hands, when he took them, were icy; it shocked him to see how worn, how weary she had grown.

It was several hours later. In the parlor of the new suite, a spacious, sunny room, fragrant with flowers and cheerful with brilliant cretonnes, Gray and Briskow were talking. Allie and her mother could be seen in their bedrooms putting away the last of their belongings. Gray's eyes had been drawn, at frequent intervals, to the younger woman, for the change in her became the more amazing the more he observed her, and he was still striving to reconcile this creature to the picture he had held in his mind. In a few months Allie had become almost a stranger to him. It was a marked and yet a subtle change that had come over her; she was anything but a polished young woman, of course; nevertheless she had been modified, toned down, vastly improved, and not until her first queer emotion at seeing him had disappeared was the full extent of that improvement manifest to the newcomer. He wondered why she had acted so oddly at first; surely she did not fear him. No, Allie's face at this moment was alight with supreme joy and satisfaction; she appeared to be quite as happily at her ease as Ma, who was singing steadily in a thin, rusty voice.

Gray sent the father away on some pretext, finally; then he called to Allie: "Come in here and talk to me. I am a guest and I demand entertainment." He observed with silent approval her carriage as she entered the room and accepted the chair he offered her. Faint trace of the nester's daughter here. "I want a good chance to look at you."

Allie colored faintly. "I guess I'm not much to look at."

"Hm-m! You don't in the least resemble that girl I found hoeing in the garden. You are terribly thin."

"Spinach!" said Allie.

"Dieting, eh?"

"Yes. Spinach and water and a rubber suit. Sometimes I have a party and eat a whole soda cracker."

"It isn't too high a price to pay for beauty—beauty, 'the fading rainbow's pride.' We men should thank Heaven for women's courage in pursuing it. It is all that makes this world an attractive dwelling place for nice people."

"Sometimes I think it's kind of wicked to spend so much time and money that way, but—I guess it's all right. I want to look as good as other people."

"I'm in a mood for quotations. 'Is beauty vain because it will fade? Then are earth's green robe and heaven's light vain.'

Pride, even vanity, is less of a vice than slovenliness, my dear. Now then, do you like Mrs. Ring?"

Allie nodded. "I like her, but—I hate her. She makes me feel awful mad because she can't understand that I ain't—I am not mad at her, but at myself. I don't hardly know how to explain it. If I was her I'd hate me, like I do."

"Would you like to have her remain?"

"Oh, I would! She knows everything, and she makes me learn. But she won't stay. I just found out that she's been quitting every few weeks, and Pa's been raising her wages. No, the disgrace, and our being thrown out—"

"My dear girl, let me assure you, once for all, there is no suggestion of disgrace about this affair. You behaved with spirit, and those who have heard about it admire you. I have talked with a number of them, and I know. I had a talk with Mrs. Ring also, and she will remain if you wish her to do so."

"You're a—a good man, ain't—"

"Aren't!"

"—aren't you, Mr. Gray? You fix everything."

"Not a good, but a convenient man. My specialty is making things easier for my friends."

"Are these other folks, these rich ones around the hotel, like you?"

"Oh, much nicer than I!" Gray laughed. "You must meet some of them."

Allie's face whitened at this suggestion. "Please, sir—I'm scared!"

"Very well. As you wish. Tell me, what are you going to do with me this afternoon?"

"I dunno!" Allie looked blank. "I don't do anything but study. I s'pose I got to study."

"Nothing of the sort. You have circles under your eyes now from overwork, and this is your vacation. I am a visitor, a restless visitor; I abhor being asked to make myself at home, and I never do. I demand amusement. Do you know what I'd like to do best of all?" Allie did not know. "I'd like to sit here and smoke while you show me all your pretty dresses. Ah! Those dark eyes brighten. You're dying to show them to me, aren't you?"

"*Would* you? Honest?"

"Cross my heart. But remember, I have a color sense and I'm not easily pleased. I'll probably condemn some of them."

Allie breathed deeply. "Oh, Gee!" she said.

"Run along and try them on, then I'll borrow a pair of puttees and we'll go for a ride."

For the next two hours Allegheny Briskow was in heaven. Never had she dreamed of anything like this. To have Calvin Gray alone, all to herself—Ma, as usual, had disappeared—and to discuss with him exciting questions of dress and good taste that she could not discuss with her own people; to meet his occasional hearty approval—well, it was enough to make a girl drunk with happiness. Gowns that he liked became precious; she hated those that he condemned. Her fingers grew clumsy with haste, her cheeks burned. He said she wore her clothes well, that she carried herself well. He approved of her—liked her! God above! And to think that she had contemplated suicide! Of course she was pitifully ignorant as yet, and she had not even learned to talk as he talked, but there were books. She would study. Oh, the fury with which she would apply herself after this! She would beat the contents of those books into her head with her fists, if necessary; she would show him how fast she could learn; she would astonish him. Her heart sang at the thought that she was rich—richer than he. That would count, too, for men liked money.

"Where is Ma?" Gray inquired, when the last gown had been paraded and when Allie appeared in her riding suit.

"Out with the fairies, I suppose. She won't tell Pa or me where she goes or what she does—says it's all foolishness."

"Perhaps she will tell me, for I believe in fairies," Gray said, seriously.

Allie smiled at him. "I reckon she will. Folks tell you 'most anything you want them to, I reckon."

This was the busiest hour of the afternoon. Gray had purposely ordered the horses sent around at a time when he knew that the veranda, the walks, and the tennis courts would be filled, for ever since his interview with the hotel manager a plan had been shaping in his mind and already he had dropped a few words, a hint or two here and there, that were calculated to stimulate interest in Allie Briskow.

It gratified his craving for the theatric now to lead the girl out before so many curious eyes. For himself, he knew that he commanded attention, and as he noted the lines of this young Juno he could find nothing in her that needed betterment. Allie's suit was the latest, smartest thing in riding habits, and it set off her magnificent figure as nothing else could. Systematic exercise and hard work, like the final touch of a skilled sculptor, had given it beauty and refinement; harmony and proportion had destroyed the impression of unusual size. How deep was her bosom, how smooth and flowing were her curves, how superbly tall she was! As a thing of flesh and blood, she made these other women look like females of an insignificant race.

It thrilled him pleasantly to observe the confidence with which she swung herself into the saddle and the instant mastery she exercised over her restless mount. No timidity there, no need of assistance; no absurd, hampering skirts and artificial posture, either, but a seat astride as befits anyone who chooses to honor the king of four-footed creatures.

Under cover, Gray noted Allie's effect upon her attentive audience, and he smiled. If only he could spend a few days here he would make her a woman to be sought after by some of the best people. She refused to meet them, eh? Well, that would be as it was to be.

"We've been having supper in our rooms lately," she told him, when they returned at dark. "You're going to eat with us, ain—aren't you?"

"I am, to be sure. But not in your rooms," he declared.

"I'd rather—"

"You'd rather do exactly what would please me, now wouldn't you?"

"Yes, sir."

"Then run along and put on that dinner dress that I liked best. And tell Ma to look her prettiest, too. We'll not spoil this day."

It was seven-thirty when Gray, in evening clothes, appeared at the Briskow suite. Allie told herself there had never been a man so handsome, so distinguished, so Godlike as he. God, she now felt sure, must wear full dress.

Gus Briskow beamed as the visitor smiled approvingly at his daughter. "She is purty, ain't she? Don't look much like the girl I sent to Dallas for fixin's."

"Allie is more then pretty, she's regal. 'Such another peerless queen only could her mirror show.' But—her head is turned already, Gus. Don't spoil her." The speaker stood with arms folded and head lowered while he studied the girl impersonally. Allie wore an expensive black lace dress, sleeveless and sufficiently low of neck to display her charms. "Plain! A little too somber," Gray declared. "She can afford colors, ornaments. Jove! I'd like some time to see her in something Oriental, something barbaric. The next time I'm in New York I'll select a gown—"

Ma Briskow entered at the moment, greatly flustered and extremely self-conscious, and here, certainly, was no lack of ornamentation or of color. Ma wore all her jewelry, and her dress was an elaborate creation of brilliant jade green, from one shoulder of which depended a filmy streamer of green chiffon. In her desire to gild the lily she had knotted a Roman scarf about her waist—a scarf of many colors, of red, of yellow, of purple, of blue, of orange—a very spectrum of vivid stripes, and it utterly ruined her. It lent her an air of extreme superfluity; it was as if she had put on everything except the bedspread.

"You said to look my nicest," she bubbled, "so I done the best I could."

"You *are* lovely, both of you, but—this is my party, isn't it? I can do anything I please?" Gray looked from one to the other in eager inquiry. "Then let me fix you my way. Ma Briskow, your face is too sweet, too gentle, to be spoiled. Your charm is in your simplicity. Here, I have it!"

With swift impetuosity he untied the scarf and whipped it from Ma's waist. "Watch me now and you'll see I'm right." With his penknife he cut the threads that held the chiffon streamer in place and removed it. "*Voila*! Even so little, and we see an adorable motherly person, richly but unostenta-tiously gowned. Don't you agree with me?"

Without pausing for an answer, he wheeled upon the daughter and drew her into the range of a pier glass. "Now close your eyes and keep them closed." Around Allie's hips he flung the scarf, drew it snug and smooth, then knotted it. Next he snatched the length of chiffon and bound it about her head. His touch was deft and certain; a moment and it had been fashioned to suit him. Then he stood back and eyed the *tout ensemble*.

"Gorgeous!" he cried, genuinely enthusiastic. "That was the touch. I defy any costumer to better it. Open your eyes, oh, gypsy princess! And what do you see?"

"It—it sort of makes a difference, doesn't it?" Allie said. "A *difference*!" Gray flung aloft his hands in exaggerated despair. "Heaven help me! I am inspired; I have a flash of genius, a divine impulse, and with a magic pass I work a miracle. I transform you from something somber, dark, morose, into a creature of life, of passion, of allurement." He groaned. "And you stand there like a stalagmite. Why, girl, *look* at yourself!"

"Darned if she don't look like a pitcher I seen som'er's—on an almanac," Gus declared.

"Aha! A man with a soul! A human being who sees beauty where I see it. An artist with my fire!" Gray burst into infectious laughter, and the others joined him.

This proved to be an evening when people really did turn their heads as the Briskows were shown to their table, but for once Allie suffered no embarrassment, for she felt sure they were looking at Calvin Gray, and in the shining glory of his presence she knew that she and her parents were invisible.

It was the sort of situation in which Gray appeared to best advantage, so he talked incessantly during the meal, and in a key that kept his companions unconscious of their surroundings. On their way out they passed the entrance to the ballroom and paused to look in. The beat of the music swayed

Allie unconsciously; then, before she knew it, Gray's arm was around her waist and he was guiding her out upon the floor.

"Oh, n-no!" she gasped. She stumbled, but he drew her closer, saying:

"I'm proud of you, and I want you to show these people that you dance even better than you ride."

Allie rose to the challenge.

About midnight Calvin Gray strolled outdoors for a breath of fresh air before retiring. He glowed with the consciousness of a worthy deed well done. He had come to the Notch expecting to spend one night, but events of the last few hours had induced him to change his plans, and he now made up his mind to stay several days. He was burning to be back in the oil fields, to be sure; every hour away from them was an hour wasted, and although he told himself it was his feud that drew him, he knew better. As a matter of fact, when he thought of Texas it was of Wichita Falls, and when he visualized the latter place it was to picture a cottage with the paint off or a small office with the sign, "Tom and Bob Parker, Real Estate and Insurance."

He had been eagerly, selfishly, counting the hours until his return, but here, it seemed, was work to be done, a task that he alone could accomplish, and his decision to remain had been made final when Allie Briskow told him with tremulous earnestness that he had saved her life—when she confessed that she had intended to kill herself, and why.

Naturally Gray had put no faith in that wild declaration, nevertheless it was plain that the girl—that all three Briskows —needed a friend to guide them. He sighed with resignation, but reflected that, inasmuch as he had put his hand to the plow, he must turn the furrow. After all, he could well afford to spare a week to put that girl on the road to happiness.

CHAPTER XVI

From the day of their first meeting, Henry Nelson and Calvin Gray had clashed. No two people could be more different in disposition and temper, hence it was only natural that every characteristic, every action of the one should have aroused the other's antagonism. Nelson was a cool, selfish, calculating plodder with little imagination and less originality; he thought in grooves. His was a splendid type of mind for a banker. He had but one weak point—*viz.*, a villainous temper, a capacity for blind, vindictive rage—a weakness, truly, for a man who dealt in money—but a weakness that lent him a certain humanity and without which he would have been altogether too mechanical, too colorless, too efficient. Nature seldom errs by making supermen. A drab man, in many ways, Nelson was extraordinary mainly in this, that his mind followed straight, obvious channels, and that never, except under the urge of extreme passion, did he depart from the strictly logical line of action. In this, of course, he was superior to the average person, who too frequently undertakes the unusual. Calvin Gray's ebullience, his dash, his magnificence of demeanor, could be nothing less than an affront to such a man; Nelson could see in him only a pompous braggart, an empty, arrogant strutter.

Age and easy success had not improved the banker's apoplectic turn of mind, hence Gray's defiant declaration of war, his impudent assurance that the recent misfortunes to the house of Nelson were the direct results of his own deliberate efforts, had proven almost unendurable. In the first place, Nelson could not imagine a man making such a declaration; it was new to his entire experience and contrary to his code. It was unconservative, therefore it staggered him. It was, in fact, a phenomenon so unique as to leave him numb. He told himself that it must have been the act of a madman or a fool. Under no circumstances could he conceive of himself warning an enemy of his intentions; on the contrary, when he undertook to crush a rival he went about it slyly, secretly, in the only regular and proper way. As a matter of fact, it had come as a disagreeable surprise to learn that his former comrade at arms cherished any resentment whatever toward him, for he had thought his tracks were well covered.

What left the banker actually gasping, however, that which he came back to with unfailing astonishment, was Gray's effrontery in coming to Wichita Falls to boast of his accomplishments. That bespoke such contempt, such supreme self-confidence in his ability to wreak further damage, that Nelson wanted to shout aloud his rage and his defiance.

Following the departure of his two callers on that day of the meeting in the bank, Nelson closed his desk and went home. He could work no more. For several days thereafter he was an unpleasant person to do business with.

On mature consideration, what amazed him as much as anything else was the fact that Gray had made good in so short a time and in such a big way. Evidently, however, it was only another story of a lucky break and an overnight fortune—a common occurrence these days. But it was doubly unfortunate under the circumstances, for already Nelson was carrying a load equal to his strength, and he told himself that he could not afford to be distracted, even temporarily, by the irresponsible actions of a maniac. One never could tell what a madman would do. And Gray had confessed himself a madman—a fanatic of the most dangerous type. There was but one course of action open—viz., to eliminate him, destroy him without delay. That was no easy task, even in these lawless times, but the stakes were too high to permit of half measures.

There must be a way.

One would have to be careful, of course, not to put oneself too much in the power of unscrupulous people, and, alas! the world was full of unscrupulous people. It was a pity that people could be so unscrupulous as to take advantage of a bargain made in good faith. That was blackmail. However, the prestige of the Nelson name was great, the power of its money was potent, and Henry believed that he could protect himself from eventualities. After cautious deliberation he sent word to one of his men in the Ranger field that he wished to see him.

The man came promptly, and when he left Henry Nelson's house after a conference he carried with him a perfectly clear idea why he had been sent for. This despite the fact that he had not been told in so many words. He knew, for instance, that a certain Calvin Gray had become a menace to his employers, so dangerous that it was worth to them a substantial fortune to be rid of him, and that while Henry Nelson could under no circumstances countenance anything illegal, anything savoring of violence, nevertheless if some accident should befall Gray, if some act of God should put an end to him, there would be no disposition on Henry's part to question the divine origin of that calamity. Furthermore, the speaker had made it plain that if Providence did take a hand in some such mysterious manner, he would then be in a position amply to reward his employee for many acts of loyalty that had apparently passed unrecognized. For instance, profitable deals were forever coming up, new acreage was constantly being acquired, and it would be easy to carry a third party for an interest which was bound to make that third party rich.

All this was expressed with admirable vagueness, but the man understood.

So much accomplished, Nelson went to Dallas and there undertook to learn something about the size of Calvin Gray's profits, who was behind him and the extent of their backing, and what his prospects were. He followed every avenue of information; he even went so far as to hire an investigator and send him north to look up Gray's record and to follow his tracks as far back as possible. Nelson was reconnoitering behind the enemy's lines and testing the strength of his position.

When he returned home Gray was gone, whither he could not learn. As the days passed without further developments, Nelson began to believe that he had had a bad dream and that Gray had merely been talking to hear his own voice. He devoutly hoped that such would prove to be the case.

A time came, however, when his apprehensions were roused afresh, and it was Barbara Parker who rekindled them. She had come to the bank with an excellent proposition and was doing her best to sell it; in the course of her conversation she referred to Gray in a manner that gave Nelson cause for thought.

"I've looked this lease over," "Bob" was saying, "and I've seen the books. It has been producing a hundred and fifty barrels a day steadily. Production like that is cheap at a thousand dollars a barrel. It is worth a hundred and fifty thousand dollars, Henry."

"Why is it offered for seventy-five?"

"Bob" shrugged. "How did a 'boll weevil' like this Jackson ever make even a hundred-and-fifty-barrel well, in the first place? Where did he get the money to drill? He is sick of the game, I suppose, and would be satisfied to get his money back with a reasonable profit. It is a find, really."

"Looks so, for a fact. How did you get on to it, 'Bob'?"

"Purely by chance. Through a man named Mallow, a 'scientist' of some sort with a magic tester." The girl laughed.

"Don't know him."

"Mallow is as queer as the rest of his kind, and I put no faith in his story until I investigated. But the well is there and doing a hundred and fifty barrels as regular as clockwork."

"You'll have no trouble in selling it."

"Then you're not interested?"

"Interested? Yes, indeed." Nelson nodded. "I'm quite excited, as a matter of fact, but—I can't handle it at this particular time."

"Frankly, I'm glad you can't," Barbara told him, "for now I can sell it to Mr. Gray."

"Gray?" Henry looked up quickly. "If you wanted it for him, why did you bring it to me?"

"Because Mr. Mallow insisted. He felt sure you'd jump at it. Besides, Mr. Gray is away and prompt action is necessary. I'll wire him at once and ask him to accept my judgment."

"Will he do so?"

The girl colored faintly at the tone of this inquiry. "Perhaps. I think he believes in me, and—that's more than you do. It's mighty flattering to a girl to have a man like Mr. Gray believe in her. Why, I am practically his agent! He buys and sells through me whenever he can."

"He's buying and selling, is he? He said something about entering this field in a big way—"

"He's in." "Bob's" eyes were sparkling. "Oh, things are looking up for dad and me. Mr. Gray is a real miracle man, isn't he?" When this question evoked no response, the girl inquired, curiously, "Tell me, are you and he such good friends as he says you are?"

"Does he say we are good friends?"

"Um-m—well, he speaks admiringly of you, and if people admire me I *love* them. He thinks you are a remarkably capable person. 'A determined fighter,' I think he called you. That should be high praise, coming from a fellow officer. He probably outlined his plans to you."

"He did." Nelson spoke dryly.

"I assumed that he was relying on your judgment and taking your tips." "Why? How so?"

"Because he has bought so much land alongside of yours."

"Where?"

Barbara was surprised. "I—why, I supposed you knew!" After a moment of hesitation she said: "I think I'd better keep my mouth closed. Just the same, he couldn't have done better than to follow your lead. That is the first compliment I ever paid you, Henry."

"I've paid you enough. And I do believe in you, 'Bob,' but I'm not the flattering kind. He's a great ladies' man. I wonder if he is going to make me jealous."

"You? Jealous? Coming from Wichita's most emotionless banker, from the cold county Croesus, that speech is almost a—a declaration." Miss Parker laughed frankly. "Why, Henry! My haughty little nose is turning up—I can feel it. But, alas! it proves your insincerity. If you had faith in my judgment you'd pick up this snap."

With some hesitation the man said: "We're in deep, 'Bob.' Awfully deep! And things haven't gone as well as they should, lately. It's temporary, of course, but it would require an extraordinary effort at this time to take on anything new. That's the worst of this oil game, it takes so much money to protect your holdings. It doesn't pay to prospect land for the benefit of your neighbor; the risks are too great. Gray has been pretty attentive to you, hasn't he?"

"That's a part of the man; he is attentive to everybody. I have received more candy and flowers and delightful little surprises than in all my short, neglected life."

"I didn't know you liked candy."

"I don't. But I adore getting it. The thought counts. I don't care much for canaries, either—I have such bad luck with them—but he sent me the dearest thing from New York. A tiny mechanical bird with actual feathers. And it sings! It is a really, truly yellow canary in a beautiful gold cage, and when you press a spring it perks its head, opens its beak, flirts its tail, and utters the most angelic song. It must have cost a fortune. Couldn't you *love* a man who would think of a present like that?"

"Hm-m! Could *you*?"

"Oh, I'm joking, of course," "Bob" said, seriously. "We are merely business associates, Mr. Gray and I, but he has the faculty of taking his personality into his business, and that's why I know he is bound to make a great success."

"Some day," Nelson said, with an effort at lightness, "when we have finished with this infernal oil excitement and the fever has subsided, perhaps I'll have a chance to—well, to play ladies' man. It won't last long—"

"I'm sure it won't," laughed the girl. "You'd never make a go of it, Henry."

"I mean this boom won't last. These fools think it will, but it won't. While it does last, we busy men have no time for anything else, no chance to think of anything, no room in our minds—" The speaker stared gloomily into space. He shook his head. "When a fellow is worried about important matters, he neglects the little; things."

"To me that is the tragedy of this oil excitement. It devours everything fine in us. I wonder if the 'little things' of life aren't, after all, the most important. Mind you, I'm not hinting —I don't want your attentions—I wouldn't have time for them, anyhow, for I'm just as feverish as anybody else. But in the midst of all these new concerns, these sudden millions, this overnight success, our ambitious schemes, we are forgetting the things that really count. Gentleness, courtesy, love, home, children: they're pretty big, Henry. Candy and roses and yellow canaries, too. But"—the speaker rose, briskly—"I didn't come here to talk about them; I came here to sell you an oil well. Sorry you can't take it."

When she had gone Nelson sat in a frowning study for some time. So, it was not all a bad dream. What could be Gray's object in buying acreage adjoining his? Was it faith in his, Nelson's, judgment, a desire to ride to success on the tail of his enemy's kite, or did it mean a war of offsets, drilling operations the instant a well came in? More likely the latter, if the maniac really meant what he had said. That promised to be an expensive and a hazardous undertaking on Gray's part; that was playing the game on a scale too big for the fellow's limited resources, and yet—it might be well to study the maps. Yes, and it was like Gray's effrontery to pay deliberate court to "Bob" Parker, knowing his rival's feelings toward the girl. Another insult! The upstart certainly possessed an uncanny dexterity in pricking armor joints. But what if Gray were in earnest? "Bob" had become a wonderfully desirable creature, she was the most attractive girl in Wichita Falls—

It was a thought that had not previously presented itself to Henry Wilson, and it disturbed him now. He was glad, indeed, that he had sent to Ranger for that field man.

In and around the office of McWade & Stoner these were busy days, what with a couple of new wildcat promotions and a well going down on semiproven ground—that lease which cornered into the Nelson holdings, and to which Stoner had called attention. It had been easy to sell stock in the latter enterprise, and now the deeper went the hole, the higher rose the hopes of the promoters. Stoner himself was directing operations, and he had named the well "Avenger Number One."

To-day he and his partner had been listening to Mallow, who concluded an earnest discourse with these words:

"Nelson and her are pardners in one deal and he's stuck on her. If anybody can put it over, she's the one."

"If he buys that well it'll be the biggest laugh this town ever had," McWade declared.

"Buy it? A hundred and fifty barrels in the heart of settled production for seventy-five thousand? I bet he'll buy it."

"Think the boss will stand for that kind of a deal?"

"Why not? They can't hang it on him, and Heaven knows I'm honest."

"He said 'nothing crooked'—"

Mallow snorted. "Say, I bet you believe in Santa Claus! Gray's a great man, and what makes him great is that he does his own crooked work."

Stoner was inclined to agree with Mallow's measure of their associate. "That's how I got him figgered. His honesty talk didn't go far with me, and I don't believe he'll kick at anything. He's willing to pay any price to break this banker, but you can't bankrupt a feller unless you rip his coin loose; you can't *ask* him to please loosen. If we make a well of the Avenger we'll force him to shoot maybe a hundred thousand right away, and that may cramp him for a while; but suppose he makes the turn and hits it like we do? We've made him that much stronger, haven't we? Gray plans to keep him spending faster than he can get it in, and that's all right—if it works, but if Mallow can bilk him for seventy-five thousand at one fell swipe—Well, I'll bet my best gold tooth that the boss will stand the shock like a man."

"I think you've both got Gray all wrong," said McWade. "He's too smart to be crooked."

This was a statement so absurd that Mallow proceeded to riddle it. It was, upon its face, a contradiction, for none but smart men could be crooked, and the laws of logic proved the converse to be equally true.

Stoner sat in frowning silence while the argument raged, but he broke in finally: "I've always wanted to pull a real salting job, just to show how easy it is to gyp the cagy ones—not an oil-can job like this, but something big. This looks like the piscological moment."

"Lay off, I tell you!" McWade cried. "We're a legitimate firm,' solid as Gibraltar and safe as a church.' That's our motto, and we've got to live up to it. I came into Wichita on the roof of a Pullman; I'm going out in a drawing-room. Me and sin are strangers." "Nothing sinful about my idea, Mac. One fall or two won't break Nelson; we've got to spill him hard. If we can pick up a few pennies ourselves in the process, why, that's legitimate. The dealer is entitled to his percentage, ain't he? Now listen. Everybody's getting set for a big play over in Arkansas, as you know—salting away cheap acreage and waiting for some of the wildcats to come in. Well, last year I had a tool dresser from up there; nice boy, but he got pneumonia and it turned into the 'con,' so I took him home. He's back on his farm now, coughing his life away and doing a little bootleggin' to keep body and cough together. He's got a big place, but it's all run down and so poor you couldn't raise a dust on it with a bellows. It would be a Christian act to help him sell that goat pasture for enough to go to some nice warm country where he'd get well and they couldn't extradite him."

"Of course, if you've got a scheme that is perfectly safe," McWade ventured, charitably, "and our bit was worth it—"

"I been thinking we might help the boy sell that farm to Nelson."

"How?"

Mallow, too, was curious. "Nelson's lungs are healthy; he wouldn't cough a nickel unless the place had oil on it."

"I meant to tell you it's got oil on it. Best indications I ever saw. There's a drinking well, only the water ain't fit to drink till you skim off the 'rainbow.' Then there's a wonderful seepage into the creek. You can see the oil oozing out from under the bank, in one place. Certainly is pretty."

Stoner's hearers were intent; they exchanged puzzled glances.

Mallow was the first to speak. "Come on. What's the joker? I ain't saying you'd murder the guy for that farm, but if it's as good as that he'd of died of the plague or something, and left it to you long before this."

"In a way, I'm getting ahead of my story," Stoner continued, imperturbably. "The oil ain't actually visible, but it will be if, when, and as, Henry Nelson gets ready to buy it."

"Easy enough to pour oil into a water well, I suppose, but that wouldn't fool a child. As for salting *running* water, a creek— show me."

"There's a lot for you to learn in this business, Mallow. The point is, can we lay Nelson against a bunch of acreage like that?"

"You could lay *me* against it if it looks like you say it does," McWade declared.

"This bootlegger, being half dead and non compost mentis, would help put it over with a man like Nelson; he'd set him in a draught while he was signing the option. I'll guarantee the seepage to last for a month, even if he has the well bailed out every day, and the creek will carry oil for half a mile."

"Would your one-lunged friend know how to play in?"

"*Would* he? It was his idea, and all that kept us off of it last year was the fact that the oil would have to be hauled about thirty miles, and we didn't have the price between us to hire a truck."

For some time the trio discussed the various angles of Stoner's proposition, endeavoring if possible to devise some natural way of intriguing the interest of Henry Nelson. On this score McWade had fewer apprehensions than did his companions, his contention being that it mattered not how the matter was brought to the banker's attention so long as the property would stand investigation. Nelson was bound to be suspicious, anyhow, and a sale depended entirely upon the character of the oil showing. McWade's coolness toward the enterprise, it transpired, was occasioned not by a loftier sense of rectitude than his associates displayed, but by lingering doubts as to the profits involved.

Not until Brick declared that his tubercular friend would accede to any arrangement he saw fit to make did the junior partner fall in with the proposal. "If it's a fair, square deal all around, I'm for it," the latter finally agreed. "But we can't afford to have any guy squawking that we did him up—especially if he's only got one lung to holler with. We're a legitimate firm, and we've got to treat our clients right. I think a fifty-fifty split would be reasonable."

Stoner, too, thought that would be about right, and so it was left.

Mallow was highly enthusiastic. "This will be a great surprise to Gray," he said, with animation. "It's mighty lucky he's got a gang like us to help him."

CHAPTER XVII

To learn that her mountain retreat had been invaded and that she had been spied upon filled Ma Briskow with dismay, but when Allie found fault with her behavior the elder woman burned with resentment.

"We're queer enough," the girl said, "without you cutting up crazy and making folks talk. If you want to dance, for goodness' sake hire somebody to lear—to teach you, same as I did."

Mrs. Briskow had silently endured her daughter's criticism up to this point, but now her lips tightened and there was a defiant tilt to her head.

"Who says I want to dance?" she demanded. "I can dance good enough."

"What was you up to the other day? That Delamater man said you was acting plumb nutty."

"I wasn't doin' anything."

"Where do you go every day, Ma? You stay around nice and quiet till Miz' Ring or I look the other way, then—you're gone."

"I kinda—visit around."

"Who d'you visit with? You don't know anybody. Nobody ever speaks to us. You ain't in earnest about those fairies and things, are you?"

"It ain't anybody's business where I go or what I do," Ma declared, in sullen exasperation. "I ain't bothering anybody, am I?"

"Don't say 'ain't,' say 'isn't.'"

For once in her patient life the mother flamed into open rebellion. "Don't 'don't' me!" she cried. "You're gettin' the 'don't' habit off Miz' Ring an' nothin' I say or do is right any more. You mind your own 'isn'ts' an' I'll handle my 'ain'ts.' I got places where I go an' things I do an' I don't bother nobody. I guess we got enough money so I can do things I want to, as long as I don't bother nobody."

"Why don't you take Pa along? He'd go, then people—"

"Mind your own business!" the old woman snapped. She flounced out of the room, leaving Allie amazed and indignant at this burst of temper.

That day Ma Briskow abandoned her mountain fastness. She took her faithful retainers with her and led them farther up the ravine to a retreat that was truly inaccessible. She moved them, bag and baggage. Of course, there was a scene; the children cried, the women wailed, the men wept. But she told them that traitors had betrayed their hiding place to the dastardly Duke of Dallas, and any moment might bring his cutthroat crew upon them. Some of the younger bloods were for remaining and selling their lives dearly, but Ma would not hear to it.

It was quite an undertaking to move a whole nomad tribe, for there were all the household belongings, the rattle, the sheep, the goats, the milk-white Arabian steeds, the butter and eggs and homemade preserves, and all the paraphernalia of a warlike people. It is surprising how stuff accumulates in a mountain fastness. But she managed the retreat with conspicuous ability. Ma led the long caravan into the bed of a running stream, so that there would remain not a single footprint to guide pursuers, then she sat in her saddle and gazed back at the silent camping place.

Trap her, eh? Come upon her unprepared, would they? Ha! ha! She laughed scornfully and tossed her head of midnight hair as she pictured the duke's rage at finding he had been foiled again, and by a mere slip of a girl!

This was a good game and exciting, too. Fetch Pa Briskow along, indeed! Why, these wild mountain folk would kill him; in their present mood they would rend a stranger hip from thigh. If they dreamed, for instance, that she, their queen, was married—

Here was a new thought, and Ma's imagination leaped at it. If these passionate people suspected that she had contracted a secret marriage with the—the Earl of Briskow, their jealousy would know no bounds. They would probably slay Pa. Ma shuddered at the horrid vision of what would happen to Pa. This was truly thrilling.

Later on in the morning Mrs. Briskow discovered that she possessed another amazing accomplishment—*viz.*, the ability to walk on a ceiling, upside down, like a fly. It was extremely amusing, for it enabled a person to see right into everything. Pa and Allie looked very funny from above.

The next day, when she stealthily slipped out of her French window, she found Calvin Gray idly rocking on the veranda. He welcomed her appearance and pretended not to see her embarrassment at the meeting; he was glad of this chance for a visit with her alone. Perhaps she was going for a walk and would take him along?

Ma was annoyed and suspicious. She liked Gray, but—she was

as wary as a trout and she refused to be baited. She would allow him to walk with her—but lead him to the retreat? Well, hardly.

The man was piqued, for suspicion irked him. It was a tribute to his patience and to his knack of inspiring confidence that Ma finally told him about Allie's criticism and her resentment thereat.

"I got my own way of enjoyin' myself, an' I don't care what people think," she declared, with some heat.

"Quite right. It's none of their darned business, Ma."

"She thinks I'm kind of crazy an'—I guess I am. But it comes from livin' so long in the heat an' the drought an' allus wantin' things I couldn't have—allus bein' sort of thirsty in the head. When you want things all your life an' never have 'em, you get so you *play* you've got 'em."

The man nodded. "You had a hard time. Your life was starved. I'm so glad the money came in time." "You see, I never had time to play, or a good place to play in, even when I was a little girl. But this is like—like books I've read."

"Are these mountains what you thought they would be?"

"Oh, they're better!" Ma breathed. "It's too bad Allie's got to spoil ever'thing."

"I shall speak to her. We won't let her spoil anything. Now tell me how you play."

But Ma flushed faintly, and for some time longer she refused her confidence. It didn't matter; it was all an old woman's foolishness; nobody would understand. Gray was not insistent; nevertheless, before long they were on their way toward the glen.

It was a glorious morning, the forest was beautiful, and as the two strolled through it Ma's companion told her many things about trees and flowers and birds and bees that she had never dreamed of. Now Gray's natural history was shockingly inaccurate, nevertheless it was interesting, and it was told in a manner both whimsical and sprightly. He made up outrageous stories, and he took no shame in seriously recounting experiences of his own that Ma knew were wholly imaginary. She told him, finally:

"Sakes alive! You're as crazy as I am."

This he denied with spirit. Forests were enchanted places, and trolls dwelt in the mountains. There was no question about that; most people never took time to see them, that was all. Now as for him, he had actually beheld naiads and dryads, nixies and pixies, at play—at least he had practically been upon the point of seeing them. Ma, herself, must have come across places they had just left, but probably she had lacked the patience to await their return or the faith to woo them into being. There were little woods people, too, no bigger than your thumb, whose drinking goblets were acorn cups, and whose plates were shiny leaves. He showed her how to set a fairy tablecloth with her handkerchief and with toadstools for seats.

In a reckless burst of confidence Ma told him how it felt to walk upside down, like a fly, and to go bounding through the woods like a thistledown. Gray had never tried it, but he was interested.

Then, finally, alas! the inconsistency of woman! she told him allabout her hidden band of mountaineers.

Now this was something he *could* understand. This was more his speed. He insisted upon making the personal acquaintance of those bold followers of hers and upon hearing the whole sad story of the Princess Pensacola. The history of her struggle against the wicked Duke of Dallas moved him; he wove new details of his own into it, and before Ma knew it he was actually playing the part of the duke.

The duke, it appeared, was a hard and haughty man, but at heart he was not all bad; when he had listened to the story of his victim's wrongs and more fully appreciated the courage, the devotion of her doughty followers, he was touched. For her sake, and theirs, he proposed a truce to this ruinous struggle. What kind of a truce? Well, he refused entirely to renounce his claim to the throne, but—they might share it. He was a handsome man and no wickeder than the general run of dukes; he would make a becoming husband to the beauteous princess, and if she set her mind to it she could probably make a better person of him. Thus would the warring factions be united, thus would the blessings of peace descend—

But the princess raised her slim, jeweled hand, and spoke thus: "Too late, Your Honor! I been married to His Royal Highness the Earl of Briskow, and it serves you right the way you done both of us."

The duke fell into a great rage at this. He refused to believe it, and threatened to annul the marriage.

"Oh, you can't do that," tittered the princess. "We was married by the Royal Justice of the Peace and—we got two children."

Here *was* a blow! The duke was crushed, until a happy thought came to him. If cruel fate prevented him from claiming the Princess Pensacola for a bride he would take her for a mother. He had always wanted a mother, anyhow; lack of maternal care it was that accounted for his wildness—it was enough to ruin any duke—and mothers were much nicer than wives. They were much harder to get, also.

"Lord! I wish you meant it!" Ma exclaimed, in a matter-of-fact tone. "I wish Allie was a real princess. Mebbe—"

Gray broke in with a laugh. "There! You've spoiled the play.

The duke has fled."

Mrs. Briskow's wrinkled face beamed. "Think of a gre't big man like you playin' 'pretend' with a foolish old woman like me! I thought you had more sense."

"I live in my own land of 'pretend,' just as you do. Why, I have a real princess of my own."

"Honest?"

Gray nodded. "The Princess of Wichita Falls. Would you like to hear about her? Well, she's small and dainty, as princesses should be, and her eyes are like bluebells, Ma. They are brave, honest eyes that can laugh or cry—the sort of eyes that make a man's head swim when he looks into them too long. She carries herself like a great lady, and she's very cool and business—I mean princess-like, to men. But in reality she's just an adorable feminine creature who wants to be loved. When she laughs two deep dimples come into her cheeks—marks of royal favor. Some people may consider her too stern, too matter-of-fact, but she isn't; in her boudoir there is scent and sachet and frilly, ribbony things that nobody ever sees. And flowers from me. She loves roses best of all and she says she buries her face in them. I send her roses, mostly, so they can kiss her cheeks for me. A tiny yellow love bird in a tiny yellow cage sings her awake every morning. I taught it the song it warbles, but—she'll never understand what the little bird is trying to say."

Ma Briskow had listened with rapt attention. Now, she inquired, "Does she love you?"

"Didn't I tell you this was my game of pretense?" Gray said, gayly. "Do you really think that an adorable creature whose head is full of girlish notions and youthful ideals could care for the worldly, wicked old Duke of Dallas? I am old, Ma, and I've gone the gait."

"Pshaw! You ain't any such thing."

"Well, perhaps I'm a better lover than I believe. Who knows? Fortunately, however, it is all just an amusing game." The speaker rose and looked at his watch. "It is lunch time, Mother Briskow, and I'm famished."

As the two entered the hotel grounds, Gus and Allie hurried to meet them, and the latter exclaimed, irritably: "It's about time you showed up. We've been looking everywhere for you."

At sight of her husband's face Ma inquired, in sudden anxiety, "What's wrong, Gus?"

"It's Buddy," Allie declared.

"'Tain't serious," Briskow said. "And it is, too. He's left school —run away! Here, Mr. Gray, see what you make out of it."

Gray read aloud the letter that was handed to him, a letter from the principal of the institution that he himself had recommended, stating that Ozark had disappeared without doing the college authorities the courtesy of leaving an address. Inasmuch as he had never expressed the slightest dissatisfaction with his surroundings, the writer was at a loss to explain the reason for this disappearance. As to Ozark's safety, there was no immediate cause for apprehension, for he had taken with him three trunks of clothing, a high-powered touring car, and a Belgian police dog; but certain of the young man's exploits that had come to light since his departure aroused grave doubts in the principal's mind of his moral well-being.

"What's it mean?" the mother inquired.

"It means that Buddy has taken a vacation. How much money has he?"

"He's got plenty," Gus declared. "More 'n is good for him if—"

"If what?" Ma queried.

Gus halted; it was Allie who answered: "If he's done what we think he's done—gone away after some woman."

"Some *woman?*" Ma stared blankly from one face to another. "Buddy in love? Why, he never wrote me nothing about bein' in love." Reading a further message in her husband's expression, she cried, fiercely: "He's a good boy. He wouldn't take up with—with nobody that wasn't nice. What makes you think it's a girl?"

"I didn't say 'girl,' Ma, I said '*woman.*' Buddy's been writin' to me and—"

"What's the difference? Mebbe he's in love with some nice young woman an' they've run away to git married. Buddy's han'some, and they got nice women everywhere—"

"*Love?* With all his money? And him only up to fractions?" Allegheny laughed scornfully.

Gus Briskow wiped his face with a nervous hand. "I'm 'most sick over it," he confessed. "The perfessor has written me a coupla times about him. Buddy's gone kinda wild, I guess, drinkin' an'—"

"Drinking?" Gray interrupted, sharply. "Why didn't you tell me? So, you gave him unlimited money, in spite of my warning?"

"He wanted his own bank account; his share of the royalties. Made him feel more like a man, he said. I—I never learned how to say 'no' to him or Allie. Ma an' I allus said 'no' to each other, but it was allus 'yes' to them. We never had much to give 'em, noway."

"Drinking, eh?" Gray was frowning. "The woman part I don't care so much about—he'll probably get over that if it isn't too serious. But whisky! That's different. I'm responsible for that boy; in a manner of speaking, I adopted him because—well, because he flattered me by pretending to admire me. It was a unique experience. I took Buddy for my own. Will you let me handle this matter?" The speaker looked from one parent to the other, and they saw that his face was grimly set. "Give me my way and I'll bring that young rascal to time or—" He shrugged, he smiled faintly. "Give me permission to treat him as if he really were my own, will you?"

"You got my leave," said the father; but Ma Briskow bristled.

"Don't you dast to hurt him," she cried.

Again Gray shrugged, this time with resignation. "As you will. I was wild, myself; I think I know what he needs."

"You can't beat anything into Buddy's head." It was Allie speaking. "After all, he's grown up, and what right has anybody got to interfere with him? S'pose it *is* a woman? S'pose she *is* after his money? It's his. Men can get what they want by payin' for it. An hour, a day, a week of happiness! Ain't that worth all Buddy 'll have to pay? I'd pay. I'd go through torture the rest of my life—"

"*Allegheny Briskow!*" the mother exclaimed.

"Well, I would." The girl's voice broke, a sudden agitation seized her; in passionate defiance she went on: "What's the use of wanting something all your life and never getting it? What's money for if you can't buy the one thing you want worst of all? That's where men have got the best of it; they can buy love. I wish I was a man; I wish I was Buddy! I'd have my day, my week—and as much more as I could pay for. I'd have happiness that long if it broke my heart. But I'm a *girl!*"

It was with a sudden interest that Gray studied the speaker. Here was a side to the Briskow character that he had not suspected, and it gave him a new light upon Buddy, for brother and sister were much alike; it showed him more clearly the size of the task he had volunteered to undertake. He heard the father speaking, and reluctantly withdrew his eyes from Allie's flaming face.

"He likes you, Mr. Gray, an' mebbe you could keep him from spoilin' his hull life. That's what he's liable to do an'—I'm skeered. He wouldn't listen to me. Boys don't listen to their fathers."

"I'll find him, Gus, and I'll make him listen to me. If it is drink, I'll break him of it. If it is a woman—I'll break him of that, too, for it can't be more than a passing fancy." Noting the tragic concern that wrinkled Ma Briskow's. face, he put an arm about her, saying more gently: "Now, now! I won't deny you the luxury of worrying, Ma dear. That is a mother's divine prerogative, but rest assured Buddy sha'n't do himself any great harm. Now then, let's get to a long-distance phone."

It was perhaps two hours before Gray reported to Gus Briskow: "They don't know much more at the school than was written in that letter. He has been going a rather lively pace lately, it seems."

"Did you find out anything about the—the woman?"

"Nothing definite. I have put detectives on the case, and they will report to me at Wichita Falls. As soon as they uncover his trail, I'll go to Buddy at once."

"You goin' to leave us?"

"I must. I've just received a telegram from my—my agent. About the purchase of a well. It is a matter that can't wait."

"I can't thank you for all you done for us. We was in bad shape till you come. Now—"

"Now everything is straight again. That's my job, Gus—to do little odd favors for those I love. You must stay here, for Ma is happy, and this place is making a girl of her. Allie is doing wonders with herself, too. By the way, she needn't be lonely any more; I've talked to some of the guests, and they want to make friends with her. She'll find them nice people, and you must make her meet them halfway. Perhaps she'll become interested in some decent young fellow. I'd like that, wouldn't you?"

"Would ye?"

The tone of this inquiry caused Gray to glance more keenly at the speaker, but Briskow's bright eyes told him nothing.

"Why, naturally. Allie is becoming more attractive every day, and she is going to make something of herself. She is going to 'do us all proud.'"

As soon as he was alone Gray eagerly reread his telegram from Wichita Falls. It was from Barbara Parker—the first, by the way, that he had ever received—and he smiled at the girl's effort to be thoroughly businesslike, and at the same time to convey the full urgency of her message. Why had she economized on words when every one was precious to him? Buy that well? Of course he would, if she so earnestly desired it. But what was better by far than the prospect of a profitable purchase was the fact of her personal interest in him. When it came to the last line of her message, "Bob" had plunged into a ten-word riot of extravagance.

"The bird is darling. I have named him after you."

Gray wondered if these words really meant what they seemed to imply, or if it was merely her bubbling, enthusiasm that spoke. Well, he would soon find out. Already he had wasted too much time on the Briskows—a man's duty ever lies in the way of his desire—but once he had rounded up Buddy perhaps the family would be able to take care of itself. He hoped so, for it was assuming the character of a liability.

It was late that night. The southbound flyer had gone through. The Briskows were sitting in the pleasant parlor of their handsome suite, but they were like three mourners. Ma and Pa were soberly discussing the news about Buddy, Allegheny was staring in somber meditation at nothing. The girl was bitter, rebellious, for never had she felt so utterly alone as at this moment. To that question which monotonously repeated itself, she could form no answer. Did he care, or was it all pity—just his way?

She heard his name and her own mentioned, and she became attentive. "What's that? He wants me to meet these people halfway?" she inquired. "What for? I don't like 'em."

"He says you'll git to like 'em, an' they'll git to like you. He says you're goin' ahead tremendous, and we'll all be proud of you. Mebbe you'll meet some nice young feller—"

"He said that, did he?" Allie's voice was sharp.

"N-not exactly, but—"

"He asked 'em to be nice to me—he fixed it all up. Is that it? I got lots of money; some man 'll make love to me and I'll—I'll fall in love with him. Is that what he said?"

"He didn't put it that way. What he said was more—"

Allegheny rose with an exclamation of anger. "Well, I won't meet 'em. He'd better mind his own business."

"Why, *Allie!*" the mother exclaimed, in mild reproach.

"I won't! I hate 'em. I hate everybody. Him, with his high an' fancy ways—" the girl choked. "He looks down on us the same as other folks does, an' I don't blame him. He acts like we was cattle, an' we are." Her own scorn appeared to whip the speaker into a higher frenzy. "Now he's gone off to spoil Buddy's doin's. Buttin' in, that's what it is. If I knew where Buddy is, I'd warn him. I'd tell him to look out. I'd tell him to grab his chance when it comes along, if it takes all the Briskow money, all the Briskow wells. He's lucky, Buddy is. It don't make any difference *who* he took up with, if he loves her."

Never but once before had the Briskows seen their daughter in a mood like this, and that was on the occasion of their first visit to Dallas. Now they sat numb and speechless as she raved on:

"Playin' with us to amuse himself! It's a game with him. He 'ain't got anything better to do. Why, he even shows us how to dress! 'With a touch,' he says, 'I work miracles. I transfer—transform you from something dark an'—an' common into a thing of passion.' *Passion!* What the hell does he know about passion? He's a doctor, he is, cuttin' up a live dog to see what ails it. A live dog that's tied down! Cuttin' it up—Oh, my God, I wish I was Buddy!" It was several moments after the door of Allie's room had slammed behind her before Gus Briskow spoke, and then it was with a deep sigh.

"I been afraid of something like this, Ma. I reckon we're goin' to pay dear for our money before we get through."

"An' him with a princess in Wichita Falls!" the mother quavered.

CHAPTER XVIII

There are many arguments against industry; much is to be said against its wholesale practice. For one thing, habitual diligence, of whatever sort, begets other habits hard to break, habits that persist in plaguing a man during his periods of indolence and perhaps during his whole life. Early rising is one of the most annoying of these habits. While it cannot be said that Tom Parker had ever labored arduously at anything, nevertheless he had followed his calling faithfully, and the peculiar exigencies of that calling had made of him a light and fitful sleeper. He had so often used the earth as a mattress and his saddle as a pillow, that sunup invariably roused him, and as a consequence he liked to tell people that he could do with less sleep than any man in Texas. That was, in fact, one of his pet complaints.

It was true that Old Tom never slept long, but it was also true that he slept oftener than any man in Texas. He was up and dressed by daylight, and until breakfast time he engaged himself in purposeless and noisy pursuits. This futile energy, however, diminished steadily until about nine-thirty, after which his day was punctuated by a series of cat naps, as a broken sentence is punctuated by dots and dashes.

That small room at the rear of his office Barbara had cleared of its dusty accumulations—of its saddles and saddle-bags, its rusty Winchesters, its old newspapers and disorderly files—and had transformed into a retreat for him. She had overcome his inherent prejudice against innovations of any sort by arguing gravely that the head of every firm should, nay must, have a private sanctum.

Tom approved of the change after he became accustomed to it, for he was subjected to fewer irritating distractions there than elsewhere. Before long, in fact, he acquired the ability to doze placidly through almost any sort of business conference in the outer office. It was his practice to sleep from nine-thirty until eleven, when "Bob" fetched him a glass of orange juice with a "spike" in it. This refreshing beverage filled him with new energy to tackle the issues of the day, and thereupon began a routine as fixed as some religious ritual. First, he smacked his lips, then he cleared his throat loudly several times, after which his chair creaked as he massaged his rheumatic leg. Promptly upon the count of twenty he emerged from the inner office, slamming the door energetically behind him.

Whether "Bob" was alone or engaged with clients, Old Tom's air was always the same; it was that of a busy man weighted with grave responsibilities. He frowned; he muttered, hurriedly:

"Got to see a man; back in an hour. Anybody calls, tell 'em to wait."

This took him to the front door, which he also slammed behind him—there being a certain force and determination to the sound of a slamming door. Then he limped down the street to Judge Halloran's office. The judge usually had the checkerboard out and set when Tom arrived.

Afternoons passed in much the same manner, and night found Tom, if not actually exhausted from the unceasing grind, at least pleasurably fatigued thereby and ready for an after-dinner doze. He considered himself seriously overworked.

This morning "Bob" was alone at her desk when he came out, and something about her appearance caused the old warrior to look twice. He was exactly on time, but the judge could wait. He was a cranky old scoundrel anyhow, was Judge Halloran, and it would do him good to cool his heels for a few minutes. Tom paused with his hand upon the door knob.

"My goodness! son, you're all dressed up!" he said, as he noted "Bob's" crisp white dress, the rose upon her bosom, the floppy hat that framed her face. "Church sociable som'er's?"

"No, dad."

"What's going on?"

"Nothing in particular."

"You certainly are sweet." Tom's bleak, gray face softened, then some vague regret peered forth from his eyes. "Certainly are sweet, but—"

"But what?" The girl smiled up at him.

"Oh, I don't know—seems like you ain't quite the same boy you was. You're changing lately, somehow. Getting more like your mother every week. I like that, of course," he said, quickly, "but—I'd like awful well to see you in your ranch clothes again. I bet you've clean forgot how to ride and rope and—"

"You know very well I haven't. I'm a little bit rusty, perhaps, but remember I'm a pretty busy girl these days."

"I know." Tom sighed. "I'm wore out, too. What d'you say we close up the ol' factory and take a rest? Let's get us a couple of broncs and go up to the Territory for a spell. Used to be a lot of wild turkeys in a place I know. It'd do us a lot of good."

"Why, dad, we can't do that! And, besides, those turkeys were killed out years ago."

"Um-m! I s'pose so. Ain't much left to shoot at but tin cans, come to think of it." There was a pause. "I don't reckon you could han'le a six gun like you used to, 'Bob.'"

"You think not? Try me sometime and see," said the girl. Apparently Tom believed there was no time like the present, for he slid his right hand under the left lapel of his coat, and when he brought it away there was a large single-action Colt's revolver in it—a massive weapon upon the mother-of-pearl handle plates of which were carved two steers' heads. Those steers' heads Tom had removed from a gun belonging to a famous bad man, suddenly deceased, and there was a story that went with them.

"Now see here," "Bob" protested, "one of these new policemen will pick you up some day."

"Pshaw! Nobody wouldn't pick me up, just for totin' a gun," the old man declared. With practiced fingers he extracted the shells, one by one. "I feel right naked without a six-shooter. I feel like I'd cast a shoe, or something."

"I wish you'd give up carrying it."

"Lessee you do a few tricks,'Bob'. Do the roll. Remember she don't stand cocked."

Miss Parker rose to her feet and took the weapon. She balanced it in her hand, then she spun it, rolled it, fanned it, went through a routine of lightninglike sleight-of-hand that Tom had taught her long before.

"Lessee you do a few shots," her father urged, when she handed it back to him.

"In *here?*"

"Sure! It's our shanty. Drive a few nails or—I'll tell you; kill that bear and save that tenderfoot's life." Tom pointed to a Winchester calendar on the rear wall, which bore the lithographic likeness of an enraged grizzly upon the point of helping himself to a hunter.

"Why, we'd have the whole town running in."

"Go on, son. Make it speak. Bears is easy killed."

"Nonsense."

Reluctantly Tom reloaded his weapon and thrust it back into its shoulder holster; regretfully he murmured: "Doggone! We never have any more fun." He turned toward the door.

"Where are you going, dad?"

"I got to see a man; back in an hour. Anybody calls—"

"You know you won't be back in an hour. Where are you going?"

"I got to see—What is it?"

"Bob" hesitated. "I wish you'd stay here. I think Mr. Gray arrived this morning, and I expect him in."

Tom decided that he had made Judge Halloran wait long enough. He should have been in the old rascal's king row by this time. So he said, briskly, "Wish I could, son, but I got to see a man."

"Mr. Gray was here several times before he went away, but you were always out." When her father showed no inclination to tarry, Barbara spoke with more impatience than she had ever used toward him. "I want him to meet you, dad, for he has come back on purpose to take up that Jackson well. If I devote all my time to business, it seems to me you could afford to sacrifice an hour to it, just this once. That checker game can wait."

Tom Parker stiffened. Sacrifice an hour to business, just once!

That *was* a blow. As if his nose was not at the grindstone day in and day out! As if he were not practically chained to this office! As if unremitting application to business had not wrecked him—worn him to the bone—made an insomniac of him! That was the worst about children, boys especially; they twitted their elders; they thought they were the whole works; they assumed undue importance. Tom was offended, and, being a stubborn man, he bowed his back.

"Tell him to wait," he said, curtly. "I'll get around to it soon as I can."

"Why, *dad*! He isn't a man who can wait. This deal won't wait, either."

"I been talking over that Jackson well with—with a man, and I got him—"

"I asked you not to mention it—not to a soul. It is a very important matter and—"

Now Tom had not discussed the Jackson well, except casually with Judge Halloran, but every word that "Bob" spoke rankled, so he interrupted with a resentful query:

"Ain't I equal to han'le an important deal?"

"Bob" acknowledged quickly that he was. She had not meant to criticize his ability to conduct negotiations of the very highest importance, but she was surprised, in view of her earnest request, that he had even mentioned this particular matter to anybody. She reminded him that insurance was his forte, and that their understanding had been that she was to take exclusive charge of their oil business. While she was talking, Tom realized with a disagreeable shock that of late there had been no insurance written, none whatever. He had given the matter no thought, but such was undoubtedly the case, and in his daughter's words he felt a rebuke. Now he could not abide rebukes; he had never permitted anybody to criticize him. For once that unconscious irritation that had been slowly accumulating within him flamed up. It was an irritation too vague, too formless to put into words, especially inasmuch as words did not come easily to Tom Parker when he was mad.

Without further comment the old man pulled his gray wide-awake lower over his eyes and limped out of the room. But he did not go to Judge Halloran's office; he was too sore to risk further offense at the hands of one who took malicious delight in antagonizing him, so he walked the streets. The more he pondered "Bob's" accusation—and accusation it surely was—the angrier he became; not at her, of course, for she was blood of his blood, his other and better self; but angry at himself for allowing the reins to slip out of his fingers. He was the head of the firm. It was due to his ripe judgment and keen common sense that the business ran on; his name and standing it was that gave it stability. Perhaps he had permitted the girl to do more than her share of the work, and hence her inclination to take all the credit for their joint success was only natural, but it was time to change all that; time to turn a big deal without her assistance. That was the thing to do, handle the Jackson lease in his own way and turn it over for a price far in excess of seventy-five thousand dollars. Anybody could sell things for less than they were worth, but it took real ability to realize their full value. Here was a snap, a chance to clean up big money—"Bob" said so—why not, then, take over the lease for himself and her, pay something down, hold it for a few weeks, and then resell it at a staggering profit? Such things were being done—Tom did not know just how, but he could easily find out—and there were several thousand dollars in the bank to the firm's account. If that was not enough to meet the first payment he could probably get Bell Nelson to give him another mortgage on something. Or was it he that would have to give the mortgage to Bell? It didn't matter. The thing to do was to jump out to the Extension, buy the well, and show "Bob" that he was as good a business man as she—better, in fact.

A bus was about to leave, so Tom clambered in.

Barbara Parker had to acknowledge that she was more than a little bit thrilled at the prospect of seeing Calvin Gray again. She had assured her father glibly enough that there was nothing "going on" that day, but—there was. It was something to realize that a mere telegram from her had brought a man of Mr. Gray's importance clear across the country, and that he was coming straight to her. What mysterious magic lay in the telegraph!

Ever since their first meeting he had awakened in her a sort of breathless excitement, the precise significance of which she could not fathom, and that excitement now was growing hourly. It could not mean love—"Bob" flushed at the thought, for she had no intention of falling in love with anybody. She was too young; the world was too new and too exciting for that, and, besides, her life was too full, her obligations were too many to permit of distractions, agreeable or disagreeable. Nor, for that matter, was Gray the sort of man to become seriously interested in a simple person like her; he was complex, many-sided, cosmopolitan. His extravagant attentions were meaning-less—And yet, one could never tell; men were queer creatures; perhaps—

Little prickles ran over "Bob"; she felt her whole body galvanize when she saw Gray coming.

He entered, as she knew he would enter, with the suggestion of having been blown thither upon the breast of a gale. He was electric; he throbbed with energy; he was bursting with enthusiasm, and his delight at seeing her was boyish.

"Bob" colored rosily at his instant and extravagant appreciation of her effort to look more pleasing than usual, but embarrass-ment followed her first thrill. She could not believe his compli-ments were entirely genuine, therefore she took refuge behind her coolest, her most businesslike demeanor. For a while they talked about nothing, although to each the other was eloquent, then "Bob" came as quickly as might be to the matter she had wired him about.

He listened with smiling lips and shining eyes, but he heard only the bare essentials of her story, for his thoughts were galloping, his mind was busy with new impressions of her, other voices than hers were in his ears. That was his rose at her breast. She had been pleased at his coming, otherwise she would not have paid him the girlish compliment of wearing her best. Evidently she cared for him—or was she merely impressed, flattered? Women had called him romantic, whereas he knew himself to be theatric; he wondered if she—

"I told Jackson you'd be out to look at the well and the books to-day," "Bob" was saying. "He won't wait an hour longer."

"Splendid! I came the instant you telegraphed—dropped everything, in fact. Some of my men are waiting to see me, but I haven't even notified them of my arrival. Important business, too; nevertheless, I hurried right here. They can wait." Gray laughed gladly. "Jove! How becoming that hat is. I hired the best-looking car I could find, and it will be here in a minute. I told myself I had earned a day with you, and I wouldn't spoil it by permitting you to drive. I've so much to talk to you about—business of all sorts—that I scarcely know where to begin."

Now "Bob" had expected to drive to the Northwest Ex tension with Gray; nothing else had been in her mind; her field clothing was even laid out ready for a quick change, but a sudden contrariness took hold of her; she experienced a shy perversity that she could not explain.

"Oh, I'm sorry! I—can't go. I simply can't," she declared.

He was so obviously disappointed that her determination gained strength; she was surprised at her own mendacity when she explained the utter impossibility of leaving the office, and told a circumstantial fib about a title that had to be closed with people from out of town. The more she talked the more panicky she became at thought of being for hours alone with this forceful, this magnetic, this overwhelming person. Strange, in view of the fact that she had been looking forward to it for days!

In order finally to get him away before she could change her mind, she promised to hurry through her affairs and then drive out and bring him home. There was no time to lose; Jackson was growing impatient; it was a wonderful deal; there were other days coming—

When Gray had gone and "Bob" was alone, she drew a deep breath. Her pulse was rapid, she was tingling as if from some stimulating current. What a man! What an effect he had upon people! What a fool she had been not to go!

The road to Burkburnett is well surfaced for some distance outside of Wichita Falls, therefore Gray leaned back with eyes closed as the car sped over it, picturing again his meeting with Barbara, recalling her words of greeting, puzzling over the subtle change in her demeanor at the last. Perhaps he had frightened her. He was given to overenthusiasm; this would be a lesson.

Queer how women interfere with business. Here he was going at things backward, whirling out to the oil fields when he should be with McWade and Stoner. They would probably be distracted at his nonarrival, but—this was business, too. And she would drive out to get him. There would be the long ride back. Far away across the undulating prairie fields the horizon was broken by a low, dark barricade, the massed derricks of the town-site pool. So thickly were they grouped that they resembled a dense forest of high, black pines, and not until Gray drew closer could he note that this strange forest was leafless.

By now the roads were quagmires, and the unceasing current of traffic had thickened and slowed down until Gray's car rocked and plunged through a hub-deep channel of slime. There was but one route to the Extension, and it led through the very heart of Burkburnett; there were no detours around the town, no way of beating the traffic, therefore vehicles, no matter how urgent their business, were forced to fall in line and allow themselves to be carried along like chips in a stream of tar.

"Burk" was a one-story town, or at least most of its buildings projected only one story above the mud, and that mud was mixed with oil. Leakage from wells, pipe lines, storagetanks, had made the mass underfoot doubly foul and sticky, and where it was liquid it shone with iridescent colors. Mud was everywhere; on the sidewalks, inside the stores, on walls and signboards, on the skins and clothing of the people.

Through the main street the procession of cars plowed, then out across the railroad tracks and toward the open country beyond. When it came to a halt, as it frequently did, above the hum of idle motors could be heard the clank of pumps, the fitful coughing of gasengines, the hiss of steam. This, of course, was soon drowned in a terrific din of impatient horns, a blaring, brazen snarl at the delay. The whole line roared metallic curses at the cause of its stoppage.

Even the railroad right of way had been drilled. Switch engines shunted rows of flats almost between the straddling derrick legs.

Gray's driver had been dumb thus far, now he broke out abruptly: "Speaking about mud; I was crossing this street on a plank the other day when I saw a bran'-new derby lying in the mud and picked it up. Underneath it was a guy's head.

"'Hullo!' I said. 'You're in pretty deep, ain't you?'"

"The feller looked up at me and said: 'This ain't bad. You'd ought to see my brother. I'm standing on his shoulders!'"

The chauffeur laughed loudly at his own humor. "*Some* country, I call it! But the sun's out, so it will be blowing sand to-morrow."

When Burkburnett had been left behind, another and a vaster island of derricks came into view. It marked the Burk-Waggoner pool, part of the Northwest Extension, so called.

The car was waiting its turn to cross a tiny toll bridge spanning a sluggish creek, the bed of which ran seepage oil from the wells beyond, when the driver grumbled aloud:

"Four bits to cross a forty-foot bridge. There's a graft for you! One old nester above here tore a hole in his fence opposite a wet place in the road and charged us half a dollar to drive through his pasture. But it was cheaper than getting stuck. He had to carry his coin home in an oat sack. After a few weeks somebody got to wondering why that spot never dried out, and, come to investigate, wha' d'you think?"

"I seldom think when I am being entertained," his passenger declared.

"Well, that poor stupid had dammed the creek, and every night he shut the gate and flooded his road."

If the clustered derricks of the town-site pool were impressive, there was something positively dramatic about the Extension. Burkburnett had been laid out in lots and blocks, and the drilling had followed some sort of orderly system; but here were no streets, no visible plan. This had been a wheat field, and as well after well had come in, derricks, drilling rigs, buildings, tanks, piles of timber, and casing had been laid down with complete disregard of all save the owner's convenience. Overnight new pipe lines were being laid, for hours counted here and the crude had to find outlet—fuel had to be brought in. These pipe lines were never buried, and in consequence the ceaseless flow of traffic was forever forced to seek new channels. The place became a bewildering maze through which teams floundered and motor vehicles plunged at random.

Towns had sprung up, for this army of workers was isolated in a sea of mud, but whereas "Burk" was more or less permanent, Newtown, Bradley's Corners, Bridgetown, were cities of canvas, boards, and corrugated iron. By day they were mean, filthy, grotesque; by night they became incandescent, for every derrick was strung with lights, and the surplus supply of gas was burned in torches to prevent it from accumulating in ravines or hollows in explosive quantities. They were Mardi Gras cities.

Day by day this field spread onward toward the Red River; the whole region smelled of oil.

Fire, of course, was an ever-present menace. Newtown, for instance, had been wiped out several times, for it lay on a slope down which a broken pipe line could belch a resistless wave of flame, and even yet the place was a litter of charred timber, twisted pipe, and crumpled sheets of galvanized iron. Owing to this menace the residents had taken the only possible precaution. They had dug in. Behind each place of business was a cyclone cellar—a bomb-proof shelter—into which human bodies and stocks of merchandise could be crowded.

Gray drove directly to the lease he had come to examine, and was disappointed to learn that the owner had just left. This was annoying; "Bob" had assured him that he was expected. Inquiry elicited from the surly individual in charge no more than the reluctant admission that Jackson had been called to the nearest telephone, but would be back sometime.

There was nothing to do but wait. Gray let his car go, then made a cursory examination of the property. He could see little and learn less. The caretaker agreed that the well was pumping one hundred and fifty barrels a day.

Some evasiveness in this fellow's demeanor awoke Gray's suspicion. A sudden telephone call. The owner's absence when he expected a purchaser. Probably somebody else was after the property. It was decidedly worth while to wait.

Gray was unaccustomed to inattention, incivility, and had anybody except "Bob" Parker put him in this position he would have resented it. Under the circumstances, however, he could do nothing except cool his heels. As time passed he began to feel foolish; by late lunch time he was irritable; and as the afternoon wore on he grew angry. Why didn't "Bob" come, as she had promised? He had lost a day, and days were precious.

Evening found him wandering about aimlessly, in a villainous mood, but stubbornly determined to see this thing through at whatever cost. He had no wish to spend a night amid these surroundings, for respectable people shunned these oil-field camps after dark, and he knew himself to be conspicuous. It would add a ridiculous climax to a trying day to be "high-jacked"—to be frisked of his jewelry.

During the early dusk he returned to the lease, only to find even the greasy caretaker gone. By this time Gray was decidedly uncomfortable, and, to add to his discomfort, he conceived the notion that he was being followed. On second thought he dismissed this idea, nevertheless he took a roundabout course back toward the main street.

It seemed odd to be floundering through inky shadows, feeling a way through this miry chaos, when aloft, as far as the eye could see, the sky was lit. This phantom city of twinkling beacons gave one a sense of acute unreality, for it was an empty city, a city the work of which went on almost without the aid of human hands. The very soul of it was mechanical. Only here and there, where a drill crew was at work, did an occasional human figure move back and forth in the glare of low-hung incandescents, nevertheless the whole place breathed and throbbed; it was instinct with a tremendous vigor. From all sides came the ceaseless rhythmic clank of pumps, the hiss of gas and steam, the gurgling flow of liquid—they were the pulse beats, the respirations, the blood flow of this live thing. And its body odor stung the nostrils. All night long it panted with its heavy labors—as if the jinns that lifted those giant pump beams were vying with one another in a desperate endeavor. They were, for a fact. Haste, avarice, an arduous diligence, was in the very air.

Gray stared and marveled, for imagination was not lacking in him. Those derricks with their fires were high altars upon which were heaped ten thousand hopes and prayers. Altars of Avarice! Towers of Greed! That is what they were.

He marvelled, too, at the extremes these last few days had brought him; at the long cry from the luxurious Burlington Notch to this primitive land of fire worshipers. Here, only a few hours by motor from paved streets and comfortable homes, was a section of the real frontier, as crude and as lawless as any he had ever seen. Yonder, for instance, was the Red Lion, a regular Klondike dance hall.

He looked in for a moment, but the sight of hard-faced houris revolving cheek to cheek with men in overalls and boots was nothing new. It did remind him of the march of progress, however, to notice that the bartenders served coca-cola instead of "hootch." Hygienic, but vain, he reflected. Not at all like the brave old days.

Farther up the street was a flaming theater decorated with gaudy lithographs of women in tights. That awoke a familiar echo. The grimy figures headed thither might well be miners just in from Eldorado or Anvil Creek.

Gambling was practically wide open, too, and before long Gray found himself in a superheated, overcrowded back room with a stack of silver dollars which he scattered carelessly upon the numbers of a roulette table. Roulette was much like the oil game. This was a good way in which to kill an hour.

Absorbed in his own thoughts, Gray paid little heed to those about him, until a large hand picked up one of his bets. Then he raised his eyes. The hand was attached to a muscular arm, which in turn was attached to a burly stranger of unpleasant mien. Gray voiced a good-natured protest, but the fellow scowled and refused to acknowledge his mistake. Noting that the man was flushed, Gray shrugged and allowed the incident to pass. This bootleg whisky from across Red River was of a quality to scatter a person's eyesight.

For some time the game continued before Gray won again, and the dealer deposited thirty-five silver dollars beside his bet. Again that sun-browned hand reached forth, but this time Gray seized it by the wrist. He and the stranger eyed each other for a silent moment, during which the other players looked on.

Gray was the first to speak. "If you're not as drunk as you seem," he said, easily, "you'll excuse yourself. If you are, you need sobering."

With a wrench the man undertook to free his hand; he uttered a threatening oath. The next instant he was treated to a surprise, for Gray jerked him forward and simultaneously his empty palm struck the fellow a blinding, a resounding smack. Twice he smote that reddened cheek with the sound of an explosion, then, as the victim flung his body backward, Gray kicked his feet from under him. Again he cuffed the fellow's face, this time from the other side. When he finally desisted the stranger rocked in his tracks; he shook his head; he blinked and he cursed; it was a moment before he could focus his whirling sight upon his assailant. When he succeeded it was to behold the latter staring at him with a mocking, threatening smile.

The drunken man hesitated, he cast a slow glance around the room, then muttering, hoarsely, he turned and made for the door. He was followed by a burst of derisive laughter that grew louder as he went.

Gray was in a better mood now than for several hours; he had vented his irritation; the air had cleared. After a while he discovered that he was hungry; no longer was he too resentful to heed the healthy warning of his stomach, so he left the place.

CHAPTER XIX

Newton's eating places were not appetizing at best, but a meal could be endured with less discomfort by night than by day, for at such times most of the flies were on the ceilings. The restaurant Gray entered was about what he had expected; along one side ran a quick-order counter at which were seated several customers; across from it was an oilcloth-covered table, perfectly bare except for a revolving centerpiece—one of those silver-plated whirligigs fitted with a glass salt-and-pepper shaker, a toothpick holder, an unpleasant oil bottle, and a cruet intended for vinegar, but now filled with some mysterious embalming fluid acting as a preservative of numerous lifelike insect remains. Here, facing an elderly man in a wide gray-felt hat, Gray seated himself.

Gray's neighbor was in no pleasant mood, for he whacked impatiently at such buzzing pests as were still on the wing, and when a perspiring Greek set a plate of soup before him he took umbrage at the presence of the fellow's thumb in the liquid. The argument that followed angered the old man still further, for it arrived nowhere except to prove that the offending thumb was the property of the proprietor of the restaurant, and by inference, therefore, a privileged digit.

When a departing customer left the door open, the elderly diner grumbled bitterly at the draught and draped his overcoat over his bent shoulders.

"Dam' Eskimos!" he muttered. "—raised in a chicken coop—

Windy as a derrick!"

Gray liked old people, and he was tolerant of their crotchets. Irascibility indicates force of character, at least so he believed, and old folks are apt to accept too meekly the approach of decay. Here was a spirit that time had not dulled—it was like wine soured in an old cask. At any rate, wine it had been, not water, and that was something.

Most of the counter customers had drifted out when, without warning, the screen door banged loudly open and Gray looked up from his plate to see his recent acquaintance of the gambling table approaching. This time purpose was stamped upon the man's face, but whether it was deliberate or merely the result of more drinking there was no telling. He lurched directly up to the table and stared across at Gray.

"Slapped my face, didn't you?" he cried, after a menacing moment.

"I did, indeed," the speaker nodded, pleasantly.

"You ain't going to slap it again. You ain't going to slap anybody's—"

"What makes you think I won't?" Gray became aware as he spoke that his elderly neighbor had raised to the intruder a countenance stamped with a peculiar expression of incredulity, almost of anger, at the interruption, and that the two remaining counter customers had turned startled faces over their shoulders, while the proprietor, his arms full of dishes, had paused beside the swinging door to the kitchen.

That which occurred next came unexpectedly. The stranger whipped out from under his coat a revolver, at the same time voicing a profane answer to the challenge. The proprietor uttered a bleat of terror; he dropped his dishes and dived out of the room; the men on the stools scrambled down and plunged after him.

As Calvin Gray rose to his feet it was with a flash of mingled anger and impatience. This quarrel was so utterly senseless, it served so little purpose.

"My friend," he cried, sharply, "if you don't put up that gun, one of us will go to a hospital."

In spite of the intruder's haste in drawing his weapon, he appeared now to lack the will promptly to use it—his laggard spirit required a further scourge, so it seemed; something more to goad it into final fury. It was a phenomenon by no means uncommon, for it is not easy to shoot down an unarmed victim.

By way of rousing his savagery, the fellow uttered a bellow, then, like a warrior smiting his shield with his spear before the charge, he swung his heavy weapon, smashing at one blow that silver-plated merry-go-round with its cluster of bottles.

A shower of toothpicks, fragments of glass, a spatter of oil and vinegar covered the old man in the end chair, and he rose with a cry that drew a swift glance from the desperado.

Gray was upon the point of launching himself over the table when he witnessed a peculiar transformation in his assailant. The man's expression altered with almost comic suddenness, he lowered his weapon and took a backward step. Gray, too, had cause for astonishment, for the elderly man was moving slowly toward the disturber, his overcoat, meanwhile, hanging loosely from his left shoulder, like a mantle. His gray face had grown white, malignant, threatening; he advanced with a queer, sidling gait, edging forward behind the shelter of his garment as if behind a barricade. But what challenged Gray's instant attention was the certainty of purpose, the cold, confident menace behind the old fellow's demeanor. There was something appalling about him; he had suddenly become huge and dominant.

That he had been recognized was plain, for the armed man

cried, agitatedly: "Look out, Tom! I don't want any truck with *you*."

The deliberate advance continued; in a harsh voice Tom answered: "I don't allow anybody to interfere with me when I'm eating!" For every step he shuffled forward the man before him fell back a corresponding distance.

Again the newcomer rasped out his warning, and Gray, too, added his voice, saying: "Leave him to me, old man. This is my quarrel." As he spoke he moved around the end of the table, but the mantled figure halted him with an imperious jerk of the head. Without in the slightest diverting his steady gaze, Tom snapped:

"Hands off, stranger! I won't have you buttin' in, either. I don't allow anybody to interfere with me when I'm eating."

Gray was checked less by the exasperation, by the authority in the speaker's tone, than by the fact that the entire complexion of the affair had changed. The ruffian, who had entered so confidently, was no longer the aggressor; a mere look, a word, a gesture from this aged, unknown person had put him upon the defensive. More extraordinary still was the fact that his power of initiative was for the moment completely paralyzed, and that he was tortured by a deplorable indecision. He was furious, that was plain, nevertheless his anger had been halted in mid-flight, as it were; desperation battled with an inexplicable dread. He raised his hands now, but more in a gesture of surrender than of threat.

"Don't come any closer," he cried, hoarsely. "Don't do it, I tell you! *Don't—do it!*" There was no longer any thickness to his tongue; he spoke as one quite sober.

When for the third time that malevolent voice repeated, "I don't allow anybody to interfere with me when I'm eating," the solitary onlooker felt an absurd desire to laugh. During intensely dramatic moments nervous laughter is near the surface, and there was something rigidly dramatic about the methodical, sidling advance of that man half crouched behind his overcoat. Tom, as he had been called, gave Gray the impression of Death itself marching slowly forward to drape that black shroud upon his cowering victim.

Brief as had been the whole episode, already passers-by had halted, staring faces were glued to the front windows of the cafe. Well they might stare at those two tense figures, one advancing, the other retreating, as if to the measures of some slow dance.

But the tempo changed abruptly. The desperado's back brought up against the swinging kitchen door; it gave to his weight and decision was born of that instant. With a cry he flung himself backward, the spring door snapped to and swallowed him up with the speed of a camera shutter; then followed the sound of his heavy rushing footsteps.

"Hell!" exclaimed the old man. "I had his buttons counted!" With the words he let fall his overcoat, and there, beneath it, Gray beheld what he had more than half suspected, what indeed was ample cause for the quarrelsome stranger's apprehension. Held close to the owner's body was what in the inelegant jargon of the West is known as a "dog leg." The weapon, a frontier Colt's of heavy caliber, was full cocked under the old man's thumb; the hand holding it was as steady as the blazing eyes above.

With a smile Gray said, "Allow me to congratulate you, sir, upon a most impressive demonstration of the power of mind over matter."

"A little killin' helps those scoun'rels," breathed the white-haired warrior. "Surgin' around, wreakin' vengeance on vinegar bottles! And me with a bad indigestion!"

"I don't often permit others to do my fighting. But you wouldn't let—"

"I don't allow anybody—" doggedly began the former speaker, but the street door burst open, a noisy crowd poured into the room, a volley of excited questions was raised. Amid the confusion Gray heard his own name shouted, and found himself set upon by two agitated friends, Mallow and Stoner. They had been combing Newtown for him, so they declared, and were near by when attracted by the excitement on the sidewalk. What was the trouble? Was Gray hurt?

He assured them that he was not, and explained in a few words the origin of the encounter. But other concerns, it seemed, occupied the minds of the pair, and before he had finished Mallow was dragging him towards the door, crying, breathlessly: "Gee, Governor! You gave us a run. We've been coming since noon."

"It was only by the grace of God," Stoner declared, "that we heard you were out here and why you'd come. We managed to get a phone call through to Jackson, but it was—"

"Jackson? I've been looking for him all the afternoon."

"Sure! Mallow swore he was all right, but Mac and I don't know him, and we figured he might turn a trick. Anyhow, Mallow and I jumped the Lizzie and looped it. Boy! I tramped on her some, until we hit bottom the other side of Burk. Mallow went clean through the top. I guess I smashed the whole rear end, but we couldn't wait to see. They'll have her stripped naked, tires, cushions, and all, before we get back. Motor, too, probably. We've been hitting it afoot, on wagons and pipe trucks—managed to get a service car finally, but it fell open like a book. Just one of those dam' unlucky trips."

"Jackson didn't get to you, did he?" Mallow inquired, anxiously.

"Get to me? No. Nor I to him." Gray spoke impatiently. "What is this all about?"

"Simply this, Governor: Jackson's well is a 'set-up'! For Nelson! We nearly dropped dead when we found out that Parker kid had laid *you* against it. Why didn't you *tell us*—?"

"What are you saying? I don't—"

"The well's phony. Dry as a pretzel."

"In what way? I saw the oil—"

"Never mind. Lay off!"

"I think I'm entitled to an explanation."

"Well, then, it's salted!"

"Impossible! I saw it pumping."

"I'll say you did." Mallow chuckled. "Live oil, too; right out of old Mamma Earth. Cheap lease at seventy-five thousand, eh? It's like this: the pipe line of the Atlantic runs across Jackson's lease, and one dark and stormy night he tapped it. It wasn't a hard thing to do; just took a little care and some digging. Now he runs the oil in, pumps it out and sells it back to them. He's a regular subsidiary of the great and only Atlantic Petroleum Company. It can't last long, of course, but—oh, what a well to hand Nelson! What a laugh it would have been!"

"Outrageous!" Gray exclaimed. "I can't believe you are in earnest."

"It *is* shocking, isn't it? Such dishonesty is incredible. And what an unhappy surprise for the company when they finally locate the leak!"

Gray clamped a heavy hand upon the speaker's shoulder; harshly he inquired, "Do you mean to say that Miss Parker deliberately—"

"She don't know anything about it."

"You said she 'laid me' against it."

"No, no! I merely tipped her to it because she's one of Nelson's brokers."

"She's his sweetie," Stoner added. "He's going to marry her, so Mallow thought he'd surely fall for it, coming from her."

"You—you're not fit to mention that girl's name, either of you." Gray's tone was one of quivering anger. "If you involve her in your crooked dealings, even indirectly, I'll—God! What a dirty trick." He flung Mallow aside in disgust. "You ought to be shot."

"Why, Governor! We wouldn't hurt that kid. She's aces."

"I told you my fight with Nelson was to be fair and square."

There followed a moment of silence. Mallow and Stoner exchanged glances. "What percentage of that goes?" the former finally inquired.

"One hundred."

"So? Then it's lucky Nelson didn't fall. But there's no harm done—nobody's hurt."

"It is lucky, indeed-for me. I'd have felt bound to make good his loss, if you had hooked him. I presume I ought to expose this swindle."

"Expose Jackson?" Stoner inquired, quickly. When Gray nodded, there was another brief silence before the speaker ventured to say: "I know this bird Nelson, and, take it from me, you're giving him the best of it. If I hadn't known him as well as I do, I wouldn't of put in with you to break him. It's all right to trim a sucker once; it's like letting the blood of a sick man—he's better for it. But to ride a square guy to death, to keep his veins open—well, I ain't in that kind of business. Now about this Jackson; you can land him, I s'pose, if you try, but it would be lower than a frog's foot, after him playing square with you."

"What do you mean by that?"

"He could have stung you, easy, couldn't he? You surged out here on purpose to buy the lease, but he hid out all afternoon to avoid you."

"He is a thief. He is stealing hundreds of dollars a day."

"Sure! From the Atlantic, that has stolen hundreds of thousands from the likes of him—yes, millions. It was the Atlantic that broke the market to sixty-five cents, filled their storage tanks and contracted a million barrels more than they had tankage for, then gypped the price to three dollars. I can't shed any tears over that outfit."

"Let's not argue the ethics of big business. The law of supply and demand—"

"Supply and demand, eh? Ever strike you as queer that crude never breaks as long as the big companies have got their tanks full? The price always toboggans when they're empty, and comes back when they're filled up. That's supply and demand with the reverse English, ain't it? Say, the Atlantic and those others play with us outsiders like we was mice. When their bellies get empty they eat as many of us as they want, then they let the rest of us scurry around and hunt up new fields. We run all the risks; we spend our coin, and when we strike a new pool they burgle us over again." Stoner was speaking with a good deal of heat. "Big business, eh? Well, here's some little business—dam' little. The Atlantic leased a lot of scattered acreage I know about and drilled it. Pulled off their crews at the top of the sand and drilled in with men they could trust. It turned out good, but they capped their wells, wrecked their rigs, and, of course, that condemned the whole territory. Then they set about buying it all in, cheap—through dummies. Double-crossed the farmers, see? Friend of mine took a chance; put down a well on his own. The usual thing happened; they broke him. It took a lot of doing, but they broke him. One little trick they did was to cock a bit and drop it in the hole. That prank cost him sixteen thousand dollars before he could 'side track' the tool. He quit, finally, less 'n a hundred feet from big pay. Then, having bought up solid for near nothing they came back and started business, laughing merrily. That's the Atlantic."

"A splendid lecture on commercial honesty. I am inspired by it, and I reverence your scruples, but—I grope for the moral of the story."

"The moral is, mind your own business and—and give a guy a chance."

"Um-m! Suppose we leave it at that for the present."

Mallow, who had remained silent during his friend's argument, greeted this suggestion with relief. He was glad to change the subject. "Good!" he cried, heartily. "I'd about as soon face Old Tom Parker, like that fellow in the restaurant did, as to face Jackson. He'd sink a stillson in my head, sure, if—"

"Parker? Was that old man Miss Parker's father?"

"Certainly! What d'you think ailed that gunman? D'you think he got the flu or something, all of a sudden? There ain't anybody left tough enough to hanker for Tom's scalp. He's pinned a rose on all of those old-timers, and he's deadly poison to the new crop."

For the first time Calvin Gray understood clearly the reason for the unexpected outcome of that encounter in the cafe. No wonder the stranger's trigger finger had been paralyzed.

Barbara's father, indeed! How stupid of him not to guess. On the heels of his first surprise came another thought; suppose that old Paladin should consider that he, Gray, had shown weakness in allowing another to assume the burden of his quarrel? And suppose he should tell his daughter about it! That would be a situation, indeed.

"I must find him, quickly," Gray declared. "Perhaps he'll ride back to town with us."

It was not a difficult task to locate the veteran officer, and Tom was delighted at the chance to ride home with his new acquaintance.

That journey back to civilization was doubly pleasant, for Mr. Parker cherished no such feelings as Gray had feared, and, moreover, he responded quickly to the younger man's efforts to engage his liking. They got along famously from the start, and Tom positively blossomed under the attentions he received. It had been a trying day for him, but his ill humor quickly disappeared in the warmth of a new-found friendship, and he talked more than was his custom. He was even led to speak of old days, old combats, of which the bloodless encounter that evening was but a tame reminder. The pictures he conjured up were colorful.

A unique and an engaging person he proved to be; an odd compound of gentleness and acerbity, of kindliness and rancor; a quiet, guileless, stubborn, violent old man-at-arms, who would not be interrupted while he was eating. He was both scornful and contemptuous of evildoers. All needed killing.

"Hard luck, I call it, for a budding desperado to wreck a career of promise the way that wretched fellow did," Gray told him with a laugh. "Out of all the men in Texas, to pick you—"

"Oh, he ain't a bud! He's quite a killer."

"Indeed?"

"He kills Mexicans and niggers and folks without guns, mostly. Low-down stuff! He's got three or four, I believe. I never could see why the Nelsons kep' him."

There was a brief silence. "I beg pardon?" said Gray.

"He's been on the Nelson pay roll for years—doing odd jobs that wasn't fit to be done. But I guess they got tired of him, anyhow he's been hanging around Wichita for the last two or three weeks. He's been in an out of our office quite a bit."

"Your office? What for?"

"I dunno, unless he took a shine to 'Bob.'"

"Not—really?"

Mr. Parker uttered an unpleasant sound. "She never said anything about it, but I suspicioned she had to order him out, finally. I'd of split his third shirt button if he'd stood his ground. He knew I had something on him, but he couldn't figure just what it was." Old Tom's teeth shone through the gloom. "A man will 'most always act like that when he don't know just where he's at. I knew where *I* was at, all the time, only I wanted to see that button plain. I allus know where *I'm* at."

Later, when the journey was over and Tom Parker had been dropped at his gate, Gray spoke to his two companions.

"Did you hear what he said?"

"We did."

"Do you believe I was framed?"

Both Mallow and Stoner nodded. "Don't you?" the former inquired.

When no answer was forthcoming, he said: "Better give us the flag, Governor. We're rar'ing to go."

"You mean—?"

"You know what I mean. Nelson's so crooked his bedclothes fall off. We pulled a boner this time, but Brick has got another window dressed for him."

"I'll think it over," said Gray.

CHAPTER XX

Ozark Briskow, like his sister Allegheny, was studying hard and learning rapidly, but he had adopted an educational plan, a curriculum, so to speak, far different from hers. Whereas she lived between book covers and the thousand and one details of her daily existence were governed by a bewildering army of "don'ts," Buddy had devised his own peculiar system of acquiring wisdom, and from it the word "don't" had been deliberately dropped. His excursion into the halls of learning, brief as it had been, had convinced him that books could teach him only words, whereas he craved experiences, ideas, adventures. Adventure comes at night; pleasure walks by gaslight. Young Briskow told himself that he had missed a lot of late hours and would have to work diligently to catch up, but he undertook the effort with commendable courage.

It is said that all wish to possess knowledge, but few are willing to pay the price. Buddy was one of the minority. Early he adopted the motto, "Money no object," and it provoked him not at all to learn that there is a scale of night prices considerably higher than the scale of day prices; to find, for instance, that a nocturnal highball costs twice as much as one purchased during daylight hours. That phenomenon, by the way, had nothing to do with the provisions of the Eighteenth Amendment, it merely explained why farmers went to bed early—they couldn't afford to sit up, so Buddy decided.

He had learned a lot since leaving school, not only about prohibition, but also about speed laws, men's fashions, facial

Rex Beach

massage, the fox trot and the shimmy, caviar, silk pajamas, bromo-seltzer, the language of flowers, and many of the pleasures and displeasures of the higher intellectual life, such as love and insomnia.

His education was progressing apace, for love is the greatest of educators, and Buddy was in love—madly, extravagantly in love. Love it was that accounted for his presence in Dallas, and his occupancy of the Governor's suite at the Ajax. A fellow in love with the most wonderful woman in the world couldn't afford to look cheap in his home town, could he?

Of course Dallas was not Buddy's home town, but it had been his point of departure into the world, and it was the home of his bank account, hence some pride of proprietorship was pardonable. It gave him such a pleasing sense of importance to adopt the city as his own that he adopted everything and everybody in it.

In spite of the fact that the train from Wichita Falls was behind time, one morning shortly after Buddy's arrival, he was still abed when Calvin Gray arrived at the hotel. Instead of disturbing the slumbers of youth, Gray went directly to the detective who had telegraphed him, and for half an hour or more the two talked.

Later, during the course of a leisurely bath and shave, the new arrival pondered the information he had received. Here was a problem. Having dressed himself, he strolled around to Coverly's place of business and interviewed the jeweler.

"Sure! He has bought quite a bit of stuff in the last few days," Coverly told him. "He was in only yesterday and ordered a fine piece made up. He wanted a ruby heart pierced with a diamond arrow, but I got him off that and onto a blue Brazilian solitaire. We're mounting it in a platinum lady's ring."

"What is the price?"

"Forty-five hundred, and the value is there."

"Have you seen the woman?"

Coverly nodded. "The boy is a good picker. I don't blame her much, either, for I've seen a lot of worse-looking fellows than Buddy."

"Hold the ring. He may change his mind."

"I say!" Coverly was in dismay. "Are you going to spoil the best sale I've made in two weeks?"

"Oh, I'll take it off your hands if he doesn't. Make some excuse not to deliver it until I say the word. You don't know the woman, eh?"

"Never saw her before."

Gray knocked several times at the Governor's suite before a sleepy response, a succession of yawns and mutterings, told him that he had been heard. The door opened finally and the pride of the Briskow family, his eyes all but swelled shut, his muscular figure splendidly arrayed in futuristic silken pajamas, mumbled:

"What's eatin' you, any—?" The eyes opened wider, Buddy's face broke into a slow smile. "Why, Mr. Gray!" He extended a palm, a bit dry and feverish, and drew his caller inside. "Dawg-gone! I'm glad to see you."

Gray entered with a buoyant laugh and a hearty greeting; he clapped the young giant heavily upon the back. At the blow Buddy voiced a sharp cry and seized his head.

"Easy over the bumps! I'm carryin' a cargo of nitroglycerine, and I'll let go if you jar me," he explained.

"Sorry! I know how it feels. But, man alive, it's afternoon! I began to think you were dead."

Buddy led the way into his bedroom, piled his pillows together and gingerly lowered himself upon them. He showed his strong white teeth in a wide grin and winked meaningly. "I'll be all right directly. It's this here sim—sympathetic booze they talk about. Have a drink, Mr. Gray? There's a coupla bottles of real liquor in the closet—not this tiger's milk you get—"

The caller declined the invitation. "Where the devil have you been, Buddy? We were getting worried."

"Who, me? Oh, I been—lookin' around."

"Your mother is nearly frantic."

Buddy stirred uneasily. "Pshaw! I'm fine. I can take keer of myself. Nobody don't need to worry about me."

"Good! Now then, you young scoundrel, I'm going to order you the sort of breakfast that goes with what ails you, and while it is coming up, you are going to jump under the shower."

"Where d'you get that 'jump' stuff?" the youth inquired, faintly. "Besides, I'm clean."

But Gray had seized the phone, and as soon as he had given his order he strode into the bathroom and turned on the water. He was out again in a moment, then laughingly he dragged the aching Texan from his couch. "Under you go," he insisted, "or I'll wet down your whole Japanese flower garden."

"Some pajamas, ain't they? I got a dozen pairs," Buddy said, proudly.

"Quick! If you think I'll consent to hang around a lonesome hotel while you sleep, you're mistaken. I can't tell you how glad I am to run into you, Buddy. I'm dying to have a riotous time."

"Eh?" Briskow turned an inquiring face to the speaker.

"I've been hibernating in the wilderness, sucking my paw and living off my fat, like a bear. I want you to shown me this town."

A bath, a brisk rubdown, and breakfast put Buddy in fairly good fettle once more; so marked was his improvement, in fact, that Gray envied him his glorious gift of youth.

"Flying pretty high, aren't you?" the elder man inquired, with a wave of the hand that took in the expensive suite.

"Well, I ain't exactly broke."

"True. But I know what these rooms cost. That's going strong for a lad like you."

"You took 'em, didn't you, when you had less 'n I got?"

"Ahem! It is embarrassing to be held up as an example. I've done a good many things, Buddy, that I wouldn't like to see you do."

"If they wouldn't hurt me any more 'n they've hurt you I'd like to try'em."

"Another proof that you are still in short pants. I'm a bad person to copy. By the way, why did you quit school?"

Buddy considered his reply, then: "I reckon it was because of them short pants you speak about. I can't stand bein' laughed at, Mr. Gray. It comes hard to stand up in a class along with a bunch of children and make mistakes and have a little boy in a lace collar and spring heels snap his fingers and sing out in a sweet soprano, 'Oh, tee-*cher!* Then have him show you up. They put me in with a lot of nursin' babes. What the hell? I weigh a hundred and ninety and I got a beard!"

"Didn't you learn anything?"

Buddy closed a meaning eye, and his pleasant features wrinkled into that infectious smile. "I'll tell the world I did! After the whistlin' squabs was asleep in their nests I went out among the whippoorwills an' the bats. Ain't it funny how quick folks can learn to put up with bad grammar when you got a jingle in your jeans? I guess I've got enough education to do me; anyhow, I can write Ozark Briskow in the lower right-hand corner and that seems to get me by."

"You wouldn't consent to go back or—have a tutor, like Allie?"

"Who, *me?*" Briskow laughed scornfully.

"Um-m! Merely a suggestion. You are the architect of your own career."

"I'm fed up on that kind of schoolin', Mr. Gray. I—" Buddy's facereddened, he dropped his eyes. "I don't mind tellin' *you*— I—It's like this—I kinda got a girl!"

"*No!*" The speaker was surprised, incredulous.

"Sure have. She's—wonderful. She's right here in this hotel!"

"Buddy, you're developing!" Gray exclaimed, with apparent admiration.

"I been showin" her the sights—that's what ails me this morning. She lets me take her around to places—trusts me, you understand? She thinks I'm aces."

"Splendid! I wish you'd ask her to dig up a friend."

"How d'you mean?"

"Why, ask her to find another good-looking girl for me—I assume she *is* good looking—then we can make it a foursome. I'm a great entertainer, and, while I don't drink, I haven't the slightest objection to ladies who do. Dallas, I believe, is a pretty lively—"

"She's a stranger here," Buddy broke in, stiffly. His enthusiasm had cooled; he regarded Gray with veiled displeasure. "An" besides, she ain't that kind of a girl."

"Oh! Sorry! I thought from what you said—that headache—bottles in your closet, too! My mistake, Buddy."

"She'll take a drink, with me," the youth confessed. "Anyhow, she's gettin' so she will. I don't see anything wrong in a woman takin' a drink now an' then with a man she—with a man that's honorable." The last words were voiced defiantly.

Hastily Buddy's caller averred: "Nor do I. We sha'n't come to blows over an abstract moral issue like that. This is an age of tolerance, an age of equality. I flatter myself that I'm quite as lawless and broad minded as the average bachelor of our very smartest set."

"I'm—" the speaker gulped. "I'm goin' to marry her."

"Oh, fine!" Gray's enthusiasm was positively electric. He seized Buddy's hand and crushed it. "Education, indeed! No use for that now, is there?"

"I mean I'm goin' to, if I can; if she'll let me."

"Let you? With your money? Why, she'll jump at the chance. No doubt you have already asked her—or she suspects—"

The lad shook his head. "She don't have to marry nobody. She's got money—an *es*-tate. You think it's all right for me to do it?"

"Simpler men than you have asked that question, and wiser men than I have refused to answer. As for me, I've never had the courage to take the plunge. However, the worst you can get is a heartbreak and a lifetime of regrets. But, of course, the woman takes some chances, too. Tell me about her."

"Well—" Buddy beamed fatuously. "I dunno hardly where to begin." Into his voice, as he spoke, there crept a breathless excitement, into his eyes a dumb adoration. "She's— wonderful! She's too good for me."

"Once and a while they are."

"She's educated, too—more in your class, Mr. Gray. I dunno how she stands for me. She's the smartest, purtiest girl—"

"She's young, eh?"

"She's—older 'n I am. I reckon she's mebbe twenty-five. I never ast her."

"Naturally. How did you meet her? When? Where? I'm a terribly romantic old fool." Gray hitched his chair closer and leaned forward, his face keen with interest.

"Well, sir, it's a regular story, like in a book. I was in a restaurant with a coupla fellers an' a feller she was with struck her—"

"Struck her?"

"Yep. He was her brother, so she told me. Anyhow, I bounced him. I sure spoiled him up a lot. She was cryin' an' she ast me to take her home. That's how I got to know her. I s'pose she cottoned to me for takin' her part that-a-way. She didn't know the sort of place it was her brother had took her. Pore kid! She's had a hard time, an' every man she ever knew, but me, done her dirt. Even her husband." Buddy scowled.

After a moment Gray said, quietly, "So, she's married?"

"She was. He's dead, or something. I was bashful about callin' around to see her, not havin' anything to talk about but school an' oil wells, but she took an interest right away, 'specially in the wells. You'd ought to hear the story of her life, Mr. Gray. It's as sad as any novel. You see, her folks had lots of money, but her ma died an' her pa was too busy to be bothered, so he sent her off to a convent. Them nuns at the convent was so cruel to her that she run away—"

"And went on the stage."

"How'd you know?"

"I didn't. But—the stage is the usual refuge for convent-bred girls who are abused. I've met several. Did she—Was the old home in Virginia?"

"Sure! Mebbe you know her!" Buddy cried.

"Perhaps. I seem to remember the story. What is her name?"

"Arline Montague."

The elder man shook his head. "You said something about a marriage. I dare say she married some rich John whose family disapproved of the match—so many show girls have been deceived like that. You can't imagine the prejudice of those Fifth Avenue parents—"

"That's what she done. An' he went off an' joined the French Legion of Honor an' was killed."

"Foreign Legion, no doubt."

"Anyhow, he never made no pervision for her. But she wouldn't of touched a penny of his money if he'd left it to her, she's that honorable." Now that the lover had fairly launched himself upon the engrossing life story of his sweetheart he was in deep earnest, and his listener's quick understanding, his sympathy, his grasp of the situation, was a spur to further confidences. It was a blessing to have a friend so old, so wise, and so worldly.

"What is the estate you mentioned?"

"Oh, that's her own! It's all she had to fall back on. It's bein' settled up now an' she'll have her money before long."

"The old Virginia homestead and the slaves—?"

"Good thing she met me when she did, for them lawyers had it all tied up in court and wouldn't let go till she paid their fees."

"A providential meeting, truly. You fixed that up, of course, and got rid of the wretched bloodsuckers. I've done much the same thing, more than once. Now, one other question—how does she happen to be in Dallas? I infer from your account that she is a model of virtue, and that she accepted your aid only upon the condition that your attentions to her should be characterized by the deepest respect. So? Well then, 'how come'?"

"That was just a lucky chance. She's got some interests here; stocks an' things, belongin' to the *es*-tate. She dunno, herself, how valuable they are, but me comin' right from Texas an' bein' in oil an' all, she ast me to he'p her out. So I got her to come. All that had kep' her back was the expense. Mind you"—Buddy's tone became one of deeper admiration—"she ain't blue, or anything. No sir-ee! Her life's been sad, but you'd never know it. She's full of pep; allus out for fun, an'— that's what I like about her. Gee! You gotta meet her, Mr. Gray."

"Well, rather! But meanwhile, we must telegraph your parents not only that you have been found, but also the further good news."

"I—We better not say anything about my gettin' married."

"Why not? They'd like to know."

"I'd oughta wired 'em long ago, but—you understand! Miss Montague ain't exactly Ma an' Allie's kind."

"You're not ashamed of her?"

"Hunh!" The tone of this exclamation was an eloquent denial.

"Then let's have them come on and get acquainted. They'll probably take right to her." But when this suggestion met with disapproval, Gray inquired: "Is it because you are ashamed of *them*—of your mother and sister?"

Buddy stirred uneasily. "Pshaw, no!" A sudden thought came to him. "Why, it's this way: I haven't ast her yet. Mebbe she won't have me. If she says yes—I'll let 'em know."

"Good! We'll make it, for the time being, a mere message of reassurance. To-night you and Miss Montague shall dine with me and we'll go to a theater." This arrangement met with young Briskow's enthusiastic approval, and so it was left.

It was with something more than mere impatience that Calvin Gray awaited the dinner hour; he was angry, restless; his mind was back in Wichita Falls, whence the message from his detective had abruptly summoned him. Matters of moment were at issue there, and with a love affair of his own upon his mind he could think of no undertaking less to his taste than this: of saving a young fool from his folly. He could expect no thanks, if he succeeded, and if he failed he would in all probability incur Buddy's enmity, if not that of the whole Briskow family. Families are like that. It would all take time, and meanwhile his business was bound to suffer. However, he was not one to turn back, and he remembered with a pang the last look he had seen in Ma Briskow's eyes.

Gray was prepared to find his young friend's light o' love superficially attractive, and she was all of that. He was not prepared, however, to find her quite as good an actress as she appeared to be. In spite of the fact that she probably took less pleasure in the meeting than did he, she admirably covered her feelings. She was delighted, flattered—Buddy had so often spoken of him that she almost felt acquainted—She was quite excited at knowing the famous Colonel Gray—She would have recognized him anywhere from Buddy's glowing description.

Gray's heart sank as he studied Miss Montague. She was blond—to his suspicious eye a trifle too blond—and she wore her hair bobbed. She was petite and, both in appearance and in mannerism, she was girlish; nevertheless, she was self-reliant, and there was a certain maturity to her well-rounded figure, a suggestion of weariness about her eyes, that told a story.

Following his first critical appraisal, Gray was vaguely conscious of something familiar about her; somewhere within him the chords of remembrance were lightly brushed; but try as he would he could not make himself believe that he had ever seen her. Probably it was the type that was familiar. He undertook to make sure by talking "show business" at the first opportunity; she responded with enough spontaneity to give an impression of candor, but her theatrical experience was limited and that line of exploration led nowhere.

Whatever the pose she had adopted for Buddy's benefit, it was evident now that she credited his friend with intelligence equal to her own, and recognized the futility of deceit, therefore she made no attempt to pass as anything except an experienced young woman of the world, and Gray admired her for it. She smoked a good many cigarettes; her taste in amusements was broad; she had sparkle and enthusiasm. She was, in fact, a vibrant young person, and referred gayly to a road house whither Buddy had taken her on the night before and where they had danced until all hours. She loved to dance.

The elder man played host in his best and easiest style, both at dinner and at the theater; then he passed the burden of entertainment over to Buddy, first cheerfully declaring that he would not be sidetracked and that he intended to impose his company upon the young couple whether they wanted him or not. This was precisely to young Briskow's liking, and soon they were speeding out to that road house mentioned earlier in the evening.

Buddy drove, with Miss Montague by his side, the while Gray sat alone in the back seat of the car quietly objurgating the follies of youth and mournfully estimating his chances of surviving the night. Frankly, those chances appeared pretty slim, for Buddy drove with a death-defying carelessness. By the time they had arrived at their destination, Gray's respect for the girl had increased; she had nerves of steel.

The resort was run on rather liberal principles; a number of flushed and noisy couples were dancing to the music of a colored orchestra. It was a "hip-pocket" crowd, and while there was no public drinking, the high-pitched volubility of the merrymakers was plainly of alcoholic origin. Gray realized that he was in for an ordeal, for he had become too well known to escape notice. Consternation filled him, therefore, at thought of the effect his presence here might have. But the music went straight to Buddy's feet; syncopation intoxicated him much as the throbbing of midnight drums and the pounding of tom-toms mesmerizes a voodoo worshiper, and he whirled Miss Montague away in his arms without so much as an apology to his other guest.

There was nothing conservative about Buddy's dancing. He embellished his steps with capricious figures, and when he led his partner back to the table where he had left Gray, like a sailor marooned upon a thirsty atoll, he was red faced and perspiring; his enthusiasm was boiling over. "Dawg-*gone!*" he cried. "Now, if we had something wet, eh? These pants is cut purpose for a brace of form-fittin' flasks, but I left 'em in the room on account of you not drinkin', Mr. Gray."

"Miss Montague," the elder man exclaimed, "I am not a kill-joy and I hastily resent Buddy's accusation. I have pursued folly as far as any man of my years."

"I bet him that you were a good fellow," the girl said, with a smile.

"Exactly! Abstinence comes as much from old age as from principle, and I am in my very prime. With all vigor I defend myself against the odious charge of virtuousness. Dyspepsia alone accounts for it."

"You don't object to drinking?"

"A wiser man that I has said, 'There are many things which we can afford to forget which it is yet well to learn.' I have had my day. May I claim the next dance?"

In spite of the fact that Ozark Briskow was compelled to sit out every alternate dance in a distressing condition of sobriety, he enjoyed himself, for he was playing host to the one woman and the one man for whom he cared most. He had dreaded meeting Gray, fearing the effect of an open confession, expecting opposition, but Gray was broad minded, he was a regular guy. In the relief of this hour, Buddy could have worshiped him except for the fact that he was too darned nice to Arline—nobody had the right to show her attentions as marked as his own—Gray was a man no woman could help loving—

Before long Buddy experienced a new sensation—jealousy. It was mild, to be sure, but it hurt a little.

Once Miss Montague's suspicions had been allayed, she, too, devoted herself to having a good time. She rather enjoyed Gray and her sense of victory over him. She retired to the ladies' room, finally, to powder her nose, and when she reappeared it was with added animation and with a new sparkle to her eyes. When next it came the elder man's turn to dance with her, he caught upon her breath a faint familiar odor, only half disguised by the peppermint lozenge that was dissolving upon her tongue, and he smiled. Evidently this charmer maintained herself in a state of constant preparedness, and her vanity bag hid secrets even from Buddy.

Where had he seen her? For the hundredth time he asked himself that question, for amid these hectic surroundings that first haunting suggestion of familiarity had become more pronounced. But patient delving into the dark corners of his memory was unavailing, and her conversation afforded him no clue.

As time passed the young woman made other trips to the dressing room, returning always with an access of brightness and a stronger breath; she assumed with Gray a coquetry which Buddy did not like. Buddy, indeed, strongly disapproved of it, but that only drove her to more daring lengths. She ventured, at last, to discuss the young millionaire with his friend.

"He's a dear boy, isn't he? And so innocent."

"He's learning."

"I'll say he is. He has learned a lot from me."

"'Delightful task, to rear the tender thought.' But aren't you afraid he'll learn, for instance, why you are eating peppermints?"

"Oho!" Gray's petite partner lifted her head and eyed him curiously. "Do you know why?"

"I have a suspicion," he said, with a smile, "that when a girl deliberately perfumes her breath it is in preparation for the struggle in the cab."

Miss Montague laughed unaffectedly. "Say! I could like you,

Mr. Wisenblum, in spite of the fact that I ought to hate you."

"Hate me? But why?"

"Why shouldn't I?"

"Because—I'm rather nice; I dance well."

"You are, and you do. You'd be a perfect dear if you'd only mind your own business. Buddy is of age, and you and I will get along like ham and eggs if you'll remember that."

CHAPTER XXI

"Why the SOS?" Mallow voiced this question as he entered Gray's hotel room early the following evening.

"I'm in a predicament and I hope you can help me," the latter explained. "I'm trying to remember something and I can't. I have a cold spot in my head."

Mallow deposited his bag with a sigh of relief. "Glad it's no worse. Anybody can cure a cold in the head."

"Sit down and light up while I tell you about it." In a few sentences Gray made known the story of Ozark Briskow's infatuation, and the reason for his own interest therein. "The woman is of the common 'get-rich-quick' variety," he concluded, "and she won't do."

"She didn't pull the family estate and her father's slaves and the orange grove on you, did she?"

"Oh no. She used that on Buddy and he believes it implicitly —so implicitly that she warned me to keep off the track. She showed her teeth, in a nice way. I've seen her somewhere; in some place where I should not have been. But where? It must have been in this country, too—not abroad—or I'd remember her."

"Maybe I haven't been as wild as you, Governor. This is a big country and I've missed a lot of disreputable joints."

The former speaker smiled. "You have trained yourself to remember faces, Mallow. Your researches—scientific researches, my dear Professor—have led you into quarters which I have never explored. I must identify this venturesome little gold digger without delay, for Buddy yearns to make her all his; matrimony is becoming the one object of his life."

"Why not let the poor carp have her? It's tough enough for a dame to get by since prohibition. I don't see how they make it, with everybody sober. Chances are she'd get the worst of the swap, at that."

"Not unlikely, but that is neither here nor there. Understand me, I'm no seraph; I pose as no model of rectitude, and, unfortunately for my peace of mind, Miss Montague is a really likable young person. But Buddy has a mother and a sister, and they hold me responsible for him. We three are dining downstairs in an hour; perhaps you could look in on us?"

"Sure. I'll give her the once over," Mallow agreed. "If she's anybody in our set, I'll know her."

The dinner had scarcely started when Gray heard his name paged and left the table. In the lobby Mallow was waiting with a grin upon his face.

"Is that her?" he inquired.

"That is the girl."

"*Girl?* 'Arline Montague,' eh? Her name is Margie Fulton and she had her hair up when they built the Union Pacific."

"Nonsense! You're mistaken. She can't be more than twenty-five—thirty at most."

"A woman can be as young as she wants to be if she'll pay the price. Margie had her face tucked up two years ago. Cost her five thousand bucks."

"I—can't believe it."

"You see it every day. Look at the accordion-pleated beauts in the movies. Why, some of those dolls nursed in the Civil War! Those face surgeons have ironed the wrinkles out of many a withered peach, and you're dining with Margie Fulton, the Suicide Blonde. I know her kid."

"Her *what?*" Mallow's hearer gasped.

"Sure. She was married to Bennie Fulton, the jockey, and they had a boy. Bennie was ruled off in New Orleans and started a gambling house."

"New Orleans! Wait—I'm beginning to remember."

Into Gray's mind came an indistinct memory; the blurred picture of a race track with its shouting thousands, a crowded betting ring; then, more clearly, a garish, over-furnished room in a Southern mansion; clouds of tobacco smoke rising in the cones of bright light above roulette and poker tables; negro servants in white, with trays; mint juleps in tall, frosted glasses; a pretty girl with straw-colored hair—"You're right!" he agreed, finally. "She was a 'come-on.'"

"That's her. She worked the betting ring daytimes and boosted in Bennie's place at night. Whenever she was caught she suicided. That's how she got her name."

"Just what do you mean by that?"

"Why, the usual stuff. A bottle of water with a poison label. If a mullet threatened to call the police, she'd cry, 'You have ruined my life!' Then with shaking hand she'd pull the old skull bottle and drink herself to death. Of course, the poor leaping tuna usually got the acid out of her hand in time to save her. She saw to that."

Gray was laughing silently. "My dear Professor," he confessed, "wisdom, of a sort, is mine; sometimes I grow weary with the weight of my experiences and wonder why the world so seldom shows me something new. But beside you I am as a babe. Tell me, what has become of the ex-jockey husband?"

"She divorced him. Mind you, Margie was square, like most of those 'come-ons.' She'd 'how dare' a guy that so much as looked at her. You know the kind I mean."

"And the child? Where do you suppose she keeps it?"

Mallow reflected. "The last time I saw the little cherub he was singing bass in a bellboys' quartette at Hot Springs. He hops bells at the Arlington summers and butchers peanuts at the track during the season—you know, hollers 'Here they come!' before they start, then when the women jump up he pinches the betting tickets out of their laps and cashes them with the bookies."

"Could you get hold of this—this boy basso and bring him here without letting him or his mother know?" "I can if he's still at Hot Springs, and I saw him there the last time I was up. The little darling got me into a crap game and ran in some shaped dice. Of course, it would cost something to get him."

"How much?"

Mallow "shot" his cuff and upon it gravely figured up the probable expense. "Well, there would be the fares and the eats and his bit—he wouldn't come for nothing. He'd gyp me for ten dollars, but he'd probably come for five. I'd offer him three—"

"There is a thousand dollars in it if you can produce him within the next forty-eight hours. I doubt my ability to sit on the safety valve much longer than that, for Buddy Briskow is rapidly breaking out with matrimonial measles. If I throw cold water on him it will only aggravate the disease."

"A thousand dollars!" Mallow cried. "Why, for a thousand berries I'll bring you his head on a platter. I'll car the little devil down and lock him in a suitcase." The speaker hesitated a moment before concluding. "It's a dirty trick on Margie, though."

"I know. But I'm thinking of Buddy. Now, in Heaven's name, hurry! My constitution may survive a few more road houses, but my reputation will not."

That night was a repetition of the one before, but with variations and with trimmings, for Buddy wore his "two-pint trousers" again, and this time they were loaded, hence Gray had a chance to observe him at his best—or worst. A little liquor went a long way with the boy; he derived much effect, many by-products, so to speak, from even a few drinks, and the elder man was forcibly reminded of Gus Briskow's statement that his son had a streak of the Old Nick in him. It was true; Buddy was indeed like a wild horse. Artificially stimulated, he became a creature of pure impulse, and those impulses ran the entire gamut of hilarity: he played the drum; he wrestled with a burly doorman; he yelled, whenever he found what he called a good "yelling place"; he demonstrated his ability to sing "Silver Threads Among the Gold" to the accompaniment of a four-piece orchestra energetically engaged in playing something quite modern and altogether different. These, and many other accomplishments equally unsuspected, he displayed. On the way from one lively resort to a livelier he conceived the unique idea that he could "swap ends" with his touring car in much the same manner that he could turn a nimble cow pony, and he tried it. Happily, the asphalt was wet, and in consequence the maneuver was not a total failure, although it did result in a crumpled mud guard and a runaway. Milk-wagon horses in Dallas, it appeared, were not schooled to the sight of spinning motor cars, and the phenomenon filled at least one with abysmal horror.

Gray felt sure that he had visibly aged as a result of that ride, and he began to understand why a new crop of wrinkles was appearing about the corners of Margie Fulton's eyes. No wonder she was beginning to look a trifle weary.

Fearing that Buddy was likely to turn sentimental without warning, the elder man monopolized as much of "Miss Montague's" time and attention as possible; he danced with her frequently, and he assiduously devoted himself to winning her favor. The result was a tribute to his acting and to his magnetism. In a moment of abandon she confided to him that she wished he had Buddy's money or—that he was a marrying man. Both of Buddy's flasks had been emptied by this time, however, so Gray was not unduly beguiled by this flattery.

On the whole, it was a horrible night.

As Gray languidly crept into bed about daylight he had the satisfaction of knowing that he had at least excited his young friend's open jealousy. That might act as a stay. On the other hand, of course, it might have directly the opposite effect—one could never tell—and it might be the part of wisdom, therefore, to gain possession of that diamond ring.

Buddy sought him out in the lobby, early the next afternoon, and after a colorless greeting, said, queerly, "Would you mind comin' up to my room for a minute?"

"Certainly not. I'd have looked in on you before this if I'd thought you were up." As the two mounted the wide marble stairs Gray went on, cheerfully: "Not looking your best this morn—afternoon, my lad. As for me, I am, in a manner of speaking, reborn. I have taken a new start. Careful reflection upon the providential outcome of that amazing skid has convinced me that whatever joys or sorrows assail me hereafter, however much or little of life is spared me, it will be all 'velvet.' A touch of mascaro about my temples and I shall look as young as I did yesterday. What are we going to do to-night?"

"I dunno."

Once inside his spacious suite, Buddy flung himself into a chair and with trembling fingers lit a cigarette. It was evident that he had something to say, but either dreaded saying it or knew not where to begin. His companion, meanwhile, pretended to look out upon the street below. In reality, he was observing the young giant. Poor Buddy! He was suffering.

The latter cleared his throat several times before he managed to say, "You don't want me to marry Arline, do you, Mr. Gray?"

"Frankly, my boy, I do not."

"Why?"

"There are many reasons."

"What's one?"

"I don't think you love her."

Briskow stirred. "Is that why you—went an' got that di'mon' ring I had made?" When this query met with a nod the young Texan's face flamed and his eyes glowed. "What in hell—" He swallowed his anger, rose to his feet and made a nervous circuit of the room before coming to a pause at Gray's side. His lips were working; there was a tragic, a piteous appeal in his eyes; his voice shook as he stammered: "I didn't mean to break out at you, Mr. Gray. I like you. Gee! I—You're kinda like God to me. I'd ruther be like you than—well, there ain't nobody I like like I like you—You could get her away from me if you wanted to, but—you wouldn't do a trick like that, would you? I was mighty happy till you came—You—got that ring with you?"

"I have it in my pocket."

"I want it." Buddy extended a quivering hand.

"Why?"

"I'm goin' to ask her to marry me, to-day. If she won't I'm goin' to—"

"She will."

Buddy gasped. "You *sure?*"

"I'm quite sure she would if you asked her. But I don't want you to ask her." When an expression of pained reproach leaped into the lad's face, the speaker explained, quickly: "Don't think for a moment that I care for her, nor that she has the slightest interest in me. It is you that I care for. What you just said pleased me, touched me. I wish you could understand how much I really do care for you, Buddy. Won't you wait—a few days, before you—"

"I *can't* wait."

"You must."

The men eyed each other steadily for a moment, then Buddy demanded, querulously, "What have you got against her, anyhow?"

"You wouldn't believe me if I told you."

"She told me everything there is to tell an' I told you. I don't care what she's done—if she ever done anything. She's had a hard time."

"Will you wait forty-eight hours?"

"No."

"Twenty-four?"

"Gimme that ring!" When Gray made no move the speaker ran on, excitedly: "I'm a man. I'm of age. It's none of your business what I do—nor Pa's or Ma's, either. It won't do no good for them to come."

Gray went to the door, locked it and pocketed the key. "Buddy"—his voice was firm, his face was set—"you are a man, yes, although you were only a boy a few weeks ago. You are going to act like a man, now."

"You goin' to try an' *hold* me here?" The inquiry was one of mingled astonishment and anger, for young Briskow could scarcely believe his eyes. "Don't do that, Mr. Gray. I— Nobody can't *make* me do anything. Please don't! That's plumb foolish."

"What if I told you that Miss Montague is—"

Buddy interrupted with a harsh cry. "Damn it! I said I wouldn't listen to anything against her. I'm tellin' you, again, keep your mouth shut about her." The youth's face was purple; he was trembling; his fists were clenched, and with difficulty he restrained even a wilder outburst. "You can have the ring, but—you lemme out of here, quick." When this command went unheeded he strode toward the bedroom, intending to use the other exit, but his caller intercepted him. "Lemme out!" the young man shouted.

"One of us is going to remain in this room, and I think it will be you." As Gray spoke he jerked off his coat and flung it aside. "Better strip, Buddy, if you mean to try it."

Buddy recoiled a step. Incredulously he exclaimed: "You—you wouldn't try *that*! This is my room. You must be crazy."

"I think I am, indeed, to endure what I have endured these last two days; to make myself ridiculous; to be humiliated; to risk my business ruin just to save a young fool from his folly." Impatience, resentment, anger were in the speaker's tone.

"I never ast you. You butted in—tried to cut me out. That's dirty. You was lyin' when you said—"

"Have it that way. I've run out of patience."

Ozark Briskow, too, had reached the limit of his endurance; he exploded. Momentarily he lost his head and cursed Gray vilely. For answer the latter moved close and slapped him across the mouth, saying: "Fight, you idiot!"

Buddy's low, gasping cry had the effect of a roar; it left the room echoing, then savagely he lunged at his assailant. He was blind, in him was a sudden maniacal impulse to destroy; he had no thought of consequences. Gray knocked him down.

It was a blow that would have felled an ox. As the youth lay half dazed, he heard the other taunting him, mocking him. "Get up, you lummox, and defend yourself. You'll be a man when I get through with you."

Codes of combat are peculiar to localities. In the north woods, for instance, lumberjacks fight with fist and heel; in the Southwest, when a man is mad enough to fight at all, he is usually mad enough to kill. As Buddy Briskow rose to his knees he groped for the nearest weapon, the nearest missile, something—anything with which to slay. His hand fell upon a heavy metal vase, and with this he struck wickedly as Gray closed with him. This time they went down together and rolled across the floor. The legs of a desk crashed and a litter of writing materials was spilled over them.

Gray was the first to regain his feet, but his shirt had been torn half off and he tasted blood upon his lips. He had met strong men in his time, but never had he felt such a rocklike mass of bone and muscle as now. Buddy was like a kicking horse; his fists were as hard as hoofs, and that which they smote they crushed or bruised or lacerated. He possessed now the supreme strength of a madman, and he was quite insensible to pain. He was uttering strange animal sounds.

"Shut up!" Gray panted. "Have the guts to—keep still. You'll —rouse the—"

He dodged an awkward swinging blow from the giant and sent him reeling. Buddy fetched up against the solid wall with a crash, for Gray had centered every pound of his weight behind his punch, but the countryman rebounded like a thing of rubber and again they clinched.

A room cluttered with heavy furniture is not like a boxing ring. In spite of Gray's skill and an agility uncommon in a man of his size, it was impossible to stop the other's rushes or to avoid them. Straining with each other they ricocheted against tables and chairs, and only the fact that much of the furniture was padded, and the floor thickly carpeted, prevented the sound of their struggle from alarming the occupants of the halls and the lobby. They fought furiously, moving the while like two wrestlers trying for flying holds; time and again they fell with first one on top and then the other; their flesh suffered and they grew bloody. The room soon became a litter, for its fittings were upset, flung about, splintered, as if the room itself had been picked up and shaken like a doll's house.

Gray managed to floor his antagonist whenever he had time and space in which to set himself, but this was not often, for Buddy closed with him at every opportunity. At such times it was the elder man who suffered most.

In a way it was an unequal struggle, for youth, ablaze with a holy fire, was matched against age, stiffened only by stubborn determination. Neither man longer had any compunctions; each fought with a ferocious singleness of purpose.

Buddy's face had been hammered to a pulp, but Gray was groaning; he could breathe only from the top of his lungs, and the bones of his left hand had been telescoped. Agonizing pains ran clear to his shoulder, and the hand itself was well-nigh useless.

It was an extraordinary combat; certainly the walls of this luxurious suite had never looked down upon a scene so strange as this fight between friends. How long it continued, neither man knew—not a great while, surely, measured by the clock; but an interminable time as they gauged it. Nor could Calvin Gray afterward recall just how it came to an end. He vaguely remembered Buddy Briskow weaving loosely, rocking forward upon uncertain legs, blindly groping for him—the memory was like that of a figure seen dimly through a mist of dreams— then he remembered calling up his last reserve of failing vigor. Even as he launched the blow he knew it was a knockout. The colossus fell, lay motionless.

It was a moment or two before Gray could summon strength to lend succor, then he righted an armchair and dragged Buddy into it. He reeled as he made for the bathroom, for he was desperately sick; as he wet a towel, meanwhile clinging dizzily to the faucet, his reflection leered forth from the mirror—a battered, repulsive countenance, shockingly unlike his own.

He was gently mopping young Briskow's face when the latter revived. Buddy's eyes were wild, he did not recognize this unpleasant stranger until a familiar voice issued from the shapeless lips.

"You'll be all right in a few minutes, my lad."

Briskow lifted his head; he tried to rise, but fell back limply, for as yet his body refused to obey his will.

"You—licked me," he declared, faintly. "Licked me good, didn't you?"

"*Buddy!* Oh, Buddy—" It was a yearning cry; Gray's streaked, swollen features were grotesquely contorted. "You won't be mad with me, will you?"

"Want to fight any more?"

The victor groaned. "My God, *no!* You nearly killed me."

This time Buddy managed to gain his feet. "Then I reckon I'll—go to bed. I feel purty rotten."

Gray laughed aloud, in his deep relief. "Righto! And after I've phoned for a doctor, if you don't mind, I'll crawl in with you."

CHAPTER XXII

On the morning after the fight Mallow knocked at Gray's door, then in answer to an indistinct and irritable command to be gone, he made himself known.

"It's me, Governor. And I've got Exhibit A."

"Really?" came the startled query. There was a stir from within, the lock snapped and the door opened.

"I've got a little friend here that I want you to—" Mallow paused inside the threshold, his mouth fell open, he stared in frank amazement. "Sweet spirits of niter!" he gasped. "What happened to *you?*"

"I was playing tag in the hall with some other old men, and one of them struck me."

"My God, you're a sight!" Mallow remained petrified. "I never saw a worse mess."

"Come in and close the door. I am vain, therefore I have a certain shyness about exposing my beauty to the curious gaze. Pardon me if I seat myself first; I find it more comfortable to sit than to stand, to recline than to sit." Stiffly the speaker let himself into an upholstered divan and fitted the cushions to his aches and his pains, his bruises and his abrasions. He sighed miserably. His features were discolored, shapeless; his lips were cut; strips of adhesive tape held the edges of a wound together;

his left hand was tightly bandaged and the room reeked with the odor of liniment.

"You've been hit with a safe, or something," Mallow declared. "Evidences of some blunt instrument, as the newspapers say; maybe a pair of chain tongs."

"Blunt and heavy, yes. Buddy Briskow and I had an argument—"

"That big bum? Did he lay it on you like that? Say, he's got the makings of a champ!"

"Pride impels me to state that he got the worst of it. He is scarcely presentable, while I—"

"Your side won?"

"It did. Now, where is the boy?"

"He's outside." Without shifting his astonished gaze, Mallow raised his voice and cried, "Hey, Bennie!" The door opened, a trim, diminutive figure entered. "Bennie, mit my friend Colonel Gray."

The youngster, a boy of indeterminate age, advanced and shook hands. There was no mistaking him; he was Margie Fulton's son in size, in coloring, in features. "I told Bennie you could use a bright kid about his age. And he's bright."

It required no clever analysis of the lad to convince Gray that he was indeed bright, as bright—and as hard—as a silver dollar. He had a likable face, or it would have been likable had it been in repose. It was twitching now, and Gray said, with a smile, "Go ahead and laugh, son."

The urchin's lips parted in a wide grin, and he spoke for the first time. "Did the Germans do that?" The effect of his voice was startling, for it was deep and husky; it was the older man's turn to be astonished.

"He could pass for fifteen on the street," Mallow said; "but when he talks I chalk him down for thirty-five. How old are you, Ben?"

"Seventeen. What's the big idea, anyhow?" The question was directed impudently at the occupant of the divan. "Did you send all the way to Hot Springs to get a guy you can lick?"

"Your mother is here in Dallas, my boy."

"Yeah?" There was a pause. "How's it breaking for her?"

"Um-m, very well. I thought she'd like to see you."

Bennie cocked his head, he eyed the speaker curiously, suspiciously. "Come clean," he rumbled. "Mallow said you could use me." "I can. I will." The boy shrugged. "All right, Sharkey. I s'pose it'll come out, in time. Only remember, I've got twenty coming, win or lose."

"Of course" Gray waved toward the dresser, upon which was a handful of bills. "Help yourself. Better make it twenty-five. Then wait outside, please. We will join you in a few minutes."

"And don't make it thirty," Bennie's traveling companion sharply cautioned.

When the door had closed, Gray gave his friend certain instructions, after which he limped to the telephone and called Arline Montague. "May I ask you to step down to Buddy's room?" he inquired, after making himself known. "Oh, it will be quite all right—We three must have a little talk—But he *couldn't* see you last night. He was quite ill, really; I sat up with him most of—" There was a longer hiatus then. "Hadn't we better argue that in Buddy's presence? Thank you. In five minutes, then."

As he and Gray prepared to leave, Mallow said, sourly: "Margie is a good little dame, in her way, and I feel like a—like a damned'stool.'"

"My dear fellow," the other told him, "I understand, and I'd gladly take another beating like this one to escape this wretched denouement."

When Ozark Briskow answered Gray's request for admittance, he was deeply embarrassed to find Miss Montague also waiting; his stammered protest was interrupted by her sharp inquiry:

"What is the meaning of all this mystery? He said you were too sick to see me."

"Permit me to explain," Gray began, as he closed the door behind them. "Buddy and I came to blows over you; you were, in a manner of speaking, an apple of discord between us, and the melancholy results you behold. Jealousy of your charms was not my motive; I merely asked Buddy to defer a contemplated action. He refused; I insisted. Argument failed to budge either of us and—"

The young woman's sympathetic regard of Gray's victim changed to a glare of hostility as she turned upon the speaker, crying: "You *brute!* You ought to be arrested!"

"He ast me to wait, Arline—"

"To delay asking you a question which I felt should be more seriously considered. In the absence of his family I took it upon myself to—"

"To butt in!" Miss Montague exclaimed, with curling lip.

"Quite so. I merit your disapproval, but not your disdain."

With some heat Buddy declared: "Pa an' Ma know that I got a

mind of my own. It won't do 'em any good to come."

"See here," the woman demanded. "What have you been telling Buddy about me? I told him all there was to tell."

"Quite all? I fear you have not been as frank as you would have me believe. That, in fact, explains my connection with the affair. Believe me when I say that I am interested only in seeing justice done to both of you young people, and in making sure that you do not deceive each other. It is an impulse of artless youth to trick itself in glowing colors, but you should know the whole truth about Buddy and he about you. If, after you are thoroughly acquainted with each other, you still maintain a mutual regard I shall have nothing further to say—except to beg that I be allowed to show my true friendship for both of you."

"Well, spring the bad news," said Miss Montague. Briskow now displayed the first open resentment he had shown since his defeat of the day before. "You licked me, Mr. Gray, an' I took my medicine," he growled. "You changed my looks, but you didn't change my mind. I'm waitin' for the folks to come, but I ain't goin' to listen to 'em."

"Let him get this off his chest, Buddy. Go ahead with the scandal, Saint Anthony."

Gray bowed. "Suppose we ignore the early convent training and the Old Kentucky Home and agree that they are pleasant fictions, like the estate which you are in such imminent danger of inheriting. Those, I'm sure you will admit, are entirely imaginary." Buddy Briskow's swollen eyelids opened wider, his tumid lips parted, and an expression of surprise spread over his dropsical countenance.

"Step on it," sneered Miss Montague. "Dish the dirt!"

"Buddy's belief, however, that your stage career was blasted and your young life laid waste by the scion of a rich New York house should, in the interests of truth, be corrected."

"He knows I was married."

"True. But not to Bennie Fulton, the jockey."

"That is a—lie!"

"Nor that the estimable Mr. Fulton, instead of perishing upon the field of glory, dodged the draft and is doing as well as could be expected of a jockey who has been ruled off every track in the country, and is now a common gambler against whom the finger of suspicion is leveled—"

"It's a lie!" the woman stormed. Of Buddy she inquired: "You don't believe that, do you? You don't intend to listen to that sort of stuff?"

The object of this appeal was torn by conflicting emotions. Doubt is a weed that sprouts fastest in dull minds; suspicion is the ready armor of ignorance; to young Briskow came the unwelcome vision of those oil wells. Was Gray telling the truth? Could it be that Arline had made a fool of him? But no, she was smaller, prettier, more adorable than ever, now that she was whipped by this gale of anger, and a girl like that could not be a deceiver. Buddy longed desperately to believe her refutation of the charge. He closed his eyes and made himself believe.

"Even now," Gray was saying, "if you would tell the boy all he ought to know, I would take myself off and have nothing more to say."

"You-you make me *sick!*" Miss Montague cried, vibrantly. "What right have *you* to preach? What kind of a man are you? If he believed your lies for a minute I'd never want to see him again. He has been a true friend to me"—her voice quavered, caught in her throat—"the only true friend I ever had. *I* don't care whether he's rich or poor, but men like you are all alike.

What chance has a girl got against you? You want to use his money, so you p-poison his mind—break a woman's heart—just b-because you—hate me." The last words were sobbed forth. Miss Montague broke down.

"Hell!" hoarsely exclaimed young Briskow. "You're makin' her cry!"

Gray sighed; he stepped to the door, opened it and called, "Come in, both of you."

Arline Montague's shoulders ceased to shake, she lifted her blond head alertly. Then she uttered a breathless exclamation.

Buddy, meanwhile, had been staring at the door, and he was surprised when, instead of his family, he saw entering a strange man and a boy small of stature but old of face, a boy insouciant, impudent, swaggering. It was this boy who spoke first.

"Hello, momma!" he cried.

At sound of that voice Buddy recoiled, for it was deeper than his own. His expression of dismay was no doubt ludicrous, at any rate the urchin's lively eyes leaped to his face and remained there, while a grin spread over his features.

"Hully Gee!" rumbled the lad. "Here's *another* one that ought to be buried!"

"Mrs. Fulton"—it was Gray speaking—"I took the liberty of asking your son—"

Buddy Briskow heard no more, for his ears were roaring. Her son! That voice! Being little more than a boy himself, nothing could have hurt him more cruelly than this; his impulse was to flee the room, for his world had come down in crashing ruin. She *had* lied! She *had* made a fool of him. Gray had been right. The others were still talking when Buddy broke in faintly. His battered visage was white, his lips were colorless. "I reckon this—ends my part of the entertainment," said he. Slowly he seated himself and bowed his head in his hands, for he had become quite ill.

Arline Montague—Margie Fulton—once the blow had fallen, behaved rather well; she took Bennie in her arms and kissed him, then in answer to his quick look of dismay at her agitation, she patted him on the shoulder and said: "It's all right, son. You didn't know."

"Didn't know what?" demanded the lad. "Say—" He stared angrily from one face to another. "Is it a plant?"

"Hush! You wouldn't understand."

Bennie's suspicions now were in full play, and his gaze came to rest upon Calvin Gray; his eyes began to blaze. "You—you big bum!" he cried. "I might have known you were a double-crosser."

"Hush, Bennie, please!"

"I'll get you for this." The midget was quivering with rage. "You'll look worse 'n that, you—you big bum!"

"Take my key. Here!" The mother thrust her room key into the boy's hand. "Run along. I—I'll see you in a few minutes." To Mallow she said: "Take him out, please. You brought him."

Mallow, flushing uncomfortably, took Bennie by the wrist and dragged him to the door.

"Dirty work!" said the woman, when the two had gone. Her eyes were dark with anger as she stared at Gray.

"It must look so to you," he agreed. "Frankly, I didn't enjoy it."

"Bah!" Margie turned to Briskow, but in his attitude, his averted gaze, she read the doom of her hopes. One final chance remained, however, and desperately she snatched at it. "Buddy!" she cried. "*Buddy!*" Her voice was poignant as she pleaded. "I couldn't tell you the truth. I wanted to—I laid awake nights trying to get the courage, but I was afraid you wouldn't understand. I'd have told you the whole thing, if you'd ever given me the chance. You know I've been married; does it make so much difference that I have a son?" When the object of her appeal only stirred, she went on, reproachfully: "Are you going to allow this—this man to—come between us?"

"I wouldn't believe you now, if—" Buddy choked. "I'm through!"

"You mean that?" The young fellow nodded. "Very well!" Something in the tone of the last words, some accent of desperation, caused Buddy to raise his head. He was in time to see Margie fumble with her purse and extract something therefrom; to Buddy's eyes it resembled a bottle. "There is no use fighting any more. You have ruined my life."

"My God!" young Briskow yelled, in dismay. "Don't do that! Stop her!" He leaped to his feet and lunged for the poison vial which was trembling upon Arline's lips. Gray, too, had been galvanized into action, but of an unexpected nature; he grappled with Buddy and held him. "Look out!" the latter gasped. "She's killin' herself." The Texan was weak with horror; he could only paw impotently at his captor and cry: "Arline! You wouldn't do *that?* For *me?* Lemme go. Arline—"

"This is the end," moaned the woman, still holding the bottle to her lips. Her despair was tragic; nevertheless, she did not instantly hurl herself into the hereafter. This hesitation at meeting death was only natural, perhaps, for none but the bravest can leap into the unknown without a moment of farewell.

"Drink hearty!" Gray exclaimed, over his shoulder, meanwhile closing tighter his embrace of the terrified youth.

Buddy's struggles suddenly ceased, for at last the bottle had been drained; the girl was groping blindly toward the nearest chair.

"God'lmighty! You let her do it!" he cried, hoarsely. "You—you *murderer*! We—we gotta get a doctor, quick."

"Nonsense! Water won't hurt her; and that's all it is. She's known as 'the Suicide Blonde.'"

"Say! You're bursting with information, aren't you?" It was Miss Montague, tottering upon the brink of the grave, who voiced this explosive inquiry. Her drooping shoulders straightened, she raised her head and flung the empty bottle violently from her. Her face was deathly white, to be sure, but not with darting agonies. "You know *everything*, don't you? You make plain the past, the present, and the future. Well, Madame Thebes, you're under the wire with the horseshoe on your neck." With head erect and with firm tread she moved to the door; she turned there and blazed forth in bitter scorn, her bobbed curls shaking as she spoke: "Take that selling plater back to the car barn, where he belongs. I'm off boobs for life. I knew you had a jinx on me the minute I saw you, for I broke my mirror the day you breezed in. Seven years bad luck? My God, you're all of that and more! Why, you'd bring bad luck to a church! I'll beat it now while you give little Rollo his bottle and rock him to sleep. If he cries, tell me and—and I'll furnish the rock."

The door slammed to behind the diminutive fury, and Gray sank feebly into a chair. He was laughing silently.

"By Jove! She's splendid!" he chuckled. "Buddy, I—I like that woman."

It was midforenoon of the next day. Mrs. Fulton, after a

restless night, was packing her trunks; her room was in disarray, what with open suitcases and piles of dresses, lingerie, shoes and the like strewn carelessly about. She had halted her labors for a second time to scan a brief note that had arrived a few moments before and ran as follows:

DEAR MRS. FULTON,—I am not really such a bad sort as you consider me, and I'm genuinely interested in that boy of yours. Let's cry quits and have a serious talk about him and—perhaps other things.

Sincerely yours,

CALVIN GRAY. She was thus engaged when there came a knock, and in answer to her voice the writer entered.

"Thank you for letting me come up," he began. "I'm becoming accustomed to dodging chambermaids and scurrying up back stairs. But I'm looking better, don't you think?"

"There's only one way you'd look better to me," the woman said, unsmilingly, "and that is laid out."

"Please put me at my ease. I am physically sore and mentally distressed."

"*You* sore, distressed! Humph! I wouldn't have consented to see you except for what Mallow told me. After what he said I'd like to give you a piece of my mind. What right have *you* doing a thing like this? Do you know what I think of you?"

"I do. Also what Mallow thinks of me, for he told me. You see, he believes firmly that I am a—well, a person of much looser principles than I really am, and my protestations of honesty only excite his veiled derision."

"He says he's sorry. Sorry! After spilling the beans."

"Mrs. Fulton, I have learned that life is a mixed affair, and that most of our actions are the results of conflicting motives. Yes, and that we ourselves are products of conflicting forces, good and evil. Few of us are as good as we would like to have people believe nor as bad as we appear. I wonder if you will believe me when I say that I—like you."

"Certainly not."

"Nevertheless, I do. For one thing, you are a good fighter and a good loser. I try to be, but I fear I lack your spirit. I would not have hurt you willingly."

The woman tossed her head and turned away; when she spoke, it was wearily: "I might have known I couldn't make the jump. I never did win a big race. A good loser, eh? Well, I've had enough practice at it. How is Buddy? Hurt, I suppose. His young life is blasted; he'll never trust another woman."

"He is standing it pretty well, and is greatly cheered by the fact that he can see out of his left eye practically as well as ever. He is going back to the oil fields and learn the business. I am going to put him to work. What are you going to do with Bennie?"

"Do with him? What can I do with him?"

"He is a bright boy."

"I'm bright, too, but I have all I can do to get by."

"It is a shame to think he will grow up into what his father was."

Margie Fulton wheeled and her blue eyes were dark. "I suppose you think I'm a bad mother. But what do you know about it? How do you know what I've gone through for him; the sacrifices I've made? I've made plenty and they came hard."

"I'd like to help you make a man of him."

"What? *You?* How?"

"I'd like to put him in business and teach him that there is no profit in short-changing customers; that the real wise guy isn't the fellow who gets the best of every bag of peanuts, but the one who can go back to the same customer and sell him another bag. The abstract principle has been put much more succinctly, but I doubt if it would carry the same weight with him. I'd enjoy giving the boy a hand up, but—he is more than I'd care to tackle alone."

"There's Mallow to help you. He'd be a refining influence." The mother's lip curled.

"How about you?"

"Me?"

"Isn't the—sort of life you are living becoming a bit tiresome? Aren't you about fed up on uncertainties?" The object of these queries drew a deep breath; her eyelids flickered, but she continued to stare at the speaker. "Worry brings deeper wrinkles than old age. Wouldn't you like to tie to something solid and be able to show Bennie that you are, at heart, the sort of woman I consider you? He'll soon be getting old enough to wonder if you are what he thinks you are or if—" "I suppose you learned this—bayonet practice in the army," Mrs. Fulton said, hoarsely.

"Anybody can make a good living in a country like this if he cares enough to try. I'll back you if you need money."

"And—what's the price?"

"My price? Oh, I'd feel well repaid if some day Bennie acknowledged that I was a 'regular guy,' and if you agreed."

"Is that all?"

"Quite all. Is there something you do—well?"

"I can cook. I'm a good cook. Women like me usually have hobbies they never can follow—and I have two. I can make a fool of a stove, and I—I can design children's clothes, wonderful things, new things—"

"Will you come to Wichita Falls and start a restaurant and make good things to eat, if I supply the money and the customers?"

"*Will* I?" The speaker's face had flushed, her eyes had begun to sparkle. "Then it's a bargain," Gray declared, gayly. "Why, you'll get rich, for it is the chance of a lifetime. I'll guarantee patronage; I'll drum up trade if I have to turn sandwich man and ring a bell. Leave the details to me."

Margie Fulton sank slowly into the nearest chair, regardless of the fact that it was piled full of lacy, white, expensive things; her voice quavered, broke, as she said: "Gee, Mr. Gray! I figured there must be some decent men in the world, but—I never thought I'd meet one."

CHAPTER XXIII

In a long, relentless struggle between two men psychology may play a part as important as in a campaign between two opposing armies, or so at least Calvin Gray believed. That, in fact, was one of his pet theories and from the first he had planned to test it. It was characteristic of Henry Nelson, on the other hand, that he put no faith whatever in "imponderables," hence Gray's reference to morale, on that day of their first meeting, had amused him. Morale, indeed! As if a man of his tough fiber could be affected by the mere chanting of a Hymn of Hate! He considered himself the captain of his soul, and the antics of a malicious enemy, the wild waving of false danger signals, instead of distracting a resolute mariner, would merely cause him to steer a truer course.

But Nelson was a brooder. Time came when doubts distressed him, when he began to put faith in "malicious animal magnetism" and, despite his better sense, to wonder if some evil spell really had not been put upon him.

In his arrogance it had seemed at first a simple matter to do away with Gray. That had been mistake number one. The miserable breakdown of that plan, the refusal of his hireling to go forward, and the impossibility of securing a trustworthy substitute convinced him finally that he had erred grievously in his method. Some men are invulnerable to open attack, and Gray, it seemed, had been wet in the waters of the Styx. No, that had been a bad beginning and Nelson regretted it, for he feared it had served as a warning.

So, indeed, it appeared, for not long thereafter he actually felt, or thought he felt, the vengeful claws of his enemy. A new strike in one of the western counties had become public, and a brand-new oil excitement was born overnight. Trains were crowded, roads were jammed with racing automobiles; in the neighborhood of the new well ensued scenes to duplicate those of other pools. For the first week or two there was a frenzy of buying and selling, a speculation in oil acreage and town lots.

The Nelsons, of course, were early on the ground, for in spite of the father's contention that they could ill afford, at the moment, to tie up more money in unproductive properties, the son had argued that they must have "protection," and his arguments had prevailed.

Henry went in person, and he was disagreeably surprised to discover Gray on the ground ahead of him. The latter bore evidences of hard usage in the shape of a black eye and numerous bandages, reputed to be the result of an automobile collision. Henry regretted that his enemy's injuries were so trivial. It was indeed a pity that so few accidents are fatal.

He bought rapidly, right and left, as much to forestall Gray as anything else, and he was back at the bank shortly with a number of leases. Not until some time later did he learn that he had paid a price for them twice as high as that charged for properties closer in.

It was Bell who brought this unwelcome information home to him—brought it home in his characteristic manner.

"What the hell ails you, anyhow?" the father inquired, in apoplectic wrath. "Have you gone clean crazy?"

After some inquiry Henry realized what ailed him and who had caused him to throw away his money, but he did not apprise Bell. More than once they had been parties to "wash sales," and had helped to establish artificial values, but to be victimized in the same manner was like the taste of poison.

Of course, it meant little in the big game. At most, the firm had been "gypped" only a comparatively few thousand dollars, and the loss could probably be recouped by a resale; nevertheless, the incident was significant, and, upon second thought, it appeared to shed light upon certain other expensive transactions in other fields.

Now, oddly enough, this new oil discovery did not develop as had been expected—in fact, the excitement died out quickly— and when Henry Nelson undertook to dispose of his holdings he was faced by a heavy loss, for Gray was offering adjoining acreage at low prices.

Following this unhappy experience, the scandal about the Jackson well became public—the Atlantic Company having at last located the leak in its pipe line—and the whole Red River district enjoyed a great laugh. Henry Nelson did not laugh. He turned green when he realized how close he had come to buying that lease. Of course, here was a swindle that Gray could have had nothing to do with, and yet—Nelson wondered why "Bob" Parker had failed to sell it to him. "Bob" had tied it upon an option, awaiting his return, and he had hurried back on purpose to examine it. Why hadn't he bought it? Henry asked that question of the girl, and, when she told him as much as she knew, he began to believe that the whole thing was, indeed, an incredibly bold attempt to swindle him, and him alone.

Miss Parker, of course, was deeply chagrined at her connection with the fraud; nevertheless, the banker felt his flesh turn cold at the narrowness of his escape. He assured himself, upon calmer thought, that his imagination was running away with him; this was too devilishly ingenious, too crooked! And besides, Gray had promised to fight fair. All the same, the thing had a suspicious odor, and Nelson slept badly for a few nights. He decided to use extra caution thereafter and see that he neither paid more for leases than they were worth nor permitted anybody to "salt" him. Salting, after all, was rare; one read about it in books, but no experienced operator had ever been fooled in that way.

About this time a big gasser blew in north of the Louisiana fields, and wise oil men began to talk about Arkansas and quietly to gather in acreage. Less than a week later one of Nelson's field men brought into the bank a youth who owned some property in the latter state. This yokel was a sick man; he was thin and white; he had a racking cough, and he knew nothing about oil except from hearsay. All he knew was that he would die if he didn't get to a warmer, drier climate; but the story he told caused Henry Nelson to stare queerly at his field man. That very night the latter left town.

On the third night thereafter, in answer to a telegram, Nelson and the Arkansas farmer slipped unobtrusively out of Wichita Falls. It so happened that Brick Stoner, en route to Hot Springs for a little rest, was a passenger on the same train.

Stoner returned in due time, much rested, and he brought with him a large check to the firm's account.

"We timed it to the minute," he told McWade and Mallow. "That gasser couldn't have come in better if we'd ordered it. Nelson's dickering under cover for more acreage near what he's got, but I tipped off who he was."

"He fell easy, eh?"

Stoner grinned. "He was so pleased with himself at swindling an invalid, and so scared somebody would discover those seepages that he couldn't hardly wait to sign up. If it hadn't of been for the general excitement, he might of insisted on time to do some exploring, but he's pulled a rig off another job and he's sending it right up."

"We've got some good news, too," McWade asserted. "Avenger Number One is trying hard to come in."

"No?"

"I tell you Gray's got a rabbit foot. If we continue to trail along with him, I'll be losing you as a partner, Brick."

"How so?"

"Why, I'll be turning honest. It seems to pay."

"Um-m. Probably I'd better keep all this Nelson money and leave you—"

"Oh, not at all," the junior partner said, quickly. "That isn't an oil deal, strictly speaking, for you say there ain't oil enough on the land to grease a jackknife. I look on it as a real-estate speculation."

With a laugh Stoner accepted this explanation, and then announced that he was hungry for his breakfast.

This time Mallow spoke up. "I'm bally-hooing for a new joint; Fulton's Fancy Waffle Foundry. Follow me and I'll try to wedge you in. But you'll have to eat fast and pick your teeth on the sidewalk, for we need the room." In answer to Stoner's stare, the speaker explained his interest in the welfare of Wichita Falls's newest eating place, and en route thereto he told how Margie Fulton came to be running it. "Gray did it. He got the Parker girl to help us, and we had the place all fixed up by the time Margie got here. She's tickled pink, and it'll coin money—if it isn't pinched."

"Pinched?"

"Sure! Bennie's the cashier, and he palms everything from dimes to dishtowels. Force of habit! Better count your change till I break him of short-changing the customers."

"*You*—" Stoner stopped in his tracks.

"Oh, I'm giving him lessons in elemental honesty."

"My God! Are you turning honest, too?" the other man exclaimed. "Seems like that's all I hear lately."

It was a blue day for Henry Nelson when Avenger Number One came in, for it made necessary immediate drilling operations on his part. And the worst of it was the well was not big enough to establish a high value for his holdings. It was just enough of a producer to force him to begin three offsets and that, for the moment, was an undertaking decidedly inconvenient.

Bell Nelson was even more dismayed at the prospect than was his son, for upon him fell the necessity of raising the money. "Hell of a note," the old fellow grumbled, "when a wet well puts a crimp in us! A little more good luck like this and we'll go broke." "We can't afford to let go, or to sub-lease—"

"Of course not, after the stand we've taken. There's talk on the street about the bank, now, and—I'd give a good deal to know where it comes from." The junior Nelson had heard similar echoes, but he held his tongue. "I never did like your way of doing business," the speaker resumed, fretfully. "We've overreached. You wanted it all and—this is the result."

Now Henry Nelson was warranted in resenting this accusation, for it had ever been Bell's way to pursue a grasping policy, therefore he cried, angrily:

"That's right; pass the buck. You know you wouldn't listen to anything else. If we're in deep, you're more to blame than I."

"Nothing of the sort." Old Bell began a profane denial, but the younger man broke in, irritably:

"I've never won an argument with you, so have it your own way. But while you're raising money for the Avenger offsets, you'd better raise plenty, for Gray is going to punch holes down as fast as ever he can."

"Who is this Gray? What's he got against you?"

Henry's eyes shifted. "Has he got anything against me? He bought a good lease and was wise enough to get somebody to make a well for him—"

"Those crooks! Those wildcatters!"

"Now, he proposes to develop his acreage as rapidly as possible. Nothing strange about that, is there?"

"Is he sore at you?"

"We didn't get along very well in France."

"Humph! I suppose that means you fought like hell. And now he's getting even. By the way, where am I going to get this money?"

"That is up to you," said Henry, with a disagreeable grin, whereupon his father stamped into his own office in a fine fury.

Not long after this father and son quarreled again, for of a sudden a perfect avalanche of lawsuits was released, the mysterious origin and purpose of which completely mystified Old Bell. The Nelsons, like everybody else, had unsuccessfully dabbled in oil stocks and drilling companies for some time before the boom started, also during its early stages, and most of those failures had been forgotten. They were painfully brought to mind, however, when Henry was served with a dozen or more citations, and when inquiry elicited the reluctant admission from the bank's attorney that a genuine liability existed—a liability which included the entire debts of those defunct joint-stock associations in which he and his father had invested. This was enough to enrage a saint.

Henry argued that he had invariably signed those articles of association with the words, in parentheses, "No personal liability," and he was genuinely amazed to learn that this precaution had been useless. He protested that scores—nay, hundreds—of other people were in the same fix as he, and that if this outrageous provision of the law were strictly enforced and judgments rendered widespread ruin would result. His lawyer agreed to this in all sympathy, but read aloud the provisions of the statute, and Nelson derived no comfort from the reading. The lawyer was curious to know, by the way, who had taken the trouble to acquire all of these claims—a task of heroic size—but about all the encouragement he could offer was the probability of a long and expensive series of legal battles, the outcome of which was problematical. That meant annoyance, at best, and a possible impairment of credit, and the Nelson credit right now was a precious thing, as Henry well knew. Eloquently he cursed the day he had met Calvin Gray. What next, he wondered.

He discovered what next when the driller he had sent up to Arkansas in charge of his rig one day came into the office in great agitation. The man's story caused his employer's face to whiten.

"*Salted!* I—don't believe it." Nelson seized his head in his hands. "Oh, my God!" he gasped. Misfortunes were coming with a swiftness incredible. Salted! Victimized, like the greenest tenderfoot! A small fortune sunk while the whole country was still chuckling over the Jackson scandal! This *was* a nightmare.

Henry was glad that his father was in Tulsa in conference with some other bankers over that Avenger offset money, otherwise there was no telling to what extreme the old man's rage would have carried him at this final calamity. And that whining, coughing crook, that bogus farmer, was in Arizona—or elsewhere—out of reach of the law! The younger Nelson turned desperately sick. If this was not more of Gray's work, it was the direct result of the curse he had called down.

"Does anybody know?" Henry inquired, after he had somewhat recovered his equilibrium.

"Nobody but us fellows."

"You—you mustn't shut down. You've got to keep up the bluff until—until I get time to turn."

"You going to bump off that land to somebody else?"

"What do you think I'm going to do?" Nelson was on his feet now and pacing his office with jerky strides. "Take a loss like that?" He paused and glared at the bearer of bad tidings, then growled: "What are you grinning about? Oh, you needn't say it. You want yours, eh? Is that it?"

"Well—it's worth something to turn a trick like this."

"How much?"

"It's a big deal. It'll take something substantial—something substantial and paid in advance—to make our boys forget all the interesting sights they've seen. But I'd rather leave the amount to you, Henry. You know me; I wouldn't be a party to a crooked deal, not for anything, except to help you out—"

"How much?" the banker repeated, hoarsely.

But the field man merely smiled and shrugged, so, with a grunt of understanding, Henry seated himself and wrote out a check to bearer, the amount of which caused him to grind his teeth.

Now it was impossible to dispose of a large holding like that Arkansas tract at a moment's notice. In order to evade suspicion, it was necessary to go about it slowly, tactfully, hence the financier moved with as much circumspection as possible. His careful plans exploded, however, when he met Calvin Gray a day or so later.

Gray had made it an invariable practice to speak affably to his enemy in passing, mainly because it so angered the latter; this time he insisted upon stopping. He was debonair and smiling, as always, but there was more than a trace of mockery in his tone as he said:

"So your luck has changed, hasn't it? That Avenger well of mine has put a good value on your property. I congratulate you, Colonel."

"Humph! I don't believe in luck," Nelson mumbled. "And the Avenger isn't enough of a well to brag about."

"So? You don't believe in luck? It seems to be our lot invariably to differ, doesn't it? Now, my dear Colonel, I'm not ashamed to confess that I am deeply superstitious, and that I believe implicitly in signs and prodigies. You see, I was born under a happy star; 'at my nativity the front of heaven was full of fiery shapes,' as it were. Comfortable feeling, I assure you. Take that incident at New-town, not long ago; doesn't that prove my contention?"

"What incident?"

Gray's brows lifted whimsically. "Of course. How should you know? There was a clumsy attempt to do me bodily harm, to—assassinate me. Funny, isn't it? So ill considered and so impracticable.—But about this Avenger matter, if you find it inconvenient to offset my wells as fast as I put them down, perhaps you'd consider selling—"

"*Inconvenient?*" Nelson felt the blood rush to his face at this insufferable insult, but he calmed himself with the thought that his opponent was deliberately goading him. After all, it served him right for permitting the fellow to stop him. "Inconvenient! Ha!" He turned away carelessly.

"No offense, my dear Colonel. I thought, after your Arkansas fiasco, you might wish—"

"What Arkansas fiasco?" Nelson wheeled, and in spite of himself his voice cracked.

"Ah! Another secret, eh?" Gray winked elaborately—nothing could have been more deliberately offensive than that counterfeit of a friendly understanding. "Very well, I sha'n't say a word."

"You—" The banker was gasping. "You're doing your damnedest to—to start something, aren't you?"

"Every day. Every hour. Every minute." The speaker bowed. "In defense of my promise to fight fair, let me assure you, however, that I did not start this. As a matter of fact, I knew nothing about it until you had been hooked. Apropos of that quixotic promise, please remember that your own actions have absolved me from it."

The men stared at each other for a moment that seemed interminable. Gray was watchful, expectant; Nelson was plainly shaken by a desire so desperate that resistance left him weak. He was like an animal frozen in the very attitude of springing.

"Foxy, aren't you?" he managed to say, at last. "Tempting me to—make the first move." With a mighty effort of will he forced his tense body to relax. "The act of a bully! Bah! Wouldn't I be a fool—"

"A bully is usually a coward," Gray said, slowly. "Neither of us is a coward. I'm not ready to—join the issue that way, especially in a place like this. The game is too exciting to—"

"You'll get all the excitement you're looking for," Nelson cried, wrathfully. "You've cost me a lot of money, but you could have cost me a lot more if you hadn't been fool enough to brag about it and give me warning. Now—I'll send you out of Texas afoot."

"On my back, perhaps, but never on my feet."

Without another word the banker passed on, but he went

blindly, for his mind was in black chaos. No chance now for secrecy; he was in for a bit of hell. He managed to kill the story in the local papers, but it appeared in the Dallas journals, which was even worse, and for the first time in his life he found himself an object of ridicule. The Arkansas transaction was made to appear the most outrageous swindle of recent oil history, and, coming so quickly after the Jackson exposure, it excited double interest and amusement.

In truth, the facts about the salting of that Arkansas tract did make a story, for the methods employed had been both new and ingenious. Nelson had been fooled by a showing of oil in an ordinary farm well, and by a generous seepage into a running stream some distance away. Not until a considerable sum had been spent in actual drilling operations, however, did those seepages diminish sufficiently to excite suspicion sufficiently, in fact, to induce the crew to pump the water well dry. This done, an amazing fraud had been discovered. It had been found that the vendor of the land had removed the rock curbing and behind it had packed a liberal quantity of petroleum-soaked cotton waste. Naturally, when the well had been walled up again and permitted to resume its natural level, the result was all that the unscrupulous owner could have expected.

The creek seepage had turned out to be equally counterfeit, but even more ingeniously contrived. It had manifested itself where a stratum of clean white sand, underlaid with clay, outcropped at the foot of a high bank. In the undergrowth, quite a way back from the stream, tardy investigation disclosed that a hole had been dug down to that layer of sand and into the hole had been poured several barrels of "crude." The earth from the digging had been removed and the hole had been cunningly covered up. Naturally, the oil from this reservoir had followed the sand stratum and—the resultant phenomenon at the water's edge had been well calculated to excite even the coldest-blooded observer. It had excited Henry Nelson to such an extent that he had bought not only this farm, but a lot of other farms. And Nelson was shrewd. Oh, it was a great joke! The whole mid-continent field rocked with laughter at it.

Nelson, senior, returned from Tulsa bull-mad, and he came without the money he had expected to get. What went on in his office that morning after he sent for his son none of the bank's employees ever knew, but they could guess, for the rumblings of the old man's rage penetrated even the mahogany-paneled walls.

CHAPTER XXIV

Gray had once told Barbara Parker that there was no one quite like him—a remark more egotistical in the sound than in the meaning. Unusual in many ways he probably was, but, like most men, the discovery that his proudest virtues were linked with vices of which he was ashamed struck him as extraordinary. As if nature were not forever aiming at a balance.

In spite of the fact that he was impulsive, headstrong, swift in most things, this girl possessed the unique faculty of rendering him acutely self-conscious, and it annoyed him the more, therefore, to find how timorous he could be in putting her feelings to the test. That was the one thing he could never quite summon courage to do. She was so young, so cool, so disconcertingly straightforward that, in contrast, his own age appeared the greater, and his many counterfeit qualities were thrown into uglier relief.

Then, too, her answer meant so much that fear of refusal became an actual torture, and the mere thought of it left his arrogant spirit strangely humble. To a man in his vengeful mood, to a men whipped by one savage purpose, love had come as a blessed relief; and, in consequence, anger at his indecision was the greater. Sometimes he told himself that he deserved to lose her.

One such occasion was after he had taken her out to the Avenger lease.

There was more than one well by this time; Avenger Number Two and Three and Four were going down, and offsetting the first Avenger were three of Nelson's rigs. "Bob" studied the situation briefly, then, with a dubious shake of her head, she announced: "You are taking a big risk, Mr. Gray."

"You mean these new holes may come dry? Of course, but I believe in crowding my luck. I don't know any other way to work."

"You *have* been lucky, haven't you?" She stared at him with a detached, impersonal interest. "Everything is coming your way, even down in the Ranger district."

"Oh, I have my share of troubles. I lost a crooked hole, recently—had to skid the derrick and start over. Then a pair of chaintongs was dropped into another hole—"

"That makes an expensive fishing job."

"The worst ever."

"Somebody must have it in for you." When Gray nodded, "Bob's" face lit up with surprise. "Really. Do you suspect someone in particular?"

"I know."

"How interesting." After a moment had passed and he had explained no further, the girl went on: "Everybody is talking about you and your success. They say you have the golden touch."

"That is a good reputation to enjoy; but this country is full of fellows who came here knowing as little about oil as I knew and who have accomplished more sensational results. I've come up like a rocket, to be sure; it remains to be seen whether I shall fall like a stick."

"You won't fall."

"Do you really believe that?" The inquiry was eagerly put. "I'd trust your intuition, Miss—"Bob." Sometimes I have moments of uneasiness, for, you see, I'm drilling more wells than I should. It is double or quits, you understand? If my luck breaks, so do I."

"You have always impressed me as a—a man of destiny. I think fate has selected you as an instrument with which to do big things. That's why I'm always a bit overawed by you."

"Overawed?" Gray laughed. "Why, I feel the same with you. If you knew how little I am, how little it all signifies, except as a means to an end. If you only knew what it is that I want so much more than oil, or money, or—"

"I thought you were like all the others here—absorbed only in the game."

"I was, at first. I had reason to be; a very great reason, I assure you. Then I saw something far more desirable than fortune, far more absorbing than—than the motive that brought me here. Some days, like today, I think I'm going to win it, then again I grow faint-hearted."

"Faint-hearted? *You?*" There was an elaborate skepticism in "Bob's" tone, but as the meaning of Gray's ardent gaze struck home to her, she turned her head with a lightly affected laugh. She was coloring, but she knew that her companion's agitation was so much greater than hers that he did not notice it.

"Fair lady," he said, a bit uncertainly, "you multiply my courage tenfold, and I shall retain the guerdon of your faith. But we swashbuckling fellows are proud; we must come as victors or not at all, and I am anything but victorious, yet. I've had many a fall, and my armor is dented in a dozen places. I have a record of failures that only a lasting success can wipe out. When, if ever, that record is wiped out, why—my tongue shall be my heart's ambassador." This was the boldest speech that Gray had ever permitted himself.

Never had he felt "Bob" to be so close to him as on this day, and in consequence he made of it a festival. He played the lover with a respectful ardor, doubly thrilling by reason of its restraint, and that night it was not Henry Nelson's face that lingered last in his memory. He wondered, before he fell asleep, if he had acted wisely in letting slip his hour. Opportunity has a fickle way of jilting those who ignore her, and yet—how could he speak with honor to himself?

It must not be inferred that Henry Nelson endured with patience the blows that were rained upon him. On the contrary, he fought back with every weapon he could lay hands upon, and there were many. In this he was aided by Old Bell, for father and son were much alike and their friction had been only such as results from the rubbing of two hard bodies of identical composition; now that they were put under heavy pressure, they adhered and functioned without heat.

They were handicapped, however, in that they had the bank to think about, and, in times of frenzied finance such as this, a banking business is more of a liability than an asset. Under normal conditions no single individual of Gray's limited resources could have caused them more than temporary annoyance; but in the midst of a speculative frenzy, in a time of vast "paper profits" and overnight losses, at an hour when they themselves were overextended and the financial fabric of the whole oil industry was stretched to a point of inflation where a pin prick was apt to cause complete collapse, the feat of warding off a lance in the hands of a destructive enemy was one that kept them in a constant state of nervous panic.

To make matters worse, the crest of the wave had passed, the boom was nearly over, and money was no longer easy. Outside investors were cooling; mysterious and powerful influences were at work, and there were rumors of a break in the price of crude. Meanwhile, so far as the Nelsons were concerned, it was necessary to pour a steady stream of dollars into the earth in order to save that which had been accomplished at immense cost, and such oil as their producing wells gave forth was swallowed up in other holes. It became, with them, a problem of how to hold on, how to finance from day to day until production returns overtook exploitation expense—a problem that put gray hairs in their heads and lines about their eyes. They were forced to many expedients.

How they managed it at all baffled Gray, and worried him, too, for he knew that if ever they turned the corne to the ground. One big well would set them up, and there was always that danger, for scarcely a week went by without news of some gigantic gusher. Knowing all there was to know about their field activities, he set himself to the task of learning more about the bank itself and about their method of operating it. This was a task, indeed, and he spent much time at it—time he could ill afford, by the way, for he, too, had about exhausted his last resource.

He was surprised one day to receive from Roswell, the banker who had first backed him, an almost peremptory summons to Dallas. Gray had made much money for Roswell and his crowd; they were still heavily interested with him, and he was counting upon their further support. The tone of this letter, therefore, gave him a disagreeable shock. On the whole, however, he was glad of an excuse to go, for the Briskows had returned and had bought a home in Dallas, and he was eager for a sight of them.

Mr. Roswell's greeting was quite as cool as his letter; but he betrayed a keen interest in the progress of their joint affairs and asked a good many searching questions. Gray answered frankly.

"You surprise me," the banker announced, finally, "for you confirm something I did not wish to believe. I have just learned that you are using us to further a private grudge and to ruin a reputable man. I couldn't credit such a statement without—"

"It is quite true, except that I haven't 'used' you. Not, at least, in the sense you imply."

"You have used our money. It is the same thing."

"Oh, not at all I have handled a number of speculations—investments is a better word—for you and your group and I've made a lot of money for you. That's the most you expected; that's all I promised. So long as I continue to do that, my motives, my personal likes and dislikes, concern you in no wise. Neither are you concerned in the use I make of my winnings." "Legitimate competition is one thing; malice, double-dealing, dishonesty is—"

"Dishonesty?" Gray interrupted, sharply. "I am a quick-tempered man, Mr. Roswell. I'll ask you to choose your words more carefully."

"Don't you call salting a well dishonest?"

"I do. I didn't salt that Arkansas property—and I assume you refer to that. In fact, I knew nothing about it, and I so informed Nelson. Evidently he didn't believe me, and I don't expect you to do so. Nevertheless, it is true. I have never lied to you, and I never shall. Now, malice—Yes, I bear malice toward Henry Nelson and I shall continue to bear him malice long after I have put him in his grave." Roswell's startled eyes leaped to the speaker's face. "Exactly! I propose to put him in his grave, and he knows it."

"Nonsense! That's wild talk and you'll regret it. What has he done to you?"

The object of this inquiry shrugged. "A private matter, purely. As to double-dealing—is it double-dealing to go to an enemy and tell him frankly that you intend to down him and how you propose to do it?"

"Did you do that?"

"I did. What is more, I offered to fight fair and he agreed. But, of course, he broke that, as he feels free to break any agreement when it becomes onerous or unprofitable. He began by trying to assassinate me."

"What are you saying?" Roswell cried. "This is incredible."

Gray's cigar had gone out; he lighted it with steady and deliberate fingers before he said: "I am giving you facts. The fighting has not been all on my side. For instance, I haven't hired men to drop tools in his wells or run crooked holes, and that sort of thing, as he has. Not that I wouldn't follow his lead if he forced me to, but I haven't had to resort to petty annoyances. I haven't had to make any 'small change,' for I have originality, imagination—even a small amount of daring, while he—Well, he is obvious. He has nothing except physical courage. Thank God, he's not a coward! He'll die hard."

"Amazing!" The banker was at a loss for words. After a moment, he inquired: "What about Bell Nelson?"

"A harsh, headstrong, ruthless old man whose history will not bear careful reading. His sins shall be visited upon him through his offspring. He will have to go, too."

Roswell stirred as if to shake off the effect of some oppressive, mesmeric influence; reluctantly he admitted, "All I can say is you have a colossal nerve—"

"Precisely. And that is all I had when I came to Texas."

"I was coming to that. You deceived me, Gray. You said you represented big capital; had friends and connections—"

"A pardonable deceit, under the circumstances, was it not? As a matter of fact, I said nothing of the sort; I merely allowed you to infer—"

"You're splitting hairs." The banker was impatient. "The fact remains that you led me to make a fool of myself. Why, man alive, I have your whole history here, and it's a record of one sensational failure after another. You had no backing whatever, no—"

"Is that the result of your own investigation?"

"Partly."

"For the rest, you took Nelson's word, eh? Very well, I've beaten him out from cover sooner than I expected. Now as to my failures. Failure proves only this: that one's determination to succeed is not strong enough. Who fail, except those who try? You have not always succeeded; neither have I invariably failed. Your report is a bit unfair."

"You will fail now. And you deserve to fail."

"Indeed? Why?"

"Because you're doing an outrageous thing; because—See here, Gray, I know why you hate Nelson." There ensued a moment of silence.

"He told you that?" The younger man's face had slowly whitened; he spoke with difficulty.

"He told me everything. He told me that you were dishonorably discharged from the army—cashiered, we used to call it—and that you blame him. I don't mind saying it was a shock—worst I've had in years. In time of war, too! The army doesn't do that unless—without ample—Well, Gray, it's damned nasty!"

"Quite the nastiest thing that can happen to a man," the other agreed in a thin, flat voice.

"I couldn't, wouldn't believe it."

"Why not? You believed everything else he told you."

"I wouldn't accept his word on a thing like *that* without asking you." Another pause followed. "There's probably some explanation. I told him so—" Mr. Roswell showed his genuine distress by the frown upon his brow and by his averted eyes. He stirred uncomfortably, then he broke out, irritably: "Well, well? Why in hell don't you say something?"

"There is nothing to say."

"What? My God, man! You don't mean—See here, you're not a coward, or a thief, or an incompetent. What's your side of the story? What's the explanation?"

"Explanations are hateful. The man who makes them deceives either himself or the other fellow—usually both. It is easy to be plausible. Would a mere statement from me, unsupported by proof, convince you where it failed to convince a court martial? Of course not. Then why make you uncomfortable by doubting my word?" Gray's smile was like the mirthless grin of a mummy. "I was found guilty, all in due military order, and—disgraced, branded! My uniform was taken from me, and I can't wear it again. I can never again serve my country. It was handled quietly, with admirable discretion, for those things are bad for the morale, you understand? Very few know about it. I'm a proud man, a vain man; I assure you the death penalty would have been much easier to bear."

"What did Henry Nelson have to do with it?"

"He alone can answer that."

"An extraordinary situation! This is your revenge, eh?"

"As a man of spirit, I had a choice of but two things, revenge or—suicide."

"Hm-m! It is an embarrassing situation for me."

"Indeed?"

"Nelson has sold a large block of his bank stock to one of our directors."

"Tell him to get out from under, quick," Gray said, sharply, "for I'll break Henry Nelson or—I'll kill him!"

"Tut, tut! You're excited. You mustn't talk like that. I give you credit for an honest hatred, but—I can't sympathize with it. Neither can I believe so ill of Henry Nelson. Remember, I've known him and Bell for years." With a complete finality the banker concluded, "You'll have to give it up, Gray."

"I beg pardon?"

"I say we sha'n't permit you to go on with this murderous feud. We can't be parties to it. What you've told me warrants us in withdrawing our support instantly, but I—I—Damn it all, I can't help liking you and believing in you! Frankly, there's something sublime about a grudge like yours. However, we can't go on like this. We can't put up more money now that we know what you have in mind. Call this thing off and perhaps I can induce our crowd to leave their money in until it can be worked out. That's the most I can undertake."

"I need your money and your support now more than ever," the other man gravely confessed. "I need it at once; to-day. Nevertheless, I sha'n't quit."

"You *must!*" Roswell cried, impatiently. "You can't defy us."

"The devil I can't!" It was Gray's turn to blaze. "That's exactly what I'm doing. I defy you to get your money out. I defy you to interfere with me in the slightest or to wring a particle of mercy out of me. I knew this would come, sooner or later, and I planned accordingly. What d'you think I am, eh? I tell you I've got him! Otherwise he'd never squeal about this—army matter. Now then, tell your crowd to try and pull out! That's not a threat, sir, for they have played fair with me, and I sha'n't sacrifice a penny of their money—unless they force me to do so. But—I'm in control. I'm sitting pretty. They can't unseat me, and I warn them not to try."

"You are making a great mistake. We will find a way to—to *pull* you off."

"Ever try to pull a bulldog out of a fight when he had the other dog down and his teeth in its throat? I have. There's something rather horrible about it—rather beastly and shocking. And there's always the danger of losing a hand." The speaker rose. He hesitated, before leaving, to say: "Your son served with honor, Mr. Roswell. I know how you must feel about this— other matter, therefore I shall spare you the embarrassment of declining my hand."

The financier's face reddened; rather stiffly he said, "You know whether you have a right to offer it."

Instantly the departing visitor extended his palm, and Roswell realized that he had seldom seen a man more deeply moved. "Thanks! I—It is a blow to lose your support, but—nothing can swerve me. Meanwhile, I'm glad that we do not part as enemies."

When he had gone, when he had passed out with head up and shoulders square, the banker shivered slightly. Audibly he murmured: "God, what a man! What a hatred!"

The Briskows had just moved into their new home, and the place was still in some confusion when Gray mounted the steps. Pa answered the bell in his shirt sleeves and with a claw hammer in his hand, for he had been hanging pictures. He favored his visitor with a wide smile of welcome and a hearty greeting-quite a feat, inasmuch as his mouth was full of nails—then, having rid it of its contents, he explained:

"We got a slave that tends the door, but I 'ain't got gentled up to bells an' things yet. Allie's away an' Ma's layin' down, so—"

"Ma isn't ill, I hope?"

"N—no. Just ailin'. I thought mebbe one of the neighbors had run in to see her, but—I guess they're busy. We got lots of neighbors here, rich ones, an' we made up our minds to like 'em, if they'll give us a chance."

"You were in luck to find a house in such a smart neighborhood, Gus. Now show me around, quickly, for I'm dying to see it."

"Lord, I'm dyin' to show it to *somebody!* You're the first one that's dropped in an' we been here 'most two weeks. Say, you'll stay an' eat supper, won't you?"

"Of course I will, and breakfast, too, if you can take care of me."

"Pshaw! Didn't we take keer of you when you come to the ranch? We got three niggers now, just doin' the housework." As if in justification of this riotous mode of life, the oil man explained: "Ma wanted to do it herself, but she's porely, an' Allie vetoed it complete. She says we'll be stylish an' enjoy life if it kills all three of us. I'd of bought a bigger house if they'd of let me, but—"

"It is large enough. Anything more would merely add to your cares."

"Her and Ma picked out the furniture. Swell, ain't it?"

"Beautiful!" Gray exclaimed. Inwardly he groaned, for,

although the contents of the home appeared to be expensive, almost ostentatious, they nevertheless betrayed a conspicuous lack of taste both in character and in arrangement. Here and there were color combinations so atrocious that they positively hurt the caller. On the whole, however, the place looked better than he had expected, and such indications of harmony and restraint as he detected he attributed to Allie. It was a nice enough home, and with a little change, a little rearrangement, it could be made attractive even to one of elegant tastes. Those changes, of course, Gray determined to make.

Gus, plainly, was not yet accustomed to the sense of owner-ship, and he hung with eagerness upon his guest's expressions of approval. After a tour of inspection the men wound up in the library—an absurd misnomer under the circumstances, inasmuch as the shelves were entirely bare except for Allie's dog-eared school books—and there, before a blazing gas log, they discussed the miracle.

"Allie's gone out to the old farm to get some stuff for Ma," the father explained in due time. "Some pitchers of her an' Buddy when they was little, an' a rockin'-chair, an' Ma's favorite bedspread, an' some other things she likes."

Gray remembered the portraits, executed by a St. Louis "enlargement" concern. They had wide gilt frames, and were protected from ravaging flies by mosquito netting. He hoped that Ma would not hang them in the hall or the living-room. And that rocker, for which she yearned, was probably the one with the creaking coiled springs—the one that had leaped after him and clashed its jaws like an alligator.

"By the way, how does Buddy like the new home?" the latter inquired.

"He 'ain't seen it yet. Says he's too busy to leave the job. What you done to that boy, anyhow?"

"I'm making a real man out of him—and an oil man, too. He

knew how to dress tools when I got him, but he's a pretty good driller now. Before long he'll be able to take charge of your property and run it on practical lines. I told you he had it in him, and that he'd make a 'hand.'"

"You never wrote us nothin' about his—his trouble."

"I left the explaining for him."

Gus smiled meditatively. "First we knew that you an' him had been fightin' was when he wrote us a letter sayin' he was doin' great an' could see out of one eye." Then, more gravely: "It was worryin' over Buddy's affair that got Ma to ailin'. She 'ain't been right well since. Say, wha'd you do with that—woman?" Briskow pronounced the last word with an accent of scorn and hatred.

"I gave her a chance to make an honest, decent living. I set her up in business."

"*What?*"

"And she is making good." When the elder man shook his head impatiently Gray went on, "I'm pretty worldly and calloused, but if one virtue has been spared me, it is charity."

For a moment the father studied his caller. "Tell me," he began, "was it altogether on Buddy's account that you an' him tied into one another?"

Gray threw back his head and laughed frankly. "Altogether, I assure you. That's why I found it so hard."

"He *oughta* been licked! Takin' up with a—a thing like her." Gus was groping for words more eloquent of his displeasure at his son and his hatred for the object of Buddy's misplaced affections, when Gray forestalled him.

"Just a minute. You are a rich man and you are growing richer.

Careful, frugal, prosperous people like you are apt to become unduly hard and oversuspicious; but you mustn't permit it. Think, for instance, what environment did to your children, then remember that under slightly different circumstances it might have made evildoers even of them. Most people would like to run straight, and would do so if they had a chance. Anyhow, it is an interesting experiment to put the chance in their way. Tell me, Gus, how much money have you got?"

"I dunno. Figgers over a thousand dollars don't mean much to me."

Gray searched the speaker's face with a speculative gaze. "It's mostly liquid, I presume." There was a pause. "I mean it's in cash or the equivalent?"

"Oh, sure! These bonds an' stocks an' things—" Briskow shook his head disapprovingly. "Land ain't any too safe, either. It's rainin' now, an' it 'll keep on rainin' till the farmers is all drowned out. Next year it'll be droughty an' fry 'em to a crisp. No, I'm skeered of land. I'm skeered of everything!" This last was said plaintively. "Why, lookit these Liberty bonds! Goin' down steady. I wouldn't put no money into the gov'ment unless I had something to say about runnin' it. An' s'pose I did? I wouldn't know how it oughta be run."

"How about oil properties? Wouldn't you like to invest in a good, safe proposition, with the prospect of big—"

"Gosh, *no!* I'm skeerder of oil than anything, 'cause I know somethin' about it. Feller been tryin' to sell me life insurance, lately, but you gotta die to get your money back. No; there's a catch in all them propositions. Sometimes I wake up nights dreamin' we're all back at the old place an' pore again. That ends my sleepin'. You see, Allie's a lady now, an' she's used to silk stockin's, an' Buddy's been out in the world spendin' money on women, an' Ma's gettin' old. I could go back to corn bread, but it would kill them. Worst of it is, the black lime ain't holdin' up, an' our wells will give out some day."

Briskow sighed heavily and his brows drew together in an anxious pucker.

"You'll have enough money in bank to do you."

"Banks bust. I tell you the hull world's full of skullduggery. Suspicious? I should say I was! I use' to think if we had money our troubles would be over, but—Lord, that's when they begin! You see, if I was bright an' knew what slick people is up to, I'd be all right; but—Why, I'm like a settin' hen. I can feel the eggs under me, but how am I goin' to keep the skunks away when they smell the nest? I'm 'most tempted to turn everything I got over to some honest man an' let him han'le it. Some feller that had the savvy."

"Unfortunately, such people are rare."

"I don't know but one."

"Indeed? Who is he?"

"I reckon you know," said Briskow.

The listener looked up with quickened interest; there was a sharp ring to his voice when he said: "Let me get this right."

"You're the only man I ever knowed that I'd bank my life on. An' you're smart. You wouldn't take Buddy, but mebbe you'd kinda—take me; take all of us. I tell you I'm skeered!"

"Just how much confidence do I inspire in you?" Gray's expression was peculiar, for amazement, doubt, eagerness were equally blended.

"This much: I'd turn the hull works over to you, if you'd look out for us."

"You—scarcely know me."

"Oh, I know you well enough!" Briskow smiled his slow, shrewd smile. "So does Ma. So does Allie an' Bud."

For quite a while the caller sat with head bowed, with his gaze fixed upon the flames; when he looked up his face was red, his eyes were brighter than usual.

"To be trusted is a greater compliment than to be loved. Yes, and it's hell to be born with a conscience." He fell silent again, for this was a moment to be treasured and he could not let it pass too quickly. "You say you want nothing to do with oil?"

"Anything but that. I know it so well, an'—Ma's gettin' feeble." Again silence. "Of course, if you'd do it, I wouldn't ask no questions. I'd rather shut my eyes an' trust you than keep 'em open an'—"

"You don't know how much I'd like to say yes, but I fought Buddy to prevent him from making a mistake, and I sha'n't allow you to make this one."

"Hm-m! Will you keep me from makin' *other* mistakes?"

"I will, if I can."

"Mebbe that's enough. Anyhow, I'll sleep better to-night for seein' you."

"I think I hear Ma stirring," said Gray, as he rose. "I brought her a few little presents, and I'd like to take them up to her." As he left the room there was the same queer light in his eyes; nevertheless, he moved slowly, like a man tired.

CHAPTER XXV

Gray was shocked at the change in Ma Briskow. She had failed surprisingly. Pleasure lit her face, and she fell into a brief flutter of delight at seeing him; but as soon as their first greeting was over he led her to her lounge and insisted upon making her comfortable. He had tricks with cushions and pillows, so he declared; they became his obedient servants, and there was a knack in arranging them—the same knack that a robin uses in building its nest. This he demonstrated quite conclusively.

It was nice to have a great, masterful man like this take charge of one, and Ma sighed gratefully as she lay back. "It does kinda feel like a bird's nest," she declared. "And you kinda look like a robin, too; you're allus dressed so neat."

"Exactly," he chuckled. "Robins are the very neatest dressers of all the birds. But look! Like a real robin, I've brought spring with me." He opened a huge box of long-stemmed roses and held their cool, dewy buds against Ma Briskow's withered face, then, laughing and chatting, he arranged them in vases where she could see them. Next, he drew down the shades, shutting out the dreary afternoon, after which he lit the gas log, and soon the room, whether by reason of his glowing personality or his deft rearrangement of its contents, or both, became a warm and cheerful place.

He had brought other gifts than flowers, too; thoughtful, expensive things that fairly took Ma's breath. No one had ever given her presents; to be remembered, therefore, with useless, delightful little luxuries filled her gentle soul with a guilty rapture.

But these were not gifts in the ordinary sense; they were offerings from the Duke of Dallas, and his manner of presenting them invested every article with ducal dignity. The Princess Pensacola had not played for a long time, and so to recline languidly in a beautiful Japanese kimono, with her feet in a pair of wonderful soft boudoir slippers spun by the duke's private silkworms and knit by his own oriental knitting slaves, while he paid court to her, was doubly thrilling.

The duke certainly was a reckless spender, but thank goodness he hadn't bought things for the house—things just to *look* at and to share with other people! He knew enough to buy intimate things, things a woman could wear and feel rich in. Ma hugged herself and tried to look beautiful.

Gray was seated on the side of her couch with her cold hand between his warm palms, and he was telling her about the princess of Wichita Falls when the summons to dinner interrupted them.

Ma was not hungry, and she had expected to have a bite in her own room; but her caller was so vigorous in his objections to this plan that she finally agreed to come downstairs.

The Briskow household was poorly organized as yet, and it was only natural that it should function imperfectly; nevertheless, Gray was annoyed at the clumsy manner in which the dinner was served. Being a meticulous man and accustomed to comfort, incompetent servants distressed him beyond measure, and he soon discovered that the Briskow help was as completely incompetent as any he had ever seen. The butler, for instance, a pleasant-faced colored man, had evidently come straight from the docks, for he passed the food much as a stoker passes coal to a boiler, while the sound of a crashing platter in the butler's pantry gave evidence that the second girl was a house wrecker.

"See here, Ma!" Gray threw down his napkin. "You have a beautiful home, and you want it to be perfect, don't you?"

"Why, of Course. We bought everything we' could buy—"

"Everything except skillful servants, and they are hard to find. You are capable of training your cook and teaching your upstairs girl to sweep and make beds; but the test of a well-run house is a well-served meal. Dish-breaking ought to be a felony, and when I become President I propose to make the spoiling of food a capital offense. Now then, you're not eating a bite, anyhow, and Gus won't mind waiting awhile for his dinner. With your permission, I'd like to take things in hand and add a hundred per cent to your future comfort?"

In some bewilderment Ma agreed that she would do anything her guest suggested, whereupon he rose energetically and called the three domestics into the dining room.

"We are going to start this dinner all over again," he announced, "and we are going to begin by swapping places. I am going to serve it as a dinner should be served, and you are going to eat it as—Well, I dare say nature will have to take its course. I shall explain, as I go along, and I want you to remember every word I say, every move I make. Mr. and Mrs. Briskow are going to look on. After we have finished you are going to serve us exactly as I served you."

Naturally, this proposition amazed the "help"; in fact, its absurdity convulsed them. The man laughed loudly; the cook buried her ebony face in her apron; the second girl bent double with mirth. Here was a quaint gentleman, indeed, and a great joker. But the gentleman was not joking. On the contrary, he brought this levity to an abrupt end, then, gravely, ceremoniously, he seated the trio. They sobered quickly enough at this; they became, in fact, as funereal as three crows; but their astonishment at what followed was no greater than that of the Briskows.

Gray played butler with a correctness and a poise deeply impressive to his round-eyed audience, and as he served the courses he delivered a lecture upon the etiquette of domestic service, the art of cooking, and the various niceties of a servant's calling. Nothing could have been more impressive than being waited upon by a person of his magnificence, and his lecture, moreover, was delivered in a way that drove understanding into their thick heads.

It was an uncomfortable experience for all except Gray himself —he actually enjoyed it—and when the last dish had been removed, and he had given instructions to serve the meal over again exactly as he had served it, the three negroes were glad to obey. Of course they made mistakes, but these Gray instantly corrected, and the results of his dress rehearsal were, on the whole, surprising.

"There!" he said, when the ordeal had finally come to an end. "A little patience, a little practice, and you'll be proud of them. Incidentally, I have saved you a fortune in dishes."

"I wish Allie'd been here. She'd remember everything you said," Ma declared.

"Lord! Think of Mr. Gray waitin' on them niggers!" Gus was still deeply shocked.

"You see what a meddlesome busybody I am," the guest laughed. "I don't know how to mind my own business, and the one luxury I enjoy most of all is regulating other people's affairs." He was still talking, still lecturing his hearers upon the obligations prosperity had put upon them, when he was summoned to the telephone by a long-distance call. He returned in some agitation to announce: "Well, at last I have business of my own to attend."

"Was that Buddy talkin'?"

"It was, and he gave me some good news. He says that well on thirty-five is liable to come in at any minute, and it looks like a big one." The speaker's eyes were glowing, and he ran on, breathlessly, "He says they're betting it will do better than ten thousand barrels!"

"*Ten thousand bar'ls!*" Briskow echoed.

"That's what he said. Of course, they can't tell a thing about it. Buddy's only guessing, but—I haven't had a big well yet." Gray took a nervous turn about the room.

"Ten thousand barrels! Lord! That would help. That would do the trick. And to think that it should come now, this very day—" He laughed triumphantly and ran on as if talking to himself: "'The wicked are fatted for destruction. Their happiness shall pass away like a torrent.' Pull out and leave me, eh?" A second time he laughed, more loudly. "Luck? It isn't luck, it's Destiny. The mills of the Gods are grinding. Ma Briskow, the fairy ladies danced upon the hearth when I was born. Do you know what that means?"

"Ten thousand bar'ls a day, an' you buttlin' for three niggers!" gasped the head of the house.

"I'm going out on to-night's train and see it come in—if it does come in. I told Buddy to stop work; not to drop another tool until I arrived. 'Fatted for destruction.' I like the sound of that. Ten thousand barrels! Ho! I'll write this day in brass. Why, that lease will sell for a million. It—it may mean the end."

Gray brought himself to with an effort, hastily he kissed Ma Briskow's faded cheek and wrung her husband's hand. A moment later he was gone.

"Thirty-five," where Buddy was working, was only a few miles from the Briskow ranch, therefore the boy was able to meet his sister at Ranger and drive her directly to the old home. The place was much the same as when they had left it, thanks to the watchful attention of the men in charge of the Briskow wells, and there they spent the night. Buddy and his sister had always been close confidants, and their long separation, their varied experiences, left many things to be discussed.

The ranch house seemed very mean, very insignificant to Allie, but she slipped into one of her old dresses and prepared the supper while Buddy straddled a kitchen chair and chattered upon ten thousand topics of mutual interest.

"Doggone!" he exclaimed, finally. "I hardly knew you when you stepped off that train, but it seems like old times now, with you hustlin' around in that gingham."

"I wish it was."

"Hunh?"

"I wish, sometimes, that we'd never struck oil."

"Good Lord! Why?"

"Oh"—Allie turned her back and bent over the stove—"for lots of reasons! Ma never had a sick day till lately. Now she's failin' fast." Buddy frowned at this intelligence. "And Pa's as restless as a squirrel. All the time scared of losing his money."

"Well, *you* got no kick coming, sis. You've sure made good."

"How?"

"I dunno—You've got rich ways. An' rich *looks*, too!"

Allie lifted an interested face, and her brother undertook, somewhat awkwardly, to tell her wherein she had improved. She listened with greedy delight, but when he had finished she shook her head skeptically and declared: "It sounds nice, and God knows I've tried hard enough, but-there's a difference,

Bud. We're 'trash' and always will be."

Of course young Briskow's mind was full of business, and he could not long stay off that absorbing topic. When, during their supper, he announced the fact that the well on thirty-five showed signs of coming in shortly, and that he intended to send for Calvin Gray, Allie changed her mind about returning home and decided to wait over until the latter arrived.

She and Buddy talked until a late hour that night, but although she was dying to have him tell her about his romance, his dream of love, he never so much as referred to it, and she could not bring herself to disregard his reticence. Nor could she bear to discuss with him the problem that lay nearest her own heart. She had brooded long over that problem, and her soul was hungry to share its bitter secret; nevertheless, she could not do so, for it is often easier to bare our wounds to strangers than to those we love. If her breedings, her bitterness of spirit manifested themselves, it was in a fixed undertone of pessimism and in an occasional outburst of recklessness that bewildered her brother.

On the morning of Gray's coming she rode with Buddy over to thirty-five. It was a wretched, rainy day, and nothing is more bleak than a rainy day in a drilling camp. Work had been halted and the men were loafing in their bunk house. Brother and sister spent the impatient hours in the mess tent. As usual, they talked a good deal about Calvin Gray.

"Funny, him comin' here a stranger, an' gettin' to run our whole family, ain't it?" Buddy said.

Allie nodded. "Funnier thing than that is your working for him." Buddy was surprised, so she asked him: "Aren't you sore at him for—what he did? For breaking up that affair?" It was a question that had been upon her lips more than once; she could not credit her brother with entire sincerity when he answered, frankly enough:

"Sore? Not the least bit."

"Didn't you—care for her?"

"Why, sure. I was all tore up, at first. But he did me the biggest kind of a favor."

Allie shook her head uncomprehendingly. "Men are queer things. You *must* have loved her, for a while."

"I reckon I did, if you're a mind to call it that. But he says that sort of thing ain't real love."

"'*He says*'!" the girl cried, scornfully. "My God, Buddy! Would you let *him* tell you—? Is he pickin' out women for you like he picks out a dress for me and a hotel for Ma? How does *he* know what's the real thing?"

"She was a—grafter," the brother explained, with a flush of embarrassment. "She'd of probably took my money an' quit me cold."

"Bah!" The girl rose and, with somber defiance in her smoldering eyes, stared out at the desolate day. "You'd have had her for a while, wouldn't you? You'd have lived while it lasted. What's the difference if she was a grafter? D'you think you're going to fall in love and marry a duchess, or something? I wish I'd had your chance, that's all."

"What d'you mean by that?" Buddy queried, sharply.

"I mean this," Allie flamed at him. "We're nobodies and we've got nothing but our money. A counterfeit is as good as ever we'll get—and it's as good as we're entitled to. I'd rather know what it is to live for an hour than to go on forever just pretending to live. If I've got to be unhappy, then give me something to be unhappy over; something to look back on. I'd rather be—But, pshaw! You don't understand. You couldn't."

"I dunno what's got into you lately," Buddy declared, with a frown.

"Nothing's got into me. Only, what's the use of starving when the world's full of good things and you've got the price to buy them? *I* won't do it. If ever I get my chance, you watch me!"

Gray's trip from the railroad was more like a voyage than a motor journey, for the creek beds, usually dry, were angry torrents, and the 'dobe flats were quagmires through which his vehicle plowed hub deep; nevertheless, he was fresh and alert when he arrived. After a buoyant greeting to Allie, he and Buddy inspected the well, then he issued orders for work to be resumed.

"We're gettin' close to something," young Briskow declared. "She's making gas an' rumblin' like she'd let go any minute. We got reservoys built an' the boiler's moved back, so we can douse the fire when she starts. I figger she'll drownd us out."

"What are the indications at Nelson's well?" Gray turned his eyes in the direction of a derrick on the adjoining property, the top of which showed over the mesquite.

"Nothin' extra. They won't tell us anything, but they're deeper 'n we are."

"How do you know?"

Buddy winked wisely. "We counted the layers of cable on the bull-wheel drum. Checked up their casing, too, an' watched their cuttin's. They got their eye on us, too, an' they'll be over when we blow in."

That was an anxious afternoon, for as the drill bit deeper into the rock it provoked indications of a terrific force imprisoned far below. To the observers it seemed as if that sharp-edged tool was tap-tapping upon the thin shell of some vast reservoir already leaking and charged to the bursting point with a mighty pressure. An odor of gas escaped from the casing mouth, occasionally there came hoarse, throaty gurglings of the thick liquid at the bottom of the well. The bailer was run frequently.

Word had gone forth that there was something doing on thirty-five, and from the chaparral emerged muddy motor cars bringing scouts, neighboring lease owners, and even the members of a near-by casing crew.

Supper was a jumpy meal, and nobody had much to say, Allie Briskow least of all. She was silent, intense; she curtly refused Buddy's offer to send her home, and when the meal was over she followed Gray back to the derrick. He was on edge, of course. It seemed to him that every blow of that bit was struck upon his naked nerves, for he had a deep conviction that this was to prove the night of his life, and the strain of waiting was becoming onerous. This well meant so much. Ten thousand barrels, fifteen, five—even one thousand; it mattered little how heavy the flow, for a good-paying well would see him through his immediate troubles. And this was a well of some sort, or else indications meant nothing and everybody was greatly mistaken. Of course, a big well, something to create a furor— that was what he needed, for that not only would bridge his financial crisis, but also it would mean a frenzy of quick drilling, new wells crowded close together, hundreds of thousands of dollars poured into the earth, and the Nelsons couldn't stand that. It would break them—break them, and he would taste the full sweetness of revenge. Oh, he had waited long! Nor was that all. Once he had Henry Nelson down, and his foot on the fellow's throat, he'd have something to say to Barbara Parker. He could say it then and look her in the eyes. He wished she was here to-night while he stood on the top of the world. Ten thousand barrels! Twenty thousand! Twenty-thousand-barrel gushers were not unknown. A well like that would mean a fortune every day. But why didn't it start?

They were bailing again and curiosity drew the owner in upon the derrick floor. This time the flow might begin; at any moment now oil might come with the water. There is some danger in standing close to a well during this bailing process, but Gray was like a bit of iron in the field of a magnet; spellbound, he watched the cable as it ran smoothly off the drum, flowed up over the crown block and down into the casing mouth. That heavy, torpedolike weight on the end of the line was dropping almost half a mile. Up it came swiftly, as if greased; up, up, until it emerged into the glare of the incandescent overhead and hung there dripping. It was swung aside and lowered, and out gushed its muddy contents.

Water! Black and thick as molasses, but water nevertheless.

Buddy Briskow was running the rig, and the dexterity with which he handled brake and control rod gave him pride. He had seated his sister on a bench out of the way, where she was protected from the drizzle, and he felt her eyes upon him. It gave him a sense of importance to have Allie watching him at such a crisis; he wished his parents were with her. If this well blew in big, as it seemed bound to do, it would be a personal triumph, for not many cub drillers could boast of bringing in a gusher the first time. It was, in fact, no mean accomplishment to make any sort of a well; to pierce the earth with an absolutely vertical shaft a half mile deep and line it with tons upon tons of heavy casing joined air-tight and fitted to a hair's breadth was an engineering feat in itself. It was something that only an oil man could appreciate. And he was an oil man; a darn good one, too, so Buddy told himself.

He eased the brake and the massive bailer slid into the casing as a heavy shell slips into the breech of a cannon. As he further released his pressure, the cable began to pour serpentlike from the drum. Buddy turned his wet, grimy face and flashed a grin at Allie. She smiled back at him faintly. Some lightninglike change in her expression, or perhaps some occult sense of the untoward warned him that all was not as it should be, and he jerked his head back to attention.

There are moments of catastrophe when for a brief interval

nature slows, time stops, and we are carried in suspense. Such an instant Buddy Briskow experienced now. He knew at first glance what had happened, and a frightened cry burst from his throat, but it was a cry too short, too hoarse, to serve as a warning.

During that moment of inattention the bailer had stuck. Perhaps five hundred feet below, friction had checked its plunge, and meanwhile the velvet-running drum, spinning at its maximum velocity by reason of the whirling bull wheel, was unreeling its cable down upon the derrick platform. Down it poured in giant loops, and within those coils, either unconscious of his danger or paralyzed by its suddenness, stood Calvin Gray.

Men schooled in hazardous enterprises carry subconscious mental photographs of the perils with which their callings are invested and they react involuntarily to them. Buddy had heard of drillers decapitated by flying cables, of human bodies caught within those wire loops and cut in twain as if made of lard, for when a wedged tool resumes its downward plunge it straightens those coils above ground in the twinkling of an eye. Instinct, rather than reason, warned Buddy not to check the blinding revolutions of the bull wheel. Without thought he leaped forward into the midst of those swiftly forming loops, and as he landed upon the slippery floor he clenched his fist and struck with all the power he could put behind his massive arm. Gray's back was to him, the blow was like that of a walking beam, and it sent the elder man flying as a tenpin is hurled ahead of a bowling ball. Buddy fell, too. He went sprawling. As he slid across the muddy floor he felt the steel cable writhing under him like a thing alive, and the touch of it as it streamed into the well burned his flesh. He kicked and fought it as he would have fought the closing folds of a python, for the bailer was falling again and the wire loops were vanishing as the coils in a whiplash vanish during its flight.

Buddy's booted legs were thrown high, he was tossed aside like a thing of paper, but blind, half stunned, he scrambled back to his post. By this time the whole structure of the derrick was rocking to the mad gyrations of the bull wheel; the giant spool was spinning with a speed that threatened to send it flying, like the fragments of a bursting bomb, but the youth understood dimly the danger of stopping it too suddenly—to fetch up that plunging weight at the cable end might snap the line, collapse the derrick, "jim" the well. Buddy weaved dizzily in his tracks; nevertheless, his hand was steady, and he applied a gradually increasing pressure to the brake. Nor did he take his eyes from his task until the drum had ceased revolving and the runaway bailer hung motionless in the well.

When he finally looked about it seemed to him that he had lived a long time and was very old. Gray lay motionless where he had fallen, and his body was twisted into a shockingly unnatural posture. He was bleeding. Allie Briskow was bending over him. Other dim, dreamlike figures were swarming out of the gloom and into the radiance of the derrick lights; there was a far-away clamor of shouting voices. Buddy Briskow felt himself growing deathly sick.

They carried Gray to the bunk house, and his limbs hung loosely, his head lolled in a manner terrifying to Buddy and his sister. As they stumbled along beside the group, the girl cried:

"Oh, my God! Oh, my God!" She repeated the cry over and over again in a voice strange to her brother's ears.

"It—it wasn't my fault," he told her, hoarsely. "I aimed to save him."

"You killed him!"

"He ain't—" Buddy choked and clung to her. "He's just stunned like. He ain't—that!" The youth was amazed when Allie turned and cursed him with oaths that he himself seldom ventured to employ.

But Gray was not dead. Buddy's blow had well-nigh broken

his neck, and he had suffered a further injury to his head in falling; nevertheless, he responded to such medical aid as they could supply, and in time he opened his eyes. His gaze was dull, however, and for a long while he lay in a sort of coma, quite as alarming as his former condition. They brought him to at last long enough to acquaint him with what had happened, and although it was plain that he understood their words only dimly, he ordered the work resumed.

When for a second time he lapsed into semiconsciousness, it was Allie Briskow who put his orders into execution. "You ain't doing any good standing around staring at him and whispering. Bring in that well, as fast as ever you can, and bring it in *big*. Now, get out and leave him to me."

Buddy was the last to go. He inquired, miserably: "Honest, he ain't hurt bad, is he? You don't think—"

"Get out!"

"He won't—die? Ain't no chance of him doin' that, is there?"

"If he does, I'll—" The speaker's face was ashen, but her eyes blazed. "I'll fix you, Buddy Briskow. I will, so help me God!"

It was late that night when the well came in. It came with a rush and a roar, drenching the derrick with a geyser of muddy water and driving both crew and spectators out into the gloom. Up, up the column rose, spraying itself into mist, and from its iron throat issued a sound unlike that of any other phenomenon. It was a hoarse, rumbling bellow, growing in volume and rising in pitch second by second until it finally attained a shrieking crescendo. Ten thousand safety valves had let go, and they steadily gathered strength and shrillness as they functioned. A shocking sound it became, a sound that carried for miles, rocking the air and stunning the senses. It beat upon the eardrums, pierced them; men shouted at each other, but heard their own voices only faintly.

Calvin Gray had recovered his senses sufficiently to understand the meaning of that uproar, and he tried to get up, but Allie held him down upon his bed. She was still struggling with him when her brother burst into the house, shouting:

"It's a gasser, Mr. Gray! Biggest I ever seen."

"Gas?" the latter mumbled, indistinctly. "Isn't there any—oil?" His words were almost like a whisper because of the noise.

"Not yet. May be later. Say, she's a heller, ain't she? I'll bet she's makin' twenty million feet—"

"Gasser's no good."

"Can't tell yet. We gotta shut her down easy so she don't blow the casing out—run wild on us, understand?" Buddy was still breathless, but he plunged out the door and back into that sea of sound.

With a tragic intensity akin to wildness, Gray stared up into Allie Briskow's face. "Worthless, eh? And they told me ten thousand barrels." He carried a shaking hand to his bandaged head and tried vainly to collect his wits. "What's matter?" he queried, thickly. "Everything whirling—sick—"

"You had an accident, but it's all right; all right—No, no! Please lie still."

"Running wild, eh? Tha's what hurts my head so. Blown the casing out—Bad, isn't it? Sometimes they run wild for weeks, years—ruin everything." He tried again to rise, then insisted, querulously: "Goto get oil in this well! I've got to! Last chance, Allie. Got to get ten thousand barrels!"

"Please! You mustn't—" Allie had her strong hands upon his shoulders; she was arguing firmly but as gently as possible under the circumstances, when something occurred so extraordinary, so unexpected, as to paralyze her. Of a sudden the interior of the dim-lit, canvas-roofed shack was illuminated as if by a searchlight, and she turned her head to see that the whole out-of-doors was visible and that the night itself had turned into day.

With a cry that died weakly amid the chaos of sound beating over her, the girl ran to the window and looked out. What she beheld was a nightmare scene. The well was afire. It had exploded into flame. Where, a moment before, it had been belching skyward an enormous stream of gaseous vapor, all but invisible except at the casing head, now it was a monstrous blow torch, the flaming crest of which was tossed a hundred feet high. Nothing in the nature of a conflagration could have been more awe-inspiring, more confounding to the faculties than that roaring column of consuming fire. It was a thing incredibly huge, incredibly furious, incredibly wild. Human figures, black against its glare, were flying to safety, near-by silhouettes were flinging their arms aloft and dashing backward and forward; faces upturned to it were white and terrified. The scattered mesquite stood against the night like a wall, spotted with inky shadows, and, above, the heavens resembled a boiling caldron.

It was a hellish picture; it remained indelibly fixed upon Allie Briskow's mind. As she looked on in horrid fascination, she saw the derrick change into a latticelike tower of flame, saw its upper part begin slowly to crumble and disintegrate. The force with which the gas issued blew the blaze high and held it dancing, tumbling in mid-air, a phenomenon indescribably weird and impressive. The men who stood nearest bent their heads and shielded their faces from the heat.

Allie tore her eyes away from the spectacle finally. She turned back to the bed, then she halted, for it was empty. The door, still ajar from Buddy's headlong exit, informed her whence her patient had gone, and she flew after him.

She found him not half a dozen paces away. In fact, she stumbled over his prostrate body. With an amazon's strength, she gathered him into her arms, then staggered with him back to his couch, and as she strained him to herself she loudly called his name. Amid that demoniac din, amid the shrieking of those million devils, freed from the black chasms of the rock, her voice was as feeble as the wail of a sick child.

When she had laid her inert burden upon the bed, Allie knelt and took Gray's head upon her bosom. Then, for the first time, those forces imprisoned deep within her being ran wild, and under the red glare of that flaming geyser she kissed his hair, his eyes, his lips. Over and over again she kissed them with the hungry passion of a woman starved.

CHAPTER XXVI

A subdued but continuous whispering irritated Calvin Gray. When it persisted, minute after minute, he opened his eyes, asking himself, dully, why it was that people couldn't let a fellow sleep. He lay, for some time, trying to recognize his unfamiliar surroundings; oddly enough, he could not discover the origin of that low-pitched murmur, since there was nobody in his bedroom. Evidently he had slept too hard, for his eyes were heavy, his vision was distorted, and an unaccustomed lassitude bore down his body and stupefied his brain. A thousand indistinct memories were moving about in the penumbral borderland of consciousness, but they refused to take shape. They would emerge into the light presently, of course. Meanwhile, it was restful to remain in this state of semi-stupefaction. He was pretty tired.

That whispering, he realized after a while, was nothing more than the monotonous murmur of rain upon a shingle roof, and the gurgle from dripping eaves. Oh yes! It had been pouring for several days; raining buckets, barrels—Ten thousand barrels a day!

Yonder was something familiar; a patent, spring rocking-chair. Gray knew it well. It creaked miserably when you sat in it, and when you got up to look at diamond rings it snapped its jaws at you like an alligator. Odd that they'd let an alligator into the Ajax Hotel. Nelson's doings, probably. Always up to some deviltry, that Nelson. But, thank God, the fire was out, and that ear-splitting racket that hurt his head had changed into

Rex Beach

the soothing patter of raindrops. There couldn't be any fire with ten thousand barrels of rain falling.

Gray closed his eyes and dozed briefly. But he had dreams; calamity haunted him; he awoke to the realization of some horror. Slowly his brain began to function, then more swiftly, until, like a flood released, memory returned. He groaned aloud.

Allegheny Briskow appeared out of nowhere and laid a soothing hand upon his brow. When she saw the light of sanity in his eyes, her face brightened and she cried, eagerly:

"You're coming around all right, aren't you?"

"Ten thousand barrels!" he mumbled. "They said it would be a big well and I counted on it."

"Don't try to think—"

"But it came in a gasser. I remember it all now—nearly all. I —I'm about ruined, I guess."

"No, no!"

"It caught fire."

"You mustn't talk. Everything is all right—all right, honestly. I'll tell you everything, but just you rest now until Buddy comes." There was magnetism to the girl's touch and comfort in her voice.

It was some time later that Gray opened his eyes and spoke in a more natural voice, saying, "How do I happen to be here in your house, Allie?"

"We brought you over at daylight. Buddy's gone for a doctor, but he'll be back." The girl averted her face quickly and moved toward the window.

"I remember being hurt in some way—derrick fell on me, or something. Then the well caught fire. What time is it?"

"It's afternoon. About four o'clock. Buddy 'll be back—" Allie's voice caught queerly. "He'll get back somehow."

"He ought to be at the well—putting it out. God! What a sight! I see it yet!"

"The well is out!" Allie returned and seated herself beside the bed. "You probably won't understand it or believe it—I can scarcely believe it myself, for it's a miracle. All the same, it is out, shut in, and not much damage done. You're not ruined, either, for Buddy says they're short of fuel here, and a gasser this size is worth a good deal—'most as much as a fair oil well.'"

"How can it be shut in? It was blazing, roaring—a tower of flame. The derrick itself was going—"

"I know, but the strangest thing—" Allie spoke breathlessly. "Let me do the talking, please. You remember the drill stems were standing over in one corner? Well, the fire drove everybody off, of course; there was no facing it, and they thought sure they'd have a job—have to send for boilers and smother it down with steam, maybe, or tunnel under, or something—work for days, maybe weeks, and spend a fortune. Anyhow, they were in a panic, but when the derrick went down what do you think? That stack of drill stems fell in such a way as to close the gate valve at the top of the casing."

Gray frowned, he shook his head. "Impossible. You're trying to ease my mind."

"Of course it's impossible. But it happened, just as I tell you. Buddy had a bar fixed in the valve wheel, like a long handle, so that a half turn, or maybe a quarter, would shut it. Anyhow, those drill stems caught that bar in falling and closed the valve. Somebody said it happened once before, to an oil well over in Louisiana—"

"It—sounds incredible." The speaker made an effort to collect himself, he raised an uncertain hand to his bandaged head. "What ails me? I recall a lot of things, but they're pretty well confused."

Allie made known, the nature of the accident resulting in Gray's injury, and he nodded his understanding. "So Buddy saved my life!" He smiled. "Great boy, Buddy! I'll know better than to mix it with him again—he learns too quickly."

"Oh, it was terrible! I've been so—so frightened!" Allie Briskow suddenly lost control of herself and, bowing her head, she hid her face in the musty patchwork quilt. Her shoulders shook, her whole strong body twitched and trembled. "You've b-been awful sick. I did the best I could, but—"

"There, there!" Gray placed his hand upon the girl's head; he took her palm in his and stroked it. "I'm not worth your tears, child. And, anyhow, I'm all right again; I am, indeed. I'm as well as ever, so far as I can tell. By the way, what set the well afire?"

"Buddy thinks somebody must have dropped a cigarette when the stampede came." The girl raised her face and wiped the tears from it. "It doesn't seem possible anybody would be so careless as to smoke near a well that was coming in, but—Just think, Mr. Gray, those drill stems shut it off! Why, it was the hand of God!"

"It seems so. My luck hasn't run out, that's plain." The speaker pondered briefly, then he said: "Shut in! Safe! Jove, it's wonderful! Buddy can take me to the railroad to-night and—"

"Oh, you can't leave. You're not able."

"I must. This gasser was a great disappointment to me. I allowed myself to count on a big well, and now I have a serious problem to meet. It must be met without delay. Buddy will soon be back, I dare say?" Allie undertook to evade the speaker's eye, but unsuccessfully, and he inquired, sharply: "What's wrong? What's happened to him?"

"Nothing. He's all right, but"—Gray's evident alarm demanded the truth, therefore she explained—"but I don't know when he'll be back. That's why I've been so frightened. It has been raining cats and dogs; the creek has overflowed and everything is under water."

"Under water? Here? Why, that can't be." Gray insisted upon rising, and Allie finally consented to his doing so; then, despite his protest that ha was quite able to take care of himself, she helped him to the window. From that position he beheld a surprising scene.

The Briskow farm lay in a flat, saucerlike valley, arid and dusty at most seasons of the year, but now a shallow lake, the surface of which was broken by occasional fences, misty clumps of bushes, or the tops of dead weeds. The nearest Briskow derrick was dimly visible, its floor awash, its shape suggestive of the battle mast of a sunken man-of-war.

"It's not more than a foot or two deep on the level," Allie explained, "but that's enough. And it has come up six inches since Buddy left. He'd have been back before this if he could have made it."

"Did you ever see it like this before?"

"Once, when I was a little girl. Some years the creek never has a drop in it."

"Then we're marooned."

"We were cut off for three days that time."

Gray frowned. What next? he asked himself. Here was a

calamity that could not be dodged. He shrugged, finally. "No use to fret. No use to crouch beneath a load. I'd give my right arm to be back in Dallas, but—this is our chance to cultivate the Christian virtue of submission. So be it! One must have a heart for every fate, but," he smiled at the girl, "it is hard to be philosophical when you're hungry. And I'm hungry."

"Oh, you *are* better!"

"I'm well, I tell you, except for the bruises bequeathed me by your brutal brother. Three days—a week, maybe! My God! By the way, is there any food in the house?"

"Plenty."

"Then—we've nothing to do except get better acquainted, and that is something I've wanted to do for some time."

Allegheny Briskow sang while she prepared supper, for the reaction from the strain of the last twelve hours was like an intoxication. Mr. Gray was in no further danger; he was well except for a bandaged head and some bruises. And he was here alone with her. They were as completely cut off from the outside world as if shipwrecked on some island, and, for the time being at least, he was hers to look out for, hers to wait upon and to guard. Allie laughed at the drumming of the rain upon the kitchen roof, and she thrilled at memory of some of the things she had done. She could feel again Gray's head upon her bosom, his lips against hers, his body strained to hers. She had listened to his heartbeats; with her own abundant strength she had shielded him, fought for him, drawn him, by very force of her will, back to life; the anguish she had suffered during those long hours became, in retrospect, a poignant pleasure.

She wondered if by any chance he would remember—there had been times when he had seemed to be almost rational. She hoped not. And yet—why not? If he did remember, if indeed he had felt her kisses or heard her pleadings, that memory, even if subconscious, might serve to awaken him. It might evoke some response to the flaming passion that had finally escaped her control. Gray was a strong man; his emotions, once roused, were probably as wild as hers, therefore who could tell what might happen? Irresistible forces, fire and flood, had thrown them together. They were at the mercy of elemental powers, and they were alone with each other—a man and a woman. Allie hoped against hope; she prayed recklessly, defiantly, that her hour had struck.

Gray came into the kitchen after a while to warm himself over the stove. He was still a little bit unsteady on his feet, and his head felt queer; but he assumed a certain gayety and insisted upon bearing an awkward hand with the cooking and the dishes. He had never seen Allie as she was now, nor in a mood to compare with this, and for the first time he realized how fully she had developed. It was not surprising that her metamorphosis had escaped his attention, for he had never taken time to do more than briefly appraise her. With leisure for observation, however, he noted that she had made good her promise of rare physical charm, and that her comeliness had ripened into real beauty—beauty built on an overwhelming scale, to be sure, and hence doubly striking—moreover, he saw that all traces of her stolidity had vanished. She was an intelligent, wide-awake, vibrant person, and at this moment a genial fire, a breathless excitement, was ablaze within her. Gray complimented her frankly, and she was extravagantly pleased.

"Buddy said almost the same thing," she told him. "I don't care whether it's true or not, if you believe it."

"Oh, it's true! I saw great things in you, but—"

"Even when you saw me hoeing in the garden that first day?"

"Even then; but I wasn't prepared for a miracle. You were an enchanted princess, and it required only a magic word to break the spell."

"It is all your doings, Mr. Gray. Whatever I am I owe it all to you. And it's the same with the rest of the family. I—" Allie hesitated, looked up from her work, then shook her head smilingly.

"What?"

"I feel as if—well, as if you'd made me and I—belonged to you." It was dusk by this time; the girl's face was lit only by the indirect glow from the open door of the stove, therefore Gray could make nothing of her expression.

"How very flattering!" he laughed. "As a real matter of fact, I had almost nothing to do with it."

"All the same that's how I feel—as if I owed you everything and had to give something back. Women are queer, I guess. They love to give. And yet they're selfish—more selfish than men."

"I wouldn't say so."

"You don't know how bad hurt you were, Mr. Gray. I saved your life as much as Buddy did. You'd have died only for—only I wouldn't let you."

"I believe it. So, you see, you have more than evened the score. After all, I merely awakened the Sleeping Beauty, while you—"

"The prince woke her up with a kiss, didn't he?" Allie said, with a smile.

"So the story goes. Fairy stories, by the way, are the only kind one can afford to believe."

"Then I've got—something coming to me, haven't I?"

This time the girl turned her face invitingly to the speaker and waited.

Here was a new Allie Briskow, indeed, and one that amazed, nay, disturbed, Gray. Romance, he told himself. The girl meant nothing by this; nevertheless, her fancy had run far enough. He ignored her invitation, and instead of kissing her he patted her shoulder affectionately, saying:

"You're a dear child, and I can never repay you for mending my poor cracked head."

He turned his back, went to the table and lit the lamp, uncomfortably aware of the fact, meanwhile, that Allie remained motionless where he had left her. He ran on, casually, during the time he adjusted chimney and wick: "I was on the porch just now and found a rabbit crouching there. The poor thing was too wet and frightened to move." Allie did not seem to hear him. "All sorts of things are floating about; dead chickens, rattlesnakes, and—Oh yes, another thing I noticed; there's a good deal of oil on the water! I wonder where it comes from?"

Allie stirred herself; she jerked open the oven door, peered in, then slammed it shut. Her voice was sullen as she said: "They've been expecting a gusher on sixteen. Maybe the reservoirs have overflowed, or a pipe line has broken. Maybe it came in wild, you can't tell. This flood will cost a good many people a lot."

Supper, when the two sat down to it, proved to be a pleasant meal, for the soft glow of the lamp, the warmth from the stove, made of the Briskow kitchen a cozy place, while the drumming of the rain overhead enhanced their feeling of comfort and security. Gray's appetite was not that of a sick man, and Allie, who had regained her agreeable humor by this time, waited upon him with eager face and shining eyes. He paused, finally, to say:

"See here! You're not eating a bite."

"I'm not hungry. I couldn't eat, to-night. Please—I'm perfectly happy. I feel like a slave at the great lord's table; all I care to do is look on." After a moment she continued: "It couldn't have been so bad to be a slave—a girl slave. Somebody owned them, anyhow; they belonged to their masters, body and soul, and that's something. Women are like that. They've got to belong to somebody to be happy."

Gray was a talkative man, therefore he argued this point until he began to suspect that his companion was not heeding his words so much as the sound of his voice. More plainly than before he realized that there was something about Allie to-night utterly strange and quite contrary to his conception of her, but, because he believed her to be unlike other women, he did not try to understand it.

During the night an explosive crash followed by a loud reverberation awoke Calvin Gray and brought him up sitting. His room was lit by white flickers, against which he saw that the rain still sheeted his windows; he fumbled for his watch and found that it was two o'clock. This was a storm, indeed, and he began to fear that this deluge might swell the waters to a danger point; therefore he rose, struck a light, and dressed himself. Sleep was out of the question, anyhow, amid such an uproar. As he stepped out upon the front porch, his attention was instantly drawn to a yellow glow in the west, a distant torch, the flame of which illuminated the angry night. He stared at it for a moment before he realized its meaning. A well was afire! Lightning had wrecked a derrick and ignited the stream of oil. No wonder, he told himself, for this field was dotted with towers well calculated to lead lightning out of the skies, and amid a play of destructive forces such as this nothing less than a miracle could have prevented something of the sort. But it was a pity, for yonder a small-sized fortune was going up in smoke.

By the next flare he saw that the waters had crept higher. They were nearly up to the porch floor now, and, obviously, they were still rising. That rabbit was crouched where he had last seen it, a wet ball of fur with round, black eyes. The heavens echoed almost constantly, now to a thick, distant rumble, again to an appalling din directly overhead; for seconds at a time there was light enough to read by. The house, Gray decided, was in no danger, except from a direct bolt, for the valley was nothing more than a shallow lake; nevertheless—

A blinding, blue-white streak came, and he counted the seconds before the sound reached him. Sound traveled something like a thousand feet a second, he reflected; that bolt must have struck about a mile distant. Nothing alarming about that, surely. A moment, then he blinked and rubbed his eyes, for out of the murk was born another bonfire like that to the westward.

Hearing an exclamation behind him, Gray turned to behold Allie Briskow's dim figure in the door.

"Hello!" he cried, excitedly. "Did you see that? Yonder are two wells afire."

"I know. I haven't closed my eyes. You can see another one from my window." Allia snapped the light from a pocket flash upon Gray, and, noting that he was only partly clad, she urged him to come into the house. When he ignored the request she joined him, and together they stared at the mounting flames.

"Jove! That's terrible!" he muttered.

"Look here." Allie directed the beam of her light down over the edge of the porch, and moved it slowly from side to side. The surface of the water was not only burdened with debris, but also it was thick with oil. "It's just like that on the other side. That gusher on sixteen must be wild."

"Why didn't you call me?" the man inquired, sharply.

"What was the use? There's no chance for us to get out."

"How far is it back to high ground?"

"Quite a ways. Too far to wade. It would be over our heads in places, too. I don't like the look of it, do you? Not with those fires going, and—"

"I dare say it won't get any worse." Gray spoke with a carelessness that he was far from feeling, but his tone did not deceive the girl.

"It doesn't have to get any worse," she declared, im patiently. "There's oil enough here to burn. We're in the middle of a lake of it. What 'll happen if it catches fire?"

"Frankly, I don't know. I've never been marooned in a lake of oil. Probably this rain would quench it-"

"You know better than that!" Allie cried. "Don't act as if I were a kid. We're in a bad fix, with fire on three sides of us."

"At least we'll be as well off inside as out here," Gray declared, and his companion agreed, so together they went into her room, where, side by side, they peered through her window. What Allie had said was true, and the man pinched himself to see if he were dreaming. This conflagration was even closer than the others, and he could not doubt that there was every likelihood of its spreading to the surface of the lake itself. Here was a situation, truly. For the life of him he could think of no way out of it.

"I've read about this sort of thing," Allie was saying. "Tanks bursting and rivers afire. It spreads all over, the fire does, and there's no putting it out."

"One thing sure, this lightning won't last long—"

A blue glare and a ripping explosion gave the lie to Gray's cheering words. Allie Briskow recoiled from the window.

"We'll be burned alive!" she gasped. "Roasted like rats in a trap. I—I'm frightened, Mr. Gray." She drew closer to him.

"No need of that. We'll get out of this scrape somehow—people always do." A flicker lit the room, and he saw that the face upturned to his was wide eyed, strained. That brief glimpse of Allie, like a picture seen through the shutter of a camera, remained long with the man, for her hair was unbound, her lips were parted, and her dark eyes were peculiarly brilliant; through the opening of her lacy negligee her round, white neck and swelling bosom were exposed. It was a head, a bust, to be remembered.

"I—You got to—hold me," she said, huskily, and he felt her body shrink close to his. She clung tightly to him, trembling at first, then shaking in every limb. Fright, it seemed, had suddenly mastered Allie Briskow.

Gray endeavored for a moment to soothe her, then gently to loosen her hold; he spoke to her as he would have spoken to a terrified child, but the wildness of her emotion matched the wildness of the night, and her strength was nearly equal to his. Knowing her as he did, this abysmal terror was inexplicable; such abandon was entirely out of keeping with her. But she had acted queerly ever since—Gray was ashamed of the thought that leaped into his mind; he hated himself for harboring it. He hated himself also for the thrill that coursed through him at contact with this disheveled creature. The touch of her flesh disturbed him unbearably. Roughly he tore her arms from about his neck and put her away from him; by main strength he forced her into a chair, then snatched a covering of some sort from the bed and folded it around her shoulders. His voice was hoarse—to him it sounded almost brutal as he said:

"Get hold of yourself! We're in no great danger, really. Now then, a light will help us both." With clumsy hands he struck a match and lit the lamp. "Light's a great thing—drives away foolishness—nightmares and fancies of all sorts." Without looking at her he seized the electric torch and muttered: "I'll take a look around, just to see that things are snug. Back presently."

Gray despised himself thoroughly when the turmoil within him persisted; when he still felt the unruly urge to return whence he had come. Wild horses! That was how Gus Briskow had described his children. Well, Allie had followed Buddy's example and jumped the fence. Here was something unique in the way of an experience, sure enough; here were forces at play as savage and as destructive as those that lit the heavens. The girl was magnificent, maddening—and he was running away from her! He, a man of the world, as ruthless as most men of his type! It was a phenomenon to awaken sardonic mirth. He wondered what had come over him. He had changed, indeed.

Could it be that he had read a wrong significance into Allie's actions? Thus his mind worked when he grew calmer. He tried to answer in the affirmative, but already he hated himself sufficiently. No, the night had done it. Texas cattle stampede on stormy nights. They run blindly to destruction. The very air was surcharged, electric, and the girl was untamed, only a step removed from the soil. The possibility that she could be seriously interested in him, strangely enough, never presented itself.

Gray laid strong hold of himself, but it is not easy to subdue thought, and he could feel those strong, smooth, velvet arms encircling him. Disorder without and chaos within this house! The heavens rumbled like a mighty drumhead, the lightning made useless the feeble ray in his hand. It was the place, the hour of impulse. Gray swore savagely at himself, then he stumbled into his room and dressed himself more fully.

"Well, there doesn't seem to be much change," he said, cheerfully, as he opened Allie's door awhile later. "The fires don't seem to be spreading." She was sitting where he had left her, she had not moved. "Anything new on this side?"

Allie shrugged; slowly she turned, exposing a face tragic and stony. "I guess you don't think much of me," she said.

"Indeed!" he declared, heartily. "This is enough to frighten anybody. I don't mind saying it has upset me. But the worst is over." He laid a reassuring hand upon her shoulder.

Allie moved her body convulsively. "Lemme be!" she cried, sharply. "I don't mind the lightning. I ain't scared of the fire, either—hell fire or any other kind. I ain't scared of anything, and yet—I'm a dam' coward!"

She rose, gathered her loose robe more closely about her, and made blindly toward the bed. She flung herself upon it and buried her face in the pillows. "Just a—dam' coward!" she repeated, in a muffled wail. "My God, I wish the blaze would come!"

CHAPTER XXVII

Buddy Briskow had difficulty in getting out of the valley on his way for a doctor, for never had the roads been like this. He drove recklessly; where necessary he disregarded fences and pushed across pastures that were hub deep; he even burst through occasional thickets in defiance of axle and tire. It was a mad journey, like the ride in a death-defying movie serial; only by some miraculous power of cohesion did the machine hold together and thus enable him to keep it under way and bring it out to high ground. Since he had not taken time before leaving to change into dry clothing, he was drenched to the skin; he was, in fact, sheeted with mud like the car itself.

To find a doctor, however, was a problem. Buddy tried first one camp, then another, but without success. Meanwhile, the downpour continued and the creeks rose steadily, obliging him to make numerous detours and to follow the ridge roads wherever possible. He was aching in every bone and muscle from the pounding he had received, his arms were numb, his back was broken. He drowned his motor finally in fording a roily stream and abandoned the car.

He came into Ranger that afternoon on the back of a truck horse that he had borrowed—without the owner's consent. For a time it seemed that if he got a doctor at all he would have to follow a similar procedure, but the Briskow name was powerful, and Buddy talked in big figures, so eventually he set out on the return journey—this time in a springless freight wagon drawn by the stoutest team in town. A medical man was on the seat beside him.

Progress was maddeningly slow, incredibly tedious; creek beds, long dry, had become foaming torrents; in places even the level roads were belly deep and the horses floundered. When one of them fell, it required infinite labor and patience to get it upon its feet again.

It was after midnight when Buddy and his miserable companion gained the comparatively easy going of the last ridge, that flinty range beyond which lay the Briskow farm. Here they drove in the glare of lightning and under a sky that rumbled almost steadily, for a frightful electric storm had broken. Here it was that they saw what havoc was being wrought—they counted several blazing wells ahead of them.

Buddy stopped at a drilling camp where lights showed the occupants to be astir, and there he received confirmation of his fears. The flats beyond were inundated to a depth rendering travel impossible, and although some of the men stationed out there had managed to work their way back, others were, for the time being, hopelessly cut off. What was more alarming by far, in view of these blazing beacons, was the news that a huge gusher on sixteen was wild and pouring its inflammable flood out upon the surface of the water.

Buddy stood in the midst of a spreading puddle from his streaming clothes, and through chattering teeth announced: "My sister and Mr. Gray are out there. I *gotta* get through!"

"How you going to get through, kid?" one of the drillers inquired. "Our men had to swim in places."

"I guess I can swim, if I try. Feller can do 'most anything if he has to. How about you, Doc?" Buddy turned to his traveling companion.

The latter shook his head positively. "You're crazy, Briskow. We'd probably drown. If we didn't, we'd be burned alive when that loose oil catches fire."

"Looks like it's bound to catch if this lightning keeps up," some one declared. "Listen to that!"

Buddy cursed furiously and lurched toward the door. It took force to restrain him from going.

That was indeed a night of terror in the oil fields, for destruction was wholesale, and to those who were fortunate enough to be in no danger it was scarcely less trying than for the luckless ones out in the flooded area. Buddy Briskow was half demented. At one time it seemed certain that the surface oil was aflame near his father's farm, and the pictures he conjured up were unbearable.

The rain ceased with the passing of the electrical storm, but the late hours of the night were thick and the fires continued to burn. It seemed as if morning would never come. With the first light Buddy mounted one of his horses, and, regardless of admonitions, set out. In miles he had no great distance to go; nevertheless, it was midday before he came in sight of his father's unpainted farmhouse, and when he dismounted at the front porch he fell rather than walked through the door.

He broke down and blubbered weakly when he saw Calvin Gray up and around and apparently well. He collapsed into a chair and huddled there in a wet heap, the while he sobbed and laughed hysterically. He was considerably ashamed of his show of feeling.

Even after he had been helped into the kitchen and his wet clothes had been stripped from him, he could tell little about his trip, but hot food and drink brought him around and then, indeed, his story was one that deeply touched the elder man.

Already the waters had ceased to rise, but Buddy's difficulty in getting through proved the folly of attempting escape for the time being; his horse had been forced to swim with him in more than one place; in others he had waded waist deep, stumbling through thickets, hauling the animal after him by main strength. There was nothing to do, it seemed, but await a subsidence of the flood. Then, too, the boy was half dead for sleep.

Under the circumstances it was not easy for the elder man to face this delay. His affairs were in a precarious condition and more in need of his immediate attention than ever before; to be cut off, therefore, to be lost for several days at this particular time was more than a misfortune—it was a catastrophe. Such vague plans as he had considered he was now forced to abandon. He could see ruin ahead.

One purpose this enforced idleness did serve, however; it enabled him—nay, it forced him—to evolve a new scheme of relief. Some minds become paralyzed in moments of panic, others function with unexpected clearness and ingenuity, and his was such a mind. An idea came to him, finally, which seemed sound, the more he thought about it. Indeed, its possibilities galvanized him, and he wondered why he had been so long in arriving at it. It was spectacular, daring, it might prove to be impossible of accomplishment; nevertheless, it was worth trying, and he could scarcely wait for Buddy Briskow to wake up so that he could put it to him.

Late that evening, after Allie had gone to bed, he had a long talk with his young friend, during which he told him more about his affairs than he had made known even to Roswell, the banker.

Buddy listened with the closest attention. He drew a deep breath at last and said: "I knew you was in deep, but I thought it was just your way. Now I *know* it was Nelson's crew that fired our gasser. Why, they might have cost us thousands—yes, hundreds of thousands—if it had been the kind of a gusher we figgered on! Say"—the speaker's brows drew together in an angry scowl—"what ails this Nelson, anyhow—tryin' to get you shot, an' firin' your wells, an' everything?"

"He once did me a great injury."

"What kind?"

There was a pause. "I'd rather not go into that now, Buddy. To repeat what I've been telling you, however, the situation is this: I've gone as far as I can go with the backing I have, and I must make a quick turn—strike one final blow or give up. Nelson and I are like two wrestlers floundering on the mat. We're both tired, groggy, out of breath. Whichever one gets the first hold will win, for the other lacks strength to break it. Do you think your father would trust me? Do you think he'd go it blind on my say-so?"

"If he won't, I will. I got money. So's Allie."

Gray declined this offer with a positive shake of the head. "It must appeal to him on its merits. I wouldn't permit you to go contrary to his judgment."

"Judgment? What's Pa's judgment worth? He knows it's no good, an' so do we. Everybody's tryin' to do him up but you; you're the only one he trusts. An' the same here. There's my bank roll—you can shoot the whole piece. I don't care if it never comes back. Tryin' to get you killed! An' spoilin' a well on me!"

"Thank you, Buddy! You—make me slow to trust my own judgment. I—I seem to be developing a conscience. But I'm sure this is the thing to do, for you and your father as well as for me. People can't stand still; they must go forward. The Briskow fortune must grow or it will crumble."

"I dunno if we've got as much in us as you seem to think," the boy said, doubtfully.

"Look at Allie! And, you, too! You took hold of this field work and ran it like a man. I said you'd make a hand, and you have. The day is coming when people like you, who went from poverty to affluence overnight, will retrace that journey. That's the time when the truly dramatic story of the Texas oil boom will be written. Then will come the real tragedy, and you mustn't be caught in it. Money isn't a servant, Buddy; it is a master, and a mighty stern, relentless master, at that. When your first well blew in, it didn't mean ease and enjoyment, as you thought; it meant hard work for the rest of your life."

"If you'd talked to me like this when I went off to school," the boy said, after a moment of consideration, "mebbe I'd of made myself swallow some more education, even if I had to take it out of a bottle along with the little kids."

Gray smiled. "You have common sense, at least, and that's something you can't get in school. Men wear smooth from contact with one another, and it is time you got in touch with something bigger than mere drilling. If you're willing, I'll take you to Wichita Falls with me."

"*Willing?*" Buddy's eyes sparkled. Guiltily he confessed: "It's been pretty—lonesome out here with the scorpions. But I wanted to show you I could make good."

"Do you drink any more?"

"Haven't touched a drop. I don't reckon I ever will, either. I don't take to the idea of back-trackin' to this farm an' gettin' old in overalls, like you say. I'm sort of penurious an' I aim to keep what little sense I got. A feller as dull as I am can't afford to drink."

"One thing more." Gray nodded approvingly. "I want you to promise me that you won't fall in love with the first woman you meet. I'd never be able to lick you again."

Buddy showed his strong, white teeth in a broad grin. "I promise! That boy with the bass voice cured me. I'm goin' to be a hermit."

News of the damage wrought by the recent storm was naturally of grave concern to Henry Nelson, but owing to the fact that lines were down, about his only source of information, during the days immediately following it, was the press reports. He was reading the Dallas papers with interest one morning when his attention was arrested by the name of Calvin Gray. Now Gray's name in print affected the banker almost as disagreeably as did a sight of the man himself; therefore it was with intense resentment that he read the article in which it appeared. It was a vividly written account of the former's experience during the flood, and, due no doubt to Gray's personal touch, it read a good deal like fiction. The man had a unique turn for publicity, a knack for self-advertising that infuriated Nelson. To read this anybody would think that he was one of the dominant figures in the oil industry, and that his enterprises were immensely successful. With a sneer Nelson flung the paper aside. So, that was how it had happened. The well had been fired—Henry believed he could account for that—but a miracle had quenched the flame. Falling drill stems! Who ever heard of such a thing? Such luck was uncanny—enough to give one the creeps. If Gray were tied hand and foot and thrown into a river, somebody would drag him out—with his pockets full of fish! And to be marooned for days in the midst of a blazing lake—Damnation! Well, luck like that was bound to change. It had changed. The note of assurance in this self-edited story was patently counterfeit, or so Henry told himself, for surely the fellow must know by this time that his race was run. Probably this was a desperate effort to secure further backing. If so, it would fail.

Henry believed that he had weakened his enemy's support so completely that he would fall of his own weight; he considered it, in fact, about the cleverest move he had ever made to dispose of a block of bank stock in such a way as not only to tide him over his own difficulties, but also to make allies of Gray's associates—the very men who had been fighting him. Those men were through with the scoundrel now, and who else could he appeal to, once they abandoned him? Nobody. No, the ice had been thin, at times—Henry had felt it bending under him—but he was safe at last. The crossing had been made.

So much accomplished; now that the fellow was down and could no longer fight back, it was time to see that Barbara Parker learned the truth about her gallant suitor. The next time Tom Parker came into the bank Henry called him into his private office and had a talk with him.

Old Tom listened silently; nevertheless, it was plain that he was deeply shocked.

"I s'pose you ain't lyin'," he said, coldly, when the banker had finished.

"It's a matter of record, Tom. He can't deny it."

"Why did you—hold off so long?"

"We're not exactly friends. He foolishly believes that I had something to do with his disgrace, and he has done his best to injure me. Under the circumstances, I couldn't very well say anything. I wouldn't speak now, except for the fact that 'Bob' is interested in him and—well, I'm interested in 'Bob.'"

"She's been interested in him from the first. I don't see that the circumstances are much different than they have been," Tom said, sourly.

"Put it down to jealousy, if you wish." Henry was impatient.

"And I don't know as 'Bob' ever encouraged you to think—"

"Perhaps not. But she is the only woman I ever saw that I'd make Mrs. Nelson."

"What was it he did?"

"'Conduct unbecoming an officer and a gentleman' is the way

the record stands. That covers a lot."

"Did he welch—quit under fire?"

"No."

"Steal something?"

"No."

"Woman scrape?"

"There was—a woman concerned. Pretty nasty mess, Tom. He's the sort of man to intrigue any foolish woman. Women can't see far."

"I s'pose so." Mr. Parker rose stiffly. "But we don't have to worry about 'Bob.' She ain't foolish and her eyesight is good. She's got more sense than all three of us men." With this noncommittal remark the father limped out.

But Tom was more deeply troubled than he had shown. Nothing to be said against a man could have weighed more heavily with him than this particular charge. To a man of his type dereliction of duty was a crime; dishonorable discharge from the army of his country was an appalling indictment implying utter moral turpitude. Tom had known more than one fellow who was guilty of conduct unbecoming a gentleman—as a matter of fact, he had reason to respect certain of them for some of their ungentlemanly conduct—but conduct unbecoming an officer was something altogether different. He had never met but one such, and he had shot that fellow just above the bridge of the nose. A traitor to his oath of office, a man who could dishonor his state, his country, was worse than a renegade; his name was a hissing upon the lips of decent people. Scalawags like that were not to be tolerated. It seemed incredible that Gray could be one.

Yes, and "Bob" liked the fellow—but so did he, for   that

matter. In great perturbation of spirit Tom consulted Judge Halloran.

The judge listened to him in astonishment; angrily he cried: "The idea of his paying court to 'Bob'! The insufferable insolence of it! Why, I consider it a personal affront."

"Where do *you* come in to get all het up?" Tom growled.

"*What?*" Halloran's irascible face reddened. "'Where do I—'? My God! Haven't I—? Don't I stand in *loco parentis* to the girl?"

"You ain't as *loco parentis* to her as I am. She's my son. Trouble is, I like Mr. Gray. You don't think Henry could be lying?"

"He wouldn't dare. It is too serious. No, Tom, there's just one thing to do; you and I will go directly to the scoundrel, tell him we are aware of his infamy, and order him out of town. Ha! That's the way to go about it; cut deep and quickly. Tar and feathers are too good for—"

"Trouble is," Tom repeated, with a reluctant sigh, "I like him and I ain't sure—" "The trouble is you're a weakling!" Halloran snapped. "You are a—sentimentalist. You lack my stern, uncompromising moral fiber. *Like* him? Pah! What has that to do with it? I have no weakness, no bowels of compassion. I am a Spartan. I am—"

"You're a damned old fool—if you think you can run *him*. He's liable to run you."

Judge Halloran was furious at this; he was hurt, too. He sputtered for a moment before managing to say: "Have it your own way. You are trying to be unpleasant—not that it requires conscious effort—but I won't argue with you."

"Don't! I hate arguments. That's why I don't like to talk this over with Mr. Gray. When I'm mad enough to argue I'm mad enough to fight, and I fight better than I argue."

If, indeed, Calvin Gray's affairs were in a condition as precarious as Nelson believed, he showed no signs of it when he returned to Wichita Falls. On the contrary, he was in an exultant mood, and even on the train young Briskow, who accompanied him, was amazed at the change that had come over his friend. With every mile they traveled Gray's buoyancy increased and upon his arrival he trod the street to his office like a conqueror. McWade and Stoner, who came in for a conference with minds preoccupied and faces grave, left with a smile and a jest.

When they had gone, Gray rose with relief and surprised Buddy by saying: "That's enough for now, thank goodness! Business is only one side of life, my boy. You are going to make this city your home, so you must begin by meeting the right people, the influential people. Nicest people in the world right here, Buddy; nicest place in the world, too!"

Now to a youth who, for months, had been immured in the oil fields, Wichita Falls did indeed resemble a city of marvelous portent. Pavements, large buildings, bright lights, theaters— Buddy was thrilled. He prepared himself for introduction to oil operators, to men of finance sitting in marble and mahogany offices; he made ready to step forth into the big world.

Great was his astonishment, therefore, when after a swift walk Gray turned into a tiny frame insurance office on a side street. Funny place to look for people of influence, Buddy cogitated.

A girl was seated at a desk; she rose at sight of Gray, and her face broke into a smile. Her greeting was warm; her hand lingered in his; for the moment neither of them seemed to remember Buddy's presence. When she did hear his name, however, her face lightened and she gave her hand to him as to an old friend. When she smiled at him, as she had smiled at his companion, Buddy dropped his hat. He had never seen anyone in the least like this creature and—she knew Allie! She knew his mother! That was astonishing. He wondered why they had never said anything about it. Before she had finished telling him about that meeting in the store at Dallas, Buddy realized that here indeed was an influential person, a citizen of supreme importance. He had missed her name, but probably she owned that Dallas department store, or was the Mayor of Wichita Falls. He had never before been so embarrassed.

Mr. Gray certainly was a wonderful man. His poise, his air of respectful but easy familiarity with this—this angel raised him immensely in Buddy's esteem. Think of joking, chatting, making pretty speeches to an—an angel! That was going some. The gall of it!

They were talking about that big gasser of Gray's; the fire; the overflow; and the melodramatic occurrences of the past fortnight. Gray was telling her how Buddy had saved his life at the well, how he had risked his own, later, in braving the flood, and she was listening with eager smiles and nods and exclamations. When she turned admiring, grateful eyes upon the hero of Gray's story—and the story had been told in a manner to make Buddy no less—that youth felt himself suffocating, burning up. Mr. Gray sure knew how to talk; he could sling language. And *lie*—! Gosh, how beautifully he could lie! It was splendid of him to exaggerate like this, so as to set him in solid with the most important person in town. That was noble! People were awful nice. And this certainly was a grand city. Buddy knew he was going to get along fine; and he'd never forget Mr. Gray for this.

After a while, when the two men were on the street again, Buddy inquired: "Who is that young lady? I mean—her name?"

Gray told him, then with a friendly twinkle: "Well, speak out! What do you think of her?"

"Oh—*Gee!*" Buddy cried, breathlessly, whereupon his companion laughed in perfect satisfaction.

CHAPTER XXVIII

Gray returned to his desk that morning after his call on "Bob" Parker determined to tackle energetically the numerous business details needing his attention, but he found that he could not do so. As usual, his brief sight of the girl, instead of satisfying him, had merely increased his hunger; made him the more restless, the more eager to see her again—alone. He gave up fighting his desires, presently, and invented the necessity of a hurried trip to the Avenger lease.

Her ready acceptance of the invitation he construed to indicate an eagerness akin to his own, and during the several hours they were together he had hard work to keep from breaking his resolve and telling her all she had come to mean to him.

"Bob" seemed to expect something of the sort, as a matter of fact. Her shyness, her fluttering agitation when his voice unconsciously became tender—and he realized that, in spite of himself, the tone of his voice conveyed a message quite at variance with his words—taxed his self-control to the utmost. Well, it wouldn't be long now—another two weeks perhaps! But two weeks is an eternity when hearts are pounding, when ears are strained and lips are waiting.

Two callers were awaiting Gray when, late that afternoon, he mounted the stairs to his office—Tom Parker and Judge Halloran—and something in their formal, awkward greeting sent a quick chill of alarm through him. Mechanically he ushered them into his private room and offered them chairs.

He heard himself chatting casually enough, but neither his own words nor theirs conveyed much meaning to him. Nelson, it seemed, scorned no advantage, however dishonorable. Gray's hatred of the man attained deeper, blacker depths than ever. To-day of all days! What a reckoning was due!

The two old men were talking, one lamely supplementing the other's efforts to lead up to the object of their visit. Gray turned a set face to Tom Parker finally, and interrupted by saying:

"Permit me to ease your embarrassment, sir. You object to my attentions to your daughter. Is that it?" Tom dropped his eyes and mumbled an uncomfortable affirmative. "Not, I hope, because you question the nature of my intentions?"

"Oh no!"

"I'd say yes and no to that," Halloran declared, argumentatively. "Tom and I are gentlemen of the old school; we live by the code and 'Bob' is our joint property, in a way. Any man who aspires to the honor of—well, of even paying attentions to that girl must stand the acid test. There must be no blot upon his 'scutcheon."

"You imply, then, that there is a blot upon mine?"

"That is what prompts our visit, sir. Can you assure us that there is none?"

After a moment of hesitation Gray inquired, curiously: "Judge, do you believe that a man can live down disgrace?"

"Disgrace, yes. Dishonor, never! A man's honor is so sensitive that to stain it is to wound it. Like the human eye it cannot suffer the slightest injury without serious damage."

The younger man ignored the pompous tone of this speech; he nodded. "I see. Someone said also that it is like an island, rugged and without landing place; and once outside of it we can never re-enter. That is your idea, I dare say."

"Precisely!"

Tom Parker stirred; irritably he broke out, "I'm damned if I think you did it!"

"Did what?"

Tom remained silent, but when his companion drew a deep, preparatory breath, Gray lifted a hand. He rose nervously and in a changed tone continued:

"Again let me speak for you and shorten our mutual distress. First, however, I must make my own position plain. I—love your daughter, Mr. Parker." The declaration came at great cost, the speaker turned away to hide his emotion. "I think—I hope she is not indifferent to me. I would give my life to marry her and, God willing, I shall. So much for that." He swung himself about and met the eyes of first one old man, then the other. Harshly, defiantly, he added: "Understand me, nothing you can do, nothing on earth—nothing in Heaven or in hell, for that matter—will stop me from telling her about my love, when the time comes. Now then, Henry Nelson has told you that I was—that I was sent back from overseas in disgrace. You want to know if he spoke the truth. He did!"

After a moment of silence Judge Halloran said, with stiff finality: "Under the circumstances there is nothing more to talk about. You amaze me when you say—"

"I want to know more than if he was just telling the truth," Tom interrupted, grimly. "I want to know if you were guilty."

"That was the verdict of the court martial."

"To hell with that! Innocent men have been hung."

A faint smile softened Gray's face. "And guilty men have gone to the gallows protesting their innocence. Which are you to believe? I made the best defense possible, but it was insufficient. I have no new evidence. I would rather endure the stigma of guilt than have you consider me a liar, and, of course, that is what you would think if I denied it."

Halloran was on his feet now, and evidently anxious to terminate the interview. "There are two sides to every case, of course, and justice is not always done. However, that really makes no difference in this instance. The findings of a military tribunal are as conclusive as those of any court of law, and it is not for us to question them. To repeat what I started to say just now, I fail to understand how you can expect us to tolerate your further attentions to Miss Barbara or how you can persist in your insane determination to ask her hand in marriage."

"Perhaps you'll understand when I say that I propose to clear myself."

"How? When?"

"Soon, I hope."

"And in the meantime?"

Gray considered this question briefly. "In the meantime—if you will agree to say nothing to 'Bob,' I will promise not to declare my feelings, not to see her alone."

"That's a go," said the father.

"Mind you, I may fail to right myself. In that event I shall feel at liberty to tell her the facts and ask her to believe in me against the world. I trust she will do so. If she loves me as I love her, she will marry me even though she knows I am a liar and a blackguard."

"Never!" Halloran exploded. "'Bob' isn't that sort of a girl."

"I hope it never comes to the test."

"I hope so, too," the father declared, earnestly. "I'm—right fond of 'Bob,' and I wouldn't like to see her team up with a man she couldn't be proud of. *I* wouldn't take it easy." Mild as were these words, coming from Tom Parker they had the ominous effect of a threat.

Without further ado the two old men left.

There was little sleep that night for Calvin Gray, and the days that followed were a torture. It was a torment to avoid "Bob," for self-denial only whetted his appetite to see her, and those cunning plans he had laid at the time of their last meeting— plans devised solely to bring them together—he had to alter upon one excuse or another; he even forced Buddy Briskow to substitute for him. Fortunately, there were certain negotiations requiring his presence in Dallas, in Tulsa, and elsewhere, and it some what relieved his irritation to put miles between him and the city he had come to regard as his home.

The Nelsons' bank was known as the Security National, and it represented the life work of two generations of the family. Bell's father had founded it, in the early cattle days, but to the genius and industry of Bell himself had been due its growth into one of the influential institutions of the state. Other banks had finer quarters, but none in this part of the country had a more solid standing nor more powerful names upon its directorate. Bennett Swope, for instance, was the richest of the big cattle barons; Martin Murphy was known as the Arkansas hardwood king, and Herman Gage owned and operated a chain of department stores. The other two—there were but seven, including Bell and his son—were Northern capitalists who took no very active interest in the bank and almost never attended its meetings. For that matter, the three local men above named concerned themselves little with the actual running of the institution, for the Nelsons, who owned nine-tenths of the stock, were supreme in that sphere. It was only at the annual meetings when directors were re-elected—and invariably they succeeded themselves—that they forgathered to conduct the dull routine business which is a part of all annual meetings. After they had adjourned as stockholders they reconvened as directors, and again mumbled hurried and perfunctory ayes to the motions put before them, so that Bell could the more quickly get out his bottle of fine old Bourbon, the one really ceremonious procedure of the day. The Security National was as conservative, as rock ribbed, as respectable, and as uninteresting as any bank could well be, and its directors were always bored when election time came around.

In spite of the fact that the program this year was as thoroughly cut and dried as usual, the day of the meeting found both father and son decidedly nervous, for there were certain questions of management and of policy which they did not wish to touch upon, and their nervousness manifested itself in an assumption of friendliness and good fellowship quite unusual.

Senator Lowe, the bank's attorney and secretary, was arranging his minute books, his reports, and his miscellaneous papers, Martin Murphy was telling his latest story, when a knock came at the door to the directors' room. Bell himself answered it, but his protest at the interruption died upon his lips when he beheld Calvin Gray, Gus Briskow, and the latter's son, Ozark, facing him.

Gray spoke sharply, and his words fell with the effect of a bomb, at least upon Bell and Henry, for what he said was: "We are attending this meeting as stockholders, and we came early to enable the secretary to record the necessary transfer of our shares."

Disregarding the president's gasp of astonishment, the speaker pushed past him and entered, then introduced himself and his companions to the other men present.

Henry Nelson experienced a sick moment of dizziness; the room grew black before his eyes. It was Bell who broke out, harshly:

"*Stockholders?* Where did *you* get any stock in this bank, I'd like to know?"

"We bought it. Picked it up here and there—"

"I don't believe it!" Bell glared at the speaker, then he turned his eyes upon Swope, upon Murphy, upon Gage. "Did any of you sell out?"

"We don't own enough to make it worth while," Swope said, dryly. Murphy and Gage agreed. Bell's peculiar display of emotion surprised them; they exchanged glances. "I thought there wasn't any stock outside of what's owned by our group. What's the idea?"

Gray answered, easily. "There is now a considerable amount outside of that. A very considerable amount."

Henry Nelson made himself audible for the first time, and sneered angrily. "Quite theatric, Gray, this eleventh-hour move. How much have you got? What's your—your object?" In spite of himself his voice shook.

"My object is purely selfish." Gray's tone was equally unpleasant. He had expected to create a sensation, and he was not disappointed. "Mr. Briskow and his son are looking for a secure investment, and I have convinced them of the soundness of your institution. My operations make it necessary for me to establish a close banking affiliation—one where I can ask for and receive consideration"—his mockery was now unmistakable—"so where should I turn, except to my friends? I assume you make no objection to the stock transfer? Very well." He drew from his pocket a bundle of shares and tossed them across the table to Senator Lowe.

Henry made his way to his father's side; they withdrew to a corner and bent their heads together, murmuring inaudibly.

Gray watched them with unblinking intensity; he nodded to Buddy Briskow, and the latter, as if heeding some prearranged signal, removed his hands from his pockets and stepped farther into the room. He, too, watched the agitated pair.

"Why—look here!" the secretary gasped, after a moment or two. "This—this gives you control!"

Bell Nelson raised a stricken face. "Control?" he repeated, faintly. "*Control?*" He strode to the end of the table, and with shaking hands he ran through the sheaf of neatly folded certificates. "Sold out, by God!" He fell to cursing certain men, the names of whom caused Swope and Murphy and Gage to prick up their ears.

Gray was still staring at the junior Nelson; it was to him more than to the father that he spoke: "Sold out is right! It came high, but I think it was worth the price. We intend to vote our stock."

"By that I infer that you're going to take the bank over—take its management away from Bell and Henry?" Bennett Swope ventured.

"Naturally."

The elder Nelson voiced an unintelligible exclamation.

"That's a pretty rough deal. Bell has put his life into it. It is an—an institution, a credit to the community. It would be a misfortune if it fell into the hands of—into the control of somebody who—" The ranchman hesitated, then blurted forth, angrily: "Well, I don't like the look of this thing. I want to know what it means."

"I'll tell you," Henry cried, unevenly. "I'll tell you what it means. Persecution! Revenge! Hatred! I quarreled with this man, in France. He's vindictive; he followed me here—tried every way to ruin me—cost me thousands, hundreds of thousands of dollars. Father and I were—we were pinched. We had to realize some quick money to protect our oil holdings—offsets and the like—and we sold a lot of our stock with the understanding that we could—that we would buy it back at a higher figure. We only borrowed on it, you might say—hypothecated it. We thought we were dealing with friends, but—*Friends*! My God!" The speaker seized his head.

"The stock was not hypothecated. You sold it," Gray said, quietly, "and we bought it in."

"It is all a personal matter, a grudge."

"Is that true, Mr. Gray?" Swope inquired.

"Substantially. But I'm waiting for Colonel Nelson to tell you more; to tell you the whole story of our antagonism."

Martin Murphy, who had been a silent onlooker up to this point, made himself heard. "Mr. Gray, I don't like the look of this any better than Swope does. Your quarrel with Henry is wholly your and his affair, but the welfare of the Security National is partly ours. Banks are not toys, to be juggled and played with in mischief or in spite. You say you paid high for your stock; do you intend to wreck the institution, lose a fortune—?"

"By no means."

"That's precisely what you will succeed in doing."

"I had ventured to hope that you three gentlemen would remain on the board."

"Am I dreaming?" Bell Nelson's collar appeared to be choking him, and with clumsy fingers he tugged at it. "Going to kick Henry and me off the board, eh? Rob us? Well, I'm damned if you do! You'll not kick us off—"

"He doesn't want the bank," the son exclaimed, hoarsely. "That's all a bluff. He wants blackmail. That's the kind of man he is. He wants his price. I know him. How much, Gray? What'll it cost us?"

"I'll tell you what it will cost—"

"Ha! Didn't I say so?"

"Oh, there is a price for everything! Mine will surprise you, however, it is so low. Can't you guess what it is?" The speaker's intent gaze had never left Henry Nelson's face; it was fixed there now, as cold, as relentless as the stare of a python.

Bell Nelson leaned forward, his lips parted, a new eagerness came into his purple countenance. "Well, well! What is it?" he demanded, querulously.

"Vindication!"

There was a moment of silence. "What is he talking about, Henry?" Bell's eyes were strained toward his son.

"I don't know," the latter said, in a thin voice. "He's crazy—always was."

"I'm giving you a chance, Colonel. You'd better take it. Think carefully." When there came no response to this warning, Gray shrugged. "Very well! There is nothing further, except to complete the transfer and proceed with the business of the meeting. Mr. Briskow will be the next president, and I shall occupy the position of vice-president and treasurer now held by you—"

The effect of this declaration was electric. With a cry the younger Nelson lunged forward. Confusion followed. It was of short duration, however, for Henry found himself locked in the arms of the Briskow giant. Others lent Buddy their assistance, and, in spite of his struggles, the vice-president was flung backward upon a deep leather divan. He rose unsteadily, but, meeting Buddy's threatening gaze and realizing the impossibility of getting past him, he cried: "Let me out of here! Let me out, damn you! I—I'll get you for this, Gray. Let me out, I tell you!"

"Buddy!" Gray jerked his head in the direction of the door to one of the adjoining offices. "He keeps a gun in his desk—top drawer. Get it before me makes a fool of himself." Young Briskow stepped out of the room. Gray continued, speaking to the others, "I have something to say to you gentlemen before we go on with the meeting, and I wish to say it in the presence of Colonel Nelson and his—"

"You'll not keep me here. I refuse to stay," Henry shouted, and he pushed past Swope toward the door.

"Wait!" It was the elder Nelson speaking, and in his voice was a new note—a note of triumph. "Stock can't be transferred at an annual meeting. It has to be done in advance—ten days, I think it is. Am I right, Senator?"

"That is the usual procedure," Senator Lowe agreed.

"Better look it up and make sure," Gray directed.

There followed a few moments of uncomfortable silence while the bank's attorney ran through the by-laws. It seemed to those waiting that it was a long time before he frowned and shook his head.

"I—ah—I can find nothing against it. It seems I have nothing to do except transfer the shares."

"Then there won't be any meeting!" Bell loudly declared.

The three directors greeted this remark with exclamations of genuine relief. "Sure! Let's adjourn—put it over until—" one of them began, but the bank's president was bellowing in rising fury at the interlopers:

"Get out! Get out of my office, d'you hear? Get out—"

"Looks to me like it's *my* office," Gus Briskow said, quietly, "or it will be, directly. You, Bell, put on the muffler! I came a long ways to attend this meetin'. It's the first one I ever been to, an' it's goin' to happen. Shut up your fuss! I want you to hear what Mr. Gray's got to say."

"To hell with him, and you, too!" stormed the financier. "Hold the meeting, eh? Hold it if you dare! I defy you. Steal my bank, double-cross me—We'll see about that. Come along, Henry."

"You're in," Gray said, menacingly; "you'd better stay and vote your stock or you may never get back again." But neither father nor son heeded him. When they had gone he frowned. "I'm sorry. Really I am. I hoped I could force—"

"I think we'd better go, too," some one said. "This is too extraordinary—We're in no frame of mind to go ahead—"

"I must insist that you remain long enough to hear me out. You have no right to refuse. There is something you *must* be told."

"I'll admit I'm curious to know what the devil it all means," Murphy, the lumberman, confessed; "but I don't know that I should accept an explanation from you. Not after Henry's accusations. I've known him and Bell for years—"

"I respect your friendship for them, and I sha'n't expect you to put trust in my words. It seems to me, however, that you owe it to that friendship to hear me. This incident has taken a turn wholly unexpected, and, I must confess, disappointing. I looked for a different outcome—hoped I'd be able to force an explanation—"

The speaker shook his head and frowned again, perplexedly. When, after a moment of indecisive murmuring, the three directors seated themselves, Gray thanked them with a bow. "I'll be as brief as possible, and if you don't mind I'll stand as I talk. I'm in no mood to sit. I'll have to go back a bit—" It was several seconds before he resumed.

"When it became evident that the United States was going to war, I managed to get in at Plattsburg and took the officers' training course. It was easy for me to complete that course, because I had served in the Spanish War and had kept up my interest in military affairs. Something convinced those who ought to know that I possessed qualifications of unusual value to the country—a wide business experience at home and abroad, a knowledge of languages perhaps—anyhow, I was called to Washington. There I met Henry Nelson—a valuable man, too, in his way. We were commissioned at the same time and sent overseas on the same ship to engage in the same work—military intelligence. I didn't like the job, but it was considered important, and naturally I couldn't pick and choose. Of course it was secret, confidential work. No need of going into that here.

"Nelson's and my duties were identical, our authority was equal; we were ordered to work hand in hand, and although we were commissioned together, technically, he outranked me owing to the fact that he was given his commission a moment before I got mine.

"That's where the trouble started. We clashed, even on shipboard. He proved himself to be authoritative, overbearing; he immediately assumed the position of my superior officer. I'm not a mild-tempered man, but I put up with it, figuring that our paths would soon separate. But they didn't. When we arrived in France I tackled my job with all the energy in me; I tried for results. Nelson, I discovered in time, was concerned only in taking entire credit for all that he and I and the whole organization under us accomplished and in advancing himself. I worked; he played politics.

"You are not military men, so I sha'n't bore you with army terms or technical details, but—by one means or another he managed to intrench himself in a position of actual authority over me not at all in accord with our purpose or our instructions. I swallowed my resentment, for it seemed rather petty, rather selfish, in a time like that, to divert my attention from the important work in hand to quarrel with him. You understand? Then, too, he was not making good and I was, and I thought time would surely cure the trouble. He must have appreciated my feelings—nevertheless, he persisted in abusing his powers; he began finally to really interfere with me, to call me off of important tasks and humiliate me with futile assignments, and I realized that I was threatened with failure through his meddling. This may sound trivial to you"—the speaker raised his eyes to his audience—"but, take my word for it, there were many instances of the kind over there. Jealousy, intrigue, malevolence, petty spite, drove more than one earnest, patriotic officer to rebellion and—ruined many a career.

"I rebelled. I had to, or be made ridiculous. I warned him, privately, as man to man. He ignored the warning. Then I prepared a complete report showing by the copies of his orders, by the records of our respective accomplishments, by our correspondence, how he had systematically and maliciously endeavored to nullify my work and—and the like. It was not a pretty report to read. I turned it in to him for submission higher up.

"Then it was that he outgeneraled me. He was furious, of course, but he apologized—abjectly. He admitted that he had been wrong; that he had imposed upon me. He promised to play fair if I'd permit him to withhold the report, and—I was deceived. No man likes to be thought a cry-baby. Those were eventful times; personal complaints were not welcomed in any quarter—not with the world rocking on its foundations. I was glad to accept his promises.

"For a while we worked in harmony. I became engaged in an

intricate case, having to do with a leak concerning transport sailings and routes—a matter involving the lives of thousands of our boys, millions of dollars in supplies, and I went to Brest, under cover. It had to be handled with extreme care—some danger about it, too. A very interesting case, I assure you. I lived in a house with some of the people under surveillance. One of them was a woman, extremely attractive—thoroughly unscrupulous. My avenue of approach was through her. Nelson, of course, knew what I was doing; he was about the only one who did. "I worked a long while and I was upon the verge of success—it would hare been a real accomplishment, too—when, without apparent cause, the gang took warning, scattered, the whole thing blew up. Months of work for nothing! I had made worse than a failure this time."

"You mean to accuse Henry of—of treachery of that sort?" Swope inquired.

"I do. And that's not all. Out of a clear sky charges were preferred against me. Outrageous charges in which that woman figured." Up to this point Gray had spoken smoothly, rapidly, but now his tone changed, his words became hesitant, jerky. "I was amazed! Joke, I called it at first. Sort of a blanket indictment, it was, charging me with inefficiency, negligence, exceeding my authority, dishonesty—and things even worse. Those were some of the least serious, the least—nasty. It was all too absurd! Being peculiarly vain and sensitive, my impulse was to shoot Henry Nelson. But I couldn't believe the charges would be taken seriously.

"Well, there was an investigation. I was court-martialed. I disproved a good deal; I think I'd have exonerated myself on every count only for the woman—that one I spoke about. She turned the trick. I was found guilty, disgraced, sent back. Even though you are not military men, you can appreciate the extent of my dishonor.

"There, gentlemen, you have in a few words an unconvincing summary of a long and complicated story—one that I detest telling. However, I could not permit you to sit with me at the directors' table of this bank without knowing who I am, what I am, and why I have run that rat into his hole. Colonel Nelson spoke the truth when he said this was purely a personal matter between us. It is so purely personal that I was willing to spare humiliation to his father—leave Old Bell in control of his bank and end our fight—if he'd right that old wrong. But you heard him refuse. So they must both fall. He said I've been persecuting him—" Gray smiled grimly. "Let me tell you how. That disgrace cost me my friends, and what money I had, for I tried long and earnestly to get back, to get a rehearing, to enter the navy—anything to re-establish myself. Failing that, I came to Texas. I came without a dollar, without an acquaintance, and—began my 'persecution' of Henry Nelson. I began it by coming here to the bank and telling him what I was up to. I put him on guard, and we engaged each other, as the French would say, 'to the death.' I—won. That's all there is to the story."

"Well, I'll be damned!" Martin Murphy exclaimed.

"At least Henry played fair in this; he didn't betray your secret," Gage said, coldly.

"Oh, I meant to tell you that he didn't dare betray me, for he, too, came back in disgrace. The pot couldn't very well talk about the kettle."

"*What?*"

"Henry Nelson?"

"Impossible!"

"I mean exactly what I say. No man of his type could have lasted over there. Then, too, the story of our quarrel leaked out, that old report of mine turned up—Yes, he got the same medicine he gave me. But he had influence in Washington, and he managed to delay final action almost up to the day of the armistice. Even then he succeeded in pretty well covering up the reason for his dismissal."

"Why, even Bell doesn't know that!"

"Henry's been a terrible hero, hereabouts," said Gus Briskow. After a moment he addressed the other men. "Mr. Gray told me this, an' I wanted him to tell it to you. I dunno what you-all think of his story, but I know him an' I believe every word of it. What's more, I believe this bank is goin' to be run as well as ever it was even if I am president. A man can be president an' stay at home, if he's got folks under him that know more than he does. What d'you say if we start that meetin' we been talkin' about? I'm willing to see Mr. Gray settin' in yonder at Henry's desk if you are."

"I don't see that it makes much difference whether we're willing or not," Swope confessed. "You have the votes, between you, to do about as you choose."

"Of course we have, but, with Bell an' Henry gone, it seems like some of their neighbors ought to stay an' look out for what potaters they've left in the ground. What d'you say?"

Swope eyed his companions briefly, then he nodded. "We'll stay."

"Then, Mr. Secretary, let her go!"

CHAPTER XXIX

One morning, several days after the annual meeting, Gus Briskow opened the door between his and Gray's office and inquired, "Busy?"

The new vice-president of the Security National raised a preoccupied face to the new president and said: "I'm never too busy to talk to you. What is it?"

"Nothing! I'm just kinda lonesome; kinda tired of lookin' bright about things I don't savvy." Gus seated himself and crossed his thin legs. "Folks give an owl credit for bein' wise just because he keeps his mouth shut. Prob'ly he's got nothing of interest to say."

"Perhaps. But you can say 'no,' Gus, and that's about all the average banker is called upon to say."

"Um-m!" The elder man nodded reflectively. "I heard about a captain of industry that allus smelled a pink when he did his heavy thinkin'. Now me, I'm goin' in for bananas. I keep a bag of 'em in my desk. I'most killed myself on bananas when our first well came in—never thought I'd be able to afford all I wanted. How's the bank?"

"Why, it's still here, as you see."

"I know. That's the remarkable part. I keep thinkin' it's goin' to bust—I mean blow up an' disappear. I wake up nights dreamin' it's gone. It's all right, is it?"

"Positively! I put an accountant at work on the books and he should be ready to report any time now."

"No chance of Bell Nelson throwin' us out, is there? He's in Dallas tryin' to stir up money—"

"Not a chance, unless you want him to do so; unless you're afraid we'll make a failure of the business."

"*We?*" Gus smiled quizzically. "*You* won't fail. Folks around town are talkin' about how quick you're takin' hold, an' they're beginning to think you'll make a better banker than the Nelsons. Funny, ain't it, how easy reconciled folks is to losin' a coupla prominent citizens like that? Looks like Bell an' Henry are about the only ones that take it hard."

"The funny thing is"—Gray frowned, perplexedly—"they *don't* take it hard. At least, Henry doesn't appear to do so. That's what puzzles me. No move of any sort—That's not like him."

Gus agreed to this. "I been expectin' him to cut some capers. That's why I been hangin' around so steady."

"I know."

"Every time I peel a banana I peel an eye for Henry. I worry whenever you go out alone."

The younger man rose and nervously paced the floor. "I'm completely mystified," he admitted. "The whole affair has been a great disappointment to me. I thought I'd sprung a coup, but—I'm at a standstill. I'm stumped—checkmated."

"About that trouble between you an' him, eh? Why, we took your word for that."

"Unfortunately, that didn't help me very greatly. Other people aren't so easily convinced as you and Swope and Gage and Murphy. Damnation! I thought my troubles were over."

"Well, your money troubles is over—"

"They're the smallest part. I'd go back and start all over again if I could clean up that—that army record. It's a pretty flat triumph."

"Humph! Most triumphs is. A feller has a dream—a longin', an' he bows his back an' works his life away tryin' to realize it. If he does, the chances is he's disappointed. He finds he's kep' his back bent so long he can't straighten it. Look at me—pore as dirt an' scarcely enough to eat! I used to pray for a miracle; pray for money enough to do something for Ma an' the children—for a thousan' dollars. Here I am, president of a whole bank, but Ma's sick, Allie's miserable, an' I can't sleep nights for fear I'll lose what I got!"

"Poverty wouldn't have helped Ma's health—"

"Oh, I ain't sayin' I'd trade!" Gus wagged his sandy head. "I get my shoes shined every two hours because that bootblackin' stand is a nice place to look at the bank from. I set there an' tell myself I'm president of it! But that's the biggest dividend I've got, so far—five shines a day an' all the bananas I can eat. 'Flat' is the word."

Gray smiled affectionately at the speaker. "At least Buddy is happy. He's reaping his dividends, if I'm any judge."

"I figger he's in love again."

"Good heavens!" Gray paused in his restless pacing and turned an expression of almost comic dread upon the father. "With that woman, eh? Well, I refuse to interfere again. I haven't fully recovered from his first infatuation for her."

"I can tell the boy's symptoms. I felt the same way when I was courtin' Ma. I acted just like him."

"He has been trying to tell me something for a week, but I've been too busy and too worried to listen."

Briskow's kindly face had settled into graver lines when next he spoke. "You prob'ly wonder why I take it so easy. Well, I remember what you told me once about judgin' people I don't know. Mebbe Allie was right, too, when she said a little genuine happiness is worth all it costs. Anyhow, if Buddy wants that woman, I won't say a word. She's turned out pretty good, an' people speak well of her. Buddy's a man, an' some men just *have* to get married—the sooner it's over, the better for 'em. He's like that. But what's more 'n all that, love between two young people is a pretty sacred thing, an' when old folks keep interferin' it seems to me they're settin' themselves up to be wiser than God. Ma's folks didn't care much for me."

"I feel a rebuke in your words," Gray said; "and no doubt I've earned it, for it has always been my weakness to rearrange the lives of those I love. But—who am I, after all? If I were so divinely wise, why is my own life what it is? When I marry, perhaps I shall have to ask B—ask the girl to ignore in me things as—as disagreeable to think about as those which Buddy will have to ignore in Margie's past. That boy, in fact all you Briskows, have put me so deeply in your debt that I'm afraid I shall have to conquer my meddlesome instincts." The speaker looked up suddenly. "You'll never know, by the way, how deep is my debt of gratitude. When a vainglorious, supersensitive man finds himself under a cloud, it is pretty nice to know that there is somebody whose faith is unshakable; somebody who needs no legal proof that he's—Proof! Here I am, back again right where I was when you came in; back to my own selfish concerns. I can't get away from them. What to do next? The Nelsons are on their last legs. The loss of this bank will certainly destroy what credit remained, and even a good well now would scarcely tide them over. But—damn it,

Gus, I can't kick a man if he refuses to stand up! I can't beat a corpse!"

There came a rap at the door, and the accountant whom Gray had put to work upon the bank's books entered. "I'd like to talk to you about this report," the man began.

"Don't go," Gray said, as Briskow unfolded his legs and rose.

But the president of the Security National shook his head, saying: "Bookkeepin' is all Choctaw to me. I saw one statement an' I thought 'liquid assets' meant that bottle of whisky Bell left in his desk."

"Mr. Gray," the auditor announced, when they were alone, "I wish you'd ask somebody else to take this job off my hands."

"Why?"

"Well, somebody else could probably do it better." There was a pause. "I've known Bell Nelson all my life—" "That is why I engaged you. You've been over these books before." Again there was an instant of silence, then into Gray's face there flashed a curious alertness. "Come!" he cried, sharply. "What is it?"

"I'm sorry to be the one to—" The auditor shrugged. "If you insist on an explanation, I suppose I shall have to tell you. Perhaps it's just as well, anyhow. They say figures don't lie, but you and I know better. I only wish they didn't."

"Have you caught them lying, here?"

"I have. And—it has made me rather ill. You'd better prepare yourself for a shock."

It was nearly an hour later that Gray telephoned to Senator Lowe, the bank's attorney, and to Bennett Swope, the latter being the only member of the board available at short notice.

This done, he wrote a note to Henry Nelson. In spite of his effort to control his hand, it shook when he signed his name, and on second thought he destroyed the missive. There is something ominous about the written word. If Nelson grew suspicious, he'd never come.

Gray stepped into Gus Briskow's office and asked him to call the former vice-president, first, however, explaining exactly what he wished Gus to say. The ruse succeeded; then Gray returned to his own office. He drew a deep breath. Within him he felt a ferocious eagerness take fire, for it seemed to him that the day of reckoning had come. Henry's behavior was now easily understandable; the fellow was cringing, cowering in anticipation of a second blow. Well, the whip was in Gray's hands, and he proposed to use it ruthlessly—to sink the lash, to cut to the bone, to leave scars such as Henry had left upon him. Nor was that his only weapon. There was, for instance, Old Bell Nelson's honor. If coercion failed, there were rewards, inducements. Oh, Henry would have to speak! The Nelson fortune, or what remained for salvage from the wreck thereof, the bank itself, they were pawns which Gray could, and would, sacrifice, if necessary. His hunger for a sight of "Bob" had become unbearable. Freedom to declare his overwhelming love—and that love he knew was no immature infatuation, but the deep-set passion of a full-grown man—was worth any price he might be called upon to pay. Yes, Henry would speak the truth to-day or—for one of them, at least, there would be an end to the feud.

Gray, too, kept a revolver in his desk. He removed it and placed it in his pocket.

Buddy Briskow chose this, of all moments, to thrust his grinning visage into the door and to inquire, "Got time for me now, Mr. Gray?"

"Not now, Buddy."

"When?"

"Why—almost any other time."

"I wouldn't bother you, but it's important and I—I promised a certain party—" The youth's face reddened, his smile widened vacuously.

"Later, if you don't mind."

It was plain that Buddy did mind; nevertheless, he withdrew.

When Swope and Lowe arrived, Gray could with difficulty restrain himself from blurting out the reason for his urgent summons, but he contented himself by asking them to wait in the president's office.

Henry Nelson entered the bank with his head up, with a contemptuous smile upon his lips and an easy confidence in his bearing. His hand was outstretched toward the knob of Briskow's door, when the one adjoining opened and, from the office he himself had so long occupied, Calvin Gray spoke to him.

"Please step in here, Colonel."

Nelson recoiled. "No, thank you!" he said, curtly.

"Briskow and I are amateur bankers; there is a matter upon which we need your advice."

"Indeed? Finding it isn't as easy to run a bank as a drilling rig? He said you were out, otherwise—"

"Will you come in?"

Stiffly, reluctantly, as if impelled by some force outside of himself, Nelson stepped within, but he ignored the chair that was proffered him.

Gray closed the door before saying: "The deception was mine, not Briskow's. You prefer to stand? Um-m—I appreciate your feeling of formality. I felt a bit ill at ease on the occasion of my first call here, when our positions were reversed—"

"If you got me here just to be nasty—"

"By no means. Nevertheless, it gratifies my vanity to remind you that you considered me a braggart, a bluffer, whereas—"

"I haven't changed my opinion."

"So be it. One matter, only, remains between us. I am about to ring up on the last act of our little comedy."

"Theatrical, as always, aren't you?" Nelson's lip curled.

For a moment Gray stared at the speaker curiously; his tone had altered when he said: "You're a better poker player than I thought. You're almost as good a bluffer as I am. That, by the way, is probably the last compliment I shall pay you."

"Come! I've no time to waste."

"You will soon have ample time—if not to waste, at least to meditate—"

"What do you mean by that?" The query came sharply.

"I've had an examination of the bank's books. That, as you will readily understand, explains why I sent for you."

"Why—no. I don't—"

"I wondered how you and your father got the money to keep going so long, for I discovered you were in a bad way even before I turned up. It is no longer a mystery. When you and he, as directors of the Security National, lent yourselves money, as individuals, you must have realized that you were— well, arranging ample leisure for yourselves in which to meditate upon the stringency of the banking laws—"

"Nonsense! That's n-nothing—nothing serious." Nelson's ruddy color had slowly vanished; with uncertain hand he reached for the nearest chair, and upon it he leaned as he continued, jerkily: "Irregular, perhaps—I'll admit it was irregular, but—there's nothing *wrong*—Oh, you'll make it look as bad as possible, I dare say! But you don't understand the circumstances. Anyhow, father is getting it straightened out; all he needs is time. We'll be able to handle it, all right. We're good, you know, perfectly good—"

"You're broke! Everybody else knows it, if you don't. '*Irregular*'! Ha! There's a choice of words!" The speaker laughed silently. "It is an 'irregularity' that carries with it free board and lodging at the state's expense."

An incoherent protest issued from Nelson's throat. When next he managed to make himself audible, his words were such as really to amaze his hearer. "*I* didn't do it," he cried, in a panic-stricken voice. "It was father's idea! You had us crowded—there was no other way. I warned him—"

"Wait a minute! You blame it on *him*?" Gray's inquiry was harsh, incredulous. After a momentary pause his lips moved, but for once he stammered, his ready tongue refused its duty. He exploded, finally, with an oath; he jerked open a drawer in his desk. From his pocket he removed his revolver, flung it inside, then jammed the drawer back into place with a crash. "You—*rat*!" he exclaimed. He turned his back upon Henry Nelson and made a circuit of the little room.

"It's a thing you and I can easily fix up," the latter feebly insisted. "Now that personal matter of yours—Perhaps I could help you reopen it somehow, clear it up."

"Ah! Indeed!"

"Give and take, I say. I'm willing to do anything I can, if—"

"There won't be any 'ifs'! No conditions whatever."

"Is that so?" Nelson flamed forth, in a momentary explosion of resentment. "If you think I intend to stand the brunt of this, you're crazy. I can't afford to figure in a scandal—banking scandal—like this. I'm a young man. Bell has had his day. He's old. You can hush this up. There are lots of ways to do that. Keep me out of it and—and I'll do what's right by you; I'll do anything you say."

"You'll do that, anyhow," Gray replied, in a voice that grated. He flung himself into his desk chair and, seizing pen and paper, he began to write rapidly, shakily.

"I want to see what I'm signing," Nelson warned. A growl was his answer.

For an interminable time the only sound in the office was the scratching of that pen. When at last it came to an end, Gray rose, thrust the loose sheets into Nelson's hand, then, indicating the vacant chair, said:

"Sign that!"

The wretched recipient of this curt command read the lines caiefully. He read them twice, thrice, for his mind no longer functioned clearly. He raised a sick face, finally, and shook his head.

"Wouldn't I be a fool?" he queried.

"Listen, you—" Gray's body was shaking, his words were uneven. "I'm sorry for Bell, but not for you. I'll never forget nor forgive what you did to me. Nothing can undo that. Disgrace clings to a man. You're going to get yours, now, and you can't squirm out of it, or lie out of it, no matter how you try, for I sha'n't let you. You're ruined, discredited, blown up, but—I don't think I want to send you to the penitentiary. I'd rather see you walking the streets with dandruff on your collar.

I'd rather keep you to look at. Anyhow, you'll have to sign that."

"If you'll guarantee to keep this bank matter quiet—if you'll protect me, I'll sign. Otherwise, you can go to hell. We'll beat it out, somehow. We can do it."

Inflexibly Gray asserted: "I'm going to turn you over, whether or no. But I'll help Bell get the money to repay those loans. He'll probably manage to save himself and—save you, too."

"I won't do it!" Nelson flung down the pen. "Not on those conditions. You can't bulldoze me. It's your day to crow, but, I warn you, don't push me too far."

Gray voiced an epithet. It was low pitched, but its explosive force, the impelling fury back of it, fairly caused the room to vibrate. He was white of lip, his rage had reached the foaming point.

"Don't make me lay hands on you—choke you into it," he cried, hoarsely. "If you do, by God, I'll finish you!"

Like a man fighting some hypnotic influence stronger than his will, Henry Nelson took up the pen and signed his name waveringly. The next moment Gray smote the door to Briskow's office a heavy blow and, as it flew open, he barked:

"Come in here! All three of you!" He stood aside as Gus, Bennett Swope, and Senator Lowe entered. "Yonder is a statement which I want you to read and witness. When you've done that, I'm going to tell you why Henry Nelson signed it. The rest will be up to you."

It was midafternoon. Swope and Lowe had left the bank. Briskow drew a deep breath and said, with genuine relief: "I'm glad *that's* over. We can handle the debt between us, an', after all, Old Bell's a pretty good citizen. As for Henry, I s'pose he'll wiggle out of it, somehow. I dunno as I'd of been so easy on him if I'd been in your place."

"I'll tell you why I was easy on him," Gray confessed. "I'm tired of fighting; I'm worn out. I've won my point, and he'll carry the sort of load I've been carrying. But there is this difference: for him there will be no vindication at the end." Taking from his pocket Nelson's statement, he stared at it, then slowly his face lightened. "I was blind mad at first. I felt as if I couldn't keep my hands off him. It was such a dirty trick he did me and so reasonless! He had no excuse whatever for injuring me, Gus. However, I suppose most quarrels sprout from tiny seeds. Well, I'm square with the game! I—I'm afraid, even yet, that it's all a dream. I've wanted to yell—" The speaker chuckled; the chuckle grew to a laugh. "There's magic in this document, Gus, old boy. I've grown young all at once."

"You needn't of took it so hard. Us fellers would have stood by you if you'd turned out to be a horse thief. Texas men are like that."

"You proved it. But that wasn't enough. A man's business associates will frequently overlook a lot more than their wives and daughters will overlook. There's a certain loyalty that doesn't apply outside of the office." Gray rose and filled his lungs. "D'you know why I felt this thing so keenly? Why I fought so long? Of course you don't, for I've held out on you. Fact! I've held out on my partner—had a secret from him. Now then, steel yourself for a surprise. I'm suffering from Buddy's complaint, only ten times aggravated!"

"What?" Briskow stared up at the animated countenance above him. "You thinkin' about gettin' *married*?"

"I'm thinking about nothing else. That's what ails me. Why, Gus, you've no idea what a perfectly charming person I can be when—when I can be what I am. I thought I was too old and too blase ever to become seriously interested in a woman, above all in a girl, but—Do you remember when Ma and Allie came to Dallas that first time? Something happened about then to upset all my ideas."

Briskow's sun-parched face slowly lightened, his bright, inquisitive eyes grew bluer, brighter. "I'm—mighty glad! I allus hoped—" He tried to finish his sentence, then shook his head and murmured, huskily, "Mighty glad!"

Here was a marvel, a miracle, for which he had never dared even hope. He thought of Allie and a lump came into his throat. She had reached the stars. His girl! he would be mighty glad, too—

Gray was speaking, and in his voice was a new, vibrant quality, a new vigor. "Now you'll know why this is the biggest day of my life; why I thought those men would never go. I'm shaking all over, Gus. You'll have to run the bank for a while; I'm too young and irresponsible. I'm going out to buy a hoop and a jumping rope and a pair of roller skates." Again he laughed, boyishly; then, with a slap that knocked the breath from Briskow's lungs, he walked lightly into his own office and seized his hat.

For a long time the father sat at his big, empty desk, staring, smiling into space. This would make Ma well. Money wasn't altogether a worry, after all; it bought things that nothing else could buy—stars and—and things.

From the expressions upon the faces Gray passed in leaving the bank, he realized that his own must wear a grin; but, in spite of his dignified effort to wipe it off, he felt it widening. Well, this was his day to grin; his day to dance and caper. People were too grave, anyhow. They should feel free to vent their joy in living. Why act as if the world were a place of gloom and shadow? Why shouldn't they hop, skip, and jump to and from business, if so inclined? He visualized the streets of the city peopled with pedestrians, old and young, fat and thin, thus engaged, and he laughed aloud. Nevertheless, it was a good idea, and when he became mayor, or perhaps the junior Senator from Texas, he'd advocate public playgrounds for grown-ups. "Bob" would help him put it through. There was a girl who would never grow old. They would grow young together. He caught sight of his reflection in a shop window and slowed down his gait, telling himself that pending the time his new idea was definitely planted it might be well to walk in the old-fashioned manner. Men of substance, bankers, for instance, shouldn't rush through the streets as if going to a fire; they shouldn't dash over crossings and take curbstones as if they were hurdles. It wasn't being done. No reason, however, why a banker shouldn't throw his shoulders back and walk springily upon his toes.

When he beheld the familiar painted sign, "Tom and Bob Parker. Real Estate and Insurance," he paused. The mere sight of the little wooden building, the name, gave him an odd shortness of breath. It was weeks since he had been here.

He realized of a sudden that he had brought nothing with him; no gift, not even flowers. But there was enough to talk about. She'd forget that. What a shower of gifts he would pour upon her—and upon Old Tom, too! Good Old Tom! Tom had wanted to believe. Tom and he would be great pals. They couldn't help being pals with just one thing, between them, to love; one thing in all the world!

It was a disappointment to find the office empty, except for thefather himself, but Gray began with a rush, "Well, I told you I'd clear myself, and—here I am, walking on air."

"You did it, eh? That's good news."

"We had a show-down at the bank. Henry Nelson and I locked horns and—But here! Read what he signed. That cleans the slate. He'll do anything further that may be necessary, officially. Where's "Bob"?"

"They're fishin' for a bit in one of your Avenger wells. She's out there."

"So? I'd forgotten."

"Did you see—? Did Buddy have a talk with you? To-day, I mean?"

"Buddy? Oh, Buddy Briskow! I saw him for a moment only. She'll be back soon, I dare say?"

Tom Parker stirred; it was a moment before he spoke, then it was with apparent irrelevance that he said: "I'm sorry you and he didn't have a good talk. 'Bob' asked him to see you—sent him there a-purpose." The sight of Gray's smiling, eager, uncomprehending face caused the old man's steady gaze to waver. He cleared his throat. "Buddy's a fine boy."

"Finest in the world! I claim responsibility for him, in a way. He's part mine." Gray laughed; his eyes sparkled.

"Him and 'Bob' are out there together. They've been together a lot, Mr. Gray. Both of 'em young, that-away—"

"Of course. I knew you'd both like—" Some quality in Tom's voice, some reluctant evasiveness to his eyes, bore a belated message to the younger man—snapped his chain of thought—dried the words upon his lips. Into his eyes leaped a sudden, strained incredulity. Sharply, he cried, "What do you mean?" Then, after an instant, "Why did he want to see me?" The two men gazed squarely at each other for the first time. "My God! Why—that's absurd! I—I brought him here. He's just a *boy*!"

"And she's just a girl, Mr. Gray."

The younger man shrank as if at a blow. He closed his eyes; he raised a shaking hand to his face, which was slowly assuming the color of ashes. "That's too—rottenly unfair!" he said, faintly. "I brought him here—made a man of him. Of course he doesn't know—" His eyes opened; eagerly he ran on: "Why, Tom, it's just the boy and girl of it! Puppy love! You know how that is."

"I didn't notice how things was going till if was too late. We might as well talk frankly, Mr. Gray. Prob'ly it's well you saw me first, eh? Well, when I understood where they was heading, I worried a lot—after what you said that day, understand? But those two! Pshaw! It was like they had known each other always. It was like 'Bob's' mother and me when we first met; her beautiful and fine and educated, and me rough and awkward. Only Buddy's a better boy than I was. He's got more in him. I s'pose all womenfolks have that mother feeling that makes 'em yearn over the unlikeliest fellers." Parker looked appealingly at his stricken hearer, then quickly dropped his eyes, for Gray's countenance was like that of a dying man—or of a man suffering the stroke of a surgeon's knife.

"After all, it's youth. You're a good deal older than 'Bob,' and I s'pose you sort of dazzled her. She likes you. She thinks you're great. You kinda thrill her, but—I don't believe she ever dreamed you was actually—that you actually cared for her. You've got a grand way, you know, and she ain't a bit conceited about herself. Why, I *know* she never figgered it that way, because she made Buddy promise to tell you the first thing; sent him to the bank a-purpose, thinking you'd be so glad on his account."

"Then they've—settled it between them?"

Tom nodded gravely. "She told me last night. And from the way she told me, I know it's not just boy and girl love. She's been singing like a bird all day. And Buddy! He's breathless. I know how he feels. I couldn't draw a full breath for two weeks after 'Bob's' mother—"

Gray uttered a wordless, gasping cry. He moved unsteadily toward the door, then paused with his hand upon the knob. Tom Parker was surprised when, after a moment, he saw the man's shoulders shake and heard him utter a thin, cackling laugh. "Time is a grim old joker, isn't he? No way of beating him, none at all. Now I thought I was young, but—Lucky I found you here and spared my vanity." He turned, exposing a face strangely contorted. "You won't mention my foolish mistake, will you? No use hurting the ones we love. You know how we feel—fatherly. That's it, fatherly love. I was a silly old fool. They'll be happy. Young people like that—" The speaker choked. "Young people—Well, *adios*, old man!" He opened the door and walked blindly forth.

CHAPTER XXX

Calvin Gray did not return to the bank. He went straight to his hotel and, as soon as he could sufficiently control himself to do so, he telephoned Gus Briskow, telling him that he intended to leave town. Then he began mechanically to pack his bag. He moved like a man in a trance, for the blow had fallen so suddenly as to numb him; his only impulse was to escape, to hide himself from these people who, of a sudden, had become hateful. His city of dreams had collapsed. The ruins, as they lay, meant nothing as yet, for his mind refused to envisage them and he could see them only as they had stood. He groped amid a hopeless confusion of thought—at one moment bewildered, piteously hurt, at the next suffering a sense of shameful betrayal. He had grown old and dull and feeble, too, and for the time being he was incapable of feeling the full force of a strong man's resentment. This surprised him vaguely.

Soon, however, like kindling fires among the ruins, his fury rose—fury at himself, at Buddy, at Barbara—and in the heat of those scorching flames he writhed. She *had* loved him. He'd swear to that. He had swayed her, overpowered her; he had lacked only the courage to trust his instinct. Coward's luck! It served him right. He had held her in his arms and had let her slip through; her lips had been raised to his, and he had refused to press them. Imbecile!

He groaned; he tore the collar and the tie from his neck, for they were choking him. Old, eh? Too old! That was the grimmest jest of all, for at the mere thought of Barbara's lips unruly forces took possession of him; he experienced a fierce, resistless vigor such as he had never felt in his younger days. It was a dreadful, an unappeasable yearning of soul and body, and when the paroxysm had passed, it left him weak. He sank into a chair and lay there stupid, inert, until again those fires began to lick at him and again he twisted in dumb agony. Buddy Briskow! Buddy, of all people! That lout; that awkward simpleton, who owed him everything! But Buddy was *young*!

Gray heard himself laughing in hoarse derision. He rose and tramped heavily around his room, and, as he went, he crushed and ripped and mutilated whatever his hands encountered. His slow, deliberate, murderous rage demanded some such outlet. All the while he felt within himself two conflicting impulses, heard two voices: the one voice shouted at him to search out Buddy and visit upon him the punishment warranted by a base betrayal; the other told him jeeringly to lay the scourge upon his own shoulders and endure the pain, since he had betrayed himself. His mind was like a battle ground, torn, up-heaved, obscured by a frightful murk—he remembered a night in France, a black night of rumbling, crashing terror, when, as now, the whole world rocked and tumbled. Some remnant of self-control induced him to lock his door and pocket the key, for Buddy might come. He probably would look him up, all grins and smirks and giggles, to tell him the glorious news, to acclaim the miracle. That would be too much.

One thing was certain, there was no safety except in flight, ignominious, cowardly flight... After all, how could Buddy have known? He was a good boy, and he had shown his love, his loyalty, in a thousand ways. Gray hated him at this moment, but, more bitterly even, he hated himself. It was fate.... He fell to cursing aloud, but there was no relief in that, and again the appalling irony of the situation silenced him. He had deified himself, set himself upon a high place, bent men and affairs to his own ends, until he had acquired a godlike belief in his power to accomplish all things. His victory had been complete. He had won all—except the one thing he most desired, the very fruit of victory.

Some time later he heard Buddy come whistling merrily down the hall and knock at his door. Gray cowered in his chair, listening in breathless dread until the footsteps retreated. When he rose he moved about stealthily.

When night came he took his bag and slunk out of the hotel, for it seemed that men must surely know what a fool he had made of himself. It would have been a relief to feel that he was leaving never to return; but even that was denied him, for, after his first panic, the truth had come home. He could not run away. He had forged chains for his own limbs. Like a tethered mustang he could plunge only to the end of his rope. Friendship, again! There was simple, trustful, faithful Gus Briskow. And the bank. God, what a mess things were in! Gray knew he would have to return, have to see "Bob" and Buddy day after day, month after month, and the prospect was too distressing to dwell upon. Again his mind grew weary, baffled; he experienced a wretched physical illness... Where to go, where to hide until his sickness had passed? That was the question.

For the first time he appreciated the full extent of his loneliness; his utter lack of resource in a crisis like this. Most men, however solitary, lay by material things for themselves, build homes and surround themselves with personal possessions from which, or amid which, they can gain some sort of solace in times of trial. But he had not fashioned so much as a den into which he could creep and lick his wounds. Once he had left his hotel room behind him he was in the open and without cover. Not a single soul cared whether he came or went, not another door stood ajar for him. And he had planned so much upon having a home, a real home—But he could not trust himself to think much along that line; it induced an absurd desire to weep at his plight. It made him feel like a child lost in a wood. That was silly, just an emotional reaction; nevertheless, the impulse was real and caused him to yearn poignantly for human comfort.

He thought of Ma Briskow, finally. She was human; she had a heart. And Dallas was a sort of homey place; anyhow, the bellboys at the Ajax knew and liked him. That was probably because he had tipped them handsomely, but what of that? If they'd be kind to him now he'd tip them more handsomely than ever. Lonely men—old ones—must expect to pay for what they get. He bought a ticket to Dallas.

Ma Briskow's eyes were dim; nevertheless, she saw the change in Calvin Gray when, late the following afternoon, he came to see her.

"Land sakes!" she exclaimed, in a shocked voice. "Pa never said you was ailin'. Why, Mr. Gray!"

"I'm not really ill," he told her, wearily, "just old. I've had a bad night." Seating himself beside her couch, he took her hand in his and made her tell him all about herself. He had brought her an armful of flowers, as usual, and extravagant gifts for her adornment—giving, it seemed, was his unconscious habit. While she admired them with ecstatic "Ohs!" and "Ahs!" he busied himself with bowls and vases, but Ma noted his fumbling uncertainty of touch and the evident effort with which he kept up his assumption of good cheer. She told him, finally:

"Something mighty bad has happened to you, Mr. Gray."

He gazed at her mutely, then nodded.

"Is it something about the—the Princess of Wichita Falls?"

"Yes, Ma."

"Tse! Tse! Tse!" It was a sympathetic cluck. "Was she a wicked princess?" The query was gently put, but it deeply affected the man. He tried to smile, failed, then like a forlorn little boy he came and bowed his head beneath her hand.

"I knew you'd understand, Mother Briskow, so I—I ran to you with my hurt, just as I used to run to my Mother Gray." After a while he continued in a smothered voice: "She isn't a wicked princess. She didn't mean to hurt me and—that's what makes it hurt so deep. She tumbled the old duke's castle down upon his head; tumbled the old duke out of his dreams. He isn't a duke any longer."

"He'll allus be a duke," Mrs. Briskow firmly declared. "He was born that way."

"At any rate, he's a sad old duke now; all his conceit is gone. You see, he was a vain old gentleman, and his courtiers used to tell him he was splendid, handsome—They said he looked as handsome as a king, and by and by he began to think he must be a king. His enemies sneered at this and said he was neither duke nor king, but a—a mountebank. That made him furious, so he went to war with them, and, by Jove, he fought pretty well for an old fellow! Anyhow, he licked 'em. When they fell down and begged for mercy he knew he was indeed a great person—greater even than he had suspected and worthy of any princess in the land."

"Pshaw! Ain't a duke higher than a princess?"

"No, Ma. Not higher than this princess. Her father made all the laws. She is very noble and very good. Good princesses are scarce and—and so, of course, they're very high. But the Duke of Dallas didn't stop to think of that. He told himself that he was so strong and so rich and so desirable that she would be flattered at his notice. He got all dressed up and went to call on her, and, on the way, whenever he looked into a shop window, he didn't see the buns and the candies and the dolls inside; all he saw was his own reflection. It looked so magnificent that he strutted higher and thought how proud he was going to make her.

"I guess that was the trouble with the old duke all along; he had never looked deeply enough to see what was inside.

Rex Beach

Anyhow, what do you think, Ma? While he'd been off at war conquering people and making them acknowledge that he was a king, the little princess had fallen in love with—with his nephew. Nice boy, that nephew, and the duke thought a lot of him."

Ma Briskow's hand, which had been slowly stroking Gray's bent head, ceased its movement; she drew a sharp breath.

"There happened to be an old mirror in the princess's boudoir, and while the duke was waiting for her he saw himself in it. He saw himself just as he was, not as he had looked in the shop windows, for it was a truthful mirror and it told everything. My! That was a bad moment for the Duke of Dallas, when he saw that he wasn't young and beautiful, but old and wrinkled and—funny. That was bad enough, but when he looked again and saw the princess whom he loved in the arms of his handsome nephew, why, he gave up. All his fine garments fell off and he realized with shame that, after all, he was only the withered mountebank.

"When he got home his castle had collapsed. There wasn't a stone standing, so he ran away—ran to his mother."

"Oh, Mr. Gray!" Ma Briskow quavered. "I could cry. An' after all you done for Buddy!"

The man shook his head vigorously, still with his face hidden. "It isn't Buddy. It's youth. Youth needs no fine adornment, no crown, no victory."

"What you goin' to do?" she asked him.

"Go on playing the duke, I suppose; rebuild the castle the best way I can. That's the hard part. If I could run away and forget, but—I can't. The old duke walled himself in. He must grin and strut and keep people from guessing that he's only a fraud until he can find a hole in the wall through which he can creep."

There was a long silence, then Ma inquired: "Would you like to tell me something about the little princess? Sometimes it helps, to talk."

"N-not yet."

"You're a duke, an' the best one that ever lived, Mr. Gray. You can't fool me; I've met too many of 'em. That lookin'-glass lied! Real dukes an' kings an' such people don't get old. It's only common folks. There's lots of magic, the world's full of it, an' your castle is goin' up again."

"After a fashion, perhaps"—Gray raised his head and smiled crookedly—"but it will never be a home, and that's what I wanted most of all. Do you think I'm very weak, very silly to come to you for a little mothering?"

"That's the kind of children mothers love best," the old woman said, then she drew him down to her and laid her cheek against his.

"There! I've made you cry," he exclaimed, reproachfully. "What a selfish beast I am! I'll go now."

"Won't you stay an' have supper with Allie an' me? We're awful lonesome with Pa gone. Allie's out som'er's, but—it would do me good to know you was here an' it 'll do you good to stay. You can rest yourself while I take my nap."

Ma Briskow did not wish to take a nap, but she knew that Gray needed the solace of his own thoughts just now, so, when he agreed, she sent him downstairs.

First balm, indeed, had come to the man; the smart was less intense. To put his trouble into words somehow lightened it; then, too, the grateful knowledge that some warmth of sympathy was his made it easier to bear. But it remained a cruel burden. That gentle, dreamy soul up yonder could not know how it hurt. How could she understand, for instance, what it meant to go back and face the deadly dull routine of a life from which all zest, all interest, had fled? A routine broken only by moments of downright torture. Yes, and the effort it would take to smile! God! If there were only some way to break his fetters, slip his gyves!

Gray's brain, like his body, had grown tired and feverish. To be sure, little more than a day had gone by since he had sallied forth like a knight, but it seemed a year, an age, and every hour brought a new and keener distress. He found it possible now, for the first time, to relax a bit physically, so he closed his eyes and lay back in an easy chair while the twilight stole in upon him. Sooner or later his mind, too, would cease its torment, for pain distils its own anodyne. Then he would sleep. It would be a blessing to forget for even an hour, and thus gain strength with which to carry on the fight. But what a useless battle it was! He could never win; peace would never come.

He heard Allie enter the house, but he did not stir. He would have to put on the mask soon enough, for, of course, she must never suspect, on Buddy's account. The room, which had grown agreeably dark, was suddenly illuminated, and he lurched to his feet to find the girl facing him from the door. She was neither startled nor surprised at his presence, and when he tried to smile and to greet her in his accustomed manner, she interrupted him by saying:

"I knew you were here."

"So? Then Ma is awake again?"

Allie shook her head vaguely. "I knew you were here the minute I came in. I can 'most always tell." There had been a shadow of a smile upon her lips, but it vanished; a look of growing concern crept over her face. "What's the matter? Whatever has happened, Mr. Gray?"

"Why, nothing. I was feeling tired, worn out. Indulging myself in a thoroughly enjoyable fit of the blues." His voice broke when he tried to laugh.

Allie uttered a quick, low cry, a wordless, sympathetic sound. Her dark eyes widened, grew darker; she came forward a step or two, then she halted. "Would you rather be alone?" she asked. He signified his dissent, and she went on: "I know what the blues are like. I sit alone in the dark a good deal."

She busied herself about the room for a few moments, straightening things, adjusting the window shades. Allie had the knack of silence, blessed attribute in man or woman, and to Gray's surprise he found that her mere presence was comforting. She startled him by saying, suddenly:

"You're hurt! Hurt badly!"

He looked up at her with an instinctive denial upon his lips, but, realizing the futility of deceit, he nodded. "Yes, Allie."

The girl drew a deep breath, her strong hands closed, harshly she said: "I could kill anybody that hurt you. I wanted to kill Buddy that time. Is it those Nelsons? Have they got you down?" There was something fierce and masterful in Allie's concern, and her inquiry carried with it even more than a proffer of help; she had, in fact, flung herself into a protective attitude. She suggested nothing so much as a lioness roused.

"No, no! It is nothing like that. I merely fooled myself—had a dream. You wouldn't understand, my dear."

Allie studied him soberly for a moment. "Oh yes, I would! I do! I understand perfectly. Nobody *could* understand as well as I do."

"What do you mean by that?"

"I've been hurt, too." She laid a hand upon her breast. "That's why I sit in the dark."

"My dear child! I'm sorry. Gus said you were unhappy, but I thought it was merely—the new life. You're young; you can forget. It's only us old ones who can't forget. Sometime you must tell me all about it." The girl smiled faintly, but he nodded, positively: "Oh, it's a relief to tell somebody! I feel better already for confiding in Ma. Yes, and your sympathy is mighty soothing, too. It seems almost as if I had come home." He closed his eyes and laid his head back.

Allie placed her hand upon his forehead and held it there for a moment before she moved away. It was a cool and tranquilizing palm and he wished she would hold it there for a long time, so that he could sleep, forget—

Allie Briskow went to her room, and there she studied her reflection in the mirror carefully, deliberately, before saying: "You can do it. You've *got* to do it, for he's hurt. When a girl is hurt like that, it makes a woman of her, but when a man's hurt it makes him a little boy. I—I guess it pays to keep on praying."

It was perhaps a half hour later that Ma Briskow heard a sound that caused her to rise upon her elbow and listen with astonishment. It was the sound of low, indistinct, but joyous singing; it came from Allie's room. Allie singing again! What could have happened? Slowly Ma's face became wistful, eager. "Oh, Mister Fairy King!" she whispered. "Please build up his castle again. You can do it. There's magic in the world. Make him a duke again, an' her a queen, for yours is the power an' the glory for ever an' ever. Amen!"

Choose from Thousands of 1stWorldLibrary Classics By

A. M. Barnard	Booth Tarkington	Edward Everett Hale
Ada Leverson	Boyd Cable	Edward J. O'Biren
Adolphus William Ward	Bram Stoker	Edward S. Ellis
Aesop	C. Collodi	Edwin L. Arnold
Agatha Christie	C. E. Orr	Eleanor Atkins
Alexander Aaronsohn	C. M. Ingleby	Eleanor Hallowell Abbott
Alexander Kielland	Carolyn Wells	Eliot Gregory
Alexandre Dumas	Catherine Parr Traill	Elizabeth Gaskell
Alfred Gatty	Charles A. Eastman	Elizabeth McCracken
Alfred Ollivant	Charles Amory Beach	Elizabeth Von Arnim
Alice Duer Miller	Charles Dickens	Ellem Key
Alice Turner Curtis	Charles Dudley Warner	Emerson Hough
Alice Dunbar	Charles Farrar Browne	Emilie F. Carlen
Allen Chapman	Charles Ives	Emily Bronte
Alleyne Ireland	Charles Kingsley	Emily Dickinson
Ambrose Bierce	Charles Klein	Enid Bagnold
Amelia E. Barr	Charles Hanson Towne	Enilor Macartney Lane
Amory H. Bradford	Charles Lathrop Pack	Erasmus W. Jones
Andrew Lang	Charles Romyn Dake	Ernie Howard Pie
Andrew McFarland Davis	Charles Whibley	Ethel May Dell
Andy Adams	Charles Willing Beale	Ethel Turner
Angela Brazil	Charlotte M. Braeme	Ethel Watts Mumford
Anna Alice Chapin	Charlotte M. Yonge	Eugene Sue
Anna Sewell	Charlotte Perkins Stetson	Eugenie Foa
Annie Besant	Clair W. Hayes	Eugene Wood
Annie Hamilton Donnell	Clarence Day Jr.	Eustace Hale Ball
Annie Payson Call	Clarence E. Mulford	Evelyn Everett-green
Annie Roe Carr	Clemence Housman	Everard Cotes
Annonaymous	Confucius	F. H. Cheley
Anton Chekhov	Coningsby Dawson	F. J. Cross
Archibald Lee Fletcher	Cornelis DeWitt Wilcox	F. Marion Crawford
Arnold Bennett	Cyril Burleigh	Fannie E. Newberry
Arthur C. Benson	D. H. Lawrence	Federick Austin Ogg
Arthur Conan Doyle	Daniel Defoe	Ferdinand Ossendowski
Arthur M. Winfield	David Garnett	Fergus Hume
Arthur Ransome	Dinah Craik	Florence A. Kilpatrick
Arthur Schnitzler	Don Carlos Janes	Fremont B. Deering
Arthur Train	Donald Keyhoe	Francis Bacon
Atticus	Dorothy Kilner	Francis Darwin
B.H. Baden-Powell	Dougan Clark	Frances Hodgson Burnett
B. M. Bower	Douglas Fairbanks	Frances Parkinson Keyes
B. C. Chatterjee	E. Nesbit	Frank Gee Patchin
Baroness Emmuska Orczy	E. P. Roe	Frank Harris
Baroness Orczy	E. Phillips Oppenheim	Frank Jewett Mather
Basil King	E. S. Brooks	Frank L. Packard
Bayard Taylor	Earl Barnes	Frank V. Webster
Ben Macomber	Edgar Rice Burroughs	Frederic Stewart Isham
Bertha Muzzy Bower	Edith Van Dyne	Frederick Trevor Hill
Bjornstjerne Bjornson	Edith Wharton	Frederick Winslow Taylor

Friedrich Kerst	Hayden Carruth	James Branch Cabell
Friedrich Nietzsche	Helent Hunt Jackson	James DeMille
Fyodor Dostoyevsky	Helen Nicolay	James Joyce
G.A. Henty	Hendrik Conscience	James Lane Allen
G.K. Chesterton	Hendy David Thoreau	James Lane Allen
Gabrielle E. Jackson	Henri Barbusse	James Oliver Curwood
Garrett P. Serviss	Henrik Ibsen	James Oppenheim
Gaston Leroux	Henry Adams	James Otis
George A. Warren	Henry Ford	James R. Driscoll
George Ade	Henry Frost	Jane Abbott
Geroge Bernard Shaw	Henry James	Jane Austen
George Cary Eggleston	Henry Jones Ford	Jane L. Stewart
George Durston	Henry Seton Merriman	Janet Aldridge
George Ebers	Henry W Longfellow	Jens Peter Jacobsen
George Eliot	Herbert A. Giles	Jerome K. Jerome
George Gissing	Herbert Carter	Jessie Graham Flower
George MacDonald	Herbert N. Casson	John Buchan
George Meredith	Herman Hesse	John Burroughs
George Orwell	Hildegard G. Frey	John Cournos
George Sylvester Viereck	Homer	John F. Kennedy
George Tucker	Honore De Balzac	John Gay
George W. Cable	Horace B. Day	John Glasworthy
George Wharton James	Horace Walpole	John Habberton
Gertrude Atherton	Horatio Alger Jr.	John Joy Bell
Gordon Casserly	Howard Pyle	John Kendrick Bangs
Grace E. King	Howard R. Garis	John Milton
Grace Gallatin	Hugh Lofting	John Philip Sousa
Grace Greenwood	Hugh Walpole	John Taintor Foote
Grant Allen	Humphry Ward	Jonas Lauritz Idemil Lie
Guillermo A. Sherwell	Ian Maclaren	Jonathan Swift
Gulielma Zollinger	Inez Haynes Gillmore	Joseph A. Altsheler
Gustav Flaubert	Irving Bacheller	Joseph Carey
H. A. Cody	Isabel Cecilia Williams	Joseph Conrad
H. B. Irving	Isabel Hornibrook	Joseph E. Badger Jr
H.C. Bailey	Israel Abrahams	Joseph Hergesheimer
H. G. Wells	Ivan Turgenev	Joseph Jacobs
H. H. Munro	J.G.Austin	Jules Vernes
H. Irving Hancock	J. Henri Fabre	Julian Hawthrone
H. R. Naylor	J. M. Barrie	Julie A Lippmann
H. Rider Haggard	J. M. Walsh	Justin Huntly McCarthy
H. W. C. Davis	J. Macdonald Oxley	Kakuzo Okakura
Haldeman Julius	J. R. Miller	Karle Wilson Baker
Hall Caine	J. S. Fletcher	Kate Chopin
Hamilton Wright Mabie	J. S. Knowles	Kenneth Grahame
Hans Christian Andersen	J. Storer Clouston	Kenneth McGaffey
Harold Avery	J. W. Duffield	Kate Langley Bosher
Harold McGrath	Jack London	Kate Langley Bosher
Harriet Beecher Stowe	Jacob Abbott	Katherine Cecil Thurston
Harry Castlemon	James Allen	Katherine Stokes
Harry Coghill	James Andrews	L. A. Abbot
Harry Houidini	James Baldwin	L. T. Meade

L. Frank Baum
Latta Griswold
Laura Dent Crane
Laura Lee Hope
Laurence Housman
Lawrence Beasley
Leo Tolstoy
Leonid Andreyev
Lewis Carroll
Lewis Sperry Chafer
Lilian Bell
Lloyd Osbourne
Louis Hughes
Louis Joseph Vance
Louis Tracy
Louisa May Alcott
Lucy Fitch Perkins
Lucy Maud Montgomery
Luther Benson
Lydia Miller Middleton
Lyndon Orr
M. Corvus
M. H. Adams
Margaret E. Sangster
Margret Howth
Margaret Vandercook
Margaret W. Hungerford
Margret Penrose
Maria Edgeworth
Maria Thompson Daviess
Mariano Azuela
Marion Polk Angellotti
Mark Overton
Mark Twain
Mary Austin
Mary Catherine Crowley
Mary Cole
Mary Hastings Bradley
Mary Roberts Rinehart
Mary Rowlandson
M. Wollstonecraft Shelley
Maud Lindsay
Max Beerbohm
Myra Kelly
Nathaniel Hawthrone
Nicolo Machiavelli
O. F. Walton
Oscar Wilde

Owen Johnson
P.G. Wodehouse
Paul and Mabel Thorne
Paul G. Tomlinson
Paul Severing
Percy Brebner
Percy Keese Fitzhugh
Peter B. Kyne
Plato
Quincy Allen
R. Derby Holmes
R. L. Stevenson
R. S. Ball
Rabindranath Tagore
Rahul Alvares
Ralph Bonehill
Ralph Henry Barbour
Ralph Victor
Ralph Waldo Emmerson
Rene Descartes
Ray Cummings
Rex Beach
Rex E. Beach
Richard Harding Davis
Richard Jefferies
Richard Le Gallienne
Robert Barr
Robert Frost
Robert Gordon Anderson
Robert L. Drake
Robert Lansing
Robert Lynd
Robert Michael Ballantyne
Robert W. Chambers
Rosa Nouchette Carey
Rudyard Kipling
Saint Augustine
Samuel B. Allison
Samuel Hopkins Adams
Sarah Bernhardt
Sarah C. Hallowell
Selma Lagerlof
Sherwood Anderson
Sigmund Freud
Standish O'Grady
Stanley Weyman
Stella Benson
Stella M. Francis

Stephen Crane
Stewart Edward White
Stijn Streuvels
Swami Abhedananda
Swami Parmananda
T. S. Ackland
T. S. Arthur
The Princess Der Ling
Thomas A. Janvier
Thomas A Kempis
Thomas Anderton
Thomas Bailey Aldrich
Thomas Bulfinch
Thomas De Quincey
Thomas Dixon
Thomas H. Huxley
Thomas Hardy
Thomas More
Thornton W. Burgess
U. S. Grant
Upton Sinclair
Valentine Williams
Various Authors
Vaughan Kester
Victor Appleton
Victor G. Durham
Victoria Cross
Virginia Woolf
Wadsworth Camp
Walter Camp
Walter Scott
Washington Irving
Wilbur Lawton
Wilkie Collins
Willa Cather
Willard F. Baker
William Dean Howells
William le Queux
W. Makepeace Thackeray
William W. Walter
William Shakespeare
Winston Churchill
Yei Theodora Ozaki
Yogi Ramacharaka
Young E. Allison
Zane Grey